Between Greed and Manhood

Between Greed and Manhood

Finnegan Gilhooley
Book 1

R.F. Ryan

WOLFPACK
PUBLISHING
— EST 2013 —

"If there is ever another war in this country it will be between capital and labor. I mean between greed and manhood."

—Alexander Franklin James 1897

Down the mines no sunlight shines
Those pits they're black as hell
In modest style they do their time
In Paddy's prison cell
And they curse the day they've traveled far
Then down their tears in a jar

So make way for the Molly Maguires
They're drinkers, they're liars but they're men
Make way for the Molly Maguires
You'll never see the likes of them again

—The Molly Maguires, The Dubliners

Between Greed and Manhood

Chapter 1

THE BLUE EARTH WOODS, MINNESOTA

September 14th, 1876

"ARE YOU THAT DAMN BIG YANKEE WHO SHOT ME BACK in Northfield?"

The voice drifted over from about fifty yards distance through the darkness. Moonlight cut shafts through the thick forest. All he could see of the other two men were slight silhouettes when they would blot out the light between the trees. Only flashes and flickers presented themselves, nothing that offered a useful target. The other pickets had gone home for coffee and victuals. He was alone, and it was impossible to say when the others would return or if they had heard the shots when the two strangers had first ridden up.

During the war, it had frequently occurred that the combatants found themselves in a stalemate with nothing better to do, so they had begun to palaver from cover. The practice allowed both sides time to contemplate their positions and lowered passions. It did not seem as though it could make matters any worse. "I may have shot you. You are mistaken, though, sir. I am not a Yankee; I am an Irishman. I only correct you in the hopes that you will understand that

1

God watches over all Irishmen and is benevolent towards us with his grace. If you wish to avoid perdition this night, you should surrender to me."

There was the faint sound of chuckling. "You were in Northfield?"

"I was. I shot one man in the leg. That man escaped. Do you happen to have a ball in your leg?"

"I do."

"Then there is a likelihood that I placed it there. You may be interested to know that your bullet only creased my coat sleeve."

"That is a pity. I know all too well how unfortunate it is to lose a good garment to chance." There was a rustling out in the darkness as one of them knocked leaves from a scrub oak. "Who is it I have the pleasure of addressing this fine evening?"

"Finnegan Xavier Gilhooley. Do not worry too much about the coat. Does your wound pain you much?" He moved around the log he was hiding behind to try and get a better look at his opponents, but it was in vain. "From your demeanor and your luck, I took you to be Alexander."

"Those who know me and my friends call me Frank."

"As I am neither, I suppose I should continue to call you by your Christian name." Finnegan tried peeking over the log, but could see nothing worth shooting at. When the two men had first approached the improvised picket, riding double on a horse that looked near exhaustion, Finnegan had yelled out to them to stop. The man riding in front had fired off a single round and Finnegan had fired back before taking cover behind the log. The two men had more fallen from their horse than dismounted and had then managed to drag the old nag into the trees with them. The single shot fired toward Finnegan had caused his horse to tear its reins free from the picket and bolt off toward Mankato. The ground all around the picket was so boggy that the men out in the dark would need to take the road or run the hazard of sinking their mount in the morass. Finnegan took a chance and pushed his whole head above the log before pulling it back down. He had been hoping to see the horse. Finnegan was not above shooting horses when necessary, but the mangy old swayback was hidden somewhere in the timber. "Is that your brother with you, Alexander?"

"It is."

"It is my understanding that you commonly travel with a large contingent. How is it the two of you have come to find yourselves alone?"

"Some recent prospects have not developed as we had hoped they would. Please do not concern yourself with our professional difficulties." There was the sound of more rustling in dried leaves. "How is it that you were in Northfield and now find yourself at this road picket, Mr. Gilhooley?"

"We all have difficulties specific to our professions, Mr. James."

"What profession are you currently engaged in?"

"I have been commissioned to search out you and your associates. I am not the only one, Alexander. Your predation of banks and trains has garnered a great deal of interest from those who formerly possessed the money you have purloined."

"So, you are some form of magistrate, Mr. Irishman?"

"I am a detective in private employ."

A new voice sounded off out of the darkness. "He's a damned hell-spawned Pinkerton bastard. I say we kill him and get on with our journey, Frank."

"Hello, Jesse. Nice to make your acquaintance. Were you

3

the one who killed that boy in Northfield? I dare say he could have done you no harm."

"When I deem it necessary to kill someone, I doubt I need the advice of a damned Irishman before I do it. We got enough trouble here with the Yankees. Why don't you go back to your own filthy country and leave this nation to them who have fought and bled for it?"

"Oh, I fought and bled, Jesse." Finnegan moved to the far edge of the log, hoping he could use the sound of their voices to locate the men. "I went into your army the day I got off the ship. I was only a lad, but they welcomed me well enough. The Yankees gave my father and I some fine new coats and muskets. They told us we would then have the honor of fighting for our new country."

"That wasn't my army, Irishman."

"No, I should say not." Perhaps getting the boy angry would get him to do something stupid? "From what I have heard the only fighting your regiment did was killing women and children and negros in Kansas. Are you afraid to face men, dear Jesse?"

"You yellow livered son of a bitch!"

"Shut up, Dingus. You'll get your head blown off." Frank sounded more exasperated than angry.

"Can you claim any different, Alexander? I am told you burned Lawrence with Bloody Bill. You know there were whole battalions of soldiers fighting in the east, but all you could manage was shooting a few shopkeepers and their wives. Is that what you call a military career, dear boy?"

"I think my brother is right. You should go home, Irishman." He chuckled again. "What the hell do you Irishmen come here for anyway?"

"My father thought we would all become rich and own gold mines."

"Some men get gold mines, some die behind logs. If you run right now you might still have a chance for the gold mine."

"I'm sorry, Alexander. My employer holds his people to a stringent policy in that regard." Finnegan had few preferable options to simply playing for time. "In the strictest sense, my commission only applies to you, Alexander. If he so wishes, Jesse may go. It might be for the best. He could write your epitaph and give your benediction to the newspapers. It appears as though he does his finest fighting in the newspapers."

Jesse's voice was sharp and angry. "Are you one of the bastards that burned our mama's house, Pinkerton man?"

"As it happens, I am not. Although you've burned many a house yourself, Jesse. I would not imagine one more would be of much import to you."

"You dirty Paddy bastard. You come here where you don't belong, fight for the damn Yankees, and now you're sticking your damn nose in where it don't belong. I'm gonna kill you tonight, Irishman."

"For the love of Christ, shut your hole, Dingus." There was a sigh that sounded as if it came from a very tired man. "Mr. Gilhooley, this situation we find ourselves in is a bit of foolishness. We are both professional men. Would you consider a proposition of a financial nature?"

"I have never heard of there being any harm in hearing a man out."

"What I propose is this: you shall move back from the road and allow us to pass. As we pass, by way of compensation, we will leave the funds from one of the cash drawers in Northfield. I believe that is a far more reasonable proposition than us sitting out here trying to shoot each other in the dark. You should give it your full consideration, Mr. Gilhooley.

There is no reason for us to kill each other over a few bags of Yankee money. The Yankees burned our home. They forced you into a war that was none of your affair. I see no reason either of us should do them any favors."

Finnegan slowly drew his Cloverleaf Colt out from the back of his belt. There were only four rounds left in his converted Colt Dragoon, and he might need the extra bullets. It had been damn foolish to lean his rifle against the picket gate on the other side of the road. He briefly considered taking James up on the offer of a payoff and then trying to shoot them as they rode past, but shooting at moving targets with a handgun often gave inconsistent results. There was nothing Finnegan hated more than inaction, but there in the night he had few options. It would surely be best to stall his adversaries and hope the other pickets returned or other posse members came down the road. "Round about how much are you offering to pay for passage this evening, Mr. James?"

"We have two reasonably large bags. You may have one. It is certainly more money than you will obtain dying on the side of the road."

"What assurances do I have that your brother is of the same mind as you, Alexander? He may not wish to part with a portion of your profits, or he may wish to fire on me as you pass. He does not seem to be as reasonable a man as you are."

"Dingus here won't be a problem. He gets his feathers ruffled, but I am a man of my word, and he knows better than to cross me."

"I would feel more comfortable if you could quote me an exact figure, Mr. James."

There was another tired sigh. "Mr. Gilhooley, I begin to fear that you are wasting my time in the hope that you will be relieved."

"That is a very logical deduction, Mr. James."

"It is my fervent wish to find an amicable resolution this night, Mr. Gilhooley. Can you truly not consider my offer?"

"Your offer is quite fair, Mr. James, and under differing circumstances I would give it due consideration. I cannot claim any particular love for the Yankees you referred to, and I care little about the disposition of bankers. I have, however, given my word to my employer. Like you, I believe that once my word has been given it cannot be rescinded."

Somewhere out in the dark Frank cleared his throat and the horse whinnied. "Mr. Gilhooley, can you give me your word on a particular matter?"

"If it is within my power, I would be happy to."

"If you live through this night, tell Allan Pinkerton I will see him in hell."

"I will inform him."

"Many thanks, Irishman."

Finnegan heard the sound of hooves coming up onto the hard-packed earth of the road. They had increased to a steady rhythm when he lunged up onto the log and fired with his Dragoon. The riders fired back as they neared with neither party hitting anything. As the horse was passing, Finnegan fired with both the Dragoon and the Cloverleaf from a distance of only a few feet. He heard bullets hit meat and the revolver fell from the hand of the taller man on the rear of the horse. The lead rider turned and fired. Finnegan felt something slam into his hip and the force twisted him down into the dark leaves and dirt. He heard what he thought was Jesse suggesting that they should pause to finish him, but Finnegan thrust the Cloverleaf forward and fired once more in their general direction. The bullet convinced the James brothers to travel on.

After watching his quarry depart, Finnegan lurched up to

sit on the log that had served him so well and inspected his wound. It was hard to say in the dark, but it felt as though the James boys had only struck him a glancing blow. The bullet appeared to have hit the edge of his hip bone and skittered off into the forest. Even so, it was already beginning to give torment. Finnegan slowly gained his feet and removed the handkerchief from his pocket. He wadded the cloth over his wound before moving his gun belt down to hold the bandage in place. With that seen to, he limped into the road and picked up the revolver that had been deposited there. Holding the weapon up in the moonlight he could identify it as an 1875 Army Remington. Finnegan had never seen that model of revolver in the hands of a civilian "You have no love for the Yankees, Mr. James, but you like their guns." Finnegan carefully slipped the weapon into his belt in a manner that would hopefully not aggravate his wound. "I shall have to compliment you on your taste when I see you again."

Chapter 2

PHILADELPHIA, PENNSYLVANIA

June 14th, 1877

FINNEGAN HAD SHOWN HIS BADGE TO THE NICE LADY AT the outer office desk and been granted access to the inner offices of the Philadelphia branch. He had never visited Philadelphia before, but Mr. Pinkerton had made mention of the fact several times that the agency was involved in a great deal of work in the area. Beyond that, Finnegan knew very little of the agency's business in Pennsylvania and had no interest in becoming better informed. During his many years of service to Mr. Pinkerton, Finnegan had learned that it was best to keep his attention firmly on the matters of current concern to his own work, and nothing else.

For the most part, this state of affairs was to Finnegan's liking. A system had developed where Finnegan saw to the completion of his tasks and Mr. Pinkerton gave him autonomy to complete them. That was, until a telegram had arrived ordering him to leave Missouri and travel east to Philadelphia. Since the only financial success Finnegan had ever known stemmed directly from Mr. Pinkerton's employ, he had not hesitated to purchase a train ticket and head east. As half the country scrolled by outside the train window, Finnegan could not help but wonder what could have transpired to cause his removal from his assignment. Up until that time, he had never been taken from one duty and given another until the task had been completed. Neither of the James brothers were yet dead or in the custody of the authorities. There was more than a bit of consternation in Finnegan's disposition at having been forced to leave a job half finished.

The door to the office he found himself waiting outside of in Philadelphia had the name Benjamin Franklin etched in the glass. With an imperfect knowledge of American history, Finnegan could only wonder if it was in reference to the famous statesman. Just as Finnegan was becoming bored enough to begin searching his clothing for an errant cigar to pass the time, the door to the office opened and Mr. Pinkerton's youngest son Robert stuck his head out. "We're ready for you now, Mr. Gilhooley."

Finnegan nodded and raised up from his chair. He did not know either of Pinkerton's sons socially, but they had both been working for the agency as long as Finnegan had, so they were quite familiar to one another. Finnegan nodded to the younger Pinkerton. "How have you been, Robert?"

"Well, enough, Mr. Gilhooley."

As Finnegan passed into the room Allan Pinkerton leapt from behind his desk and came forward to grasp his hand. "Ah, Finnegan, it warms my heart to see you again. Robert, how many times have I told you to call him Finnegan? This man has been with us since Antietam. He has worked for me longer than you have, my son."

The younger Pinkerton stiffened a bit. "It is only that I believe there is a time for business and a time for reminiscing. At this moment, we are discussing business and, as such, it is not proper to be overly familiar with a member of the staff."

Finnegan found the cigar that had been hiding in his coat pocket and placed it between his lips. "You have always set the example of professionalism in my opinion, Robert. I apologize if my calling you that seems overly familiar. I only use your Christian name as a mechanism to avoid confusion with your father." He patted his pockets. "Might you have a match, Robert?"

"I do not." The younger man's eyes narrowed into a squint. He raised one finger and pointed toward the holster that had been exposed during Finnegan's search for a match. "Mr. Gilhooley, is that the newly produced Remington revolver?"

"Oh, yes, and a fine weapon it is, sir."

"Where did you obtain it, Mr. Gilhooley? I was under the impression that only military personnel could possess that sidearm."

Finnegan removed the cigar from his lips. "In actuality, they sold all of the first production run to Indian agents. My guess would be that one of those agents was relieved of it by the man I obtained it from." Finnegan smiled. "Probably in much the same way I obtained it."

"Mr. Gilhooley, it has always been my opinion that receiving stolen goods is as much of a violation as..."

"Robert, we are not here to determine the provenance of Finnegan's arsenal." The elder Pinkerton slapped Finnegan on the back. "Although, I would hope you are still in possession of the Cloverleaf I gave you."

"Certainly, sir, and I have been getting fair use out of it, as well. It gave good service during my confrontation with the James brothers. Sir, I know you would not have brought me in from my assignment for anything other than a pressing need, but I ardently wish to return to Missouri as soon as circumstances will allow. I have excellent intelligence

11

regarding two possible locations. One in Texas and the other outside the brother's farmstead." Finnegan abandoned hope of finding a match and placed the cigar back in his pocket. "I have been considering our options, sir. I believe that the best course of action, assuming the opportunity to kill Alexander James does not present itself, would be to take him to Fort Smith, Arkansas."

Pinkerton moved slowly over to his desk. "Fort Smith? To what end?"

"The federal judge there has proven himself to be quite active, sir. A former litigator by the name of Isaac Parker has been placed on the bench there. He has, so far, offered up a respectable record of hanging scoundrels. I believe that if the circumstances force us to take the James brothers alive, it would behoove us to deliver them to Judge Parker to face whatever federal charges can be leveled against them first."

Pinkerton smiled and sat back in his chair. "Finnegan, you have always been a wonderfully inventive man."

Robert Pinkerton made a show of clearing his throat to get their attention. "Mr. Gilhooley, am I to understand that now, in addition to following the James contingent from Missouri to Minnesota and back again, you wish to pursue leads in Texas?"

Finnegan thought he had made himself reasonably clear, but answered just the same. "Yes, I am under the impression that my commission is to search out the James brothers and what little remains of their contingent, wherever they may be."

Robert gave an exasperated nod. "Yes, that has been your assignment, but it also represents a bone of contention."

"I am sorry, Robert; I don't believe I follow."

"Mr. Gilhooley, I am sure you are aware of the basic structure of our business. The agency is contracted by various clients to accomplish various tasks. While our work often requires nuance and the ability to make fine distinctions, the basic structure is very simple."

Finnegan nodded. "Yes, Robert, very simple. I shoot people for your father."

The elder Pinkerton let out a laugh. "And a damn fine job of it you do."

Finnegan shrugged his shoulders. "Beyond that, Robert, I am not likely to understand your bones or your contentions."

"No, you are not." Pinkerton shook his head and produced a cigar box from his desk. "Would you care for one, Finnegan?"

"Thank you, sir." He plucked one from the box and then took a match from the small silver container Pinkerton had opened. He struck the match on the buckle of his belt and lit the cigar. "It is a fine smoke, sir."

Pinkerton nodded. "Yes. Finnegan, please do not misunderstand what is being debated here. As you say, you are employed by this agency to shoot people and you have, as far as can be established, shot both of the James brothers." Finnegan had eventually discovered a doctor who had treated both of the James boys. Frank had suffered two wounds to his thigh and Jesse had been hit in the knee. It was not a bad showing for a night fight involving two moving targets.

"Thank you, sir."

"You've done very well, Finnegan. That is not in question."

Young Robert felt the need to defend his position. "What is in question is whether or not there is wisdom in allowing you to continue chasing the remaining members of a criminal organization that has, for all intents and purposes, ceased to exist. While there may be an argument to be made for continuation in principle, there is certainly no financial motivation."

Finnegan blew out a cloud of smoke. "I prefer to finish a task once begun, Robert."

"I know that, Mr. Gilhooley. However, the various investments and contracts of this company do not pivot based on your preferences. As stated before, this agency's profits are the result of clients contracting with us to accomplish various tasks. Do you, by any chance, know which client has contracted with us to effect the capture or killing of the James brothers?"

"No, I do not."

"That may be because there is no such client. Your seemingly endless tracking of the James and Younger contingent, effective as it may have been, is not in keeping with the usual nature of this firm's work. It is the result of my father's whimsy and nothing more."

The elder Pinkerton sparked a match and lit a cigar of his own. "What my youngest offspring is attempting to explain, Finnegan, is that your hunt for the James and Younger group has been a personal interest of mine, as opposed to a paid proposition. Robert feels the whole endeavor is beginning to take on an air of vendetta, especially since the Youngers are all dead or in jail now and you seem to have permanently hobbled the James brothers. They have not been charged with or taken credit for a single robbery of any sort for nearly a year now. If you did not give them a healthy fear of God that night in Minnesota, you appear to have given them a newly minted respect for justice and law."

Finnegan let out another cloud. "All the more reason to finish the job and let them be an object lesson toward those who would follow their example, sir, in my opinion."

"Finnegan, I, too, firmly believe that a job is not done to satisfaction until it is brought to its ultimate conclusion. Rest assured, I intend to put you back to work hunting the James

14

brothers at our earliest convenience. In the interim, though, another small chore has come up and it will require a man of your particular fortitude and skill to see to it." The world's most famous detective offered a knowing smile to his favorite blunt tool. "Finnegan, are you aware of the level of notoriety you have achieved since wounding the James brothers?"

Finnegan sighed. "Somewhat, sir." Such things were an annoyance for men like Finnegan.

Pinkerton grinned. "Don't be so glum, boy. What appears as a problem today is often the future's windfall. Your actions in Minnesota have been very favorably covered in the press. I dare say that whatever money has been spent on my vendetta will be readily recouped in the form of book sales." He knocked the ash from his cigar. "Allan Pinkerton's Bloodhound: Finnegan Gilhooley. It has a nice ring to it, don't you think?"

Finnegan made use of the ashtray. "You brought me to Philadelphia to help you write a book, sir?"

Pinkerton laughed. "No, Finnegan. I would no sooner make you suffer through that process than suffer it myself. I hire men to write my books." He assumed an inscrutable look. "Have you ever read one of my books, Finnegan?"

"Yes, sir."

"Did you enjoy it?"

"Not particularly, sir."

He laughed again. "Excellent. The truth is always welcome. Of course, you are not the intended audience." He knocked more ash. "But enough of this wool gathering. I only brought up your newly found notoriety to illustrate a point. Naturally, the detriment of notoriety, for a man in your profession, is that it makes unobtrusive movement difficult. It goes without saying that you will no longer be able to work in a clandestine capacity."

"Well, sir, I would imagine, if required, eventually..."

"Ah, yes, eventually all glory fades. However, for the time being, we will focus on the positive aspects of your fame. Just recently we have been presented with a fine example. An important client of ours has asked us for a — we can call it a supplemental addition to regular services — and has asked for you by name."

"By name, sir?"

Robert sighed and pressed the bridge of his nose. "As the gentleman put it, he wants the man that shot Jesse James."

Finnegan shook his head. "My intention was to shoot Alexander Franklin James. If the ball contacted Jesse, it was incidental and I have no substantial evidence that it really did, Robert."

"No, Mr. Gilhooley, you do not, and neither does anyone else. Sadly, that is immaterial to the whims of our clients. This man has read your name in the newspaper and now wishes to avail himself of your services, through the auspices of the greater Pinkerton firm, of course."

The elder Pinkerton sneered and blew smoke. "Alliteration, Finnegan. Alliteration is to blame."

"Alliteration, sir?"

"Jesse James simply rolls off the tongue. People show interest in the adventures and discoveries of Captain Cook for much the same reason, I believe."

"The man's motives are irrelevant, Father." The younger Pinkerton seemed to be losing patience with the conversation. "All that is relevant is that we have a paying client who wishes to engage our services through Mr. Gilhooley. That is the reason we have called you to Philadelphia and that is the reason your Quixotic quest for the James brothers has been suspended."

Finnegan cleared his throat. "Quixotic?"

"Uh, well..." While the younger Pinkerton had hoped to make a stern point, he found himself wishing he had made it to a man who had not killed quite so many people. "In a manner not unlike the quests undertaken by Don Quixote."

"Ignore the statement, Finnegan." Pinkerton shook his head, smiling at his son's awkward position. "If there is insult in his words it is directed at me, not you."

"I took no offense, sir. I was only unfamiliar with the term." Finnegan took a puff of his free cigar. "As you both know, I am not finicky when it comes to work. Tell me what your client requires, and I will attempt to see to it in an expeditious manner."

Robert sighed again. "It may not be that simple, Mr. Gilhooley."

"No?"

"No, the client wishes to meet with you personally. I will accompany you." The young man ran a hand through his hair and scowled.

"I have never taken a meeting with a client before, sir."

Pinkerton gave Finnegan his most fatherly smile. "Don't worry about it, my boy. Robert here is worried about molding a proper reputation for the agency. I have assured him that you are exactly what the client has in mind, but Robert will feel better if he accompanies you. Please, indulge us both."

Finnegan shook his head. "To the contrary, sir. I would prefer to have Robert with me. I would imagine your client is of a social circle I am unfamiliar with."

The aged detective nodded. "Yes, quite. Which brings us to the root of the matter; given your origins, Finnegan, I am sure you are familiar with the society known as the Molly Maguires."

Finnegan shook his head and knocked ash. "No, sir, I am not."

17

The elder Pinkerton emitted a grunt. "No? That comes as quite a surprise to me. They are a secret society originating in Ireland. Their purpose there was to confound tax collectors and, of course, to act as a guerilla group fighting the British."

Finnegan shrugged. "I left Ireland as a very young man. Any stories I've known of the old country came from my father and he has been gone some time now, sir." He smiled at his employer. "And, as you say, they are a secret society, so it would stand to reason that I should not be aware of them. When it comes to tax collectors, I have heard of White Shirts, but not Molly Maguires."

"You do, at least, read the papers?" Young Pinkerton made no attempt to disguise the shock in his voice.

Finnegan turned to him slowly. "When I have the opportunity. For the most part, I chase Alexander Franklin James, of late." Finnegan squinted and did some math in his head. "It takes up a great deal of time to pursue a man with so many relatives and coconspirators. Progress is slow, but in the last six months I have shot and killed three of his close associates and brought two before the courts." He turned to the elder Pinkerton. "Some instances require arrest when circumstances are beyond my control. At any rate, I prefer the chase to reading the papers. I would think you would have it that way."

Pinkerton grinned broadly. "Yes, Finnegan, fine work. My son is merely surprised to hear that you are unfamiliar with the Molly Maguires because this agency has garnered a great deal of press recently thanks to our successes investigating the organization."

Finnegan seemed confused. "You have been investigating an Irish secret society?"

"The society has been transferred to America, Mr.

Gilhooley. It would appear as though the Irish immigrants of the coal fields brought it along with them in their luggage." The younger Pinkerton seemed very proud of his knowledge. "The Molly Maguires of the new world have taken up the work of labor agitation. They foment strikes and indulge in the lowest kind of violence when their other methods prove fruitless. Our agent, placed within the organization by this agency, has accumulated evidence against no less than twenty men in the society. They stand guilty of crimes as heinous as murder, assault, bombing, and some others too terrible to mention. Half of the miscreants revealed by our investigation have concluded their trials and await execution. The other half will find a similar fate once the courts have seen to them."

"I see." Finnegan slowly withdrew a chair and lowered himself into it, being careful so his pistols would not scratch the finish. "Sir, it is not my place to question matters beyond my station, but if you have already placed an agent within the society, and he has amassed sufficient evidence, I fail to see why my presence is required here."

The elder Pinkerton nodded somberly. "Your talents are required for a separate matter, Finnegan. A number of separate interests contracted with this agency to ferret out the Molly Maguires and bring them to justice. One of them, Colonel Enoch McLeod, who sits on the board of the Philadelphia Reading Railroad, wishes to employ you for a personal matter. It will not necessarily involve anyone associated with the Molly Maguires. However, your work will undoubtedly find you in the coal fields in and around St. Clair. This is the very heart of the coal mining district. We still have several agents in place in this area. You will not be overtly working with these gentlemen, some of whom you may recognize from previous assignments. It is imperative that their status remains concealed until we can be certain all of the Molly Maguires have been collected and the society has been completely rooted out."

Finnegan smiled. "I have worked for you long enough, sir, to know it is poor form to call out a man's name in a crowd."

"Excellent. Now, to specifics: an atrocity has been committed against a member of the colonel's family in St. Clair. He wishes to have the perpetrator of this atrocity brought to bear in a manner you are most familiar with. Need I elaborate?"

"No, sir."

"Dependable as always, Finnegan. The colonel wishes to give you the details of his request in person later today. This agency is in the habit of seeing to the varied needs of our clients. As you know, we pride ourselves on our breadth and scope. That being said, the colonel's personal matters cannot be allowed to interfere with the larger mission we have already undertaken in the coal fields. Do you know anything of the coal industry, Finnegan?"

"Very little, sir."

Pinkerton grunted again. "A horrid bit of enterprise, but very necessary to the continued industrialization of our great nation. Men of vision, such as Mr. Gowan and, to some extent, Colonel McLeod, are working to bring the coal industry into line with the larger needs of this country. They are working to combine the mining, railroad, and steel industries into one cohesive unit, or trust, if you will. To put it in a metaphor you can better understand, they wish to bring the entire enterprise together so that its energies can be properly aimed, thus achieving far greater production and efficiency." The elder Pinkerton, who had been a rabble-rousing free labor advocate and Chartist in his native Scotland, shrugged, showing a strange bit of regret. "Aberrations such as the

Molly Maguires cannot be tolerated. The working man's lot in life can be bettered a great deal, Finnegan, but it must come part and parcel with the betterment of the entire country, or all is lost. I am sure you can appreciate such a distinction."

The hired gun knocked more ash into the tray. "In such matters I defer to you, sir."

Pinkerton smiled warmly. "And that is why I have always had a strong affection for you, Finnegan." He cleared his throat. "So then, you will do what is asked of you by Colonel McLeod. You will travel to the environs of St. Clair and discover the identity of the person or persons who have committed a vile crime against his family and... as always, use your best judgement. All the while keeping in mind that your actions can in no way interfere with our continuing investigations."

"Yes, sir."

"Excellent. Make quick work of this, my boy. I am as eager as you to resume the chase and deliver Mr. James to some form of justice."

Finnegan slowly got up from his chair. "I intend to deliver him to St. Peter, sir."

The elder Pinkerton extended his hand. "Matters pertaining to the next world are beyond my knowledge, but in the meantime, I believe delivering him to Finnegan Gilhooley will be sufficient. Do you have any questions, my boy?"

"Um, well, just one, sir."

"By all means, ask."

"Sir, the name on the door is Benjamin Franklin."

"Yes, he is in charge of this branch office. I am borrowing his office for the day."

"Mr. Pinkerton, is he the same daft bugger who got struck by lightning playing with a kite that I read about?"

Pinkerton chuckled. "No, Finnegan, that was a different gentleman and I do not believe our Mr. Franklin is a relative to him. Good luck in St. Clair."

Finnegan lingered for a moment, giving his mentor a rather pensive look. "Sir, I have one other question."

"Yes, Finnegan?"

"Sir, I have never discovered the identity of a murderer before. Is it a difficult proposition?"

Pinkerton shook his head. "Not necessarily, my boy." The great detective grinned. "My guess would be the colonel will have a few suggestions for you as to likely suspects. He is a very opinionated man. Try to take him in stride, as best you can."

"COPPERHEADS, Mr. Gilhooley! A seething nest of copperheads, the whole damn lot of them." Colonel Enoch McLeod threw both of his oversized arms into the air to emphasize the point. To Finnegan, the colonel looked more like a carefully shaved bear than a man. His chest was so broad that it appeared grossly out of proportion to the rest of his body, not that the other portions were not immense, as well. He also sported a white beard that came down several inches from his squared off chin, the sideburns of which waggled when he became agitated. "I have been informed by reliable sources that every damned labor agitator in that pit of a town is a rebel sympathizer, and it would not surprise me to learn that many of them are in fact fugitives in hiding from that yellow bastard Lee's pathetic army." He calmed a bit and took a small sip of whiskey before settling down into the chair behind his study desk, which was of equal proportion to its owner. "My apologies, gentlemen; my physician tells me that

I must learn to control my passions better. I am also not in the habit of imbibing so early in the day, but I have recently returned from inspecting several of the company's holdings in the wretched areas that comprise the coal fields. It is impossible for a man to travel there without ingesting the awful dust that infests the place. Coating my throat seems to be the only remedy for the coughing it so often causes."

Robert Pinkerton nodded to the colonel. "I fully assumed it was medicinal, sir."

"Of course." The colonel smoothed his beard with one hand. "Yes, well, as I was explaining to you, Mr. Gilhooley, I fear you have a difficult engagement ahead of you. The sheer weight of numbers stands against you. I have been informed that you specialize in shooting men who require to be shot and have great aptitude for it. Your great challenge in the coal fields will be finding a large enough supply of ammunition to be thorough. In my estimation, there cannot be more than a half dozen men in all of Schuylkill County who do not deserve to be shot. If I still had my twelve-pounders, I would load them with grapeshot and settle the problem myself."

Finnegan straightened up in his chair and smoothed his jacket lapels. He had never met an officer who did not heap disdain on the Army of Northern Virginia, and he had never met an enlisted man who was not scared stiff at the prospect of facing it. "It is unfortunate that you have experienced so much trouble in your business dealings, Colonel. While I can sympathize, I should inform you that I do not believe it will be possible for me to shoot every coal miner in Schuylkill County. I am only one man, and, as you said, we have no artillery."

The bearded giant chuckled. "Very well put, sir." He sipped a bit more whiskey. "I have read of your exploits, Mr. Gilhooley. You are a man of great determination. I have been told that the damn defeated rebels in Missouri consider the James family to be heroes and support them in their sinful pursuits. Is that true?"

"Some in Missouri give them aid and succor."

"And you have spent time searching for them there?"

"Yes, sir, a great deal of time."

"It takes grit to operate in the enemy's own country, Mr. Gilhooley. You must have felt generally surrounded and under siege."

"I found it was best to sleep where I was not expected to be and eat my meals with my back to the wall."

The colonel chuckled again. "A wise policy, to be sure. It was reading of your exploits in Minnesota that put me in mind that you would be the proper man to bring into service for my current predicament." He took a slightly larger drop of whiskey. "You will surely feel outnumbered most of the time." He sighed. "Mr. Gilhooley, do you have a family, children?"

"No, sir."

"I have no children, either. This state of affairs has led to me having an affectionate relationship with my various nieces and nephews. I have always found a considerable amount of joy in the antics of children." He sipped more whiskey. "At any rate, my eldest niece, Johanna Mary Wetherill, was a lovely girl in her younger years. Her smile could make the sun come up. As a child, she occupied a very special place in my heart. Unfortunately, as is sometimes the way of life, as she passed into her majority she became a very troubled young woman. I am sad to say that she became a fallen woman. She was taken to indulging in all manner of vice from drinking to other unacceptable behavior." He paused and stared down at his whiskey glass. "When she had misbehaved to the point that her family here in Philadelphia would no longer tolerate her, she ran off to the coal fields. I imagine it came as something of a relief to my poor sister, no longer having to witness her depraved state, but the worst was yet to come. It is my understanding that Johanna began keeping company with men in a tippling house, and then..." He finished what remained of the whiskey. "When her remains were found...someone had left her in a culm bank, and she had been...defiled. I am told that she was mutilated in the most abhorrent way, Mr. Gilhooley. The local magistrate, a truly useless tit, informed me that if he did not know better, he would have thought it to be the work of red Indians." He cleared his throat and refilled his whiskey glass. "Hard to imagine a man could be capable of such a thing, even a rebel or a copperhead."

"Some men have no decency, sir." Finnegan could not help but feel pity for the colonel.

"Yes, well. I suppose we all learned that in the war." He smoothed his beard again.

"It is hard to fathom the depths of some men's depravity, Colonel." Young Mr. Pinkerton spoke with complete sincerity, but the colonel did not appreciate the statement.

"What would you know of depravity, Pinkerton? You were a mere parlor soldier trailing behind your father like a pup during the war. What the hell would you know of cruelty?"

Robert Pinkerton simply stared at the man for a moment, trying to digest the depth of his rudeness. Before he could answer the colonel's accusation, Finnegan interjected. "Colonel, I too served under Mr. Pinkerton's father during the late hostilities. I do not hesitate to admit to my elation at finding an opportunity to leave the general ranks. I did not miss trying to live on embalmed beef and hardtack. I will also not hesitate to admit that I had hoped to avoid the more desperate dangers of the war in Mr. Pinkerton's service, such as facing the twelve pounders of the rebel army, but I was sadly disappointed on that score. The men serving under Mr. Pinkerton faced the hazard as much as any soldier. Certainly as much as any officer. I would also venture to say that attendance of such venues as Antietam or Gettysburg at a tender age, if anything, gives a man a more thorough appreciation of words such as depravity or cruelty. If Robert Pinkerton is a parlor soldier, I am as well, sir."

The colonel scowled and refilled his whiskey glass. "My apologies again, gentlemen. I meant no disrespect. Please understand that I only spoke out of grief and thoughtlessness. My recent journey and recent bereavement have had an unfortunate effect upon my disposition."

Both men nodded. Pinkerton shook his head. "Your agitation is understandable, sir. No offense taken."

"Very well, then." The colonel rose from his desk. "It has been an honor to meet you, Mr. Gilhooley. I pray that your time in the coal fields is short lived and look forward to receiving word from you when the matter is brought to a close and the fiend who has caused my family so much grief has been given over to the good Lord's justice."

"I shall inform you when it is completed, sir." Finnegan reached out and took the man's hand.

"The best to you as well, Mr. Pinkerton."

"The agency is always available should you have further need of us, sir."

The colonel took his hand. "You have certainly given good service, so far." He flashed the grin that may have formerly only occurred after a rousing artillery barrage. "More than twenty of the copperhead bastards. Fine work. I understand at least ten of them are slated for the rope." He continued to grin and raised his whiskey glass. "Here's hoping a hundred more will follow."

CINDERS FLEW into the night sky as a locomotive belched and moaned in the Philadelphia railyard terminus. Finnegan and Robert Pinkerton stood on the platform, awaiting the Philadelphia and Reading Line train that would take Finnegan to the coal fields. The only convenient aspect of Finnegan's new posting was that the trains were in almost constant motion between St. Clair and Philadelphia. The city had an endless thirst for coal and St. Clair was the fountainhead. The two men were alone on the platform. The only sounds were the clanking of rail equipment and the occasional curse of a railyard worker.

Robert motioned to the cinders. "It burns coal."

Finnegan nodded and puffed his thin cigar. "Yes, I suppose it does."

"Did you know, Mr. Gilhooley, that any given coal production operation employs no less than two steam engines and a furnace?"

"No, I did not."

"Yes. One engine provides for the operation of the breaker, the other provides the power to lift the coal cars from the mine. The furnace is placed at the top of the mine shaft and the fire within it provides ventilation for the shaft. Some mines are now employing a third steam engine which powers a large fan. It improves ventilation greatly."

"Very interesting."

"What I find most interesting about the entire operation is that all the engines and furnaces are fueled with coal." He grinned and shook his head. "The economics of industry are fascinating. I cannot help but wonder what amount of labor is required simply to produce the coal that is then burned to allow for continued operation. It is an intriguing equation, isn't it, Mr. Gilhooley?"

"You know, Robert, I believe we have known each other more than long enough for you to call me Finnegan."

The young man smiled in the dim light. "I believe I will. Thank you, Finnegan, for taking my part today with the colonel."

Finnegan laughed. "That man had no right to question your character, Robert. From what I know of colonels, they're a damnable breed. The closest that bastard ever got to a battlefield was probably cowering behind a supply train somewhere. I would wager Robert Lee's mother fought more engagements than that overgrown blowhard."

Pinkerton chuckled. "Yes. Well, I appreciated your words. Almost a pity the man is such a reliable client." He flashed a sly smile. "I could have challenged him to a duel. Of course, I would have chosen you for a second and promptly feigned an injury to my trigger finger."

Finnegan nodded emphatically. "I would have been proud to serve as your second, Robert, but I doubt your father would look favorably on the shooting of a client."

"Undoubtedly. As you know, most men are apt to be shot at for one reason or another, but never clients." Young Robert Pinkerton sighed and seated himself on the wooden bench that occupied part of the platform. "Terrible business, this investigation of the Molly Maguires. An outstanding bit of work by our primary agent, but still a shame it has to end with so many men climbing the gallows. Mr. Franklin, the man in charge of operations here in Philadelphia, also gave admirable service. It was quite difficult to bring all the threads of this particular investigation together." He chuckled. "You truly have no knowledge of any of the facts involving our investigation of the Molly Maguires?"

Finnegan shook his head. "I am sure it was a thrilling affair, Robert, but to tell you the truth, I simply take little interest in events that do not personally concern me. How precisely did you go about investigating them, anyway?"

"Oh, it was all very involved. We placed several Irish born operatives in their midst. It took some time for our men to gain the organization's confidence. With that done, they had to participate in several of the criminal acts to which the Mollies now stand accused. Very difficult, very dangerous." Robert stood up from the bench and paced a bit. "Father has never given you an infiltration assignment, has he?"

"Oh...he had me wandering around down south reporting on troop movements during the war. That was a simple business, though. I did not have to pretend to be something I was not. I acted like a scared boy who wished to avoid shells, and it was quite believable because that was exactly what I was. It required no subterfuge." He knocked the ash from his cigar. "Your father has a fine ability for understanding where a man's talents lie. He has never placed me in a clandestine position. As far as I can recall, this is the first assignment I have been given where the enemy was not previously defined. I have been calling myself a detective almost since I began working for your father, but I have done precious little detecting." He smiled. "Perhaps this assignment will reveal a new talent in me."

"You have always performed admirably, Finnegan."

"We all have our place in the grand scheme of things, I suppose. Who is it you set to infiltrating these Molly Maguires?"

"James McParlan."

"Ah." Finnegan nodded. "I have met him. He was at your

29

father's office in Chicago for some time. He worked a few counterfeiting cases, did he not?"

"Yes. He showed good prowess at that. What was your impression of the man?"

"I think he would be a fine choice for infiltration. He seemed the sort who would be more than willing to sell his own mother for a promotion, or possibly a pint." Finnegan smiled.

Robert hung his head momentarily. "Yes, Mr. McParlan does tend to keep his own self-interest in the vanguard of his strategy."

"It is not necessarily a bad trait, Robert. Many a man would find his life easier and, dare I say, more profitable, if he possessed it, and could exercise it without pausing to concern himself with the moral or spiritual implications."

Robert laughed. "Do you often find yourself shackled by moral and spiritual implications, Finnegan?"

"Not often, but my work is easier than that of Mr. McParlan. I need only fire back when fired upon, or fire first when I prognosticate firing may be imminent. Infiltration is a far messier business, requiring much more contemplation. At least I would imagine it would be. I am grateful that your father has never tasked me with attempting it." Finnegan took a short draw off his cigar. "Is Mr. McParlan a married man?"

"No, I don't believe so."

"Perhaps he has been contemplating marriage for some time. I have noticed that many men begin showing greater concern for promotion and matters of a financial nature when they are contemplating marriage or are married."

"It only stands to reason, Finnegan. A married man shoulders far greater responsibility." Robert eyed the gunman carefully. "Are you currently contemplating marriage, Finnegan?" He sat on the bench and puzzled. "Ah, let's see. I must use my family's world-renowned detective skills to seek out the truth here. If I had to venture a guess...perhaps some well-shaped banker's daughter discovered in the course of your duties? To the manor born? Well above your station? You must now try to make your fortune before approaching her father to ask for her hand?" Young Pinkerton shook his head. "A fool's errand. I would suggest elopement. Return to mend fences afterward and let her father provide the fortune you so ardently seek."

Finnegan could not help but laugh. "Very practical, Robert."

"My years in the family business have made me so. Is there truly a young lady who currently warrants your contemplation?"

"In the name of practicality, all I can currently contemplate is the discovery of the murderer in question. That is what I am tasked with, Robert. All other matters will have to wait."

"I suppose it is our cross to bear in this profession. As devoted Pinkerton agents, we must place murder before matrimony." Robert took his watch from his pocket and checked the time. "Do you really believe you can discover the identity of the fiend who murdered the colonel's niece?"

"I do not know. I have never tried to solve a crime such as this before." He thought on it for a moment. "In truth, I have never really attempted to solve any crime. Generally, your father tells me who to search out and I shoot them, if possible."

"Do not sell yourself short, Finnegan. I am sure you are as capable as any of our agents. Bear in mind, you will not be without assistance. You will be in direct contact with Charlemagne Bourne, the captain of the St. Clair Coal and Iron Police division. Despite the colonel's opinion, Captain

Bourne has been a valued asset to the agency for many years and has been quite thorough in his work."

"Still, if he had the ability to discover the murderer, I believe he would have, and I would still be pursuing the James contingent."

Robert shrugged. "He likely has no more experience chasing murderers than you do, Finnegan. Perhaps the two of you will make better progress working in cooperation." Robert gave Finnegan a small pat on the shoulder. "Bear in mind, the murder has already been committed. There is nothing that can be done for the poor girl at this point. Your actions on this assignment are more meant to placate the colonel and perhaps offer some balm to his conscience. People often feel as though they are somehow responsible when a family member passes. I wish you all the luck in the world, Finnegan, but if you do not find success, little will change. The colonel will be satisfied that he tried, and my father will be satisfied at having retained a client."

"Very practical, Robert, as always. Would you care for reports of my progress?"

"By telegraph, if you please, as developments occur."

The train approached the platform and let out a plume of steam that produced a sound more like a sigh than a whistle. "I hope to see you again soon." Finnegan shook Robert's hand and picked up his luggage. "It is a pity you do not have a sister who is not spoken for, Robert. I could elope with her and then tell your father I was only acting on your advice."

"If you are of the mind to steal a family fortune, Finnegan, I would suggest you steal another. The maintenance of ours requires far too much bootlicking. I do not believe a man of your disposition would care for it."

Chapter 3

ST. CLAIR PENNSYLVANIA
June 15th, 1877

THERE WAS DIM LIGHT SHOWING IN THE EAST AS Finnegan disembarked from the train and began to slowly trudge up what a badly mauled sign had informed him was Second Street. Roosters crowed in various locations, but they were hard to hear due to the dull roar of equipment that enveloped the town. It was a strange sound to be greeted with in what had been thoroughly pastoral country only a few miles back. The entire town hummed and clanked with noise produced from what Finnegan assumed were parts of the coal mining process. He could see some of the breakers were already in operation before the dawn had fully come on. The grinding reverberations reminded him of a grist mill. There were also the sounds from the furnaces which, if not for the man-made trappings that were visible, could have been mistaken for an unruly gang of giants struggling to breath underground. Fire belched from various places concealed within the breaker buildings, lighting up different parts of the low rolling hills.

In addition to all that, there was the dust. Every object was coated in a black film that occasionally glittered in what little light there was. It quickly covered Finnegan's boots, and after a few blocks he began to feel as though instead of being simply besmirched with the stuff, he had become somehow infested with it. There were no clean surfaces with which to remove it, so he continued on until he found himself beneath the hanging wooden sign that read BOARDING HOUSE.

Stepping through the door of the place, he was pleased to see that someone had taken what must have been a great deal of effort to clean all the coal dust from the entryway. Finnegan stomped his feet on the small rug in front of the door and hoped he did not ruin the cleanliness of the place. The noise of him cleaning his feet brought a rather sullen looking woman in a black dress out from behind a door. Steam followed the woman into the room, so Finnegan assumed she had been working at either breakfast or laundry.

"Good morning, ma'am." Finnegan set his bags down. "Do you have a room to let?"

The woman looked him up and down using her trained eye to determine whether she should ask for all the rent in advance. "I do."

"Very well." Finnegan stepped to the small front desk some carpenter had shoehorned into the entryway. He waited while the woman brought out a large ledger and flipped it open. Finnegan scribbled his name down. "What is the rate, ma'am?"

"A dollar and a half a week. That includes breakfast and the evening meal, if you are so inclined. I do not package lunches."

Finnegan set two dollars on the ledger book. "Please let me know when that runs out, ma'am."

She snatched up the money as if it were the first she had seen in quite some time. "How long do you intend to stay?"

"I do not know just as yet. Do you have room keys, ma'am?"

She looked rather offended at the question. "We certainly do not. There are no sticky fingers in this house, I assure you."

Finnegan nodded, glad to hear the woman only let rooms to saints and angels. "Very well. Do you have a room available on the ground floor, preferably toward the back of the house?"

She swept back her grey hair. "Now, what difference would that be making to you?"

"I sometimes keep odd hours, ma'am, and I would prefer to be able to come and go through the back door without waking the entire household."

"I see." She thought on it for a moment. The extra four bits she had already obtained seemed to be the deciding factor. "There is a vacant room down the hall and to the right." She glanced at the door she had originally emerged from. "Will you be wanting breakfast? It's almost ready."

"That would be lovely, ma'am. I will stow my possibles first, if that would be all right?"

"Certainly." She turned to go, but then turned back again. "If you've come looking for work in the mines, there is none. Especially for strangers."

Finnegan shook his head and picked up his bags. "I am not a miner." He paused. "What difference does it make if I am a stranger?"

She bit her lower lip, looking pensive. "Since you're not a miner, I suppose it makes no difference at all." She fled to the back room and Finnegan walked down the hall to his room.

Inside his room, Finnegan found the few accoutrements he had grown accustomed to from a long line of rented rooms. There was a bed of questionable hygiene, a small writing table, a coal oil lamp, and a thin cotton drape over the one and only window. He set his bags down and investigated the window. It was, in fact, large enough for him to fit through, which was all Finnegan Gilhooley ever really cared about pertaining to rented rooms. He surveyed the general motif of the place. It was odd how so many of the items in boarding houses or hotels appeared as though they matched the last set of items. Even the proprietor resembled the last black-clad widow who had let him a room in Missouri. He placed his bags under the bed, made a note to ask the lady of the house for a proper cuspidor since he was not in the habit of knocking ash onto the floor, and made his way to the dining room.

The woman placed a metal coffee pot on one end of a large oak table. Finnegan took note of the fact that the table-cloth was spotless. She might not have been overly friendly, but the lady was a fine housekeeper. "Thank you, ma'am." He lowered himself into one of the highbacked chairs.

"Most around here call me Mrs. Wallace. Would you prefer bacon and eggs or hotcakes?"

"If you have standing orders from the other boarders, I will take whatever remains." He poured himself a cup of coffee.

"The other boarders currently in the house do not partake of breakfast."

Finnegan sipped the coffee and found it more than tolerable. "You seemed to be whipping up a large meal when I came in, Mrs. Wallace."

She nodded. "I was. My four sons must eat before beginning work at the Hickory colliery. They are breaker boys and

36

work hard, but you are a paying guest, so you may have your pick for the meal."

"I'll have the eggs and pork, Mrs. Wallace."

She nodded again and disappeared into the kitchen. She returned a moment later with a plate of food and a set of utensils. "Here you are, sir."

"Finnegan Gilhooley, ma'am. You may call me what you like." He tried the eggs and found them palatable. "It is good that all of your boys have found steady situations."

"It is a blessing. It has been a struggle since Mr. Wallace passed, God rest his soul, but we manage. What profession do you follow, Mr. Gilhooley? I do not make a habit of asking my boarders their business, but you have said you are not a miner, and most people who stay in St. Clair for any length of time are somehow following the mining trade. I'm afraid you have piqued my curiosity."

"It is quite all right, Mrs. Wallace. I do not consider it overstepping one's place to ask a man his profession. I am a detective in private employ."

"A detective!" She shrieked out the words and took a step back pressing one hand to her chest.

Finnegan raised one eyebrow and sipped his coffee. "Do you consider that to be a disreputable profession, Mrs. Wallace?"

"I...I cannot say. Are you a Pinkerton detective?"

"I am."

"Mr. Gilhooley, I do not know if it is prudent for you to go around this town telling people you are a detective in the employ of the Pinkerton agency."

Finnegan slipped a piece of bacon into his mouth. "It rarely is, Mrs. Wallace, but I have learned to live with it." He continued to munch his breakfast.

"Mr. Gilhooley, you must know that the Pinkertons have

just recently caused a great deal of anger and excitement in this town by way of their dealings with a secret society involved in labor disputes."

Finnegan nodded and sipped his coffee. "I have recently been informed, yes."

"Sir, have you come here to continue such dealings? If that is the case..." She tossed her hands into the air in resignation. "If that is the case, sir, I will have to ask you to leave this house. I understand that each man must do his job, but after you leave this town I will still have to live here and look my neighbors in the eye as we pass on the street, sir."

Finnegan stuffed a forkful of eggs into his mouth and wiped his chin with the provided napkin. Like a lot of widows, Mrs. Wallace was proving to be a bit skittish. "You are an excellent cook, ma'am."

A young man stuck his head into the room at the kitchen door. "Is everything all right, mother?" Obviously, the lady of the house was not in the habit of raising her voice to boarders and the boy had become worried. He glanced nervously from his mother to Finnegan and back again.

Finnegan cleared his throat and drained his coffee cup. "Everything is fine, my boy. Your mother was simply enquiring as to my intentions during my stay in your town, which she has every right to do." Finnegan moved his stare from the boy to the lady. "I am not in the area for the same purposes that brought my predecessors here, ma'am." He swept the last of his eggs together and finished his breakfast. "If, however, my presence here will cause you any undo difficulties, I would be happy to move to another establishment. It is not my intention to burden you."

She took a moment to weigh the opinion of the neighbors against the money she already had in her pocket. The money won out yet again. "No, Mr. Gilhooley, it's quite all right." She turned to her son. "It's fine Michael, everything is all right. Get on back to your breakfast now."

"Yes, mother." He nodded to Finnegan and disappeared back into the kitchen.

Mrs. Wallace took a step closer to her boarder and lowered her voice. "You truly have no interest in the Molly Maguires?"

"None whatsoever." Finnegan refilled his coffee cup. "I had never even heard of them until yesterday when some of the other gentlemen at the office brought them up." He shook his head. "No, ma'am, I am here to find a murderer."

"Some say the Mollies were murderers."

"Really?" Finnegan brightened up. "It would be a definite piece of luck for me if one of them killed the woman. Would you happen to know if any of them were given to killing women?" The lady of the house slowly shook her head. "Oh, well, a pity."

The lady edged even closer. "Mr. Gilhooley, have you come here to discover the murderer of that Wetherill girl?"

Finnegan nodded. "Indeed, ma'am. Did you know the woman, by any chance?"

She stiffened at the very suggestion. "Certainly not."

"Oh, but you do know who she was?"

"This is not a bustling city, Mr. Gilhooley. I would hope that it is never too difficult to keep track of the painted harlots that wander the streets." The woman stopped and pressed her hand to her chest again. Her cheeks flushed with embarrassment. "I am sorry, sir. That was a very unchristian thing for me to say. Judgement should be left to the Almighty. Yes, she was known to the citizens of this town. More so by the fact that she was given to telling anyone within ear shot that she was the niece of Colonel Enoch Mcleod, if you can imagine."

Finnegan nodded. "In fact, she was, ma'am."

"No? In truth?"

"It is no less a personage than the colonel himself who has sent me here to deliver her killer to justice, ma'am." Finnegan wiped his mouth one last time. "You wouldn't happen to know who killed her, would you?"

"What?"

"Under normal circumstances I try not to bother other people with the particulars of my work, but in this instance, I have pressing business in Missouri that I wish to get back to directly. If you could, by some stroke of luck, tell me who it is that killed the girl it would be a great boon to me. Of course, you could keep the week's rent as a gratuity, ma'am."

"I...I am sorry, I do not know who took the poor woman's life."

"Another pity. For a moment I thought I might have found a rather helpful shortcut." He stood up from the table. "Thank you, ma'am, it was a most satisfying breakfast."

"I am glad you enjoyed it. Mr. Gilhooley, would you mind if I asked you another question pertaining to your profession?"

"Go right ahead, ma'am. I am an open book."

"Yes, well, actually, that is what I wish to inquire about. Aren't men in your profession generally...less obtrusive?"

"I suppose many are. I tend to practice different methods than my associates, ma'am. Oh, I don't suppose you could tell me where I might find a gentleman by the name of Charlemagne Bourne? I understand him to be some sort of constable hereabouts."

"I...I would assume he can be found at the offices of the Coal and Iron Police. It is a two-story house they have converted to their purposes, though I shudder to think what those might be. It is where Hancock meets Front Street." She motioned to the clock. "Although, I have never seen a man moving in the place before ten in the morning, so you may wish to wait before calling on him."

"Very helpful, Mrs. Wallace. Thank you, ma'am."

WITH SOME TIME on his hands, Finnegan returned to his room and sat down at the writing desk. For the majority of his life, Finnegan had not indulged in much correspondence. He would occasionally drop a line to the few family members he still had, and, of course, sent regular reports to Mr. Pinkerton, but that was all, until recently. Inside the provided writing desk, he found stationary of a passably good grade and a bottle of ink that had not congealed past use.

> Dearest Molly,
>
> You may find this difficult to credit, but today I became aware of a gaggle of Irishmen who are usurping your name. The company has sent me to St. Clair, Pennsylvania, and all the fuss here is about some other Pinkerton men who were investigating a bunch called the Molly Maguires. From what I can gather, they were some sort of labor union concern, though I have not taken the time to ask what it is exactly they were doing that made them worth investigating.
>
> I am here on other business. Mr. Pinkerton

has pulled me away from my pursuit of the James brothers to search out the murderer of a young woman who was formerly a resident of St. Clair. It is lovely country here and would probably make for a very peaceful bit of forest land if it were not for the coal mining. The miners and the factories for processing of the coal have made a terrible mess of the whole place and they raise an intolerable racket while they are about their work. Everything is covered in coal dust and the entire town resembles the front of a stove.

I hope your sister is in better health since last you wrote. She is a darling young lady, and it would be a pity if she has to suffer through a lasting illness. I hope you mother and father are doing well and that the heat is not bothering you too much along with the mosquitos.

The wound to my hip no longer troubles me and I credit the thorough recovery to your nursing. The scar is barely visible now and I believe the day will come when I will not have the slightest memento to remind me of the night I was shot by the famous Jesse James. That is, of course, if I do not count making your acquaintance as a result of it. Weighed and

42

measured, a small bullet wound to the hip seems a minor price to pay.

With any luck, my stay in St. Clair will not be long. Perhaps I can pass through Minnesota on my way back west to continue my previous pursuit.

Best wishes,
Finnegan

He slowly reread the letter several times before carefully folding it and placing it in an envelope. Writing to a woman was a new endeavor for Finnegan, and each letter seemed to take longer than the last as he became more and more tentative regarding what should be said or what should not.

With his correspondence seen to, Finnegan left his room and made his way out into the street. As the sun had slowly come up, Finnegan had watched as a veritable army of men, essentially the entire adult male population of the town, had slowly marched down the various streets to begin the morning shift at the mines and breakers. There had been surprisingly little banter that Finnegan could hear. All the miners and laborers seemed strangely serious, perhaps even morose as their boots kicked up coal dust and they trudged to their fate.

By the time Finnegan had finished his letter and began walking up the street his landlady had indicated, the working men had all been replaced with women out hanging laundry, beating rugs, or gossiping across fences. Without fail, the local women all cast a suspicious gaze on him as he passed. It might have only been his imagination, but they seemed to be consistently giving him the evil eye. The postmaster cast a similarly suspicious glace at him when he posted his letter. As a hired gun, Finnegan was rather inured to this treatment, but it seemed to be beginning a bit early on this particular job. Normally, the populace waited until after he had shot someone to treat him like a pariah.

By about quarter past ten, Finnegan was standing in front of what had once been some rather well-to-do fellow's home, but currently bore a wooden plaque naming it as the head-quarters for the Coal and Iron Police. The place did not appear overly professional, but then again, the standard for what a police station was supposed to look like varied greatly. The Coal and Iron Police were the result of industry lobbying after the war. Coal, steel, and railroad concerns had pointed out to the Pennsylvania legislature that they had special needs when it came to law enforcement. They owned too much property for a county sheriff or town constable to possibly give them thorough protection. Thus, one of the world's first private police forces had been born. For one dollar a corporation in good standing in the State of Pennsylvania could purchase a commission for a police officer and give the commission to whomever they judged fit for the job.

Never having spent any time around this particular brand of lawman, Finnegan did not know exactly how helpful their captain would be, though he had spent enough time around Pinkertons to know that there were essentially two types. There were the smart ones capable of working with autonomy, and there were the rest of them: dumb thugs who could no more decide who to shoot while working than who to hit on Saturday night.

Finnegan opened the front door and made his way down a short hallway. It did not appear as though the constabulary inhabiting the place were overly concerned with upkeep. The wallpaper hung in strips from some of the walls and there were holes in the few rugs scattered across the floors. He passed a room that had been converted into a holding cell. The metal door stood open and there were no inmates that morning. The next room he passed held three uniformed men snoring on cots. Not caring to disturb them, he walked down the hall to the third and final room on that story. The door was half open, so he stepped into the opening and snaked his head around. Inside the room a man with broad shoulders and a handlebar moustache sat behind a cheap desk. He looked rather haggard, with dirt and dust forming streaks on the coat of his dark blue uniform. He pulled his head up from the empty desktop he had been staring at when Finnegan entered.

The man rocked back in his desk chair. There was a marked flash of fear that played across his face. "You have business here, sir?"

"I do, if you are Captain Charlemagne Bourne."

He flopped forward in his chair. "I am." He looked Finnegan over. "And I would venture a guess to say that you are the man sent from Philadelphia by the illustrious Mr. Pinkerton."

"I am."

"Well..." He sighed and motioned to the sole extra chair in the dingy room. "Take a seat and let us get to it. What there is to get to, at any rate." He opened one of his desk drawers and removed a small bundle of papers and a smaller hunk of cheap brass. "Your badge and commission. Congratulations, you are now a captain in the Pennsylvania Coal and Iron Police. I imagine your sainted mother never thought you would rise so high in the world."

Finnegan took the items and lowered himself into the chair. "She did not." He looked around the room that might have served as a parlor for the previous owner. It had become the receptacle for all the unused furniture from the rest of the house and was now rather cramped for space. "Captain Bourne, it is not my intention to in anyway interfere with your work while I am posted here. My only intention is to complete my commission and move on, with all due haste."

The captain laughed behind his moustache. "Interfere with my work? That is rather amusing, Mr. Gilhooley. I am not sure how you could possibly do that. It also makes me think you are unfamiliar with the particulars of my commission in this town."

"I am unfamiliar with everything here, sir. I have never been here before."

"Ah, very well, then let me inform you. The job of the Coal and Iron Police here in beauteous St. Clair is very simple: I am to use all means at my disposal to make certain that the railcars are filled with coal and rolling to the docks at Philadelphia. For most of my career, that has meant breaking up strikes and nipping strikes in the bud before they get started. It is important for us to properly bust men's heads at the taverns to assure them that there is an authority greater than the union, from time to time. Of course, we guard the payroll that comes in every month so that the men can be paid and frequent the taverns where their heads are broken. It is a simple system and has worked quite well for a long time. That is, until you damned Pinkertons showed up and knocked the whole damned place into a cocked hat. Between your illustrious Mr. Pinkerton and that damned Gowan, I'll be lucky to crawl out of this place with my life when this is all said and done. Can't you fools appreciate the difference between a busted head and a stretched neck?"

"Captain Bourne, I am certain you make a very good

point, whatever that may be, but I have no idea what you are talking about, and I am certain it is none of my affair."

"Well, it damn well may be if you elect to stay in this town for any length of time openly professing to be a member of my police. Christ himself help you if you tell these people you're a Pinkerton man."

Finnegan adjusted himself in his chair so that his Remington would not dig into his back. "I assume you are warning me about the general poor favor Pinkerton men are currently held in around here due to the recent investigation and prosecutions, Captain?"

"That's a damned simple way of putting it." He rubbed the bridge of his nose and squeezed his eyes shut as though the world might look different when he opened them again. "Mr. Gilhooley, the problem around here isn't the fact that ten men from this very town are about to be hung. The problem is not that ten more will surely follow. The problem is that these poor bastards have had all their illusions stripped away. It was one thing to keep a thumb on them while they at least thought they had a fighting chance. Now..." He looked around the room rather mournfully. "The sons of bitches have nothing left to lose. Were you in the war, Mr. Gilhooley?"

"I was."

"Then you know the value of illusions, the lies we tell ourselves. All will be well, the war will end soon, I will not fall because so many men in my company already have. We lie to ourselves, and it allows us to go on, for a time. These people no longer have that ability, and I am damned worried that they will lynch us all in short order."

Finnegan chuckled at the man. "Really, Captain, that might be overreaching a bit. I doubt I have survived this long to end up swinging from a colliery."

The police captain shook one finger at the hired gun. "That is probably the same thing Jack Kehoe thought, but he's damn well going to swing. What I am trying to impress upon you, Mr. Gilhooley, is that the last thing we need around here right now is a damned Pinkerton strutting around like a bantam rooster flaunting to these people."

Finnegan rubbed his chin and pulled a cigar from his coat pocket. "Captain, if you truly feel my presence here will cause trouble, perhaps it would be best if you did all in your power to foreshorten my stay. I assure you, after I have shot the man who killed Johanna Wetherill, I will be back on the train within minutes. I have always found that a prompt departure should follow a proper shooting."

"Johanna Wetherill!" The captain flung his arms in the air before lowering both to his desk and laughing out loud. "I honestly thought it was a jest when I received the telegram, but you do not appear to be jesting me, Mr. Gilhooley."

"I never jest about my work, sir."

The captain laughed a bit more. "Good Christ, save us all. You really do wish to discover the murderer of that fallen tart?" He shook his head. "Has old Allan Pinkerton finally gone daft? Do you know how many men die in the mines here every year? How many die in barroom brawls or shootings? Do you know how many tarts end up in a ditch covered in coal dust with no one to bother burying them? Who gives a tinker's damn about a dead little tart in a culm bank?"

"Colonel Enoch Mcleod. He was the girl's uncle and has been a client of the Pinkerton agency for some time. In answer to your other enquiry: to my knowledge Mr. Pinkerton is still of sound mind. It would serve you well to cease casting aspersions on men you do not know, Captain."

He assumed a very serious countenance. "Yes, perhaps it would." The captain removed his cap and scratched the back of his head vigorously. "Mr. Gilhooley, you have arrived here at what may be the worst possible time and you ask for assistance with a labor that no man could possibly assist you with. What do I know of finding murderers? Before the war I was a slate picker in the Eagle Colliery. Do you know what it is to be a slate picker?"

"I do not."

"Twelve hours a day stooped over the coal as it rolls by. If the war had not come along, I would have eventually moved from picking slate to being a driver boy, then a miner's laborer, then a proper miner." He shook his head. "Then I would have dropped dead from black lung having barely seen the sun in this life, Mr. Gilhooley. As luck would have it, the rebels fired on Fort Sumpter. I joined the 48th, commanded by General Pleasants. I was with him for the tunneling at Petersburg. Have you heard of the work we did there to explode the ramparts?"

"I have, in fact."

"It was horrid bloody work. As I said, I was there with General Pleasants, the same man who today commands the Coal and Iron Police. That is the only reason I am not coughing up blood from inhaling anthracite, Mr. Gilhooley. This occupation constitutes the only luck I have ever had in this life. Your presence here could upset that. If this town and the surrounding country are induced to riot, we will all feel the lash in one regard or another."

"Captain, I can appreciate your position. I was raised up to my current standing in a similar manner, but fear of failing cannot rule a man. I have been sent here to do a job, and, hell be my heaven, I intend to see it through. Now, what can you do to assist me?"

The captain lowered his head and sighed. "Mr. Gilhooley, there is nothing I can do. I have just finished explaining that I am not a detective. I am merely a slate picker who did not die at Petersburg. Do you not read the papers, Mr. Gilhooley? Murder is a frequent affair in these parts. No less than twenty men will hang for it in short order, and some say that is only the beginning of Mr. Gowan's witch hunt." He waggled one finger at Finnegan. "How does this strike you? I propose a compromise. If all you require is a murderer, you have come to a fine place to find one. Almost any man you see in the streets of this damnable town could lay claim to that particular title. Choose one, shoot him, and be on your way. Tell Enoch Mcleod that you made use of some Pinkerton chicanery to determine the man's guilt and be done with it. It probably matters little to God who kills who and for what reason; why should you trouble yourself over it?"

Always the practical man, Finnegan took a moment to consider the proposition. "Would you be willing to attest to the man's guilt in the matter of Johanna Wetherill?"

"Oh, most certainly. If it will get you on your way any quicker, I can even point out a likely drunkard or two whose demise would be a great boon to this town."

Finnegan shook his head. "No, sir. At least not at present. Even Mr. Pinkerton could not claim to be able to determine the identity of a murderer in a day. For better or worse, I must remain here until I have caused a stir. You of all men can surely appreciate the necessity of making the occasional show for your employer's benefit. Men such as us must be seen to be working to draw our pay."

"Pay." The captain sniffed. "Before you leave this place there will be hell to pay. What do you intend to do here, Mr. Gilhooley? My guess would be that you could no more find a murderer than one of the lost tribes of Israel."

Finnegan rubbed his chin and withdrew a cigar. "You are correct in thinking that I know little of missing tribes.

50

Murder, on the other hand, I do know something about. During my journey here I had opportunity to consider the matter and I believe it would be best to begin by investigating some of the men you mentioned who are already known to be killers. If a man kills once he is likely to do it again. These Molly Maguires you have been hounding, they are all supposedly killers; are there any of them remaining in these parts?"

Captain burst out laughing and it took a moment for him to gain control of himself. "Any remaining? Very droll, Mr. Gilhooley." He stared at Finnegan who apparently did not see the humor in his statement. "Yes, sir, an ample supply of them remain. Every filthy son of Erin in this town could be classed as a Molly Maguire." The captain did not so much as pause to let Finnegan appreciate the insult to the Irish race. "If the Mollies do not appeal to you, there is a separate Irish group known as the Chain Gang. They sometimes work with the Mollies and sometimes shoot them down in the streets. If killing your own kind does not suit you, Mr. Gilhooley, there is a Welsh gang hereabouts known as the Modocs. They may actually be more detestable than the Mollies, but they never murder people for reasons related to labor disagreements, so Mr. Gowan has not deemed it necessary to begin hanging them, just as yet. Naturally, the Blacklegs band together when there is call for them to break strikes and they are always a revolting collection of men surely capable of the lowest acts imaginable. Oh, there are also the Schuylkill Raiders, if you prefer a more egalitarian group. I have been told they will allow any man to ride with them. Do any of these options strike your fancy?"

Finnegan bit the end off his cigar. "What kind of outfit are these Raiders?"

"God's forgotten scum." The captain pointed to Finnegan's cigar. "Would you have another one of those?"

Finnegan withdrew a spare and handed it to the man across the desk. "Thank you. The Raiders are..." He bit the end off the cigar and lit it. "You may find it difficult to lay your hands on any of them. They are not a group or a gang in the strictest sense. Their membership shifts depending on who amongst their number needs money at any given time. They primarily run amuck robbing taverns and tippling houses for liquor, then sell the liquor to the next tavern down the road." He chuckled and puffed out smoke. "On occasion, they dabble in horse thievery or highwayman robberies."

Finnegan lit his cigar. "You have never arrested any of them?"

The captain shook his head. "We are the Coal and Iron Police, Mr. Gilhooley. Theft or robbery leveled toward a person not involved in the coal or iron trade is simply none of our business."

"Where are these men in the habit of perpetrating their highwayman activities?"

"Oh, if you travel the road between here and Pottsville at night, I would say there is an excellent chance of running into a group of them."

Finnegan nodded. "Very well then, how many of your men could I borrow for some work tonight?"

The captain chuckled. "Just like that?"

"One must begin an endeavor somehow. The road between here and Pottsville seems as reasonable as the next option."

"Mr. Gilhooley, what precisely do you propose to do with the Raiders if you encounter them?"

Finnegan shrugged. "Shoot one to show them I am not to be trifled with and then interrogate the rest to determine if they have any knowledge of the Johanna Wetherill affair."

"That...that is a very interesting plan." The captain sat

back in his chair, staring at the Pinkerton. "Mr. Gilhooley, why on earth would some random highwayman know anything regarding the murder of Johanna Wetherill?"

"One must begin somewhere."

Bourne shook his head. "That may be, and if your luck is better than average you may even learn something regarding Wetherill's fate, but you will do it without the assistance of my men."

Finnegan arched one eyebrow. "Is that so?"

"Under the current circumstances, I cannot spare any of them. When this town boils over I will need them if anyone wearing this uniform is to get out alive. I cannot have them out wandering around in the dark with you chasing Raiders when they may be needed here."

Finnegan thought back on the men he had seen napping when he had first entered the house. "All right, Captain. Keep your men. Their presence would probably only mean a difference in the number of these Raiders who are left on the side of the road and those I bring in to be questioned. It should not be a problem."

The captain took a long pull off his cigar and slowly let the smoke roll out of his mouth. "I have read about you in the papers, Mr. Gilhooley. Allan Pinkerton has done an excellent job of letting every literate man in the country know you apparently knocked some hair off Jesse James in a gunfight."

"In actuality, I believe it was his older brother I hit."

The captain nodded. "Are you gambling that these Raiders will be privy to that knowledge and show you deference based on it? I should warn you, Mr. Gilhooley, those Raiders I have seen did not appear to follow the papers that well."

Finnegan smiled. "Like all men, they will show due deference to bullets." He got up from his chair and extended his hand to the captain. "Thank you for your time, sir. Perhaps, before I go, you could tell me where a man might obtain a horse?"

IT DID NOT TAKE TOO long for Finnegan to locate the livery stable and lay his hands on a grey that appeared to be capable of making it outside the town limits without expiring. Thankfully, the plans he had for the evening did not hinge on the quality of the horseflesh available. His transportation seen to, he returned to his rented room. With nothing better to do before sundown, he opened a book and began to peruse it. The volume had been given to him by Molly during his convalescence in Minnesota. It was an English translation of a German story about a doctor named Faustus who made a deal with the devil. When Molly had initially gifted it to Finnegan, she had made several references to the way the good doctor's dealings were similar to the arrangement Finnegan had with Allan Pinkerton. After working his way through most of the book, the gunman still did not really see the connection. Finnegan had certainly never seduced Helen of Troy or built his own country out of reclaimed swamp land. The book was not easy to digest, and the meaning of certain verses was difficult to discern, but he was determined to finish it, if for no other reason than he wished to inform Molly he had read it in its entirety when next they met.

Out of the corner of his eye Finnegan caught a bit of movement, so he pulled his gaze from the book to the window. Across the next lot there was what Finnegan had taken to be a Catholic church. As Finnegan watched, a boy of about twelve came rambling down the wide alley between the two buildings. He was somewhat mired in coal dust and appeared cheerful enough, given his dirty condition. What perked Finnegan's interest was that the young man approached the back of the church and then hopped up onto a barrel. Standing on the barrel, he was able to leap up onto the rear roof of the church, and that allowed him to leap once more into one of the lower windows of the bell tower, where he disappeared from view.

Finnegan closed his book and got up from the bed. "A belfry bat, no less." He smiled and opened the window. He sat on the sill, swung his legs out and meandered over to the side of the church. Finnegan wasn't as quick about it as the boy had been, but he climbed the barrel, ascended the roof, and swung up into the window the youngster had disappeared into. Finnegan dropped into the small room and the boy jolted backwards against the rear wall of the belfry, clearly surprised.

He looked properly shocked to have a man of Finnegan's size, dressed in a black suit and coat, drop into his room without warning. "What kind of balled up bastard are you?" The boy clutched a lunch bucket against his chest, which appeared to be his sole possession, aside from some bedding rolled up in the corner of the room and a few newspapers.

"I've never seen a pigeon your size, boy. How is it you have come to live in a church tower?"

"You're not a priest, so I would say it is none of your business."

"That could be argued, yes." Finnegan turned around and stared out the window. It afforded an excellent view of the window of his rented room. "This is a fine perch, boy. I take it the Father allows you to bivouac here?"

"Yes, not that it's any of your damn business. Mister, you might be a lot bigger than me, and I seen your guns when you swung through the window, but that don't give you a right to bother a man in his own home."

Finnegan slowly turned to look at the youngster. "You've a damn sharp tongue for a fellow who is still between hay and grass." He shook his head. "I only inquired, young man, because I wish to know who I should make an offer to if I wish to rent this space."

"Rent...this belfry? Mister, you been out in the sun too long?"

"I assure you, I am in as right of mind as I have ever been." Finnegan leaned against the windowsill. "The fact of the matter, young man, is that I often find it advantageous to sleep in a location other than the one most people assume I will be sleeping in."

"Say what?"

"I wish to rent this space to sleep on occasion. When it suits my needs."

"You want to sleep up here with me?" The boy squinted at Finnegan, as if that would somehow help him understand.

"No. If it suits your needs, on the nights when I sleep here, you would be welcome to sleep in my room." Finnegan pointed out the window. "Down there at Mrs. Wallace's boarding house. The room is quite nice. You should find it rather comfortable."

"This is just plain bosh, Mister. You must be out of your head."

"I can appreciate your difficulty understanding, young man. If I may..." Finnegan reached into his vest pocket. He removed a silver dollar and flipped it to the boy, who dropped his lunch pail to catch it. "As an older man, I might give you the small piece of advice that, in such cases as this, the rendering of payment is far more important than a firm understanding of the situation."

The kid gazed down at the coin in his hand. "A dollar?"

"Yes. Will that buy me one week's option on this property?"

"And you want me to sleep down at the boarding house?"

"If it suits you during the nights I sleep here. What is your name, boy?"

"Abijah Smith." He held up the coin for closer inspection. "You really want to pay me a dollar a week to sleep in this old belfry while I sleep in your rented room?"

"Indeed. I may also require your assistance in other matters, if you are available. I take it you are without family?"

"My father told me mother ran off with a hairbrush salesman. My father died last year in the St. Clair shaft."

"What are you doing to earn your living?"

He continued to stare down at the dollar. "I pick over the culm banks and sell the larger pieces to the stores for heat."

"Would you be interested in leaving that work for a temporary commission in my service?"

The young Mr. Smith looked up from the dollar. "What is it you do to earn your living?"

"I am a detective in private employ."

His eyes narrowed. "You are a Pinkerton man?"

"I am."

"Sir, I have heard that your kind is very truly in league with the devil."

"That may be the case." Finnegan smiled at the boy. "I am not privy to who Mr. Pinkerton may or may not take on as a partner. That being said, I pay two bits a day for assistance."

Abijah placed his dollar in the pocket of his ragged pants. "If you are truly a Pinkerton man, why don't you use the peelers for help?"

"You are a quicker fellow than I gave you credit for, Mr.

Smith. I suppose the simplest explanation might be to ask you if you have any experience acting as a detective?"

"I do not."

"And being willing to admit that makes you a greater asset than any member of the Coal and Iron Police. What I require is a man who can follow orders and not feel the need to make up his own. Are you that man?"

"For two bits a day, I will sure as hell try to be."

"Then we have a deal?" Finnegan extended his hand.

The boy took it. "What is your name, sir?"

"Finnegan Gilhooley."

The boy glanced to his small pile of newspapers and then back to his new employer. "Sir, are you the man who shot Jesse James?"

"You can read?"

"And write. The Father taught me."

"It is good that you have learned to read. Now you must learn not to believe everything you read." Finnegan withdrew a cigar and his matchbox. "Do you know how to ride a horse?"

"Yes, sir. Well enough."

"Good. Then tonight you will be earning two bits."

FINNEGAN LET the rented swayback plod along. There was no reason to hurry. When one is acting as bait it is often preferable to take one's time. He slopped in the saddle to feign drunkenness and hummed the *Battle Hymn of the Republic* under his breath to irritate any former rebels who might be listening. It was not the first time he had used such a ruse. It had proven quite effective in Missouri a time or two. Although the men who had fallen for the trick had never turned out to be James confederates, Finnegan was still convinced the method held promise. At a minimum, it usually led to one less highwayman in the world, which, to Finnegan's way of thinking, made it worthwhile.

"Let the hero, born of woman, crush the serpent with his heel." Finnegan lolled in the saddle. "Damned serpents be damned." He fumbled out a cigar and slowly lit a match. From experience, he knew to keep his eyes squinted shut so his night vison would not be affected. "His truth is marching on. Glory, glory..."

"Might you have another one of those, stranger?"

At the sound of the voice Finnegan brought the horse to a stop in the middle of the road. "What? What's all that? Who goes there?"

Several sets of hooves slopped in the mud from ahead and behind Finnegan. "Strangers well met, friend." The one talking approached from the front with two partners. Finnegan could hear two more come up behind him. "I was just professing to my associates how nice it would be to have some tobacco, and here you come down the road sporting some."

Finnegan leaned forward in the saddle and looked his assailant over. The man wore dirty coveralls and a hat with a badly tattered brim. His scraggly beard hung down in front of a body that was obviously better fed with whiskey than food. His mount looked healthy enough, though. A likely indication that it was stolen. His associates all sported outfits to match. Finnegan removed the cigar from his mouth before addressing them. "Who the hell do you gentleman think you are blocking the road at this time of night?"

The lead man sat up a bit in the saddle. He had a ragged Colt Navy shoved in his belt. "We make our home here, sir.

As such, we feel it is our right to inquire the purposes of those who pass on the road."

Finnegan laughed. "If I was you, I would spend less time bothering travelers and see to packing my traps so I could make my home elsewhere. This patch you have staked out for yourself here would do as a small piece of hell so long as the devil did not hold himself to a very high standard."

"Oh, that is unfortunate, sir. I am afraid that an insult such as that will cost you a heavy toll. I cannot let such an insult be directed at our hearths and homes without exacting payment."

Finnegan laughed again. "That is understandable, I can only assume you are the duly elected mayor of this place, and, as such, should be deeply offended. In recompense, let me suggest that if I were to take a long piss on the side of this road it should increase the greenback value of your township ten-fold. Is that offer to your liking?"

"You, sir, have a sharp tongue and it will cost you dearly tonight. I believe it will cost you all you've got." The leader leaned forward. "We will have your money, your horse, and, of course, all your cigars."

"Well, sir, that is very nearly all I have got. You are correct on that score."

"You would do well to remember this night the next time you cast aspersions on another man's home. You should be glad that we are leaving you with your duds and boots. A pernicious man would leave you naked and afoot."

"You are truly the soul of charity." Finnegan swung one leg over and lowered himself to the ground. "You are more than welcome to this old nag."

The leader let out a small chuckle. "You dislike the animal that much?"

"Liking has little to do with it. It is rented from the stable in St. Clair. I could not care less who claims to own it at any given time." The whole crew of highwaymen began to laugh over Finnegan's willingness to part with his rented steed. They seemed to be enjoying themselves so much that Finnegan made use of the opportunity to draw his pistols. He held his old dragoon in his left, the newly acquired Remington in his right, and thumbed back the hammers before his adversaries even noticed there had been a change in the odds. Finnegan angled the pistols at the two closest men, one up the road, the other down. "Gentlemen, there is no need for this to degenerate. Drop your pistols down to the ground and dismount, one at a time."

The leader sat stunned for a moment before speaking, "There are five of us, you damned fool..."

Finnegan fired the Remington and knocked the man out of the saddle. He fired off the dragoon at the same time without really aiming. The second man's horse bolted down the road and its rider slipped from the saddle with his foot still in the stirrup. The two disappeared into the night with the man flopping from stone to stone in the muddy road. Finnegan lit off two more shots at the next closest man, who was thrown to the ground as his horse reared up. That done, he turned on the last two highwaymen standing, and they both threw their hands into the air. Even in the pale moonlight, Finnegan could see they were little better than boys. The one who was not quite scared mute spoke first. "Please, Jesus, hold fire, mister. We ain't even armed, not really. Amos there has got his daddy's old squirrel gun, but that's it. We ain't no robbers, neither. Our uncle you just killed there said he'd tan our hides if we didn't come along tonight."

Finnegan heard a low moaning from one of the men he had shot. He fired a round off at the shape of the lump in the road and turned back to the boys. "Drop the squirrel gun and get down from your horses. Do not approach your kinfolk."

"Yes, sir." The talkative boy motioned to his associate, and he tossed a small rifle off into the brush before dismounting. The far-off sound of approaching hoof beats could be heard. "Sir, that might be some of our kinfolk coming."

"It is not." Finnegan slipped the dragoon back into his belt. "That is most likely my assistant."

"What are you, mister?"

"I am a captain in the Coal and Iron Police, and I am taking you into custody. You are certain you are not armed?"

"On our mother's grave, sir." The talkative boy stared over at the first man who had been shot. "You killed our old uncle Jim before he even had a chance to pull his gun, mister."

"That is generally the best method for victory in a gunfight, young man." Finnegan stepped to the hunched-up body in the road and kicked it out of its bent position so that it sprawled. There, face up in the mud, the man emitted a low groan. "It would appear your beloved uncle is shot, but not killed."

The two young men approached and stood over him. "Lord, mister, he looks poorly." The talkative one glanced between the bloody uncle and Finnegan. "Uncle Jim always was kind of a blowhard bastard, but I guess we ought not to let him die in the road all covered in mud like that. Is there something we can do to help him, mister?"

Finnegan stared down at the man for a moment. Plans rarely worked out exactly as he hoped they would. "Very well. One of you...quiet boy, you go and try to catch some of those horses. Try to catch mine, too, while you are about it." He glanced around. At some point during the excitement his rented equine had disappeared into the night. "And be quick about it." The lad took off up the road in search of the errant horses.

"Hey, hey, you sneaky son of a bitch." Down in the mud, Uncle Jim was clutching Finnegan's leg. "You shot me without warning, you son of a bitch."

"There was warning, you simply did not appreciate it." Finnegan knelt down by the man and held the Remington up for him to see. "If I waste my time transporting you to a doctor will you share information with me freely? If you intend to be truculent, I would just as soon shoot you again now and save us all the effort."

"You get this ball dug out of me and I'll tell you any damn thing you want to hear." He pointed up with one muddy hand. "And if you give me some of that damned tobacco. It's what got me shot, you might as well let me smoke."

Finnegan realized that he had been clutching the cigar between his teeth since dismounting. "That seems a fair trade." He placed the cigar in Uncle Jim's mouth and stood up. Just then Abijah came riding up leading the horse that had previously escaped in the direction of St. Clair. "Mr. Smith, you've obtained a spare mount."

"Yes, sir. She came up on us in the road dragging the dearly departed. I assumed you'd be wanting her back."

"Her rider is surely dead?"

"Dead as chastity, sir. If he was not, I assume he would have had words with me when I removed him from the stirrup." Abijah squinted in the darkness. "Billy Pyle, is that you standing there in the road?" He glanced downward. "With your old Uncle Jim?"

The talkative boy shrugged. "That would be us, Abijah. You working for the Coal and Iron peelers now?"

"You might say that. And I see you've found work as a road agent."

"It's been a short sort of career. Me and Amos been at it two nights. Last night nobody came along and tonight this fella here done shot up our whole gang. I fear Uncle Jim won't see morning."

Abijah handed the reins of the caught horse to Finnegan and got down out of the saddle. "Oh, he seems to be puffing on that cigar all right for a dying man. I expect he's got one or two more winters left in him. How's your dear aunt these days? I still recall how good that pie was she made for the church social."

Finnegan cleared his throat to get their attention. "If you boys are about done catching up, I believe we should get Uncle Jim loaded on a horse. At this point, I have something of an investment in him and would prefer that he lived to see sunrise. We have a great deal of labor left ahead of us yet tonight, boys. We have to get Jim to town and then come back here and bury the dead, unless you prefer to leave the remainder of your kinfolk for the crows."

Billy shrugged again. "Them two you killed dead was our cousins from over in Avondale. I never liked them much and I doubt they'll be missed much."

Finnegan sighed. "Boy, you bury the dead regardless of your feeling toward them. It sets a poor precedent to leave them to rot. Too much of that and there may not be anyone to bury you when you pass."

"What the hell do I care what's done with me when I'm past living?"

"Hell if I know, boy." Finnegan pointed down at the man enjoying his cigar. "Grab one end of your beloved uncle."

As it turned out, the second boy returned quite promptly with the rest of the horses. Finnegan was able to ride into St. Clair while it was still dark with the wounded Uncle Jim, two young miscreants, and two corpses in tow. He dropped the whole mess off with what passed for the night sergeant, a man named Rourke, at the Coal and Iron Police, and sent young Abijah to rouse the town's one and only doctor. The living miscreants went in a cell. The corpses were flopped on the porch of the undertaker down the street, and the wounded Uncle Jim was placed on a cot normally occupied by a napping policeman. Finnegan remained at the Coal and Iron house until the doctor adjudged that Uncle Jim's wound would probably not prove to be immediately fatal. It was the opinion of the doctor that Finnegan could wait until the next day to interrogate the man and that it might even be preferable to interrogate him after they had all rested a bit.

Finnegan returned to his rented room to find a note jammed into the crack on the outside windowpane in his room. He flipped it open. It read: *Creek bed behind house, S.R.* Finnegan grinned at the note and placed it in his pocket. Exiting through the window, he made his way down into the creek bed roughly a half mile off and only had to walk about a hundred yards before he came to a lanky man lolling on the creek bank. The fellow wore the outfit of a bartender, complete with the apron and prodigious side whiskers. "Good morning, Mr. Gilhooley, and how does the day find you in coal country?"

"Wishing I was elsewhere, Sam Rooney. I see you've stopped trying to convince mail agents to develop sticky fingers and moved on to bigger and better things. How is the liquor business?"

The man smiled and extended his hand, which Finnegan shook. "Oddly enough, better paying than the detective business. Around here I am known as Gus Moody, and I may remain that man when my commission here has expired. Some days I think it might be better to be a bartender than a detective. Bartenders are better liked, to say nothing of the fact that if I am discovered to be a detective in this town there is a good chance the fine citizens will hang me from a lamppost -- or would, if they had a lamppost."

Finnegan grinned. "These are the hazards you clandestine men run. I have always told you that it is better to be a shootist than a spy, but you never listen."

The bartender chuckled. "That is how I knew you were in town, old friend." He sat back down on the creek bank. "I heard the doctor being roused and asked your hired boy what was going on. He said a Pinkerton agent had killed some men on the road to Pottsville. I thought to myself that no Pinkerton other than Finnegan Gilhooley would dare begin killing men so early in the morning. I inquired of the boy where the Pinkerton was staying, and here we are, together again."

"You are quite the detective, Sam. I shall have to mention your prowess in my next telegram to Mr. Pinkerton."

"I wish you would, Finn." He produced two cigars from his apron and handed one to Finnegan. "This life in coal country is quite dreary, and I would prefer to move on to something with better prospects, although some of us have done quite well here."

Finnegan sat down on the bank next to his friend. "It is good to see you again, Sam. I believe the last time we were together we were chasing the Reno boys."

"Indeed. You shot that sharecropper who was trying to stick me with a scythe."

"That is what you get for being as skinny as a cornstalk."

"At any rate, I appreciated it." He lit his cigar and Finnegan's.

"Seeing you here explains why there are so many train robberies in this country. Are there any Pinkerton men placed elsewhere these days, or do we all linger here waiting for perdition to set in?"

"Some days it does feel as though the whole company has pulled up stakes and settled here. I preferred Chicago, personally, but they give us little choice, as you well know." The bartender-detective eyed his friend. "I can't imagine what old Allan has sent you here for, though. If the miners require shooting, the Coal and Iron thugs have always done a handy job of it in the past."

Finnegan shook his cigar at him. "Oh, yes, speaking of which, you might be able to aid me in my task. I have been sent here to find a murderer."

Rooney laughed. "It takes one to find one, I suppose. Although it should not be overly difficult here. Don't you read the papers, Finn? Most of these coal miners are murderers. Ask anyone."

"I require a specific one. I was sent here by Pinkerton to find the man who killed one Johanna Wetherill."

Rooney nodded knowingly. "Ah, the dead Wetherill girl. Interesting. Why would anyone care much one way or the other regarding a dead whore?"

"Before she took to whoring, she was the niece of Colonel Enoch Mcleod."

Rooney sneered. "I expect if I had to suffer a man like that as my uncle I might have turned to whoring and drinking, as well."

"I have seen you do plenty of drinking without the aid of a sour uncle." Finnegan grinned. "I would not imagine you could do very well whoring."

"I clean up well enough when freshly barbered."

Finnegan clapped him on the back. "Well, you do. Did you know the girl, Sam? If you did and could tell me who killed her, it would be of great help to me. I am rather in a hurry to leave this place and get back to Missouri and the James brothers."

"Oh, good Lord, do you still have your nose stuck in that? I swear, Finn, you are like a dog with a bone." Rooney knocked ash into the creek mud, where it sizzled. "I cannot say as I knew the girl personally. She came through the tavern a time or two plying her trade as best she could. Now that you mention it, I believe she even mentioned her relation to rotten old Enoch once or twice, although at the time I gave it no credit. I have met that old scoundrel a few times when he has passed through town on business. What God's purpose for colonels might be, I could not tell you."

"I am inclined to agree with you."

"Yes, well, as I recall she was living at a tippling house over at Crow Hollow. It is run by a woman of terrible reputation and quite popular with the young men in these parts. Quite popular with the men of the Coal and Iron Police, as well."

"Truly? Captain Bourne did not mention the local entertainment when I spoke with him."

"No, I do not imagine he did. I would bet a silver dollar that the good captain knew Miss Wetherill better than I did. The Coal and Iron peelers can't easily avail themselves of any entertainment at the local saloons. Those are reserved for the miners and such, so they go to Crow Hollow."

"A lovely arrangement, to be sure."

"Indeed. This place is full of lovely arrangements."

Finnegan shook his head and stared at the creek. "What

is it you lads have been up to around here, Sam? It seems a damned unfortunate business."

"It is unfortunate, Finn, that is for certain." He took a puff of his cigar. "By now you must have heard of the Molly Maguires?"

"I have."

"Well, then, you can appreciate the fact that they are a race of damned odd animals. They are making ready to hang no less than twenty of the poor bastards and I'm still not certain they truly exist."

Finnegan smiled at his old friend. "And what the hell does that mean?"

"Have you ever met the esteemed Mr. James McParlan?"

Finnegan chuckled. "Oh, yes, and it was not at Sunday Mass. All I really recall about the man was that he seemed to have an excellent working knowledge of counterfeit money, almost as though it represented something of a hobby for him, and he liked to complain about our pay."

"Yes, well, Mr. McParlan spent about a year here altogether and has now departed for the west to enjoy a big promotion. I am told Pinkerton is opening a branch office in Denver and Mr. McParlan will be in charge of it."

"And what was it that Mr. McParlan did here to earn such an accolade?"

Rooney smiled. "There is some debate regarding that, Finn. Some say he rooted out a vile conspiracy of murderers and anarchists. Others say he found the twenty dumbest bastards in the county and played them for fools. I ask you, Finn, if you had robbed a few banks with the James brothers, would you be guilty of bank robbery?"

"To be certain, and I would not waste my time talking to the likes of you, either. Not if I was a well-to-do bank robber."

Rooney continued to smile. "Our associate, Mr. McParlan, takes a wider view of the law, however. You see, he planned most of what the Mollies are to be hung for. He even traipsed along with them on several adventures. James has sat in court many a day calling it infiltration, but most around here view it as the act of a damned bunko artist, and I cannot help but see their point. It strikes me as a low thing to foment the rebellion and then call yourself a war hero for the federals when it is said and done."

Finnegan knocked ash down into the creek. "McParlan always was willing to use a hook or a crook to get things done. I suppose this will be remembered as his masterpiece."

"A damned ugly masterpiece, if I do say so myself. Twenty men dangling is the price of his new office."

Finnegan shrugged. "I have seen many more than that lying dead for much less."

"I suppose so." They sat and quietly puffed on their cigars for a moment. "The one good comment I can make, regarding the actions of Mr. McParlan, is that it has given me steady reason for contemplating my own future with the agency."

Finnegan laughed. "I thought you were only jesting about becoming an honest bartender."

"I am, of course. Regular work has never suited me any more than it suits you. No, what I have been asking myself ever since James McParlan finished testifying and fled the vicinity, is what I might have to do to obtain my own branch office as he has."

"Find twenty-five men to hang?"

"Possibly." Rooney leaned toward Finnegan. "Do you know how much these railroad men and coal dealers have paid Pinkerton to ferret out these Molly Maguires?"

"Mr. Pinkerton has not seen fit to make an accountant of me, yet."

70

"I have heard it was a hundred thousand dollars, Finnegan."

The gunman's eyes grew wide. "Ah, that is a grand number, is it not?"

"Grand indeed. Finn, you have always been Pinkerton's darling boy. What is more, you perform the ultimate enforcement of his edicts. Can a man do more for another man than you have done for Allan Pinkerton?"

"What are you getting at, Sam?"

"How much of that one hundred thousand dollars do you think is fated to end up in your pocket, Finn?"

The gunman shook his head. "Now you are talking like McParlan."

"And well I should. Finn, I have begun to believe that his sort are the only ones who get ahead in this world. These miners die of the black lung before they are forty. I will likely develop jaundice from my career as a bartender. You will eventually be shot when another man proves quicker than you."

"All men must face their fate."

"Not all men." Rooney motioned to the west with his cigar. "Somewhere out there, the James brothers are cooing into the ear of a proper harlot and drinking to your poor marksmanship. I have no reason to believe they will ever find themselves doing otherwise."

Finnegan laughed. "You have a very active imagination, Sam."

"It grows more active by the day. I think of how those men rob banks and trains and live far better than the lowly detectives tasked with chasing them. It makes me wonder, truly, are we employed on the wrong side of this particular endeavor? We will never rise as McParlan did. If we continue as we are now, we will never be as well off as the James brothers. Does the burden of self-betterment not fall to the man who wishes to be better? Do you honestly believe Mr. Pinkerton, or his sons, would ever place either of us in a managerial position?"

"Sam, you have developed the elongated tongue of a bartender, I will give you that. What exactly is it you propose?"

"I propose that we take advantage of opportunities as they present themselves. Are you aware that, since the long strike back in '75, the miners here are no longer paid in company script?"

"I am afraid I have not been in town long enough to familiarize myself with the pay schedules of these people."

Rooney stared at his cigar in deep concentration. "Since men like Mcleod and that silver-tongued prosecutor Gowan have consolidated all the workings in this place, all the pay comes once a month, on one train."

"Prosecutor?"

"You have not heard? Not only does Mr. Gowan own all the coal mines and the railroad, he is a schooled litigator. He took the liberty of prosecuting the Molly Maguires himself by acting as county attorney."

Finnegan shook his head. "It is a fine trick they have played on these miners. Did any of them truly kill the men they are to hang for?"

"I cannot say, and it is of little matter to me. All I know is that I count myself lucky not to be either among those killed or those to be hung. Finn, the payroll for the entire town comes in once a month on a Reading train, guarded only by those Coal and Iron deadbeats. It should number between ten and twelve thousand, Finnegan."

The gunman coughed and turned to his old friend. "That is a grand number, as well."

"It is, and it should all be genuine coin of the realm, no script."

"Ah, Sam. I have truly missed you. We are not reunited for more than ten minutes, and you are already trying to convince me to rob a train, even though neither of us are train robbers."

"We robbed more than our share of Confederate shipments during the war."

"Yes, my friend, but that was a war."

"Not one we started or had an interest in. By my way of thinking, one train is as good as the next, Finn."

"You would have us rob our own employer, Sam?"

"Who's employer? I am not employed as a miner or a railroad man, neither are you. I am a bartender and Pinkerton agent, and I fail to see what that has to do with Gowan, Mcleod, or any of the other bastards who got rich while we were piling up our friends to stop the grapeshot at Bull Run. I don't owe those chiselers anything, and neither do you."

Finnegan could not help but admit that the man had a point. He did, in fact, not owe anything to the Reading Railroad or its associated coal mining interests. "Truly, twelve thousand?"

"Perhaps more. There is no reason for you to give me an answer this very morning, Finn. Think on it. If we never act to change our own fortunes, I doubt we will ever see much in the way of improvement." Sam patted his fellow Pinkerton agent on the back. "In the meantime, give this some contemplation. There is a man who goes by the name of Egan. He lives in a shanty up on Mount Carbon. When he has money, he fancies to come drink at my tavern. Once, deep in his cups, he told a story about killing a whore in Kansas during the war." Sam grinned and puffed his cigar. "As you well know, I am not the high grade of detective Mr. Pinkerton would have

73

the world believe I am, but it seems to me that if a man has killed one whore, he is liable to kill another. Since you are currently in the practice of searching out whore killers, I thought I would mention it."

"Egan?"

"John Egan."

"Thank you, Sam. I will look into it."

"I will begin walking through here at the end of my day shift from now on. Post a note on the tree there if you wish to meet. Give some thought to the other proposition, as well. A man should not cast aside too many opportunities in this life. It is always hard to say if another of like value will present itself."

"I promise to give it my full consideration, old friend."

Chapter 4

ST. CLAIR, PENNSYLVANIA
June 16th, 1877

THE NEXT DAY FINNEGAN HAD NOT ROUSED HIMSELF until almost noon. After procuring what passed for a very late breakfast from his landlady, he made his way down the street to the telegraph office which, resided inside the train depot. He stepped to the small room that contained the operator and his equipment.

"Young sir, I wish to wire Philadelphia." Finnegan produced his newly-acquired badge. "I believe the service is free to agents of the railroad?"

The telegraph operator nodded. "It is. Who do you wish to contact?"

"Robert Pinkerton at the Pinkerton branch office. They will be listed in the city directory."

The clerk chuckled. "Yes, sir, I imagine they will be. What would you like the telegram to include?"

Finnegan rubbed his chin. "Robert, have shot two men dead, wounded a third. May have good intelligence regarding murderer." The clerk slowly scratched out the message and then glanced up with rather frightened eyes. "Sign it F. Gilhooley."

"Yes, sir. I will send it right away, sir."

"Thank you."

With his reporting seen to, Finnegan walked a bit farther down the street to the house occupied by the Coal and Iron Police. Once inside, he purloined a cup of coffee from the stove and made his way to the room that was currently acting as a hospital. Laid out before Finnegan on a rather nasty-looking cot was the infamous Uncle Jim that Finnegan had shot the night before. Despite having a .44 caliber bullet unceremoniously pushed through him, the man seemed little the worse for wear.

"You take having a new orifice installed quite well, sir." Finnegan sipped his coffee.

Uncle Jim sat up a bit and ran one hand over the bandages that covered his midsection. Finnegan's bullet had caught the old rascal on the end of one rib and spun him from the saddle. The fall might have hurt him more than the shot. "I might thank you for avoiding the existing holes. I'd damn well wager I was only in truly mortal danger when that doctor was at me. The man's a well-known drunkard."

"And you, a well-known road agent. It is hard to say where a man may find fame."

"I am told by these peelers that you have found fame with a gun in your hand. I dare say I am almost honored to have been shot by the illustrious likes of you."

Finnegan sipped his coffee again. "If you like, I can shoot you again, thus doubling your renown."

"A fine offer, but not necessary." Jim pointed to Finnegan's coat pocket. "Would you have another cigar?"

Finnegan pulled one from his coat and handed it to the man. "For a man with a hole in his lung, you enjoy tobacco a great deal." He lit the cigar and sat back in his chair, looking over the black crust the old man had deposited on the bed and littered about him on the floor. "Is that mud from last evening?"

The old man gave it a casual glance. "Is it. Here in the coal patch, we pride ourselves on our black mud. The coal dust creeps everywhere. Around here, all we got is twinkling black earth."

Finnegan shrugged and noticed the same substance adorned his boots. "This is an interesting place. How did you come to making your living as a highwayman?"

Jim puffed away. "Oh, one simply falls into such things. For a time, I made a fine living smuggling liquor. For several years, I stole army horses."

"Union or rebel?"

"Makes no difference, a horse is a horse. That is the glory of animals, sir, they hold no ridiculous political affiliations." Jim looked Finnegan over. "Your name is Gilhooley?"

"Indeed."

"You are Irish?"

"Indeed."

"How is it you come to find yourself engaged in the dirty business of being a Pinkerton? I would not think even the lowest man would hang his own kind."

"I have no kind and I have not come here to hang miners. I wish to know who killed Johanna Wetherill. That is my only charge."

Jim assumed a very serious countenance. "The good Lord as my witness, I've never killed no one, sir. Can't imagine why I would kill a woman."

"Truly? No one?"

"Not a soul. For all the men I have waylaid on the road to Pottsville, I have never had to draw my gun. To be honest, it came as a great shock to me when you began firing."

"What about your departed kinfolk? Did they pull their guns on the road before?"

"Oh, well, they did on occasion gun down a man or two, but such activity is required in that sort of work. Truth be told, I always appreciated them carrying the sin of that for me."

Finnegan chuckled. "That is an intriguing notion. I cannot help but wonder if my employer considers things in the same light. Did your kin kill Johanna Wetherill?"

Jim shook his head. "They had their faults, but they would not kill a woman. I do not recognize the lady's name. Where did she reside?"

"I am told she lived at a tippling house in Crow Hollow."

"Ah, that may explain it. The pleasures to be found in such places have been out of reach for me for some time. Probably will be for some time to come since you have shot my family and made it so difficult for me to ride. Of course, that assumes you are not intending to place me on the end of a rope. What do you intend to do with me and my nephews, sir?"

"What do you think should be done with you?" Finnegan drained the remainder of his coffee.

"I have given that some thought while I been lying here." Jim inhaled his cigar deeply. "Them boys are too young to swing, too young to be sitting in the hoosegow. Send them home and let me face whatever it is the old rip judge in Pottsville thinks I have coming to me."

Finnegan shook his head. "Ah, to hell with it. When you can walk, you may go, as well. Find a new profession, Uncle Jim." He stood.

"Hey, Pinkerton man," Jim let some smoke roll out of his

nose. "You've done me a good turn, so let me return the favor. I can tell you that these damn peelers enjoy the offerings of that tippling house you mentioned. A man would have to be of a damned ugly demeanor to kill a woman. From what I have seen over the years, these peelers might be fit for it."

Finnegan glanced around to make sure they had not been overheard. "There may be some substance to that theory. Have you any knowledge of a man named John Egan?"

Jim nodded vigorously. "Oh, most definitely. John and I formerly freighted spirits together. We had something of a falling out. I shot at him, and he shot at me. His shot went wide but I hit him in the leg, and we have not been partners ever since."

"I thought you were not given to shooting men, Uncle Jim?"

"I said I had never killed a man. John Egan still lives, as far as I know. He is a vile and pernicious man. Last I heard, he's taken to riding with the Raiders on some of their whiskey runs."

Finnegan shook his head. "He rides with the Raiders...I thought you and your kin were the Raiders."

"It depends on whether or not we're raiding, I suppose. Mr. Gilhooley, in the coal patch you will soon learn that it is best to keep affiliations loose. I was told recently that John had swapped a large batch of the homebrewed whale oil he calls whiskey for a young girl who found herself in the keeping of a ward in the Wyoming. I shudder to think what he might be doing with her."

Finnegan groaned. He was becoming annoyed by the digressions that seemed to continually keep him from his task. "Old man, what I wish to know is if you think John Egan killed the Wetherill girl. Not whether he is compromising another wayward waif."

Jim shrugged and then grimaced from the pain. "He might of killed that gal. John is mean as a rented mule when he's been drinking. He told me once that he killed a woman in Indian territory for making a jest regarding his manhood."

Finnegan smiled and nodded. "Very well then, good enough for me."

Jim grinned. "You going to kill Egan?"

"If he will not come quietly. I have been told he lives on Mount Carbon."

"He does. Take my nephew Billy with you and he can show you the very spot. Make sure not to injure that girl while you're about killing John." He let out a plume of smoke. "Ought to see to it that she finds a better situation, while you're at it."

"Oh, and maybe when I am done with that, I will drive all the snakes out of Pennsylvania. Is there anything else you would like while I am at your service, Uncle Jim?"

"A bottle of good bourbon might help me knit."

Finnegan left the old scoundrel to his convalescence and walked down the hall to the makeshift holding cell that contained the nephews. Finnegan rapped on the bars with one knuckle to get their attention. "Hey, Pyle boys, grown weary of jail life yet?"

Billy, the talkative one, nodded and got up from the floor where he had been sitting. "Most certainly, sir. We would be obliged to you if you could tell us when we might be let out, or stretched, or whatever it is they intend to do with us is to transpire."

Finnegan looked the young men over. They were nothing more than farm boys, dressed in coveralls, and filthy with the same coal dust that layered every other living soul in the vicinity. "Be honest and be of use and perhaps we can avoid the stretching. Do either of you know anything regarding a woman named Johanna Wetherill?"

"No, sir, not a thing." Billy shook his head.

"Uh, sir?" Amos, the quiet one, got up from the floor and approached the door. Finnegan was a bit shocked; he had begun to suspect the boy was mute. "Sir, I never made the acquaintance of that lady, but I do know something about her."

"And what is that, young Amos?"

"Your assistant, Abijah Smith, found her dead in a culm bank."

"How's that?"

"Abijah found her remains, sir, while he was picking over a culm bank one morning. He told me true, sir. Found her and then told the peelers here about her."

Finnegan sighed. Being a real detective was proving quite vexing. "I see. Thank you for informing me." He checked his watch. "You young men will remain here until later in the day when I come to collect you. I require your services. Are you able to lead me up Mount Carbon and show me the residence of a John Egan?"

Billy and Amos both nodded, but Billy confirmed. "We can lead you straight to his front step, sir."

"Very well, then. I will have the captain release you so you can obtain some victuals and tend to your uncle Jim. Be here when I come around to collect you." They both nodded and Finnegan made his way farther down the hall to Captain Bourne's office. He went through the door without knocking. Inside, he found Bourne standing stone still up against the rear wall, a look of panic in his eyes. He had clearly leapt into the position as the door opened. "Are you expecting perdition, Captain?" Finnegan stepped inside and closed the door. "Perhaps you thought the devil was coming to call?"

The captain unstiffened a bit and moved away from the wall to peek out his window. "My apologies, it feels as if there is something afoot today. Something in the air. How does the humor of the town seem to you?"

"Well enough. While I was walking here a rather large lynch mob inquired as to your whereabouts, but I informed them that it was your day off."

"You may jest less when the moment comes to pass, Mr. Gilhooley. I doubt a mob would give you exception simply because you are only passing through."

Finnegan pulled out a chair and took a seat in front of the captain's desk. "Bourne, the men that are to be hanged, did they commit the crimes for which they are being punished?"

Bourne shrugged and slowly moved to his own chair. "The majority, I would assume. They are all known ruffians and frequently boasted of being killers. As always, there is a chance we have mixed up which murder is which, but that cannot be remedied."

"So, some murderers are being hung. That occurs quite frequently, and the citizens of the towns it occurs in do not lynch the police force. What is the cause of your anxiety, sir?"

"It...it is not the normal state of affairs. All these men... they were involved with union business, and it is said they murdered to remedy labor concerns. Many claim the Coal and Iron Police have conspired with you Pinkertons and the Reading to falsely convict them."

"Did you?"

"Certainly not."

"Then you have little to worry about. You are not the first constable who has been forced into an unpopular position. Most survive; I believe you will, too."

Bourne nodded. "That...is a comforting assurance, thank

you." He cleared his throat. "What is your opinion regarding Jim Pyle? Did he kill the girl? If you wish to have him prosecuted, we can ship him to Pottsville and, in all likelihood, have him hung before the month is out."

Finnegan chuckled. "You Pennsylvania folk are too fond of hanging men for my taste." He took out a cigar. "No, I do not believe he is my quarry. A pity, it would be convenient." Finnegan lit his smoke. "Jim has seen fit to put me on another trail. Do you know a man named John Egan?"

The captain nodded with a knowing look. "Ah, yes, Egan. He would make a fine fit for your murderer. He is so generally disliked that you could shoot him without causing any kind of a stir." Bourne rapped on the desktop with his knuckles. "Yes, he would do just fine. You should kill him at your earliest convenience."

"Captain, if I did not know better, I would think you were trying to get rid of me. Do you not fancy my company?"

"I fancy the manner in which the world made sense before you Pinkertons came to town."

"I am sure you do." Finnegan lit his cigar. "If you truly wish to be rid of me quickly, why not lend a hand? I intend to go up Mount Carbon later today and locate Mr. Egan. If I can determine his guilt in the matter of Miss Wetherill, I see no reason why I should not be able to take the evening train to Philadelphia to inform Colonel McLeod that his familial duty has been seen to."

"Ah, that would be most welcome." Bourne drummed his fingers on the desk as though he were trying to decide if it was safe to leave his citadel. "Yes, if it will put you on your way, I will accompany you. I know John Egan by sight."

"Billy and Amos have agreed to act as guides to the man's cabin." Finnegan pulled out his watch once more. "Let them out to help attend to their uncle and get them some food. We will go looking for Mr. Egan about three, if that suits you?"

"Mr. Gilhooley." Bourne looked rather stern. "If Egan is not your man, he is damn well close enough. I have dragged him into that holding cell more than once for trying to butcher his fellow man. Drunken knife fighting is his only vocation aside from brewing whiskey. This town will not miss his presence, and neither will I. Remove him from our midst and be on your way."

"As always, sir, I will aim to please."

FINNEGAN BROUGHT his horse up alongside the mare Abijah was riding as they climbed past abandoned collieries and half-burned breakers on the side of Mount Carbon. It appeared as though there was no corner of Schuylkill County that remained untouched by the predations of the coal miners. All around them there were cuts in the tender earth made decades earlier, when men were content to go after the coal that lay close to the surface. Finnegan could not help but think what a sad day it must have been when the miners were first forced to descend into the shafts.

"Mr. Smith?"

"Yes, sir." Abijah reined in his horse to keep it from stumbling in the undergrowth that had begun to reclaim the ground since the miners had left. There had been a time when the mountain had been home to many stately trees, but they had all been sacrificed to serve as bracing in the mines. It was odd to imagine an entire forest having been moved underground over time.

"Why is it that you failed to mention the fact that you discovered the body of Miss Johanna Wetherill?"

"Discovered...is that the name of the woman I found dead in the culm bank?"

"It is."

"Of what interest is that to you?"

"Discovering her murderer is my purpose here, young man."

Abijah shook his head. "Mr. Gilhooley, I am new to this detective work, but I cannot help but think you may find your labor to be eased if you would see fit to make your purposes known to those you are working with."

Finnegan thought back and came to the conclusion that he had, in fact, not yet mentioned to Abijah what the eventual goal of their work might be. "Ah, yes. You point out a deficiency. You will have to excuse my mistake. I have rarely worked with a partner in the past. From now on, I will share information more freely."

"You may find it saves you effort, sir. I could have told you that old Jim Pyle didn't kill that gal."

"How would you know that to a certainty?"

"I know to a certainty that old Jim Pyle is far too lazy to kill anyone without gain to motivate him."

Finnegan laughed. "I do not know if that is precisely the deductive reasoning Mr. Pinkerton suggests his agents make use of, but it will do for our purposes here. What condition was Miss Wetherill in when you came across her, Abijah?"

"She was a fearsome sight, sir. Please don't think less of me, sir, for saying it, but I still see her from time to time when I close my eyes to go to sleep. I know a man should leave such fussing behind as he leaves boyhood behind, but, God save me, I cannot."

"It is no mark against you, son. I too have seen my share of things I will never forget. Such is life, and growing older does little to remedy it. I know it may be difficult to speak of it, but there are things I must know."

"I will help in any way I can, sir."

They paused in their conversation to jump their horses up onto a small roadway that had been cut into the side of the hill. "Were you able to draw any conclusions regarding the manner in which she may have been killed?"

"Sir, she appeared as though a wild animal had been at her, or one of those maniacs I read about in the *Police Gazette*. She looked as though she had been...eaten, or pummeled with an axe. I cannot imagine what would possess a man to do that to a woman."

"It is the devil's stock and trade, my boy. How long do you believe she could have been lying in that culm bank before you found her?"

"Oh, it could not have been more than just that night, sir. I had taken to working over that bank regular-like. Many men would have walked past it the previous evening on their way home from the mine and would have been walking by only an hour or so after I saw her. It is a well-traveled route by many men, and she was near the bottom of the bank."

"One night." Finnegan brought his horse to a stop when he saw the Pyle boys riding back down the half-overgrown road toward them. "Very interesting."

Billy Pyle reined in his horse. "Sir, you asked us to let you know when we were close. The cabin lies no more than a half mile off." The young man pointed up the road. "Captain Bourne and my brother can see it from where they are."

"You have performed admirably, Billy. Collect your brother and go back down the mountain with Abijah. You may take your leave from St. Clair, if you please." Finnegan turned to his assistant. "Do Captain Bourne and I the favor of loading their uncle Jim on a horse and returning him to...

86

wherever he chooses to go, within reason. When you have completed that, return the horse to the livery and wait for me at the boarding house."

"You will not require me for your business on this mountain, sir?"

"No, Abijah. Captain Bourne and I will see to our business today. Your task is to see to it that Uncle Jim is delivered."

"Very well, sir."

They rode forward and the boys split off from the men. Finnegan sat in the saddle and puffed a cigar as he watched the younger set snake their way down the mountain. He turned to Captain Bourne. "How do you think it will go with Egan?"

Bourne stiffened in the saddle. "It will go quite well if properly executed."

"Properly?"

"I would sincerely hope that we can dispense with some of the rather silly formalities you have suggested, Mr. Gilhooley."

"Such as?"

"I would suggest moving in close to the cabin and shooting Egan when we lay sight on him." Bourne pointed to the Spencer carbine Finnegan carried under his leg in a scabbard. "That is a fine rifle."

Finnegan puffed his cigar. It could not be denied that the captain's suggestion would not save both time and effort. "I am sorry, Captain. I must insist on speaking with the man first. It seems foolish to come all this way without attempting to determine if I have found the right man to wear the guilt of this crime."

Bourne scowled. "By the time the sun sets tonight you may damn well regret your attention to detail, sir."

Finnegan threw down his cigar. "It will not be the first time experience has proven me a fool, Captain. Let us move on to Egan's place and see to our labors."

They slowly made their way down the wide, brushy ridge that led to John Egan's cabin. It was not difficult to aim at the small homestead, thanks to the winding column of white smoke that was rising from the general area of the building. Bourne motioned to the smoke. "He is boiling his bust head today."

Finnegan gave the captain a stern look and whispered back. "Perhaps we can catch him in the open, then. Keep noise to a minimum as we approach."

Bourne nodded and they continued on. As the woods cleared, they came into a small opening where Egan or some former resident had cut off most of the timber. Finnegan drew his rifle out of the scabbard. Some fifty or sixty yards off they could see a man of great girth hunched over a horsehead whiskey still. Smoke rolled from the boiler and the smell of half-rotten corn drifted over the air. Finnegan and Bourne rode past the cabin and were approaching the lean-to that contained the still before the man turned and noticed them. He cast down the stir stick he held and looked furtively all around before focusing on the two riders.

"What the hell gives you two bastards the right to ride up on a man without announcing yourselves?" He rubbed his hands together and kept glancing to one corner of the lean-to. "I see you there, Bourne. There ain't no coal nor iron up here. Why don't you go back to town and pucker on Frank Gowan's ass like every other day?"

A small shiver ran through Bourne. "You have a damned ugly tongue, John Egan."

"I believe I'll speak any damn way I please in my own damn home." He sneered at Finnegan. "Is that a scarecrow you brung with you? He seems damned proud of that musket in his hand. You proud to point a gun at a man on his own front pasture, peeler bastard?"

"I have not pointed it at you yet, John Egan. If I do, you will be aware of it, I assure you." Finnegan looked around at the rather shabby homestead. "Come out of there, Mr. Egan. We wish to have a word with you."

"I have nothing to say to the likes of you." He sneered again. "Is that the Emerald Isle I hear in your voice? Here you are, riding with the peelers. You proud to hang your own kind, Irishman?"

Finnegan sighed. "Mr. Egan, please do not misunderstand me; it would brighten my spirits to shoot a man such as you, but I would rather only talk. Come out of the shed."

"You're too far up the mountain, peeler!" The yell came from behind them from the front porch of the cabin. It was promptly followed by a clicking sound.

Finnegan slowly turned to see a ragged fellow with a dirty beard and coveralls holding a shotgun. He had the hammers thumbed back and an ugly look that bespoke of a poor disposition. Finnegan sighed again and wrapped the reins around the horn of his saddle so his right hand would be free. "Whoever you are, sir, I would recommend you go back in that domicile and allow me to do my work. I do not appreciate having a gun pointed in my direction any more than your associate Mr. Egan does."

"I'll flop you right out of that saddle. I'll be damned if..."

Finnegan had pulled the dragoon out of his belt underneath his jacket. He fired backwards with the revolver still concealed. The action blew a hole in his coat, lit the fabric inside the coat on fire, and caused his horse to rear up. Luck alone caused the bullet to impact the rearward hillbilly in the elbow. As Finnegan fell to the ground the man dropped his shotgun. "Damn it to hell!" Finnegan made a best effort at heaving himself up out of the dirt with a rifle in one hand and his revolver in the other. Out of the corner of his eye, he saw Egan throw himself into the interior of the lean-to that he had been eyeballing since the visitors arrived. "Don't let him get armed, Bourne." Finnegan turned to the cabin and saw another man emerge with an old Kentucky rifle in his hands. "Drop that musket, damn you!"

The fellow looked to the man who had formerly held the shotgun. "You son of a bitch, you shot my daddy."

The fellow raised the old weapon and Finnegan began firing at him with his dragoon while working to get into a standing position. Three of the rounds went wide, but were close enough so that they spooked the fellow and kept him from shooting. As the last chamber in the dragoon rotated under the hammer Finnegan felt sure of a hit. He had the front sight leveled directly on the fellow's chest. As the hammer was falling the fellow's elbow-shot daddy stepped in front of the bullet. The old man fell face down in the mud and never so much as twitched. Finnegan leveled the revolver at the recently created orphan. "I am sorry, sir, that was not my intention. Drop your..." All of a sudden Finnegan smelled smoke and felt heat. The lining of his coat was fully on fire. "Holy hell!" Finnegan dropped his guns, intent on removing his coat. Naturally, the remaining fellow took the opportunity to fire at Finnegan. The ball flew through the flaming coat as Finnegan cast it aside. With no better option, Finnegan ran a few steps backward and flopped into the brush as the fellow was picking up his dead father's shotgun.

By the time Finnegan found a tree large enough to act as proper cover and got turned around, he could see Bourne dismounting and going into the lean-to. He could also see the fellow running toward the brush. Having left his other arms out in the open Finnegan drew his Remington. "Damn you, sir, drop that scattergun." The fellow turned toward Finnegan's voice and raised the shotgun. Finnegan fired three rounds at the man, and he fell to the ground. Both barrels of the shotgun blasted skyward as the fellow landed in the mud. The sound of a shot came from the lean-to, then another, then another. "Damn it to holy hell." Finnegan approached the dead fellow and checked to make certain he was finished. "Bourne! What's become of you?"

"I...Egan...I have killed John Egan."

"Damn you, Bourne." Finnegan hung his head and holstered his Remington. He retrieved his other two guns from the mud in front of the cabin where they lay with what was left of his jacket and made his way over to the lean-to where his rented horse stood nibbling grass as if nothing much had occurred in the preceding minute. Finnegan fought off the urge to put one of the Spencer's bullets into the animal. "Inconstant whore." He stepped into the lean-to where Egan lay dead with Bourne standing over him. A rotten old Harper's Ferry musket leaned in the corner. Finnegan shook his head. "He is surely dead?"

Bourne holstered the 1873 Colt issued to him by the Coal and Iron Police. "He made a move for his rifle. I...I had no choice."

Finnegan looked at the musket. It might have been in service for the south during the past unpleasantness or, judging by its condition, it might have been last coveted by John Brown. "Captain Bourne, I wanted this man alive. Today I have killed a man I did not intend to. I have been thrown from my horse and nearly incinerated by my own coat. That is to say nothing of the loss of the garment itself, which had given good service for many years. The fact that you have killed this man before I could speak with him is damned vexing."

Bourne merely shrugged. "I would think the death of his kinfolk is equally vexing to Uncle Jim Pyle, but you killed them last night just the same. I think it is a bit hypocritical of you to suggest you are the lone arbiter of who should or should not be shot in this county."

Finnegan withdrew his Remington and began reloading it. "One more mistake such as this, sir, and you may be surprised who the next man shot is." He slipped the last round into its chamber and closed the loading gate.

"What is that supposed to mean, Mr. Gilhooley?"

"Take it to mean what you will, Captain Bourne." He pulled out the dragoon and reloaded that, as well.

"Gilhooley, this man as much as admitted to me that he killed the Wetherill girl."

Finnegan slipped the dragoon into his belt. "This sodden whiskey peddler felt the need to confess while he reached for his gun?"

"He yelled out and asked if I was here about the girl. What else can it mean?"

"He asked if you were here about the girl?" Finnegan shook his head. "That means nothing. He could have been speaking of any girl or any of the women he has violated in the past. The man was well known to attack women."

Bourne threw his hands in the air. "He was well known to hurt women. He died yelling about a girl. You have come here about a dead girl. What the hell more could you hope to find?"

"I had hoped to hear him confess his sins when asked directly."

"How on earth did you intend to accomplish that?"

Finnegan sighed and took out a cigar. "There is a bit of a

blacksmith forge in the other half of this lean-to. I had intended to put iron to him until he informed me of his guilt. It has been my experience that when a man feels hellfire nipping at him, he often offers the most honest testimony."

Bourne grimaced. "My God, sir. You would torture him?"

"I will do whatever is required to execute my commission here." Finnegan lit his cigar. "You would do well to remember that the next time you see fit to interfere in my work."

Bourne let a small shiver pass through him. "Your work here is done, sir." He pointed to the body. "That is your man. Wire Mr. Pinkerton, place an advertisement in the paper, hang the body on Enoch McLeod's front gate, but be on your way, sir."

Finnegan puffed his cigar and scowled down at the body. "We will take him with us." He spit down into the hay that covered the lean-to floor. "Damn it, there are no survivors to identify anyone... We must take all three down the mountain to see if anyone knows these men."

Bourne chuckled "Egan's company was undoubtedly as loathsome as he was. No one can much care they have perished."

"The damned census taker cares about all souls, loathsome or not. We will take them down the mountain. They can be buried in St. Clair if no one claims them for another plot."

"Who the hell is meant to pay for that?"

"You should not kill men if you cannot afford the price of their burial, Captain. If it is too much of an imposition for you, I would suggest you take the money out of your deputies' pay." Finnegan picked up his Spencer and left the lean-to. He was making his way toward Egan's corral to investigate the available horseflesh when he heard a voice come from one of the cabin's windows.

"You some kind of law?"

Finnegan considered raising his rifle, but the voice sounded so small and scared that it was hard to credit it with bad intentions. He took a few steps toward the window. "I am a detective in private employ. The other man there is a member of the Coal and Iron Police. Who are you?"

"Annabel Lee."

"Bloody hell." Finnegan hung his head, recalling that Uncle Jim had mentioned a young girl. Unforeseen occurrences continued to complicate Finnegan's murder investigation and it was beginning to aggravate. "What is your situation here, young lady?"

"I been...I been kept by a man they call John for some time now. I cook and do the cleaning as best I can."

"I am sure you do. Is there anyone else with you in there?"

"No, sir."

"Is there anyone else in the vicinity that you know of?"

"I don't believe so, sir. Sir, did you kill all three of them?"

"Yes, young lady. That was not my intention, but it is what happened." Finnegan rubbed his forehead. "Collect your traps, girl, and come out here. We will be leaving presently." He sighed once more. "Girl?"

"Yes?"

"Consider anything of value in there to be your property now."

"Thank you, sir."

Finnegan turned away and began to walk to the corral again. "Do not thank me. I am certain your former caretaker would want you to be provided for."

FINNEGAN DID NOT CARE for the look of the undertaker at St. Clair. To Finnegan's way of thinking, an undertaker should be properly proportioned to put one in mind of the angel of death. The correct mortician should be tall and thin -- a classic wraith. Bones should poke out from the man's clothing, making the casual observer believe that nothing more than a skeleton might reside beneath. Boatmen, in charge of guiding souls to the other side, should be underfed. That was not the case with the undertaker in St. Clair.

Abraham Milton was the polar opposite of a wraith. He was short, perhaps only five-foot-five. He was fat, his collar could barely contain his jowls. Perhaps most disturbing of all, he was happy. Finnegan did not ask so much that an undertaker needed to be morose. Somber, or at a minimum, respectful would do, but the son of a bitch Milton seemed damn-near gleeful to see Finnegan approaching again. The fat man rushed out onto his porch, rubbing his flabby hands together.

"Oh, three more so quickly." He smiled up at Finnegan and Captain Bourne. "Wonderful, gentlemen, just wonderful." His countenance darkened for a split second. "Were their deaths a personal matter?"

Finnegan scowled. "They were killed in the course of our duties, carrion bird."

Milton grinned as a great weight was lifted from him. "Oh, fine, just fine. Shall I send the bill to Mr. Franklin in Philadelphia, as I did with the last batch?"

Finnegan shot an icy stare toward the captain who shivered once again. "Send the bill over to the Coal and Iron house." The captain cleared his throat. "General Pleasants will foot the bill for this one."

"Very magnanimous of you, Captain." Finnegan tossed the reins of the horses he had been leading to Bourne and wheeled his horse. "Miss Annabel, follow me." Milton tipped his bowler hat to the young lady. "No need to assess her too closely, vulture. God willing, she'll outlive us all."

"Oh, yes, God willing, sir." Milton greedily approached the closest horse holding a body. "And God bless you for doing such fine work defending our community from these scoundrels."

Finnegan hollered back over one shoulder. "I would be careful about suggesting the shooting of scoundrels if I were you, pudgy ghoul." He turned and led the girl down the street to the boarding house. After helping her down from her horse, he led her up to the front door and let her inside. "Mrs. Wallace..." He looked around the parlor. "If you are available, I would speak with you, ma'am."

The lady of the house came out of the kitchen toweling her hands off on her apron. She stopped short in the kitchen doorway, appearing quite shocked to see Finnegan in the company of an adolescent girl. "Mr. Gilhooley?" She looked around her own house, trying to determine what was underway. "What...what do you require?"

Finnegan held his hat in his hand and motioned to Annabel. "Ma'am, I wish for you to take this young lady into your employ. She appears to be capable of good service and requires a situation superior to the one I found her in recently." He produced a dollar from his pocket. "I am willing to supplement her boarding for the first week. If you prefer not to be responsible for her, I can find another placement for her in that amount of time."

Mrs. Wallace rushed forward and took the girl by the hand. She moved so quickly Finnegan barely noticed the coin being removed from his grip. The lady of the house brushed some of Annabel's matted hair from her face. "Sweet Moses, girl, what has happened to you?" She began leading the girl off. "Of course, she can stay here, Mr. Gilhooley. I am a Christian woman and would never think of turning away such a waif."

"Thank you, ma'am." Finnegan turned to go, but stopped. "Ah, ma'am? Have you seen Abijah Smith, the young man in my employ?"

"Last I seen him, he was sitting on the back porch waiting for you."

"Thank you again, ma'am." Finnegan walked down the hallway, past his room, and out onto the rear porch of the house. Abijah sat on the steps, staring over at the church where he lived. "Hello, young man. I see you made it back without incident."

"Oh, I don't know if I would go that far. Uncle Jim made an attempt at convincing me that he needed to be moved into a fine townhouse in Philadelphia. Instead, I deposited him in the old shack over by Patterson that I damn well know he inhabits."

"Good boy. Well done."

"Did you complete your business on Mount Carbon, sir?"

"In a certain sense." Finnegan watched as the boy produced a bag of tobacco from his pocket, along with rolling papers. "You enjoy tobacco, Abijah?"

"When I am in funds." He held up the bag. "Would you care for a quirley? You provided the funds."

Finnegan smiled and nodded. "I would be honored." He took a seat next to the boy.

Abijah began rolling a smoke. "Did you make progress in your investigation today?"

"I may have completed it."

"Truly?" The boy put the finishing touches on the hand-made cigarette and handed it to Finnegan. "Well, sir, I am always glad to have been of service in a job well done, but I must admit, I was rather hoping I would be in your employ for a longer time. It pays better than picking the culm banks and is more to my liking."

Finnegan lit the smoke. "All things come to an end. I suppose I have good cause to wrap up my labor here." Finnegan took a moment to assess the boy. "Is it your intention to seek work in the mines someday soon, Abijah?"

"I have considered the notion." He popped his own cigarette into his mouth and lit it. "It was not what my father wanted for me, but he failed to suggest another course of action before he passed."

Finnegan looked over what he could see of the coal patch from the porch. "It may behoove you to seek work out west, Abijah. Almost any type of labor would be more healthsome and offer superior compensation. There is farmland available to people with initiative in both Missouri and Kansas. The cattle industry in Texas is quite active. You can ride well enough; you should consider it. A man should not be wary of investigating new country or new opportunities. Do not let the cost of the journey dissuade you. An active young man such as yourself can easily earn his way west."

"I shall give it my consideration, sir." The boy knocked the ash from his cigarette. "Up on Mount Carbon today, sir, you discovered the man who killed Miss Wetherill?"

"Oh, that depends on the vantage point from which you observe the thing. I would know with more certainty if Captain Bourne had not knocked it into a cocked hat." Finnegan shook his head disdainfully. "There was only one man in the wretched county I did not want shot and the good captain shot him." He took a drag on his cigarette. "Perhaps it will all be for the best. We removed a young lady from the keeping of a thoroughly vile fellow. A whiskey peddler by the name of Egan. As things shook out, we were forced to shoot him and all his kinfolk. Three dead men in all."

"Sir, if you don't mind my saying so, you shoot a somewhat greater number of men than the average fellow."

"It is an unfortunate happenstance of my profession."

"Sir?" Abijah appeared quite deep in thought. "That deductive reasoning you made mention of earlier, how exactly would you say that is brought to bear?"

"Uh, well, as Mr. Pinkerton once explained it to me, you disregard what proves to be impossible until you are left with what is possible and therein lies your answer."

"That is very interesting, sir. So then, if that last fellow you and the captain killed, John Egan..."

"You knew him?"

"He is a well-known scoundrel, sir. A man of very poor disposition. Or was, rather."

"I see."

"Sir, as I recollect, John Egan was in one of the cells at the Coal and Iron hoosegow when I went there to tell Captain Bourne I had found a corpse. He made mention of the fact that Egan had been in there since the previous night when he had been arrested for kicking up a row at a tavern." Abijah knocked more ash from his smoke. "Sir, by that, could we deduce that John Egan could not have killed Miss Wetherill?"

Finnegan rubbed the bridge of his nose. "He was in the custody of the Coal and Iron Police?"

"Yes, sir."

"All the previous night?"

"It was my understanding, sir, that he had gotten into his cups quite early."

"Hell's bells." Finnegan hung his head. "That is a damned inconvenience."

Abijah brightened noticeably. "Sir, does this mean that you will be staying on longer?"

"It does, young man." Finnegan pointed to the boy's cigarette. "Is liquor included in your vices?"

"No, sir. My father made me promise to always abstain from it."

Finnegan nodded. "My sainted mother exacted much the same pledge from me. You will profit greatly if you stand by it as time goes by."

"I believe I will, sir."

"Abijah, I believe I will have to search out your council in the future before I maneuver. It may save me a great deal of effort."

"I would be honored, sir."

"From what I have seen so far, the honor may be all mine. Take the two horses out front back to the livery and collect the three horses at the undertaker's. Place them at the livery and let the stable keeper know I will be by presently to negotiate their sale."

"Their sale, sir?"

Finnegan tossed down his cigarette and stepped on it. "They are to be sold as part of John Egan's estate, the proceeds of which will go to his only living heir, Miss Annabel Lee. At present, I do not need to stoop quite so low as to profiting from dead men's horses. Although, the day may come. See to that and...tomorrow we will begin again." Finnegan sighed deeply. "This finding murderers is a damned difficult business."

St. Clair, Pennsylvania

June 17th, 1877

The next morning Finnegan made his way to the dining room, where he found the coffee pot sitting on the table. He drew out a chair and took a seat behind his cup. He grimaced, realizing that his spare coat, which was not as long as the coat he had lost the previous day, did not cover his guns well enough to keep from possibly scratching the landlady's chair. After only a few sips, Mrs. Wallace appeared from the kitchen. She stood on the opposite side of the table, staring quizzically at Finnegan.

"Good morning, ma'am. How does the day find you?"

"Well enough, Mr. Gilhooley." She wiped her hands on her apron. "What do you fancy for breakfast, sir?"

"Whatever you have on hand for your boys will suit me just fine, ma'am."

"Very well." She turned to go, but turned back again. "Mr. Gilhooley, the girl you brought here, Annabel, do you know anything of her?"

He shrugged. "Only that she was formerly in the keeping of a whiskey peddler and that she did not wish to remain there."

"She told me you killed the whiskey peddler, a man named Egan."

"In point of fact, Captain Bourne killed him. I shot two of his associates. In all, it was an unfortunate outing."

"God bless you for it, sir." Her voice cracked as she said the words. "You...you cannot imagine the situation that poor girl was lingering in. If...if I had experienced anything similar, I would have lost all hope, I fear. You did the good Lord's work shooting those men."

Finnegan sipped his coffee. "It is good to know I have your endorsement, Mrs. Wallace. I am sorry to report that it may not be the last of the shooting I am forced to do while visiting your community. So far, I have had no luck determining the identity of the man who killed Johanna Wetherill."

"Well, that is a pity, sir, but at least in the meantime you have done a fine thing for that young lady." She wiped her hands on her apron once more. "It may change the way people view Pinkerton agents in this town, or it will if they ask for my opinion."

Finnegan smiled. "That is very gracious of you, ma'am, but I will hopefully not be visiting long enough for community opinion to make much difference to me personally. Do you feel the girl will be all right lodging here?"

"She is a hard worker and the picture of politeness. She... Mr. Wallace and I were never blessed with a daughter."

Finnegan chuckled. "I suppose things have a way of working out."

After his breakfast, Finnegan informed his young assistant, Abijah, that they would be requiring mounts from the livery stable once again. With that seen to, he walked to the train depot and strolled up to the office of the telegraph clerk. "Young man, I have another message to be sent."

The clerk gulped. "Yes, sir. To whom, sir?"

"Robert Pinkerton at the Philadelphia branch of the Pinkerton offices."

"Very well, sir." The young clerk took up his pencil. "What would you like the message to read, sir?"

"Three more dead. Do not cover burial costs. Coal and Iron will cover." Finnegan rubbed his chin. "Investigation inconclusive thus far. Signed F. Gilhooley." Finnegan rubbed his chin once more. "What do you think of it, young man?"

"Uh, it is quite succinct, sir."

"Succinct?"

"Direct and to the point, sir."

Finnegan nodded. "Exactly what I was hoping for." He flipped a penny to the young man. "Send it on."

"I will, sir."

With what he felt was a thorough report logged in, Finnegan traveled on foot to the domicile used by the Coal and Iron Police as a headquarters. He let himself in, walked past the sleeping policemen on their cots, and swung open the door to Bourne's office. The captain leapt back from the window he had been staring out of and let a cigar fall from his hand to the floor.

"Gilhooley." He glanced down to the floor. "Damn it." He knelt and picked up his cigar. "I...I had assumed you had taken the morning train back to Philadelphia." He moved to his desk. "Do you wish for me to provide a testimonial regarding Egan's guilt?"

"What I might wish is for you to lose your fingers so that they might cease doing mischief, or possibly that your tongue may be severed from you so that organ might cease causing me trouble, as well."

"Sir, you have no right to speak to me in that manner, in my own office..."

"Captain, is it true or not that there is no way Miss Wetherill's corpse could have lain in that culm bank more than one night?"

"I suppose it would have been noticed by the men walking to work the morning after it was left, yes."

"Is it also true that you had John Egan in custody all the

previous night preceding the discovery of Miss Wetherill's remains?"

"The night before...who told you that?"

"Young Abijah Smith."

Bourne flopped down into his desk chair. "Well, I... damn it, that boy may be correct. I, I think Egan may have been here that night."

Finnegan rubbed his eyes. "This is a damn fine time for you to recall that, sir."

Bourne sighed deeply and withdrew a bottle from his desk drawer along with two glasses. "This is a damned difficult time here." He poured one glass full and looked to Finnegan.

"I do not partake."

"This town would make St. Peter into a drunkard in short order. You may change your mind the next time I offer." He slugged down the contents of the glass. "Mr. Gilhooley, what difference does it make where Egan was the night before Wetherill's corpse was discovered? She is dead, he is dead. Let us join the two and move on with our duties."

"Bourne, it is not possible that Egan could have killed the girl."

The captain hung his head. "What possible difference could that make? I do not know who killed the girl, you do not know who killed the girl. I doubt God himself knows. I find it hard to believe that the Almighty would waste his time monitoring the movements of a whore such as Johanna Wetherill."

"The disposition of God is not within my knowledge, sir. I do know that there is no way John Egan could have killed the girl. That is all that matters."

"Why does it matter? Tell McLeod Egan was the man

and let us be done with it. No one other than you, me, and that Smith boy will ever know otherwise."

"It has been said, Captain, that three can keep a secret if two are dead. Do you really believe I would sell a bill of goods to both McLeod and Mr. Pinkerton, knowing that the truth of my fabrication could be revealed by a man such as yourself?" The captain turned a bit pale. "If I am to engage in a lie, sir, I rather owe it to myself to properly conceal the falsehood completely before leaving town. Would you not agree?"

Bourne let out a small laugh, which sounded more frightened than amused. "You would threaten to shoot me, here in my own office?"

Finnegan pulled the dragoon from his belt. "Would anyone truly care? You frequently mention that you are not a well-liked man. I doubt the shot would awaken your deputies. Even if it did, they might not show much loyalty to you after they discovered you were no longer the man in charge of issuing their pay."

The captain stiffened. "You gave those men yesterday no such warning. Why are you toying with me?"

"Because I am not going to kill you, you silly buggered bastard. I shudder to imagine who would replace you." Finnegan seated the dragoon back in his belt. "From this time on you will not interfere in my investigations here, is that clear?"

There was an audible pop as the captain swallowed. "It is."

"Very well then." Finnegan turned to go.

"Mr. Gilhooley?"

He stopped by the door. "Yes."

"The Bible tells us that pride cometh before a fall, sir. I think you damned Pinkerton men walk too proudly upon the Earth. You accuse me of interfering in your business, but your coming here has interfered in mine. You threaten me with violence; do you not know that you are as mortal as I am, sir?"

"If ever you wish to test the notion you need only to give the word, Captain."

CROW HOLLOW LAY to the east of St. Clair. Instead of a real road frequented by wagons, there was only a rough path through the brush and meadows that occupied the low ground. Finnegan and Abijah slowly made their way through the brambles. Every time Finnegan began to think that they had made their way into a piece of open country, another broken down colliery or burned-out breaker would present itself. Culm banks lined the edges of the creeks they followed. There did not appear to be a single inch of the place that had not been dug into for some purpose.

"Why do all these factories and mines burn, Abijah?"

"It is the furnaces and engines, sir. Seems like only a matter of time before a cinder finds its way to the wrong spot and a fire breaks out. It is a horrid thing when fire breaks out in a tunnel. The furnace must sit on top of the shaft to draw air through the mine. At Avondale, the furnace fell into the mine. Many men died. My father spent the better part of a week helping to bring the bodies out after the fire had been extinguished. My father died when the firedamp gas was ignited in the St. Clair shaft." The boy looked sullen, thinking back on the incident. "It is said that many men in these parts joined the army during the war simply because they felt it would be safer than working in the mines."

Finnegan nodded. "It may have been, in some respects." He looked over yet another burnt-out breaker that presented itself as they rounded a bend. "Yes, young Abijah, I believe you should go west to make your fortune. Are you aware that a man can now buy a train ticket and travel all the way to the Pacific Ocean?"

"I have been told that, sir. Although, I have been told that there are dangers in the west, as well. There are wild Indians there, sir, of the stripe that murdered the valiant General Custer and all his brave men."

Finnegan laughed. "You may find this hard to credit, young man, but during the war I met a few members of the Union Cavalry who had given serious thought to murdering Custer."

"Honestly, sir?"

"They felt he made inappropriate use of the men under his command. If I were you, I would not allow Indian trouble to dissuade me from traveling west. If not for the grace of God, Custer would have never lived long enough to be killed by Indians. He was too fond of pushing his luck. It has also been my experience that newspapers tend to exaggerate Indian trouble. I spent a fair amount of time in Minnesota recently. They suffered an Indian uprising there during the war. To hear the newspapers tell it, the state was nearly lost. If you ask the people who live there, they will tell you that the only real inconvenience was hanging almost forty of the Indians." Finnegan guided his horse around a fallen log. "I did not witness the event, but I am told they hung them all at once."

"All at once, sir?"

"Yes, they erected a massive scaffold in the town of Mankato. Thousands of people came to witness it. They say it was the most men ever hung at one time. Old Abe Lincoln himself approved it."

Abijah chuckled. "He freed the slaves, but hanged Indians; it is strange what men might find themselves doing on any given day."

"It is something to consider, that is certain."

"Sir, would you mind terribly if I asked you a question about your work?"

Finnegan twisted and looked back at the boy. "I believe you have earned that right."

"Sir, the Pyle boys and a few others have told me that it is not right for an Irishman like you to work for the Pinkertons. They compare you to a man named McParlan who came to St. Clair some time ago. They say you are in the business of hanging your own kind, Mr. Gilhooley."

They were coming to a wide spot, so Finnegan reined up and let the boy come up beside him. "Abijah, as you grow older there are certain hard realities that you must come to understand in this life. Let me ask you a question: would you say the people of St. Clair are your kind?"

He shrugged. "Some are Irish, some Welsh, some were born in Pennsylvania like me. We are all living in the coal patch, so I suppose they are my kind, yes, sir."

"And after your father died, did any of them, excepting the priest who has given you a place to sleep, did any of them help you worth a tinker's damn?"

A streak of what might have been bitterness passed over the young man's face. "No, sir, they did not."

"Back in Ireland, when I was a boy younger than you, our neighbors, men my father counted as friends, informed on him to the English landlord. They claimed he had murdered a tax collector. They hoped to run him from the county so that they could make use of the land we were renting. Their plan was effective. If not for being forewarned by a true friend, my father might have ended up on the end of a rope instead of a ship to America. I may have swung with him."

"Why would they have hung you when you were only a boy, sir?"

"Because I had helped my father kill the tax collector." Finnegan rode on silently for a moment. "The old country was a hard land. We had hoped for better here, but..." He pulled a cigar from his coat. "The men who informed on my father were our kind. The people of St. Clair are your kind. If you ask me, those who have a care for your welfare are your kind. The rest can be damned." Finnegan lit his cigar. "Allan Pinkerton is my kind, Abijah. He kept me from becoming cannon fodder, which is damn well more than any Irishman has ever done for me."

"You have helped me, sir. A great deal in my opinion."

Finnegan smiled. "Very well then, young man, we will be our kind. Does that suit you? It will significantly reduce the amount of loyalty I am expected to exhibit."

The boy smiled. "I would like that very well, sir."

"Then that is how it will be." They plodded along another few steps. "What sort of place is this Crow Hollow?"

"At one time, I believe it attracted a great many birds, sir. The small patch next to it is known as Ravensdale."

"Interesting."

"They are just small places that have grown up around collieries. Both the mines they were close to are no longer going concerns. Because they are far from the mines now, the houses there are quite cheap to obtain or abandoned for the taking."

Finnegan nodded. "That stands to reason. I would assume it also makes a fine location for amoral activities. Close enough to the towns to not be an inconvenience to customers, but far enough away to avoid affecting anyone's reputation."

"Yes, sir. Crow Hollow normally has at least one tippling

house, hotel, or other establishment that is in ill repute. I have not heard of the lady who runs the current one, but my father once made mention of a lady who ran a bawdy house in Crow Hollow who died of a disease contracted in the course of her duties. He did not elaborate much."

"There are hazards to any profession." They came up over a small ridge and could view the settlement of Crow Hollow from there. "Ah, this does look like a fine place to crowd together the whores and gamblers."

Abijah nodded. "It does serve that purpose, sir." He stood in his stirrups and looked around. "The only respectable man I have ever heard of living here is John Siney. I always try to guess which house might be his when I pass through, but I can never tell. You would think it would stand out."

"Who is John Siney?"

Abijah brightened considerably upon discovering he had information to relate. "John Siney is the founder and president of the union, sir. He negotiated an end to the long strike in '75. Some say that someday he will unite all the miners in the country into one union that will be able to dictate the price of coal, or whatever ever else they dig for."

Finnegan chuckled. "I suppose then the Mollies will cease to be needed for killing foremen who do not observe proper lunch breaks."

Abijah nodded. "I suppose it would render them somewhat obsolete." He plopped back down in his saddle. "Do you hold a low opinion of the Mollies, sir?"

Finnegan shook his head. "I do not hold an opinion of them one way or the other, Abijah. They are men who did what they felt they had to do. I am no better or worse. If circumstances dictate it today, and I have no better option, I will kill some men in this grimy little town to get what I want. I will do my level best to avoid it, because violence only begets violence, and the good Lord wishes to minimize such things." He patted his pockets, looking for a cigar. "I am sure the priest has made you aware of the Sixth Commandment?"

"Surely, sir."

"Yes, well, God takes a dim view of murder, but when a man has no choice but to kill..." He found a cigar and stuck it between his teeth. "Perhaps these Mollies felt they had little choice."

"But, sir, it was your own Pinkerton men who infiltrated them and have now condemned them."

"Yes, that was their job, Abijah. What the Mollies did was outside of this nation's law. For there to be any real justice in the world the law must apply to all men. Feeling you have cause is no excuse. The Mollies knew what they were doing could have stern consequences. Now they are paying the price."

Abijah scratched one side of his face. "So, you never break the law, sir?"

Finnegan laughed. "I try to break it twice a day, before breakfast, whether I need to or not. I am no saint, young Abijah, but when I do transgress I do my best to not be caught. I would certainly never be caught in the manner the Mollies were. I know much better than to ever trust a Pinkerton." He smiled at the boy.

Abijah grinned at the joke. "Do most of the men you have chased feel they have cause for their actions, sir?"

"A good number of them."

"Do the James brothers feel that way?"

Finnegan lit his cigar. "The James brothers frequently claim that they are robbing Yankee trains and banks to take revenge on the Union and on the northern carpetbaggers."

"Do you believe it?"

"I believe the James brothers are lazy bastards who would

rather rob banks than plow." Finnegan shrugged. "But that opinion is not likely to sell many newspapers." He pointed to the small collection of buildings in front of them that was nearing with each step of the horses. "Any idea which of these abodes is the tippling house and former residence of Johanna Wetherill?"

"No, sir."

Finnegan steered his horse toward a low, one-room building with a dirt roof. Its log walls were dug in and a short dirt ramp led to the clapboard front door. It had probably once functioned to shelter livestock, but had since been repurposed. "This appears to be a sort of tavern."

"It does, sir." Abijah stared at the large pile of bottles behind the building.

They rode up to the front and Finnegan dismounted. He handed his reins to Abijah. "Keep an eye on our mounts. I will inquire within."

"I will, sir."

Finnegan straightened his guns and his coat before going inside the building through a rather small door. Inside, it was dark and the floor of the place was the same dirt, only drier, as that to be found outside. The bar at the far wall was nothing more than a few planks stretched across barrels. Seven or eight ugly-looking drunks populated the tables, which had wood blocks around them instead of chairs. Finnegan walked to the bar. Behind the planks, a man sat on an especially tall wood block. An oil lamp hung behind him that apparently provided just enough light for him to read the newspaper he looked up from as Finnegan approached.

The bartender spoke with an Irish accent that made Finnegan think he'd only gotten off the boat a few hours earlier. "What the hell kind of dandy are you?"

Finnegan looked around at the regulars. "Do you take me for a dandy because I've had a bath this month?"

The sound of a similar voice brought the bartender's dander down a notch. "What is your business here?"

"I wish to know the location of a house formerly inhabited by a Johanna Wetherill."

"What's this, now? You want to know the house of a woman, but she doesn't live there anymore?"

"Correct."

"If she's not there anymore, what the hell do you want with the house?" The bartender grinned. "Is one woman as good as the next to you as long as you like the house she's in?"

"Something like that. Johanna Wetherill lived in a house in this town, but was killed in St. Clair. I wish to speak with the people in this town who knew her."

"What the hell do you want to talk to people about a dead whore for?"

"It is my profession. I am a detective in private employ."

"A detective." The bartender's eyes narrowed. "You mean a bloody Pinkerton?"

"As it happens, yes." Behind him, Finnegan could hear the collective noise produced by every man in the bar slowly standing up. Glasses rattled and leather creaked. Having learned to take a hint over the years, Finnegan took the initiative by leaping over the bar, mostly destroying it, and pulling the bartender in front of him like a rather rotund shield. The bar patrons eyed him evilly as Finnegan brought out his Remington. "Gentlemen, I can appreciate you all having strong feelings regarding Pinkertons, given the recent unpleasantness, but there is no reason for any of us to tussle over it." He cocked back the hammer on his revolver and surveyed the group. They were plenty filthy, but not necessarily with honest toil coal dust. "You men do not appear to be miners, why do you find Pinkertons so objectionable?"

In a voice considerably less pugnacious than before, the bartender answered Finnegan's query. "These men are the Schuylkill County Raiders." The man's body stiffened as Finnegan hid behind it. "They have been told that when the Pinkertons are done with the Mollies they will be coming for them."

"I see." Finnegan placed the Remington's muzzle against his shield's neck. "Any of you men move too fast and I will be forced to shoot this formerly ornery bartender."

Quite methodically, a rawboned fellow close to where the toppled bar had stood reached into the corner of the lodge and produced a rusty rifle from under a coat. In the low light, Finnegan had to squint at the gun to identify it. The man held the weapon and smiled. "That bartender is no kin of mine. Son of a bitch only came to town some few months ago." He thumbed back the hammer of his rifle and began fiddling with the strange dispenser built into one side of the receiver.

"Don't you be fussing with that Maynard gun, sir." Finnegan let out a small chuckle. "Wherever did you get the primer tape for it?"

"This gun is solid as the dollar, you bastard." He carefully wrestled the primer tape into position.

"Don't be daft. It'll never fire." Finnegan did his best to make the statement sound certain. The man raised the rifle to his shoulder, took rather careful aim, given the short distance, and pulled the trigger. A dull click was the only result. "There now, friend." Finnegan swallowed and glanced behind him where a skinny doorway had been boarded up. It appeared as though it had once served to let the livestock come and go from the building to the pasture. Finnegan

114

kicked back and felt one of the boards give. He cleared his throat, pressing the Remington to the bartender. "I will assure you men that you are in no danger of being pursued by the Pinkerton Agency. That is so long as you refrain from doing violence to one of their agents." He kicked another board.

"Damn Pinkerton, you've cursed my rifle." The man drew out a length of the primer tape and tore off a section, leaving a hunk draped over the gun's nipple.

"Stop fussing with that rotten old Maynard, sir."

The bartender raised his hands toward the amateur gunsmith. "Bodkin, for the love of Christ, don't shoot me."

He raised up the rifle again. "This is what you get for being between me and a damned Pinkerton." He aimed and pulled the trigger once more. The roll of tape lit fire, and the gun did, in fact, go off. There was a ball of flame and the bartender lurched back against the Pinkerton behind him.

Mostly out of curiosity, Finnegan craned his head around the side of his human shield. A hole in the man's shoulder was producing blood. "I'll be damned. My apologies, bartender; I honestly did not think that old musket would fire. I would have shot the man if I thought it was serviceable."

"Damn you, you Pinkerton whore." The man flung the still smoldering rifle down to the dirt floor. "That rifle killed a score of Yankee bastards at Vicksburg before you put a damn curse on it. May you burn in hell."

"I told you to stop fussing with it."

The bartender pressed one hand to his shoulder and stared at the blood. "You shot me, Bodkin."

"That damn devil Pinkerton made me do it."

Finnegan kicked another board lose to produce a hole that he felt he might be able to fit through, although it would have to be under duress. "Now, then, gentlemen, you have had your fit and drawn some blood. I would suggest you all move away from the door over there and allow me to leave before this degenerates further. I did not come here with the intention of shooting anyone. If you will simply allow me to..."

A younger man took a step toward the fellow with the broken rifle. "Bodkin, you did the best you could. It's a pity about your old gun." He pulled a Navy Colt from his belt and held it out to Bodkin butt first. "Use mine to finish the bastard."

Finnegan, still rooted firmly behind the bartender, brought his Remington to bear on them. "Don't you touch that pistol, sir."

"Thank you much, Sloan." Bodkin reached out and gripped the revolver. He had the hammer thumbed back, still pointed directly at Sloan, when Finnegan's bullet hit him in the arm. The Navy discharged and sent a ball into Sloan's midsection. "Sloan!"

"Bloody hell." Finnegan left the bartender to his own devices and made a dive for the hole he had opened up. It was a tight fit, but with a little squirming he was able to make it through. Just outside the hole his dragoon fell from his belt, so he snatched it up and fired twice at the hole just in case some enterprising soul was following. Glancing around, he noticed a wagon parked hard up against the building. Finnegan ran to the front of it and put his shoulder into it as hard as he could, causing it to roll back and block the hole with one wheel. Feeling quite elated, he ran around the short distance to the front of the building and threw his shoulder into one of the posts that held up the overhang. The post popped free, and Finnegan jammed it against the door just as someone inside was trying to open it. He pulled the

Remington from its holster and fired once into the door. "You'll stay in there if you know what is good for you, you silly bastards." Finnegan stomped on the post for good measure to seat it firmly.

"Open this door, damned Pinkerton. Sloan is dying in here."

"Then you should not have shot him."

"The bartender is bleeding badly."

"You shot him too, half-wit."

"I am bleeding badly."

"Very well, that was certainly my intention. I..."

"Sir?"

Finnegan jumped a bit and turned to look behind him. "Uh, yes, Abijah?"

The boy sat on his horse, leaning over to see underneath the overhang. "Sir, is there something amiss?"

"No. Well, yes. The men inside were unwilling to share information with me."

"I see."

Finnegan took a step away from the door. "I think it would be best if we removed ourselves from this place. There are several men inside and that post will not..." He stopped short. "Abijah, where is my horse?"

"I am very sorry, sir, but she ran off at the sound of the gunshots. I have never seen an animal react so poorly to noise, sir. She was completely uncontrollable. She tore her reins free and ran like the wind."

"Bloody, dirty, cursed whore of a horse."

The boy looked truly heartbroken. "I would have given chase to collect her, sir, but I thought it prudent to remain here."

"You acted quite correctly." A bullet flew through the door behind Finnegan. "Bloody hell." He fired through the door once more and ran the few steps to Abijah's rearing horse. "Swing me up boy!" Finnegan grabbed Abijah's arm and managed to jump up onto the horse behind him. "Go, boy, go."

"Which way, sir?"

"Whichever way my damned horse ran off."

"Yes, sir."

FINNEGAN SAT on a tree stump attempting to brush the mud, and some other unspeakable substance, from his hat. Crawling through the hole in the rear of the makeshift saloon had not been kind to his wardrobe. "I bought this bowler hat from one of the finest shops in Chicago. I doubt it can be properly cleaned."

Abijah wandered around in a small circle, making use of a few woodland paths to look for hoof tracks. "I know your horse came this way, sir. At least, it ran toward this end of Crow Hollow."

"Hopefully the damned whore has stumbled into a hole and broken her damned neck."

"Sir, I know it may not be my place to ask, but what transpired inside the tavern?"

Finnegan sighed and stood up from the stump. "I inquired about Miss Wetherill's former place of lodging. They asked if I was a Pinkerton agent. I informed them that I was, and...the situation degenerated quickly."

"Sir, perhaps you should not have informed them you are a Pinkerton agent?"

Finnegan gave up on cleaning his hat and placed it back on his head. "Abijah, I believe, given the work my agency has already done in this area, it would be very difficult to ever convince anyone around here, ever again, that all strangers are not Pinkerton agents."

The boy kicked the dirt in front of him a bit. "Sir, I know I am new to detective work, but does it not seem as though you have been asked to accomplish something rather impossible here?" Finnegan nodded and withdrew his Remington to reload it. They had traveled more than a mile from the tavern on twisting backwoods trails and had seen no sign of the men from the tavern giving chase, but that was no reason to think they might not try it eventually. "Sir, why would anyone admit to killing Johanna Wetherill or admit to having knowledge of it now? I would think if anyone knew anything useful, they would have brought it to the attention of the Coal and Iron Police. They are not well liked, but are not so hated as to cause a citizen to conceal murder, I would think."

Finnegan nodded again. "You are, in all likelihood, correct, Abijah." He sighed. "When you are older, Abijah, you may find that men often ask you to do what cannot truly be done simply to say they have attempted an action or a remedy. The act of finding Wetherill's murderer is not nearly so important to Colonel McLeod as being able to brag that he employed the Pinkertons to search for her murderer."

"My father once told me something similar regarding the causes of the rebellion."

"Was your father native born?"

"Right here in the Commonwealth of Pennsylvania."

"He would know better than I the causes of the southern rebellion. I was young when I was pressed into the Union Army. My father and I had both just stepped onto the docks when a sergeant told us we were to become citizens and soldiers, all in one quick swindle, mind you. I can remember being told where we were marching and where we were fighting and not having the foggiest clue what in sweet hell I was being told. I had never so much as seen a map of America, you understand."

The boy let out a small laugh. "I am sorry, sir, but it is a rather funny notion. To think of you fighting for a country, but you don't know how big it is or where you are in it."

"Looking back, it is a rather ridiculous bit of fancy. Another mystery to contemplate is how my life might have gone differently if our ship had landed farther south due to wind or weather. I can only assume we would have been pressganged into Johnny Reb's army." Finnegan shrugged. "We would have been none the wiser. We had no knowledge of the politics of this nation. At that age, I had never so much as seen a negro; I certainly would have shown no interest in fighting to help one assert their rights." Finnegan grinned. "At the time, our own rights were forefront in our thinking."

"I would imagine they were, sir." The boy smiled. It was the first time anyone other than his father had ever taken the time to share a personal story with him. "Do you have family, still, sir?"

"My mother still lives. Well, I hope she does. It has been sometime since I have laid eyes on her myself. She resides in Albany, New York, along with my brother."

The boy's eyes brightened. "You have a brother?"

"His name is Francis, and he practices law in Albany." Finnegan shrugged. "It is my understanding he makes a tidy living doing it, too. He is several years younger than I, and at an early age Mr. Pinkerton was able to use his influence to get him a proper education. Under normal circumstances, I am not fond of lawyers, but Francis was always a good boy and I believe he has grown to be a good man. Although, once again, that is a supposition. I have not seen him in quite some time, either. My work for the agency keeps me quite busy."

"How is it you came to be employed by Mr. Pinkerton, sir."

"Ah, well, as I said, my father and I were plucked at the docks by the blue coats. My sainted mother and little Francis were left to more or less fend for themselves while we saw to our military service. Father and I, we were all right for some time, but ill luck is unaccountable. My father was killed at a place called Antietam. He was shot down next to a little church. I can recall thinking it odd that Americans would have a battle next to a church like that." Finnegan stared off down the path. "Well, Mr. Pinkerton had his intelligence corps deployed at that particular battle, judging troop strength on the Confederate side. I made myself useful to him at one point and he allowed for me to be transferred to his service. After that, he took an interest in my family and has been very good to us ever since. Mr. Pinkerton is a good man. There are some who would have you believe different, but it is not the case."

"He has certainly been good to you, sir."

"He has." Finnegan took his hat off and contemplated the stains once more. "Well, we should be about our business, young Abijah. We must locate that damned horse. I would not care to make the animal's acquaintance again, but the bitch still has my rifle attached to her and I have both a practical and sentimental interest in retrieving it." He pointed farther down the path. "Let us move in this direction. I believe those tavern patrons only had one old pistol between them, but there is no good reason to go in their direction and antagonize them into making use of it." They made their way down the heavily wooded path for the better part of half a mile with Finnegan leading the way and Abijah walking their remaining horse in the rear. Just as Finnegan began to feel as though he had led them into a true wilderness, the sound of music made him stop. "Do you hear that, boy?"

"Um, I do, sir. It seems to be a piano, don't you think?"

"It does, but it seems odd that there would be one here in the forest." Finnegan pulled away a few branches and attempted to look off to his left, where the sound was coming from.

"Perhaps it is the bawdy house we have been in search of, sir?"

"Here? Crow Hollow is well behind us by now."

"It is my understanding that all the houses along the length of this creek are more or less considered to be part of Crow Hollow, sir."

"This coal patch is a strange land." Finnegan pushed through the brush and Abijah followed with the horse as best he could. After some cursing and more than a few broken branches, they came out into a small clearing where a young lady held none other than Finnegan's grey horse by the bridle. Finnegan approached the pair. The girl wore a skirt almost the same color as the horse and her brown hair came down to the belt of it. "I cannot thank you enough, lass."

The girl pulled the horse's head back a bit as Finnegan reached for the bridle. "Now, how can I know this is your horse?"

Finnegan pointed back to his assistant. "That young man will attest to it, and..." He pulled a dollar from his waistcoat. "Who but the rightful owner would agree you should be paid for your time?" He flipped the coin to her.

"Thank you, sir." She stared at the dollar. "You must truly have an attachment to the horse."

"I intend to shoot it as soon as I no longer have need of it, but that is not your concern." Finnegan patted the horse. "Lass, is that a piano I hear inside the house there?"

"It is, sir."

Finnegan looked the place over. It was something of a sprawling structure that might have been meant to ape the design of a mansion before the builder lost interest or financial backing to finish. As it stood, it appeared more like a large shack had been placed on the stone foundation of that which might have grown to greatness. "Can the public enter this place and gain refreshment, lass?"

"Certainly, sir." She concealed the dollar somewhere in the folds of her skirt. "There is refreshment of all kinds offered to weary travelers here." She motioned for them to follow and the three made their way to the front of the house. The men tied their horses off on a hitching rail and stepped up onto the front porch of the place.

"Abijah, remain here and keep an eye on the animals."

The boy nodded. "Might I have a word with you first, sir?"

"Uh, yes." Finnegan turned to the girl. "Young miss, would you let the lady of the house know that I wish to speak with her in the parlor?"

The girl curtsied and patted her pocket where the dollar resided. "It would be my pleasure, sir." She bounced into the house and closed the door behind her.

Finnegan turned back to the boy. "Yes?"

"Sir, this is a bawdy house?"

Finnegan looked the place over. "It would certainly seem so."

"Only whores live here?"

"In this instance, that is probably true. I would imagine there is one old crone former whore in charge of seeing to the payroll and the proper robbing of customers."

"Sir, I do not think this is right."

Finnegan looked around once more. "Abijah, we came

here seeking information regarding the dead Wetherill girl. I do not intend to avail myself of the services of these women, and I would strongly suggest you avoid it, as well. Once gone, virtue cannot be restored."

"That is not what I mean, sir. I mean I do not think it is right to shoot women."

Finnegan ran his hand over his regularly increasing beard stubble. "Abijah, why, in the name of St. Michael, would I shoot women?"

"You shoot people wherever you go. Since there are only women here, I can only assume you will shoot women here."

"I will not be shooting anyone here, Abijah."

"That is what you claimed at the tavern and what you claimed before going to John Egan's house."

"Abijah, why would I wish to shoot women?"

"I do not know. I do not know why you wish to shoot whatever dregs occupied that tavern or those flea-bitten corpses you brought back from Mount Carbon. They do not hardly seem worth the expense of bullets, sir."

Finnegan threw his arms in the air. "I will not be shooting anyone at this establishment."

Abijah pointed down toward the side of the house. "There are horses tied there."

"They may belong to the women who live here, Abijah."

"Or they may belong to men who are visiting."

Finnegan nodded. "I suppose that may be true."

"If you intend to shoot them, I will better secure your horse."

"I am not getting into a gunfight in a damned whore-house, Abijah." Finnegan turned to go. "Just keep an eye on the horses." He walked into the house and found the parlor where the well-worn piano was being beaten on by a white haired old black man in a pink waistcoat and top hat that resembled the one Lincoln had favored. The old man turned and smiled to Finnegan. Finnegan nodded and continued into the room where a woman of at least sixty was waiting for him. "Ma'am."

She curtsied in her rather dilapidated ball gown and motioned to a bar she had set up on one side of the room. "Would you care for refreshment, sir?"

"No, thank you, ma'am." He walked to a highbacked chair and took a seat. "I am here in search of information."

"Information pertaining to what?" She slurred the words due to a very poorly fit set of dentures.

"I have been told that a woman named Johanna Wetherill once lived here."

"And who are you to ask about Johanna?"

Finnegan swallowed and took a quick glance around the room. It seemed trouble often followed him explaining himself and he did not want to prove the boy's prediction correct. "I am a detective in private employ, ma'am. I have been hired to discover the identity of Johanna Wetherill's murderer."

The lady lowered herself into a chair opposite Finnegan. "A detective?"

"Yes, ma'am."

She stared with what might be termed wonderment. "So, then, Johanna was not simply boasting about her family lineage?"

"No, ma'am."

"Sir? Sir, if that is true, why did she come to live in a place such as this?"

Finnegan had asked himself that very question many times, but had no answer to offer. "I am not privy to what might have been Miss Wetherill's motivations. I only desire to discover her murderer."

She stared unbelievingly. "I...I do not understand."

"Ma'am, do you have any knowledge regarding who killed Miss Wetherill?"

She shook her head. "No, sir, none whatsoever."

Finnegan scowled. "Ma'am, are there any men that frequent this establishment who...who have a tendency to do violence to the women?"

She laughed and her teeth flopped. "Sir, it is my experience that most men spend their whole lives waiting for some excuse to do violence to women."

Finnegan nodded somberly. "That is unfortunate, ma'am." He narrowed his gaze at the madam. "Did Miss Wetherill have any particular man who came by for visits on a regular basis?"

She shrugged. "Oh, well, several, in fact. This is a tippling house, sir." Her sad old eyes brightened. "Is Miss Wetherill's family offering a reward for information?"

Finnegan reached into his pocket and pulled out another silver dollar. "They are, and here it is."

The woman stared at the coin with hungry eyes. "Sir, I..."

"You do not know who her murderer was, ma'am, but telling me who associated with her could be of much value. Who did she keep company with, ma'am?"

"She...she favored the company of the Coal and Iron Police, sir."

Finnegan's eyes narrowed. "For what reason?"

The woman grinned with her blackened, fake teeth. "They are paid regularly, sir." She continued to stare at the coin. "Miss Wetherill had a habit that required regular funds."

"Opium?"

"Laudanum. Some of the girls here make use of it for ailments. Some become chained to it."

"It became a habit with Miss Wetherill?"

"It was a habit with her when she arrived."

"I see." Finnegan pulled a cigar from his coat with the hand that did not hold the coin. "Who among the police frequented Miss Wetherill's company?"

"All the police frequent this house. They cannot take refreshment in the towns. Men require refreshment, so they come here."

Finnegan walked the coin across his knuckles. "Did any of the men spend time with Miss Wetherill frequently? Frequently enough for you to take notice?"

"Two men come to mind."

"Name them, woman."

"One was James McKenna."

"Where can I find this man?"

The old crone raised one eyebrow. "Since being forced to remove him from this house, I have been informed that he has left the area. I have been told he was a Pinkerton agent."

Finnegan nodded sullenly. "I see. Who was the other man?"

"Thomas Duffy, a miner by trade."

"Where might I find him?"

"He resides at the Schuylkill County jail, but if you wish to speak with him you must hurry. He is set to swing from the scaffold soon."

Finnegan sighed. "He is a Molly Maguire?"

"It is my understanding that Mr. McKenna informed against him and now he is to hang."

"A very succinct arrangement."

The old woman's eyes narrowed. "Succinct?"

"Do not concern yourself with it, ma'am. Who is it the horses outside belong to?"

"Visitors."

"Of what variety are they?"

"Coal and Iron officers."

"I see." Finnegan flipped the coin to her. "I would speak with them before they leave."

"As you wish, sir. When their business is complete upstairs, I will inform them that you wish to speak with them."

"Thank you." Finnegan sat back in his chair and lit his cigar. If not for the odd construction of the house, and the omnipresent scent of cheap perfume, it would be hard to distinguish the parlor he lounged in from any other inside a respectable home. Not that Finnegan had been invited into an overly large number of parlors over the years. He was proud to say that Mr. Pinkerton had always treated Finnegan as a guest at his house in Chicago. Of course, Molly had invited him to sit with her in the parlor when he was fully ambulatory. They had spent a great deal of time there in conversation related to their various interests. Finnegan was fond of discussing the James Brothers and his chances of catching them. Molly preferred politics, a few specific points in particular. She could expound to no end on the Indian problem and suggested solutions that most would have considered provocative or, at the least, progressive. This did not bother Finnegan in the least because he had never once in his life paused to consider the Indian problem and, as a result, had no frame of reference to be astounded by some-one's suggestions.

There had been a goodly amount of laugher in that Minnesota parlor, and Finnegan was still not certain if the young lady had been laughing with him, or at him, most of the time. Molly thought it perfectly astounding that the man had no politics. Finnegan found it astounding that there were people with spare time to devote to such things. Once, in front of her father, he had informed her that if she had spent as much time at target practice as she did reading newspapers, she would be the finest shot in all of America. For some reason, that resulted in almost ten minutes of unchecked laughter from the Minnesotans.

Finnegan looked around the parlor he currently occupied. Would a woman who grew up in a house with a parlor insist on marrying a man who owned a house with a parlor? He briefly considered his current financial situation. At a minimum, a woman would probably want a house, with or without a parlor. He puffed his cigar and let his eyes wander over to the ancient black man at the piano. He had a strange glint in his eye and seemed rather proud to be tickling the keys of the instrument. He turned and smiled with a surprisingly white set of teeth. Finnegan pulled a cigar from his pocket. "Would you care for one?"

The old man ceased playing. "Oh, well, don't mind if I do." He got up from the piano and darted to the offered smoke. "Thank you, sir."

"Have a seat here to smoke it. I am sorry, but I have never cared for piano music."

"As you like it, sir." He flopped down into the chair opposite Finnegan. His practiced hands took out a match case and he lit his cigar. "What brings you by today, sir?"

"I imagine you overheard."

"I did, but it is considered polite to ask, anyway."

"Did you know the Wetherill girl?"

"Not well. I do not associate with any of them much. I am paid to play the piano and that does not pay enough to indulge in the favors offered here." He smiled around the cigar. "Even if it did, that would not be good Christian behavior, and I have grown a little old for that sort of thing."

"How old are you?"

"I cannot say to a certainty. I was born on a cane plantation in Florida and the master there was so ignorant I doubt he could keep records of such matters." He puffed out smoke. "I must be fairly old, must be. I know my hair had gone white already when the war came and it has been over a long time now, too."

Finnegan nodded. "Many years. Where did you learn to play the piano?"

He laughed. "Madam Gertrude..." The old man motioned over his shoulder at the old crone who had left. "Her daddy paid a Frenchman to teach me. I made the Frenchman mad when I took to it so well. Madam Gertrude's daddy said I played better than any man he ever heard; swore he wouldn't sell me for all the cotton in creation."

"It is always nice to receive compliments."

The old man nodded and puffed. "He wasn't lying, either. He never did sell me, he left me to Madam Gertrude, his daughter." He chuckled. "I was right there in the will next to the horses and wagons and other claptrap. 'Course, that was right near the end of the war. One day Gertrude come to me and tells me that I ain't hers no more, says I don't belong to nobody but myself." He grinned. "She tells me I'm free."

Finnegan waggled his cigar at the old man. "I have been told that a time or two myself."

"Hah, ain't all men told that? I told Gertrude that very day that I had a wife back in Florida somewheres and another wife down the road, and I don't know how many kids. How the hell was I free?"

Finnegan smiled at the man. "It is an excellent point you make."

"I felt freer when Gertrude comes to me one day and says Clanton -- that's my name, Clanton." He put out the hand that wasn't engaged in smoking.

The gunman took the proffered hand and shook it. "Finnegan Gilhooley."

"So, Gertrude come to me and says she wants to move up north and open a whorehouse. Says the Yankees love whores and they'll pay better than the deadbeat southern gentlemen who got nothing left 'cause the carpetbaggers stole it all." He shrugged. "It sounded all right to me. So, we came north, and she runs whores while I play the piano." He leaned in closer. "I would find a better situation, but I have known her since she was a girl and would feel poorly about leaving her."

Finnegan knocked ash down onto the floor. "Do many of the women in this place end up dead?"

"Some. Some go on here until they too ugly to make a living. Others, they wander off and get killed. Last winter one of 'em, she was drunk mind you, she got in a wagon with some men and halfway to Pottsville they kicked her out in the snow. Girl didn't have nothing on but bloomers and a little shirt. Girl was blue as a bottle and stiff as a board when they found her."

Finnegan contemplated it. "I have always felt freezing would be a difficult way to die."

"So have I. Often think we should have stayed in Alabama where such things could not happen. I fear the snow, I truly do."

"I had never known snow and cold that could kill a man until I came to America. Ireland is wet and cold, but it is not the kind that can kill a man. Many men freeze north of here every winter."

"Gertrude kept saying we had to move farther north to find more men with money." He motioned around at the house. "She says the coal is going to make all the men around here rich, so she bought this house last. I told her that this place sure as hell don't look like no place men going to get

131

rich. Told her we should go somewhere a man can't freeze to death, either."

Finnegan knocked more ash. "Women."

"There is no remedy."

Finnegan glanced out of the parlor and saw boots coming down the staircase. They matched those issued by the Coal and Iron Police. "Ah, good sir, I am afraid I have business with these other gentlemen. It has been nice chatting with you."

"Thanks for the cigar. Come back anytime."

Finnegan left the parlor and walked to the base of the staircase. Halfway up, a pair of Coal and Iron policemen stood adjusting their holsters and jackets. "Gentlemen, I would have a word with you."

The foremost man stared down at Finnegan's muddy clothes and befouled bowler. "Who the hell are you? You look like you just come from the gutter." He spit the words out with a thick Welsh accent.

The policeman highest on the stairs slapped the lower man on the shoulder. "That is the Pinkerton man who's been shooting highwaymen and whiskey peddlers."

The lower man looked back. "What for?"

"How the hell should I know? Some men are born mean, I suppose."

Finnegan pulled his mostly unused badge from his pocket. "You are correct; I was born mean, and the condition worsens daily. You may also take note of the fact that I outrank you."

The lower man stared down at the badge. "Where did you get that? That looks like the one Bourne's got."

"Probably because I got it from Bourne, fool." Finnegan stuffed the seemingly useless badge back in his pocket and motioned for the men to come down the stairs. "Get down here and speak with me or I will see to it that you are not wearing those uniforms soon enough."

"Uh, yes, sir." The lower one advanced a step, but stopped. "Uh, sir, I must retrieve my rifle, with your permission."

"Get to it and be quick." The lower man brushed past the upper and disappeared into the hallway above. Finnegan looked over the remaining fellow. "And where is your rifle?"

"I did not bring it, sir. I have one of the old Remingtons. They gave Albert one of the new Winchesters and he takes it everywhere with him for fear someone will make off with it if he's not watching." The man grinned. "It's like him to leave something he don't wish stolen in a whore's crib."

Finnegan pitched his cigar down to the floor and stepped on it. "Get down here."

He clomped down the stairs and joined Finnegan in the house's ill-shaped foyer. "Yes, sir."

"What is your name?"

"George Wright."

"And the one upstairs?"

"Albert Russell."

"I have some questions for the two of you regarding a woman who formerly resided here."

"I'm sorry, sir, what?"

"There was a woman who resided here by the name of Johanna Wetherill. Did you know her?"

He squinted, confused. "Sir, why would I know anything about a whore in this house?"

"Because your mother plies her trade here and she may have mentioned the lass over Christmas dinner."

"What the hell did you just say to me?" The man took a step closer, looking mad, but it was a mistake. Finnegan pulled the Remington from its holster and brought the muzzle of it up against the bottom of the policeman's chin. He crumpled to the floor, blinking in disbelief. "You, you hit me, you bastard."

"I'll do plenty more than that if I have a mind to." Finnegan holstered the revolver.

"What did you hit George for, mister?" The second policeman stood at the top of the stairs with his retrieved rifle in his hand. He appeared far more confused than angry.

Finnegan rubbed his beard gristle. "There is a trait about you two that vexes me. Get down here."

"Yes, sir." The man fairly ran down to the foyer.

"A woman who lived here, Johanna Wetherill, did you know her?"

He shook his head, glancing between Finnegan and the man who still lingered on the floor. "No, sir, I don't think so. Was she a whore?"

"She was not here in the capacity of a schoolteacher." Finnegan pointed to the man on the floor. "Get up, you oaf."

Albert pulled George to his feet and the two men stood next to each other, rather dumbfounded. Albert spoke first in their defense. "Sir, how could we know that we should have been taking an interest in the habits of whores, sir?"

Finnegan hung his head. "I suppose it is a mistake to expect any of you to take an interest in much of anything." He sighed. "Do not concern yourselves with..." He was cut off by Abijah bursting through the door. "Boy, I told you not to enter this establishment."

The young man's eyes were wide. "Sir, there are gentlemen coming up the road, well, what passes for the road. Sir, I believe they are coming in search of you."

"In search of me?"

"Sir, I believe they are the men from the tavern."

"Oh, that's...that may be a problem. How many of them?"

"Four, I think, sir."

"Well..." Finnegan glanced from the policemen to the door and back again. After a moment, he came to a decision and kicked the door shut. "Best we remain here and simply let them pass."

"And if they come here searching?"

"Then we must..."

"Let who pass?" Albert placed his fancy new Winchester '73 in a two-handed grip. "Do you presume to hide from the local ruffians?"

Finnegan sighed and shook his head. "I presume to avoid shooting any more of them than is absolutely necessary. I did not come here to eradicate the coal patch's population of drunks and loafers."

Albert worked the action on his rifle. "Sir, I do not know what you came here for, but one thing I do know is that we cannot be seen or heard of hiding from a gang of the local riffraff. Captain Bourne tells us frequently that one act of cowardice on our part can easily bring about hell to pay from the miners." Albert reached out and took hold of the doorknob.

"Mr. Russel, you would do well not to go out there. These are no ordinary ruffians. I have already shot several of them and..."

"Sir, you claimed to have only shot the one." Abijah shrugged. "That is what you claimed at the tavern."

"Regardless of how many where shot by myself or were otherwise injured, some of them have been shot, and still they persist." Finnegan scowled at his assistant. "It would be best to avoid further involvement with them if at all possible."

"I will not hide here like a woman, not from the likes of them at the tavern down the road." Albert flung the door open. "To hell with them." A bullet thudded into his upper chest. One of the brass buttons flew off his uniform and hit Abijah in the head, along with a spatter of blood. He fell backwards and the precious Winchester went sliding across the floor.

"The people of this patch have a great difficulty accepting advice." Finnegan kicked the door shut and slapped Abijah in the side of the head to break him out of the stupor the blood spatter had put him in. "Fetch me that rifle, boy."

Abijah ran his hands over his face. "Uh, yes, sir." He made a move toward the rifle, but Finnegan pushed him to the floor as more bullets shot wood splinters across the foyer. Finnegan threw himself into the corner behind the doorjamb. George, the remaining policeman, tried to follow suit, but was hit in the arm, chest, and leg as he tried to move.

The shot-up fellow fell to one knee and gave up on attempting to draw his Peacemaker. "Pinkerton man, I..." He pressed one hand to the hole in his arm. "I have been shot."

Finnegan nodded. "You are bleeding badly from that leg. You should tie something around it, or you will surely die."

"Help me, sir."

Finnegan reviewed the increasing pile of shot-to-hell men on the foyer floor. "Um, I am afraid you will have to look to it yourself."

"I...I do not feel quite right." George fell over.

"Sir, I believe he is dead." Abijah was staring at the dead policeman from his place on the floor near him.

"Yes, Abijah, he is." Finnegan craned his head forward a bit to see out the window. "Abijah, I believe we stand a much better chance of surviving this if you could fetch me that rifle."

"Oh, yes. My apologies."

"Think nothing of it, Abijah. This is your first gunfight;

some anxiety is to be expected." Another bullet split out the doorjamb just to the side of Finnegan's head. "Now, the damn gun, if you please."

"Yes, sir." Abijah crawled to the Winchester, grasped the barrel of it, and slid the gun across the floor to Finnegan's feet.

"Many thanks." He knelt to pick up the gun and made a quick check to see the chamber was loaded. He paused for a split second to appreciate how fancy the rifle was; he just couldn't help it. "Abijah, crawl into that parlor and try to get a look to see if our horses are still outside."

"Yes, sir." The boy began his crawl.

Finnegan spun to the side and sighted at a man sitting on horseback out in the front of the building. He squeezed the trigger and when the muzzle came back down the horse had fallen to the ground and the rider was trapped beneath it as it kicked. Finnegan levered the rifle's action and sighted on another mounted man. He fired and saw hair fly from the front shoulder of the horse. "Coal and Iron, jackass." He worked the action again and drew a bead on a dismounted fellow. Assuming that the rifle hit low, he held on the man's head as best he could, and squeezed. The fellow twisted as the bullet hit him in the pelvis or thereabouts. The reaction he exhibited was rather aggressive, he emptied a revolver at the front of the whorehouse and was attempting to reload when Finnegan shot him again. "Dedicated sons of bitches. Abijah! What has become of our mounts?"

"Mine remains at the hitching post, but yours has disappeared again, sir."

"Damned cancerous whore. If I ever find that horse again..." He glanced up to the top of the stairs. The lady of the house stood there, taking cover behind the banister. "Ma'am, you may not wish to remain there."

"What the hell are those drunkards doing?"

"They are trying to kill me, ma'am, but I believe they will settle with anyone they can hit. You should hide yourself behind something substantial."

"What of the girls?"

"Tell them to do the same." Wood chips flew as the men outside resumed firing. "Damn it." Finnegan heard someone step onto the porch. He had to respect the man's temerity. He spun in front of the window once more and fired at the uninvited guest. It was not a well-aimed shot and hit the floorboards of the porch. The man turned, looking quite shocked to be fired at.

"There you are, you damned Pinkerton." The man turned toward Finnegan.

Finnegan stared at the man and noticed the bandage on his arm. "Bodkin, I'll be damned. You are a daft bastard if I have ever seen one. What would possess you to come here and be shot again, much less shoot up a perfectly respectable whorehouse?"

"Call me bastard, I'll see you in hell." He moved to bring up his revolver and Finnegan shot him in the shoulder, then once more in the chest. "Shake that off, you son of a bitch." Finnegan watched him twitch on the porch for a moment, before ducking back behind the doorjamb. Outside, he could here a few voices yelling to one another. It sounded as if losing the main agitator in the conflict had caused some dissention. "Abijah, can you see anything out there? Use caution around those windows."

There was some shuffling in the parlor and some glass cracked. "Sir, I can see two men fleeing on foot and two fleeing on horseback. They are going in the direction of the tavern."

"This part of Pennsylvania houses more crazy people

than any other place I have ever been." Finnegan dropped the Winchester's hammer down to half-cock. "Piano player? Do you still live?"

"I do."

Abijah jumped at the sound of the old man's voice and turned around from the window. "Mr. Gilhooley, are you aware there is an old negro in a very fine suit of clothes hiding behind a piano in here?"

"I am. Why do you sound so surprised?"

"It is just that I have never seen that before." Abijah tipped his hat to the old man. "Abijah Smith."

"Clanton. Pleased to meet you. Young man, would you mind squishing that cigar butt out for me. I dropped it when the fracas began, and I worry it may burn the house down."

Abijah rather gingerly picked up the butt and snuffed it out on the floorboard. "Happy to help."

Finnegan slowly moved to the window he had been shooting out of and took a look around. There was no one visible outside. He set his hat on straight and took a deep breath. "This place is not very hospitable." He moved from the window and went to one of the dead policemen. "Abijah, I believe the excitement is over for the moment. Come in here." The boy presented himself in short order and Finnegan handed him a Peacemaker that had formerly been the property of the Coal and Iron Police. "Put that in your belt and secure the other, as well."

Abijah swallowed and looked at the other dead man. "We are to take their guns, sir?"

"They have no further need of them, and we very well may before this investigation is over." Finnegan assessed the way the boy was holding the revolver that had been handed to him. "You have no experience with guns?"

"No, sir."

139

"I see." Finnegan took the gun back from the boy and pointed to a burlap sack hanging on the coat rack in the corner. "Hand me that grain sack." The boy complied and Finnegan began filling it with guns and the spare ammunition the men had on them. He cursed once or twice, discovering that the revolvers had loaded rounds resting under the hammers. When everything was collected, he handed the sack back to Abijah. "Hang that from your saddle as best you can to keep it from flopping around and... ah, we should collect the guns from the men outside. I believe it would be best if the other residents of this place remained unarmed for the time being, at least while I am visiting."

"Yes, sir." Abijah glanced out one of the broken windows. "Sir, are we taking the bodies back to St. Clair?"

Finnegan contemplated it for a moment. "No, if I had killed them at the tavern I would have seen to their burial. They chose this fight, let them lay in the place they chose." He turned to the parlor where Clanton was slowly removing himself from behind the piano. "Old man, is it likely you will know the kin of the men lying outside?"

"Likely. Although it has been my experience that a man disreputable enough to shoot up a whorehouse will not have many weeping mourners at his funeral."

"Well, if anyone does come to collect the dead, inform them that any attempted retribution towards any Pinkerton men will end in the same result."

Clanton nodded. "It will not be difficult to convince them on that point."

FINNEGAN REINED up his newly acquired horse. The new animal was a large bay gelding that he had managed to catch outside the whorehouse. The beast seemed quite affable and had been of great assistance in locating the missing grey mare who had, yet again, run off with Finnegan's Spencer, which was the only reason he bothered going in search of the animal. With a fresh mount, several new firearms, and what passed for new hope, they had cut over the ridge to the south of Crow Hollow and moved toward the Reading Line. Finnegan was not precisely in the mood for a wilderness experience, but he did not wish to ride back through Crow Hollow, either.

When they made it to the tracks, Finnegan brought the gelding and the mare to a halt. "Tie off that nag and bring that grain sack over by that big tree."

"Uh, yes, sir."

Finnegan tied off his horses to a pine and walked over to the spot the train crews had been using as an air dump. He selected a couple of the used grease buckets and carried them about a hundred yards from the animals before setting them down next to the grain sack. "We will..." He looked back at the animals. "Walk one of those that way twenty paces and the other forty paces."

"Yes, sir."

Finnegan walked back to the horses and pulled a heavy hemp rope from where it was stashed in the bedroll tied to the back of the gelding's saddle. Unwinding the rope, he tied a loop in one end, which he placed around the neck of the mare, and secured the other end to the pine with a heavy square knot. The arrangement looked quite solid, but just to hedge his bets he pulled the Spencer from the scabbard. "Run all you please, lousy bitch." He walked back to the boy and the grease pails. "You have never fired a gun, Abijah?"

"Uh, no, sir."

"Then it is high time you learned. You conducted yourself quite well today. You kept your head and did not lose your composure. That is splendid behavior. The next time, however, you will not only keep your head, but act in your own defense, as well."

"Sir, I am not certain I could..."

"You can and you will. If you are going to continue tagging along with me, I feel it will become a necessity." Finnegan withdrew one of the 1873 Colts from the burlap sack and a half-empty box of cartridges he had found in a dead policeman's coat pocket. "Let's move a bit closer to that first bucket." They took about ten steps forward, where Finnegan set the box of cartridges in the grass. He pulled a tattered handkerchief from his coat pocket. "Tear a couple of pieces off that and stuff them in your ears. It is easier to learn if the noise does not scare you stiff." When the boy was done, Finnegan put the Colt in his belt and tore a couple of pieces off for himself. "It's too damn loud, no matter how old you get." He drew the Colt out again. "These cartridge pistols shoot much better than the old cap and ball guns, but they are still very hard to trust for much past ten paces. Always try to get close to the man before you fire with one of these."

"How...how does one get closer to a man? The men at the bawdy house would not have been easily approached."

"That is why it was important to fire at them with the rifle. I have found several methods that are effective for approaching men over the years. One is to come up behind them. Another method that works quite well is to tell them you do not wish to fight, approach, and then fire."

"Come up behind them?"

"Yes. I consider that the most effective."

"Is that honorable, sir?"

"I save considerations involving honor for those who abide by a sense of honor."

The boy looked a bit confused. "Who is that, sir?"

"No one I have ever met, but if I do discover someone who behaves in that manner, I will make you aware of it. Now, pay attention." Finnegan pointed the Colt downrange at the bucket. "You point it, then cock it." He slowly drew the hammer back with his thumb. "Then you put pressure to the trigger. It does not take much." Abijah saw Finnegan's finger flex the tiniest amount and flame erupted from the muzzle of the Colt. Downrange, the bucket hopped. Finnegan cocked back the hammer and fired once more. The bucket hopped again and bore a hole slightly above the first. "It seems to hit below the front sight." Finnegan sneered. "I do not care for that. If it hits in the same place for you, we will file the sight down a bit. He handed the revolver to the boy. "Use both of your hands. It will be much easier, at least until you are fully grown. In the army, I could barely lift the musket they gave me. It is something of a pity that a man is usually not big enough to use a gun when he must begin using a gun." Finnegan guided the boy's hands around the grip of the revolver. "Use this one to grip it tightly, then bring your thumb up like this to cock it." He pointed to the groove in the top strap. "You put the front sight in this. The bullet should hit somewhere around where you put the front sight."

"Will it hurt my hand to fire it, sir?"

"No. Men love to tell boys such things, but they are only talking to hear themselves spit. It is not difficult to fire a pistol or a rifle. If you keep your wits about you, it is not difficult to kill with them, either. Sometimes, I think guns make such things too easy. Perhaps it was better before the race of men had guns. Perhaps it made us think more before we tried to kill each other." He let loose of the revolver and let the boy hold it for himself. "Try to hit the bucket. Take it slow the first time." As instructed, and with very respectable deliberation, Abijah cocked back the hammer with his left hand and then wrapped his fingers around the gun's grip. He squeezed the trigger and the bullet hit above the bucket in the dirt behind it. "Try squeezing a little tighter."

"Yes, sir." He cocked the gun again and fired. The bullet hit in the dirt in front of the bucket.

"Do not pull the muzzle down trying to anticipate the shot. Put gentle pressure on the gun and let it happen."

"Yes, sir." Once more, Abijah cocked back the hammer. When the gun fired, the bucket jumped in the air. The boy turned to Finnegan smiling. "I hit it, sir!"

"You did very well." Finnegan motioned to the revolver. "Please avoid pointing that at me."

"Oh, yes sir. Sorry." He pointed the gun down at the dirt.

"It is not of much importance this time. As it happens, you are out of ammunition, but let us try to avoid it in the future."

"Yes, sir."

"Good. Now I will show you how to load it."

"Sir, how long did it take for you to learn to shoot as well as you do?"

"I am still learning. Although a man learns enough to try again the first time he must shoot." He smiled at Abijah. "Does that make sense?"

"I suppose so." Abijah stared down at the Colt. "Sir, I once read that many men hope to make their fortune in the west with a gun. Is that truly possible?"

"I have not made mine yet, so I could not tell you. Let me show you how to load it."

The boy burned his way through the half-full box of cartridges and then Finnegan took a few shots with his newly acquired 1873. Before he even began, he moved the rear sight up using the graduated wedge that was held in place by the spring pressure of the rear sight. It took about four shots for him to get it hitting where he preferred on the far bucket. Abijah sat under the shade of an oak and polished his Colt. "That seems to be a very fine rifle, sir."

Finnegan nodded approvingly. "It is. A true pity the man who owned it did not live long enough to appreciate it." He checked the chamber of the Winchester to make sure it was empty and motioned to the horses. "That lousy bitch sat there watching us shoot this whole last hour and never twitched."

Abijah looked rather wonderingly over at the mare. "That is true, sir, she did. Why is that, do you think?"

"She probably knows that she cannot leave me here to die so she does not bother running away. That horse has a damned cold heart."

THEY MADE it back to St. Clair just as the sun was sinking below the horizon. Finnegan scribbled out a quick note and instructed Abijah to attach it to a poplar in the creek bottom below the boarding house. With that seen to, Finnegan gave his landlady a few extra cents and purchased Abijah a place at the dinner table. They fairly feasted on chicken, then removed themselves to the back porch to smoke. Abijah rolled himself a cigarette and Finnegan seated a cigar between his lips.

"Do they have many stores in Pottsville?"

Abijah finished preparing his smoke. "More than here."

"This assignment has been quite rough on my wardrobe." Finnegan looked over his bowler yet again. "It is a damn shame. I could live without the hat, but I prefer a proper frock coat to keep my guns better hidden." He pointed to the

Colt Abijah proudly displayed in his belt. "We should look into getting a proper holster for that, as well."

"Truly, sir?"

"Consider it an advance on your pay. Do they have leather goods in Pottsville?"

"I would think so, yes. Are we going to Pottsville tomorrow, sir?"

"Yes. There is a man in the county jail there I must speak with before they hang him. While we are there, we may as well see to getting resupplied."

"The man you wish to speak with, he is a Molly Maguire?"

"So they say."

"He may not wish to speak with you, sir."

"That is my cross to bear in my profession."

"Do you believe the man in the county jail killed Miss Wetherill?"

Finnegan shook his head. "No. He has been residing in the jail since before Miss Wetherill was killed. Even a detective of my caliber can appreciate that simple fact."

Abijah lit his cigarette. "Then why speak to him?"

"For the simple reasons that we have nothing better to do, and I believe I can obtain a finer grade of coat in Pottsville." Finnegan stared into the darkness. "The lady proprietor of the bawdy house was only able to provide me with two names when I inquired as to Miss Wetherill's associates. Thomas Duffy was one."

"Who was the other, sir?"

Finnegan chuckled. "The other was the Pinkerton agent sent here to infiltrate the Molly Maguires."

"Oh."

"Yes. It is unfortunate. That gentleman had already departed town as well when Miss Wetherill was killed."

"Would you suspect one of your fellow agents of such a crime, sir?"

"All men are capable of evil, Abijah; it does not matter what profession they follow. James McParlan has proven himself to be capable of evil aplenty. Inconveniently, I do not feel it is the specific type of evil we are currently concerned with. Have you ever met this man Thomas Duffy? I was told he worked here in the mines."

"I do not believe so, sir. I know many of the people here, but many of the miners, especially the unmarried men, are not very gregarious with young people such as myself." Abijah flicked ash from his cigarette. "I knew Jack Kehoe, the man they claim was the leader of the Molly Maguires."

"Really?" Finnegan took a seat on the porch railing. "What kind of impression did you have of the man?"

"He seemed a good enough sort. He ran a tavern and boarding house."

Finnegan grunted. "I would have thought he would be a coal miner."

"He was, formerly. He was quite proud of the fact that he no longer had to labor in the mines. He frequented the union meetings and liked to tell the men there that the whole purpose of working in the mines was to eventually leave them. He liked to tell them that the only thing to be found at the bottom of a coal mine was hell, and that the longer a man spent in a mine the closer he would get to it." Abijah smiled. "He had a humor that I enjoyed."

"You attended union meetings?"

"At first, with my father. After he passed, I attended for the pies the ladies auxiliary would provide. All were welcome at the meetings and there was always a warm fire at whichever house the meeting was held. Mrs. Kehoe was always kind to me. She would give me hot coffee along with an extra slice of pie." Abijah took one last drag and dropped his cigarette to the floor of the porch where he stepped on it. "After my father passed, she always made a point of buying the coal for heating the boarding house and tavern from me. She could have sent her children out to collect it, as many do, but she bought it from me instead. She was very kind."

"What has become of her now?"

"She has suffered greatly. As a Christian woman, she cannot run the tavern. I do not believe the boarding house brings much money to her." Abijah turned to look at Finnegan. "It is hard for the women when they lose their men in the coal patch, sir."

"Yes, I would imagine it is." Finnegan blew out some smoke. "What, precisely, do they claim was Mr. Kehoe's crime?"

"They claim he was the..." Abijah searched for the proper word, and finally settled on a coal patch term he thought applicable. "They say he was the superintendent of the Molly Maguires. Your man McParlan has testified that Kehoe did the planning and picked many of the victims. They claim he is responsible for the killing of several foremen and intended to blow up the Reading Line when it was carrying a load of coal across one of the trestles." The boy paused and scratched one side of his face. "In the papers they always call him Black Jack Kehoe, but I never heard a man call him that in all the time I knew him."

"Such is the way with papers. Abijah, why would a man who was not even a miner anymore risk so much agitating for the miners? That hardly makes sense."

The boy shrugged. "I cannot say, sir. I know that Mr. Kehoe did dearly hate Mr. Gowan, all the railroad men, and all the mine bosses. I was at a meeting once where he said they should all be hanged." He shrugged. "Although, most miners in the patch have said much the same from time to time. I do not know if he is guilty of the crimes for which he is soon to hang, sir, if that is what you are asking me."

"I would not expect you to know what a man is or is not guilty of, Abijah. It is not of great concern. What a man is guilty of is between him and God." Finnegan dropped his cigar butt and stepped on it. "People spend too much of their lives concerning themselves with guilt, in my opinion." He sighed. "I will be bunking with you in the steeple tonight, Abijah."

"Oh. Uh, very well, sir. Do you wish for me to sleep in your rented room?"

Finnegan shook his head. "No. That would not be a good idea. I made the offer before I knew you better, Abijah. Now, I would not recommend you sleep in my room."

The young man looked a bit confused. "Uh, well, as you prefer, Mr. Gilhooley."

Finnegan pulled his watch from his pocket and held it near the house window where an oil lamp burned. "I have some business to attend to yet tonight. I will join you in the steeple rather late."

"Mr. Gilhooley, will we be informing Captain Bourne as to the fate of his men?"

Finnegan nodded. "I will see to that in the morning. The captain will simply have to begin his day early, not that he seems to sleep much." Finnegan pondered on it for a moment. "Abijah, can you think of any reason why most of Bourne's men are asleep on those damned cots up there at the Coal and Iron house every time I walk in there?"

Abijah laughed. "I believe Captain Bourne expects a retribution to be visited upon him by the citizens of the town, sir. Ever since the verdicts have come to pass, the peelers have ceased patrolling at night. Now the captain keeps them at the house, up all night, watching and waiting for a mob to come."

Finnegan grinned. "How do you come to know this?"

"I get melancholy at night on occasion, and a walk often cheers me. Before the Mollies were sent to the rope, the peelers patrolled the entire town." Abijah shrugged. "Once or twice, a patrolling policeman was given a beating. Now they claim all the drubbings were on orders from the Mollies." He shrugged again. "Still, no one knows what is true. Of late, Captain Bourne keeps all the men, all night, at the Coal and Iron house, expecting the townspeople to come lynch him. That is why they sleep all day."

Finnegan chuckled. "If you wish to see the true effects of guilt, simply look to the good captain. I would say it is obvious that he feels he has sinned, and that now the retribution for his sins is to be visited upon him." Finnegan shook one finger at the boy. "Keep such things in mind before you sin, young Abijah."

"I surely will, sir."

"Good boy." Finnegan rubbed his face. It had been a long day. "I will see you in a few hours." He motioned to his rented room. "If you would be so kind, take the rifles up to the bell tower."

"Yes, sir."

"And do not shoot me with your fancy new pistol when I come to bed."

"No, sir."

"You did very well today, Abijah. You should be proud of yourself. A man should always be proud of a job well done." Finnegan adjusted his gun belt and walked off into the darkness toward the creek bed. Once there, he settled into a comfortable place amongst the trees and waited to hear footsteps approaching. He held his Remington in one hand, just in case the person who presented themselves was not the man he had set a meeting with. When Sam Rooney came around the bend in his bartender's apron, Finnegan holstered the revolver. "You cut a fine figure in that apron, Sam. I believe if I were to begin drinking the devil rum, I would buy my first glass from you."

Rooney laughed quietly and took a seat beside Finnegan. "God save us all if you ever do. The temperance union claims liquor causes men to do violence. I shudder to think what you would be like drunk."

"I am not a violent man."

"No, brother? And how many men have you killed since you have come to town?"

He shrugged and passed a cigar to his old friend. "It is that very matter I wish to discuss. During the course of my day, I was involved in no less than two shooting scraps. One in a tavern and the other in a whorehouse. I do not know if you have heard."

"I believe everyone in Schuylkill County has heard tell of it already."

Finnegan sneered and set a cigar between his lips. "It was unfortunate. There was no need for any of it, but the people of this damnable coal patch are so very obstinate."

"As I recall, you have always had difficulties dealing with obstinate people." Rooney looked around before lighting his cigar.

"Yes, well, the day's events have brought me to the conclusion that this job I am about here may be impossible to complete. When one is tasked with an impossible job, he rapidly comes to the conclusion that he is not paid enough for his services. That consideration brings him to the conclusion that he should seek out alternative forms of income to find his fortune."

Rooney grinned. "Does it?"

Finnegan lit his cigar and leaned toward his friend. "Men like Enoch McLeod would have both of us shot for nothing more than the opportunity to brag at a dinner party that they had hired the best to do their dirty business. This state of affairs cannot go on forever. Eventually, I will step wrong and catch a bullet. Eventually, you will be discovered, and your bar patrons will swing you from a trestle."

Rooney shivered a bit and crossed his arms. "My greatest fear is that they will throw me in one of the mines." He rubbed his arms and then resumed a normal position. "You know they sent no less than three agents here before McParlan? All were killed, Finn, and two have never been found. They went into the mines one day for their shift and simply disappeared. It would be horrid, would it not? I dream sometimes of what it would be like to lie forever, tucked into some damn hole in those great endless mines."

Finnegan shook his head. "I do not believe that is a healthy habit, Sam." He patted his friend on the back. "When does the next payroll come through on the train?"

Rooney brightened up, thinking of the money. "The end of the month. It is always the same."

"This is common knowledge?"

"Oh, yes, well known. Every drunk in this town jests at doing what we are currently plotting."

"Excellent. Who guards the payroll?"

"From what I have observed, there are usually two of the Coal and Iron fools and their captain, the man called Bourne, is in the habit of accompanying them. It is an excuse for him to travel to Philadelphia, I believe. Of late, he has been making the trip alone. It looks to me as if he is loath to lower the force of Coal and Iron boys in town."

Finnegan nodded. "That man may be able to recognize me."

Rooney chuckled. "There is a simple fix for that."

"No, I do not think that will be necessary." Finnegan smiled. "In truth, I would rather leave him alive to face the consequences of having his payroll stolen. After having spent some time with him, it would amuse me greatly if he lost his position with the peelers and had to go back to the mines."

"You are a cold man, Finnegan. It would be more merciful to kill him."

"Mercy is not generally one of my concerns. Do you know how the money is transported?"

Rooney puffed his cigar. "How do you mean?"

"Is there a safe in the train car?"

Rooney grinned. "No. I know that for a fact. The train conductor and mail agent frequent my tavern. The money is in a lockbox. One of the peelers sits his fat ass down on it for the duration of the trip. I would assume the other lounges somewhere in the car."

"What about Bourne?"

Rooney's grin widened. "I am told that he is too good to ride in the mail car. He takes a seat in one of the passenger cars. The conductor claims he does nothing but read the papers and stare at the scenery. It is nothing but an amusing outing for him."

Finnegan rubbed his chin. "That is useful. So, formerly, in the mail car there were two Coal and Iron Peelers and the mail agent?"

"Yes. Now that Bourne has taken the task on himself, there is only the mail agent."

"That is good, that works in our favor. A lonely mail agent will not be difficult to handle. Does the mail car come into town every day?"

"Surely."

"Give it a good inspection next time you see it in the yard. If it has an upper hatch, that would be of use."

"Finnegan, you would propose that we take the train by ourselves? I had expected to recruit a few others to assist us. How can we stop the train and then control the passengers while we obtain the cash box? We will need assistance."

Finnegan shook his head. "It will not do for men such as ourselves to use outdated methods." He knocked ash from his cigar and smiled. "We must be on the vanguard of our industry. We would stop the trains we pilfered during the war by piling logs on the tracks. That is also the way the Reno gang effected their robberies. We will act differently."

"How so?"

"The last train robbery perpetrated by the James contingent was managed when one of their number leapt from a rock outcropping onto the train as it passed. He then ordered the engineer to stop the train and the remainder of the gang took possession of it. They robbed both the mail car and the passengers, but we have no need to rob the passengers."

"You wish to leap onto the train?" Rooney's face betrayed a hesitancy.

"It will not be an act of great heroism, Sam. I rode on the train here from Philadelphia. It follows the Schuylkill River the entire way. It slows to a crawl no faster than a man can walk on some of the curves and steeper grades. We can position ourselves above one of the cuttings and veritably step onto the mail car. It will be hardly more dangerous than swinging into the saddle."

Rooney laughed. "Oh, certainly."

"After that, one of us will open the upper hatch, assuming there is one, and the other can enter through the door at the end of the car. We can bind and gag the peelers, if

154

there are any, and the mail agent with little trouble. If they are reasonable men, there should not even be a need to do them harm. All we need to do after that is wait for another tight bend in the tracks and we can jump."

"You wish to leap *from* the train, as well?"

"Would you prefer to ride it into St. Clair so the conductor can punch your ticket?"

"No, that would not be to my liking. How do you propose we flee? We will need horses wherever it is we leap off."

"We will employ the services of my young associate, Abijah."

"The Smith boy? The one who lives in the church tower?"

"The same."

"You plan for the success of the entire venture to hinge on the abilities of one twelve-year-old boy? Finnegan, chasing the James brothers has driven you mad."

"Not mad, but amply angry. Young Mr. Smith will perform admirably. He has already done himself credit under fire several times. I have met many a grown man who does not conduct himself as well."

Rooney gave his old partner a very stern stare. "Finnegan, you may be jumping to conclusions. The boy may not wish to participate in something as sordid as a train robbery. The young oftentimes fail to appreciate the practicality of such things."

"A more practical young man you are not apt to meet. If he does suggest it is improper, I will explain to him that the money from the payroll represents the payment the young man should have received when the railroad and coal concern killed his father." Finnegan flicked more ash. "The boy told me his father was killed by firedamp; what the hell is that?"

"These coal mines have a sort of explosive gas that builds up in them." Rooney shrugged. "The miners must carry lamps with them. The lamps have flames..." He shrugged again. "They blow up frequently. So frequently, that it is impossible to say whether the Mollies are exploding them, or it is simply accidental." Rooney smoothed his apron. "I knew Abijah Smith's father, not well, but he seemed a good sort. I never once saw him lift a glass in a tavern and he was always cold sober at the union meetings."

"You attend the union meetings? I would not think bartenders would be allowed."

"Bartenders have as much interest in improving the lot of miners as anyone. The better their condition, the better ours. The meetings are dreadfully boring, but it is the place of a proper spy to sit through them. The last time they went on strike, they were out of work for six months begging for an extra nickel a month or something. When it was said and done, they came back to work for a little less than they were making when they struck. I do not believe they will allow anyone to join the union who is capable of arithmetic."

"I am certain the union bosses are properly trained in that art. Everyone I ever met in Chicago had an impressive mastery of numbers." Finnegan chuckled. "These labor men cry about the behavior of the industrialists, but if one of these union bosses ever figures a way to get a penny from every railroad worker or coal miner, he'll be the richest blighter in America. What will they say about him then?"

Rooney laughed. "That man would be forced to retire. He would, naturally, buy an iron mill and become a deeply vindictive bastard so that the next union agitator would stand a better chance of collecting pennies from the downtrodden masses."

Finnegan smiled. "By comparison, one little train robbery seems a minor matter."

"You'll hear no argument from me." Rooney grinned, showing his pearly whites in the moonlight. "A man like me never argues, he simply goes in the proper direction. I am a natural born heathen, and if that does not achieve my ends, I shall become a Baptist."

"Right after you become Pope." Finnegan sighed at his friend's constant amiability. Sam Rooney truly was ready for anything at any time. "Just see to inspecting the train car when it is next in the station."

"What will you be doing?"

"I will make use of the days we have left to pick out a spot along the tracks to jump onto and then dismount the train. With any luck, I can find two locations that will allow us to become rich without breaking our necks."

"Does having six thousand dollars make a man rich?"

Finnegan slowly removed the cigar from between his lips. "No, Sam, it does not. I have heard that a man is only rich if he can claim to possess one true friend."

Rooney stared at him suspiciously. "An interesting notion."

"Truly it is. Which is why I feel I need to inform you that if this venture of ours does in fact net us twelve thousand greenback dollars, you will not be receiving half." Rooney's eyes narrowed. "And neither will I."

"You wish to throw some of it in the river to appease God?"

"I wish for a share to go to our young friend Mr. Smith."

Rooney nodded, looking properly regretful. "Such is business. The young man must be paid for his time."

"We must also set aside a small amount for the care and maintenance of a young lady, Anabel Lee."

157

"Who?"

"I killed the man who had charge of her, or rather caused him to be killed, and she currently resides at the boarding house where I am staying. Her guardian was a loathsome sort, but still, it is the responsibility of the Pinkerton agency that she finds herself without a keeper. If we succeed, it would only be right to see to it that she has something of a pension. I will leave it in the charge of Mrs. Wallace, the proprietress of the boarding house."

"Are there any other widows or orphans here in the coal patch you presume to raise up out of poverty? Perhaps when this is all done you would suggest we take holy orders and don robes. You could use your pistol to ring the church bells and I could brew rotgut. All monks love rotgut corn liquor." Rooney smiled wide.

Finnegan shook his head. "No, simply helping the two young people should be more than sufficient."

"Very well, then, but it will be difficult for either of us to achieve sainthood if we stop there."

"I would imagine there are more than a few hurdles between us and that particular accolade. See about the train car and I will contact you with a note on the tree over there in a few days."

"Do you intend to continue shooting men around here in the meantime?"

Finnegan shrugged. "It is what I was sent here to do."

"You may find it a more difficult task in the days to come."

"It has not been precisely easy up to this point."

"What I mean, Finn, is that there has been a rumor circulating for many days that you were sent here to assassinate John Siney."

"Abijah mentioned that man earlier. Why should I want to kill him? I have never even heard of the man before today."

"That is the foolish part, Finn. Pinkerton, or his clients, would never want you to kill Siney. He is the head man at the union and has very consistently talked these ignorant miners out of striking several times. He has convinced them that the best course of action is for the union to continually negotiate with the mine owners while work goes on as usual. Mr. Gowan, the railroad, and men like Enoch McLeod never had a better friend than John Siney." Rooney tossed his cigar down into the creek. "He is a man who has found his way out of the mines. Men like that will do anything to stay out."

Finnegan chuckled. "But the miners do not understand that."

"To them the man might as well be Jesus. He gives them fresh hope that they can all be rich and prosperous at every union meeting."

"And they believe I was sent here to kill him?" Finnegan shook his head. "Since being here, I have come to surmise that these people will not improve their lot in life until they become less gullible. I got the sense there was something out of sorts today at the tavern; now I understand it."

"Be vigilant, Finn. These miners may seem like simple rubes, but they killed many a man in retribution for trespasses much smaller than what they have been told you are here to do. They will make a try for you."

"I have already made preparations for my defense. Thank you for the warning."

"I have need of you presently, Finnegan. I would hate to see anything happen to you before we are rich."

"Ever the practical man, Mr. Rooney. I will contact you soon."

Chapter 5

ST. CLAIR, PENNSYLVANIA
June 18th, 1877

FINNEGAN AWOKE TO THE BOY'S FOOT THUMPING against his shoulder. He opened his eyes and stared up at the kid. A dim light was slowly illuminating the church steeple.

"Sir, it is morning, sir."

Finnegan nodded and sat up. He glanced around to make sure his pistols were all where he had left them and that the two rifles still leaned in the corner of the steeple. "Very well. Did you see or hear anything during your watch?"

"I did not, sir. There were a few wandering drunks in the early hours, but they are to be expected. No one approached your rented room."

"Good." Finnegan rubbed his eyes and did his best to clear the cobwebs out of his head. "Come. We will get our breakfast from Mrs. Wallace and then I will inform Captain Bourne as to the fate of his men, if he has not already been made aware of it. These miners gossip more than old women making a quilt. I have never been in a place where news spreads so quickly."

"I suppose that is the result of working all day shoulder to

160

shoulder with nothing better to discuss. There is little to ruminate on in a dark hole other than what the man next to you has to say."

"I had not considered that." Finnegan cast the blanket off of him and pulled on his boots. "After I speak with Captain Bourne, we will travel to Pottsville today."

"Yes, sir."

"You will have to procure our horses from the livery. See that I do not get that damned grey again. I took the good time and effort to catch that gelding and kill his owner, I intend to keep him. Take no lip to the contrary from that stable owner."

"I will hold him to it, sir."

The two men clamored down from the steeple and made their way to the back door of the boarding house. Finnegan obtained a bowl of water from the pump and saw to his morning shave while Abijah got their breakfast ordered from Mrs. Wallace. With a clean face, Finnegan gobbled down his breakfast and parted ways with Abijah. One went east to the stable, while the other went west to the Coal and Iron house.

As Finnegan approached the house, he could not help but notice that the place appeared to be in an even worse state of disarray than usual. That morning someone had left the front door open, and it was banging around whenever the wind whipped up. Inside, Finnegan found a substantial amount of leaves that had entered the structure and had actually begun to pile up around the cots of the sleeping policemen. Finnegan sighed, staring at the men as their chests slowly moved up and down. Most of them had bellies that were falling out of their blue coats and there were bottles of various stripe littering the floor. "This is not the proper conduct for constables." He left the inert men and walked down the hall to Bourne's office. Normally, he would have swung the door open without knocking to show his disdain for the captain, but that day the door was already open. Finnegan peeked around the doorjamb to see Bourne face down on his desk. Two empty whiskey bottles adorned the desktop. Bourne's police helmet sat upside down on the desktop, as well. It appeared as though he had passed out wearing it and it had flopped from his head when he hit the desk. "For the love of St. Pete." Finnegan slammed the door shut. "Rouse yourself, Captain!"

Bourne leapt back in his chair. The force toppled it and he fell to the floor on his back. "Bastards! you won't take me without a fight!" Bourne fought his pistol from its holster.

Finnegan could hear the sound of the flap holster being opened. "Captain?" He drew his Remington.

"I'll see you in hell, you bloody..." The mumbling came from behind the desk out of sight, but the sound of a hammer being cocked was readily recognizable. "Bloody bastards." A shot went up into the ceiling.

"Captain!" Finnegan jumped forward and pulled the desk aside. Bourne stared up at him with a pair of bloodshot eyes that shown like fire pokers. Finnegan wrenched the captain's Colt away. "Drunken fool. I should shoot you and save you the shame of seeing yourself in a mirror."

Bourne licked his lips and it sounded like two pieces of leather being rubbed together. "Gilhooley?"

"Yes, imbecile. You may have killed someone upstairs discharging your pistol like that."

"Have you...have you come to finish me?"

"You have damn near finished yourself." Finnegan tossed the Colt into the corner and sat down in the chair that was still upright. "What in hell is going on here, Captain?" Finnegan gave one of the whiskey bottles a small kick. "I doubt General Pleasants would look kindly on this type of behavior. If you and your men are discovered in this condition, I should think you will all be digging coal before the month is out."

Bourne got on all fours and then used the desk to climb up onto shaky legs. Having accomplished standing on his own for a moment, he sat down on the desk. "The men..." He made an attempt at licking his lips again. "The men have been complaining. Morale has been low. I told them they could indulge. I, perhaps, overindulged, as well."

"This is pathetic, Bourne."

The captain rubbed his glowing eyes. "Why are you here? Have you found...the girl...have you found her killer?"

"No. I have come here to inform you that two of your men are dead."

"What? My men? Who?"

"If memory serves, their names were Wright and Russell."

The captain put his hands on either side of his head and squeezed, obviously to keep the vessel from splitting open. "How were they killed?"

"Shot by drunken scum at a whorehouse in Crow Hollow."

"How do you know of it?"

"I was there when it occurred."

Bourne staggered from the desk to a stove where a coffee pot resided. He felt the pot, found it cold, and promptly decided it did not matter. He poured a cup and drank. "Were you the cause of it?"

"There is no cause for something so stupid. I would add that if your men had taken my advice, they might very well still be living. I came here merely to inform you, not to discuss the matter. It is a professional courtesy and nothing more."

Bourne grimaced as he drained his coffee cup. "Fine,

Wright and Russell. I will strike them from the roster and find two other sots to take their place." He refilled the cup. "Have you any other business here?"

Finnegan got up from his chair and holstered his revolver. "No, I think not." He was half out the door when Bourne spoke again.

"Gilhooley, what became of their guns?"

Finnegan raised one eyebrow. "They were your men, Captain, I would think you would want to know where their bodies lie before inquiring about their armament."

"I place a much higher value on the weapons. They can be used against us the next time these animals riot."

"If you wish to locate them, I would suggest you ride out to Crow Hollow and look for them. You should at least make an effort to collect the bodies. If you do not, it may be observed that you and your remaining men lacked the courage to leave this hovel. That sort of cowardice has been known to cause riots, sir."

"I will take it under consideration." The captain sipped more cold coffee and sneered. "I heard a rumor regarding you, Mr. Gilhooley."

"Rumors are vile things."

"I have heard that you were not sent here to solve a murder, but to commit one. They are saying you came here to kill John Siney."

"I never heard of the man before yesterday."

"Still, it should give a man pause. Siney is very popular in this area. You speak of showing cowardice. Does the prospect of every grown man in this coal patch wishing to kill you not put a shiver up your spine?"

"I expect they wanted to kill me before anyone ever made up the story regarding Siney." Finnegan scowled at the man. "You are in a sorry state, Captain. I would recommend a bath and a shave before you go out, if you go out anymore."

With that, Finnegan left the Coal and Iron house and strolled down the street to the telegraph office. The young telegraph clerk was a pleasing switch from the debauchery he had seen at the police headquarters. The clerk looked up from the nickel book he was reading, and his face formed into a mixture of dread and surprise. "Oh, uh, good morning, sir."

"Good morning, young man."

"You wish to send another telegram, sir?"

"Yes."

"To Robert Pinkerton, care of the office in Philadelphia?"

"The same."

The clerk picked up his pencil and drew a sheet of paper from the pile near him. "Very well, sir."

Finnegan cleared his throat. "Investigation continues. Interviewing Molly Maguire in Pottsville today."

The clerk waited for a moment before raising his head from the paper. "That is all, sir?"

"Yes. Quite succinct, wouldn't you say?"

The clerk smiled, showing some relief. "Yes, sir, quite." He let a small laugh slip out. "I am glad to hear your work is becoming less fierce." He shrugged. "This is a small town, sir. We have few men to spare." He smiled at the joke.

"Oh, that reminds me. Include another bit. Two Coal and Iron men dead, unknown number of drunkards dead in same altercation."

The clerk sighed. "Very well, sir."

Finnegan pointed to the book lying on the clerk's desk. "What is it you are reading there?"

"Oh, that." The clerk held up the book to reveal its cover that depicted a vicious gun battle between one group of what appeared to be cowboys and another that were obviously meant to be some sort of Mexican bandits. "It is a rousing tale, sir. It is a story of the adventures of the James brothers in Mexico."

Finnegan chuckled. "Is that so?"

"Yes, sir. It relates how the brothers saved several Spanish ladies from the clutches of an evil Don. Have you heard of the James brothers, sir?"

"In fact, I have."

"This book claims that Jesse James is the greatest shootist to have ever lived. It says his hands are so fast that they cannot be seen to move when he draws his gun."

Finnegan picked up the book and gave it a closer look, flipping through the pages. "I would agree that it is difficult to see a man's hand move when he comes up behind you. As for speed, I would readily admit that Jesse has a claim to the world's fastest mouth."

The clerk formed a bit of a scowl. "Sir, perhaps it is not right for you to cast aspersions on a man you have not met."

Finnegan turned the book open to the first page and set it on the desk. He tapped the name and address of the publisher in New York. "I doubt the man who wrote this rag has spent much time with the James brothers, either. As far as I know, they do not often frequent Fifth Avenue." He flipped the book shut and returned it to where the clerk kept it. "You should not believe everything you read, young man."

The clerk assumed a rather huffy demeanor. "But I should believe what I am told?"

"Believe none of that." Finnegan motioned to the telegraph. "Be about your business, young man. Leave other concerns for the hours you are not at work."

FINNEGAN LOOKED himself over in the shop's full-length mirror. He was wearing the one and only black frock coat the store possessed. Traveling to the slightly larger settlement of Pottsville had not increased his selection as much as he had been hoping it would. He had not yet begun to investigate the hats.

"I am sorry, sir. We do not get much call for frock coats here. The miners prefer a shorter coat for work, and of course, they will rarely pay for wool."

"I see."

"They cannot often afford it." The shop proprietor was a small man with a pair of reading glasses perked toward the end of his nose. "I have one in grey that I keep on hand for the local preacher. He frequently ruins his. I have told him many times that a grey coat will not do in coal country, but the man is stubborn."

"What species of preacher is he?" Finnegan adjusted the coat and looked it over yet again.

"Methodist."

"As such you would think he would be more malleable." Finnegan nodded to himself in the mirror. "It will do." He turned and surveyed the rest of the shop. "Do you have leather goods; holsters, in particular?"

"Yes, sir."

Finnegan pointed to Abijah. "Find one that fits the pistol that young man has in his belt."

The shopkeeper cast a wary eye on the boy, but it only lasted a moment. Holsters were difficult items to sell. "As you wish, sir."

Finnegan checked his watch and pulled the frock coat from his shoulders. "Shopkeeper, take this garment and add it to the other purchases." Finnegan had decided to make use of the shop's stock to resupply his ammunition and to get ammunition for his newly obtained equipment. For a backwater general store, the place had an impressively wide selection. Finnegan got the sense that the owner was hoping one of Bourne's much feared riots was in the offing. "I have business at the jail that I must see to. I take it the large stone structure is that edifice?"

The shopkeeper nodded. "Yes, sir." He offered a holster up for Abijah's inspection. "Yes, sir, the one that resembles a castle. Currently, it houses some of the most ferocious men in this nation's history." The shopkeeper looked Finnegan up and down. "Are you a newspaper man?"

Finnegan hooked his thumbs into his gun belt. "Sir, do I appear to be a newspaper man?"

"No, sir, I suppose not." He held up another holster.

Finnegan motioned to the leather item. "Not that one. The boy requires his weapon to ride higher on his hip. His pistol should be concealed beneath his coat when in public." Finnegan smiled at his young associate. "He is not a road agent. He should carry his gun like a proper detective."

The shopkeeper gave Finnegan a cold stare. "You are detectives?"

"Yes."

"So, you travel to the jail to speak with the Mollies?"

"Yes."

"Better you than I, sir. I cannot say I would care to speak with any man who is so close to hanging." The man shivered. "It seems to me as though it might give a man bad luck."

"That may be why I am a detective, and you are a shop-keeper. All men eventually find their way to their proper place in this world." Finnegan shrugged and put his old coat back on. "Even if it happens to be at the end of a rope. Abijah, leave the goods here and get yourself something to eat at that café when you are done here. I will return and find you when my business is concluded."

"Yes, sir."

It was a walk of only a quarter mile to the Schuylkill County jail. It did, in fact, resemble the two castles Finnegan had seen in his homeland. One of them was Dublin Castle, from whence the English issued their proclamations. The other was a former castle, but had been repurposed and renamed. Newgate Prison was the pit where the English deposited any man they deemed a criminal, and often hung them from the battlements. Finnegan and his father had narrowly missed being among those who kicked against the cold stone wall. It seemed strangely ironic that the Americans had built a castle of their own in Pennsylvania to hang more Irishmen. Perhaps hanging Irishmen was simply something every culture got around to eventually.

Finnegan approached the large double doors at the front of the building. Just as any proper castle should, there was a lowered portcullis blocking the way. An oversized ape of a guard lounged by small door in the iron bars designed to let men pass to the inside of the prison. The ape heaved himself up from his stool and spit out a long stream of chewing tobacco, which he unceremoniously wiped away from his chin with one jacket sleeve. "What the hell do you want?" He hitched his gun belt up to the bottom of his prodigious gut and then let it fall again.

Finnegan produced his badge. "I am a captain with the Coal and Iron Police. I wish to speak to one of the prisoners you are holding."

The ape spit again. "Which one?"

"Which one? What bloody difference does that make to you?"

The ape rubbed his chin. "You don't look like one of them Coal and Iron peelers. Where's your uniform?"

"Well, you don't much resemble..." Finnegan scanned over the man. There was a revoltingly large amount of dried blood all over his clothing. "What the hell kind of jailer are you?"

"I ain't no jailer. I'm a butcher. The sheriff has got me and every other son of a bitch in the county who ain't a miner working in here this month. He thinks the miners will come to break out the Mollies." He rubbed his chin again. "Sheriff said they might try to sneak somebody in here to effect their escape. Maybe that's you."

"And maybe Jesus will walk in here and pardon them." Finnegan held the Coal and Iron badge closer to the flat-iron bars. "Here is one badge." He returned it to his coat and withdrew his Pinkerton badge. "Here is another." He put the badge away and held open his coat. "And here are my guns. Now either open this damn gate or go find me someone who is less of a fool."

"You can stand out there all damn day for all I care."

Finnegan drew his Remington. "If I shoot you, do you believe the noise might bring someone more accommodating over here?"

The ape grunted. "Fine, fine. No need to get your balls in a knot. You got them two badges; I guess if that ain't enough to get through this damn door, I shouldn't be letting anybody in." He fished a key out of his pocket and jiggled it into a rusty lock. The door creaked open.

Finnegan holstered his revolver and stepped through. "Very amiable, thank you."

"Yeah. Which piece of crow bait do you wish to commune with?"

"A Molly. By name, Thomas Duffy."

"He's in here, though not for long." The ape slowly returned to his stool. "They're keeping them Mollies in the cells on the other side of the yard there. You'll have to show them fancy badges to Mr. Mulroney to get in there."

"Mulroney is the jail sergeant?"

"He's a dairy farmer by trade. Since he ain't a miner, this week he's watching the Mollies." The ape appeared deep in thought. "I guess his wife is looking after the cows."

"Is your wife running the butcher shop?"

"Of course."

"This is all quite fascinating. I look forward to continuing this conversation with Mr. Mulroney."

The ape stared with wonderment. "Well, that's real good, I reckon." He spit out more tobacco. "Nice meting you."

"Nice meeting you." Finnegan crossed the yard and banged on a wooden door with a sally port built into it. The face of a man who looked as though he had access to an ample supply of free dairy appeared behind the tiny bars. "I wish to speak with one of the Mollies."

The moon-like face tried to see more of Finnegan but found the sally port too high. "Did Reginald let you in?"

"No, I flew over the wall."

"There are not supposed to be men coming in and out of here."

"Do you come and go from this place?"

"Yes."

"Then one more cannot make much difference." Finnegan held one of his badges to the sally port. "I only need a few moments with the man, and I will be on my way."

"A Pinkerton, by God." The face disappeared and there was a rattling noise behind the door. It creaked open to reveal a man who would have been extended on tiptoe to see anything through the hole provided. "Sir, I do not believe it is safe for you to be wandering around these parts, especially if you often inform people you are a Pinkerton."

"Yes, I have noticed that, sir." Finnegan moved past the man into the cellblock.

The dairy farmer assumed a shocked look. "You have guns?"

"Yes."

"I do not believe Reginald should have let you come in here with those."

"He did not want to, but I explained to him how very dangerous it is for a man like me in this particular town. He was, mercifully, quite accommodating."

"Oh, well, yes, I see."

"Which cell holds Thomas Duffy?"

"Duffy resides in the last cell in this corridor, sir. We have been told to keep them in separate cells and keep one empty cell between them."

Finnegan nodded. "Why?"

"I have no idea, sir. I am a dairy farmer by trade."

"Yes, Reginald informed me of that. Is your wife handling the cows well?"

"Well enough, sir. I aid her with the milking before I come here in the morning. How did you know about my wife, sir?"

"I am a detective."

"Very impressive, sir."

"I knew it would be."

Finnegan stalked down the stone corridor past a collection of men who had been made famous all over America since their arrests. Finnegan could not say for certain whether Allan Pinkerton was truly the world's greatest detective, but he was definitely world class in the field of publicity. Only men such as P.T. Barnum or Bill Cody could have claimed to be his equal. A year ago, no one outside St. Clair could have possibly cared if the six men currently held in the Schuylkill County jail were alive or dead. With only a little time, a minor amount of investigation, and a great deal of hyperbole, Allan Pinkerton had transformed those unknown men into a matter of national debate warranting two-inch tall headlines. The Molly Maguires were not simply dumb thugs pulled from a barroom. They were guerilla fighters on the vanguard of a war against capital, progress, and possibly even democracy if one were to believe prosecuting attorney Gowan. The Mollies were nothing less than hell spawn eating away at the very core of what all decent Americans held dear. Thanks to proper coverage from the eastern press, it was obvious to any literate American that Allan Pinkerton had saved the entire population from falling prey to these coal field demons. Without Allan Pinkerton and his fearless detectives, the plague of the Molly Maguires would have spread from sea to shining sea, leaving nothing but carnage and chaos in its wake.

Finnegan did not look into the other cells as he made his way down the corridor. There was no reason to; he had business with only one man. The rest did not matter to Finnegan, and he had trained himself not to contemplate the fate of men who were not of concern to his work. It was the only way to achieve anything close to efficiency in his profession. When he reached the final cell, he found a man lying on a cot within. The fellow had his feet toward the bars and lay reading what appeared to be a Bible.

Finnegan tapped the base of the bars with one boot toe. "Thomas Duffy, I would speak with you."

The man in the cell lifted his bible and stared underneath it at Finnegan. "Now who might you be? You're a tall one, aren't you? You'd make a poor coal miner, always bumping your head."

"I imagine I would."

Duffy smiled and sat up on his cot. "Yes, but you're not a miner, are you?"

"I am not. My name is Finnegan Gilhooley. I am a detective in private employ."

"Ah." Duffy nodded and set his Bible to one side. "You'll have to excuse me not shaking your hand Mr. Gilhooley. I shook another detective's hand, once upon a time, and it has caused me a great deal of consternation since."

"Yes, well, I can understand your hesitancy when it comes to keeping company with detectives, given all you have been through. Although, it seems to me that most of your current difficulties stem from the previous detective you associated with not informing you that he was a detective. I have given you ample warning regarding my profession, so you should have nothing to worry about."

Duffy nodded and grinned. "You are correct on all counts, Detective Gilhooley. You have given warning and I truly have little to worry about. That is a condition common to all men about to hang. I certainly won't be worrying about you gathering or fabricating evidence against me. If it would be of assistance to you, and you would be willing to trade some tobacco in turn, you might even find me willing to confess to any crimes that are currently troubling you. It is not as if I can be hung twice."

Finnegan pulled a cigar from his pocket and held it through the bars. Duffy reached forward and took hold of it. "That is very hospitable of you, Mr. Duffy."

"My dear mother taught me to always make the best of whatever circumstances I found myself in. I suppose there is little purpose in changing now, and I have always been pleased to make myself of use. Thinking on it, that practice may have been what has placed me here."

"You wished to be of use?" Finnegan passed him a match.

"I often saw McKenna sitting alone in the Crossed Keys. He seemed a decent sort and I would lift a glass with him from time to time. He had traveled far more than me and I enjoyed his company for the tales he told. Now, I must doubt any of them were true, but they were still fine tales, nonetheless. What was the fellow's real name? I forget."

"McParlan."

"Yes, that's it." Duffy lit his cigar and nodded approvingly. "A fine smoke, sir."

"It should be if it is to be traded for a confession."

Duffy laughed. "Confessions are trifling things compared to a good cigar, sir. Take these fellows I'm locked up in here with and myself as an example. I am told that none of them have confessed to anything and neither have I. These fine jailers have been feeding us and taking fine care of us for the better part of a year now, and no one has ever even suggested I owe a confession. I take that to mean the act would hardly offset the cost of keeping us."

"Perhaps you are right. No one has asked you to confess?"

"Not since they asked me if I was guilty or not guilty at the trial. I assume that was a roundabout way of asking me to confess. I would assume they asked the same of those other fellows -- what are their names again?"

Finnegan chuckled. "You do not know the names of your accomplices?"

"I cannot claim to have hardly made their acquaintance, sir. Some are jailed elsewhere, so I may never meet them." He pointed down the corridor and puffed his cigar. "I recall seeing a few of them at some of the town's taverns, but none of them worked at the Mammoth with me, I can tell you that.

Your friend McKenna did not know me well, either." Duffy tapped the ash from his cigar and shrugged. "Perhaps he needed a tenth name to round things out and settled on me. More than that, I could not tell you."

"So, you are not a Molly Maguire?"

"Perhaps I would have become one, given time. I never met a man who claimed to be a Molly Maguire to offer me membership, if that is, in truth, how it is done. Perhaps I would have met one, someday, if I had been given the chance. As it stands, I will not live to see my twenty-sixth birthday. It is hard to say what I might have done or not done, given the chance." He assumed a sour look. "I suppose, had I known I would hang, I would have been a Molly Maguire. If a man is to hang for some crime, he might as well have the entertainment of committing it." He shook his head and looked back to his cigar. "The smoke you offered up is almost halfway disposed of, sir. What confession would you enjoy in exchange for it?"

"Sadly, you cannot be of help to me in that regard. Your guilt in the Molly affair is not within my interest and you have been imprisoned too long to have committed the crime that is of interest to me."

"What crime is that, sir?"

"The murder of one Johanna Wetherill. Did you know the girl?"

"I knew a girl named Johanna who lived at the bawdy house in Crow Hollow. Is that the same one you speak of?"

"It is."

A flicker of sorrow passed over the young man's face. "Murdered. That is a pity. If I had not known the situation she lived in, I would have said she was a pure and darling girl. She was always pleasant, at least as far as I could say."

"How often did you call on her?"

"Call on her?" Duffy shook his head. "No, Pinkerton detective, you misunderstand. I did not know the young lady in that manner. Even if I had wished it, I could not have afforded it. I brought the woman her laudanum on a monthly basis, nothing more."

"You brought her laudanum?"

"Yes. My uncle is the apothecary here in Pottsville. I would make a circuit once a month with the dog cart and take people what they needed on a regular basis." Duffy chuckled. "If you wish to speak to some of Johanna's gentlemen callers, I would suggest you go to the Coal and Iron house in St. Clair. The peelers are the only men paid regular enough to avail themselves of the charms offered at a place such as Miss Gertrude's establishment."

"You are not the first man to suggest such a thing." Finnegan scratched one side of his face and thought for a moment. "Mr. Duffy, how much did Miss Wetherill's monthly laudanum supply cost?"

"I could not say. She did not pay me for it."

"She did not pay you?"

"No. I only dropped the bottles off with her at Gertrude's." Duffy puffed the second half of his cigar. "You can be certain someone was paying my uncle. He is not in the habit of giving free laudanum to whores. At least, not in my experience."

"I see. Your uncle has a shop here in Pottsville?"

"The one and only apothecary. You likely passed it on your way here." Duffy grinned. "Do you intend to speak with him?"

"That is my intention, yes."

"Would you mind giving him a message for me?"

"Certainly."

"Would you let him know that, just as he advised, I have stopped drinking liquor." Both men had a laugh.

"I will inform him."

"I believe he will be glad to hear it."

Finnegan took out two more cigars and set them on the horizontal flat iron that held the cell bars together. "A gratuity."

"Many thanks." Duffy took the cigars and set them on his cot. "I was always told that indulging in the sin of tobacco was a bad habit for a miner. They said it made the black lung worse, but..." He motioned around the cell. "Given my current circumstances, I believe I will chance it."

Finnegan smiled. "I have to say, Mr. Duffy, you are a surprisingly gregarious man, given your situation and my profession. I would have thought you might hold a grudge toward Pinkertons."

He shook his head. "No need to be vengeful, Mr. Gilhooley. Before I swing, I will confess my sins to the father, what few I have accumulated, and soon enough I shall find myself in heaven. I have no doubt regarding my fate." He tapped ash onto the cell floor. "Can you make the same claim?"

"That I will be admitted to heaven?"

"Yes."

Finnegan gave it some thought. "Oh, well, in all honesty, I may have a slight doubt."

Duffy nodded and contemplated what was left of his cigar. "In that case, perhaps I am not the one who should feel vengeful regarding what Mr. Pinkerton has done to me." He looked at Finnegan. "The man has only taken my life. He has left the disposition of my soul to me."

Finnegan nodded. "Thank you for your time, Mr. Duffy. You have given me a great deal to consider."

"Thank you for the cigars, Mr. Gilhooley. If you ever

require anything else you need only ask, but you best be quick about it."

FINNEGAN DISCOVERED the apothecary shop across the street from the general store where he had left Abijah. The apothecary stood inside beneath a sign that bore a large mortar and pestle. Finnegan walked to the counter. Like a lot of men who had witnessed the medical care given during the war, Finnegan was quite leery and quite skeptical when it came to physicians and other drug peddlers. He disliked any apothecary shop and always suspected that the proprietor was, probably, as likely to be an alchemist as anything else.

He cleared his throat to get the owner's attention. "Good day, sir."

The apothecary looked up from whatever concoction he had been fussing with and decided that Finnegan appeared to have enough money to purchase something. He rushed to the rear of the counter. "Yes, sir. What is it I can do for you?" The man had obviously spent far too much time listening to the pleas of the local miners who needed some sort of relief, but had no money to purchase it.

"I am not in need of a palliative."

"Oh." The man nodded knowingly. "You wish to grow more hair?"

"No."

"You wish to be more virulent in your relations?"

"No."

He gave the detective an inscrutable stare. "You wish to quit the demon rum? I have a new substance known as heroin that has offered much relief to..."

"Oh, bugger off with your damned potions. I would rather shake hands with Lucifer than drink that snake oil."

"Sorry, sir." The apothecary put the bottle back where he had found it. "I did not mean to insinuate anything."

"Are you the uncle of a man named Thomas Duffy?"

The apothecary straightened up and gave Finnegan a hard stare. "I am. Sir, I do not know what you came in here for, but I will be damned if you think you are going to get me to agree with what is being done to that young man or say anything degrading to his character. If your damned newspaper wants a quote..."

"I am not a newspaper man."

"Oh."

"I am a detective in private employ."

"I see. Sir, do you not think detectives have done quite enough to my nephew? Do you intend to investigate further so that the poor boy can be hung twice?"

Finnegan sighed. "I do not. Sir, I am not one of the detectives who investigated the Molly Maguire affair. I am charged with investigating another matter. The murder of Johanna Wetherill is my only concern. Your nephew has told me that he delivered laudanum to the woman once a month."

"What of it?"

"I have come here to inquire as to who paid for her palliatives."

The apothecary offered a cold stare. "Why should I tell you such a thing? I never even met the woman, and her life or death is no concern of mine."

"Then why not answer me?"

"Perhaps because you intend to hang my nephew presently." He held up one hand to stop Finnegan's response. "I do not care if you claim to have nothing to do with my nephew's scheduled demise. It is little to me which detective sealed his fate."

With no other reasonable option, Finnegan fell back on the one certain method he had found over the years for making a man abandon all ties of family and cast aside any particular moral principles. He slapped a silver dollar down on the countertop. "I will give you that if you tell me the name of the person paying her bills."

The apothecary stared down at the dollar. "Double it."

He set another dollar on top of the first. "I pay thy poverty and not thy will."

"What?"

"It is a line from an apothecary in a play. Who paid for Wetherill's laudanum?"

"Captain Bourne of the Coal and Iron Police brought the money every month for the laudanum delivery to Crow Hollow."

"Bourne? Why would Captain Bourne buy laudanum for a whore every month?"

"I could not say. Since you are a detective, perhaps you will be able to unravel that mystery yourself." The apothecary swept the coins from the counter and deposited them in his pocket. "Perhaps I will use this to purchase something to ease my nephew's remaining time on earth."

"Perhaps, but somehow I doubt it." Finnegan gave the man a hard stare. "You are certain it was Captain Bourne of the Coal and Iron Police? It would be unwise to lie to me."

The apothecary chuckled. "Would it? And what might you do if you did determine I have lied?"

"I will come back here and force you to drink your snake oil until you tell me the truth or expire. If you do not do it willingly, I will shove that large metal funnel in your mouth to facilitate your guzzling. Of course, that will be after a most savage beating. Now, would you care to amend your statement?"

The apothecary swallowed with an audible click. "I would not."

"Very well, sir. Oh, by the by, your nephew wishes for me to tell you that he has quit drinking liquor."

The apothecary shook his head and smiled. "The boy has always loved to jest."

"Good day, sir." Finnegan turned on one boot heel and walked out of the apothecary shop. On his way past the horses, he pulled the grain bag full of pistols from the saddle horn of his gelding and made his way back to the general store. He entered the store and looked around the place. The shopkeeper stood behind the front counter with Finnegan's purchases piled up to one side. "Has my associate gone to eat?"

"Yes, sir."

"Did he select a holster?"

"Yes, sir." The shopkeeper held up a brown number.

Finnegan took it in hand and looked over the stitching and the thong. "It should serve. What do I owe you?"

The man held out a sheet of paper with some scribblings on it. "The frock coat, holster, and ammunition come to nine dollars, sir."

"Very well, but I will be needing a proper receipt so that I can be reimbursed. The agency is quite particular about its receipts."

"Of course, sir." The shopkeeper took a printed receipt book from beneath the counter and began listing the items. "Will that be all, sir?"

Finnegan pulled a black bowler from a nearby rack and tried it on for size. "How much is this?"

"The hats are two dollars."

"Add this to the tally."

"Yes, sir." He finished out the receipt and handed it to Finnegan. "That will come to eleven dollars then, sir."

"Yes, of course." Finnegan set the bag of revolvers on the counter. "I notice that you sell firearms. Would you be interested in purchasing some?" He opened the bag.

The Shopkeeper began looking over the contents. "If they are in good condition, I have been known to purchase them." He slowly removed two of the guns and held them up to the light from a nearby window. "I would be interested in this Starr, but I will not buy a Whitney."

Finnegan pointed to the gun the man held in his right hand. "That is not a Whitney, it is a Spiller and Burr. The rebels made a much better weapon in that case, sir."

The shopkeeper looked at the pistol a second time. "I see, now, yes." He set the two guns to the side and removed the final two guns from the bag. "The dragoon I will take and... My goodness, this is a Le Mat. A grapeshot revolver."

"Yes. It is my understanding that they sell for a better price than the average piece."

The shopkeeper ogled the gun. "Yes, I should say so." He smiled. "I will give you two dollars each for the Spiller and the Starr. Three for the dragoon and..." He handled the Le Mat a bit more. "I have never seen one of these with a working secondary hammer."

"It is the first I have seen, as well."

"I will give you four dollars for it."

"Seven."

"Six."

"That is a deal."

"Ah, good." The shopkeeper smiled and set the guns off to the side of his cash register. "By my reckoning, minus the price of your goods, I owe you two dollars."

"That is what I reckon, as well."

The shopkeeper opened the cash register and removed two dollars, which he passed to Finnegan, along with his receipt. "I must confess, sir that I already have a gentleman in mind who may be interested in purchasing the Le Mat."

"Really?"

"There is a man who passes through frequently. He has often mentioned that he owns a Le Mat revolver and has often made mention that he would like to possess another. Bodkin, by name."

"I see. Well, I wish you the best of luck in selling it to him." Finnegan pocketed the two dollars. "You said my young associate has gone to the café?"

On their way out of town, Finnegan had told Abijah that he felt like riding a bit toward Reading. They paralleled the railroad track that would eventually terminate in Philadelphia as they rode. When they were a few miles out of Pottsville, Finnegan finally made some conversation.

"Does your holster ride well?"

"Oh, yes, sir." He reached back and adjusted it, just as he had a dozen or more times since mounting up. "Thank you, again. It is much preferable to carrying the gun in my belt."

"Yes, that is something of an irritant. I keep meaning to find a better debilitant for my dragoon, but I fail to get around to it."

Abijah moved the holster around on his belt once more. "It will take some getting used to."

"Yes, wearing a gun always does. Someday, if you remain in this type of work, it will feel strange not to wear it. You may indeed come to feel naked without at least a few guns close at hand." They came to the top of a cutting with the tracks running below them. "How high would you say this cliff is, Abijah?"

The boy rode over as close to the edge as he dared on a rented horse. "Oh, fifteen, twenty feet, sir."

Finnegan pointed down toward the tracks. "Do you think a man could leap from here onto the roof of a passing train?"

"Oh, as the James brothers are claimed to have done in Missouri, sir?"

"Yes." Finnegan smiled at the boy. "You follow the career of the James brothers quite closely."

"There is little else to do, living alone in a bell tower, sir." Abijah reined up his horse. "I do not know if the edge here would be close enough to a passing train to make a leap feasible, sir. I suppose the simplest solution would be for us to wait for a train to pass and see for ourselves. If the answer is important enough to warrant the wait, sir."

Finnegan nodded. "Being out of a town for a while is enough to make it worth our time today, young Abijah. I am worn out dealing with the human race for a time." He swung his leg over his horse and dismounted. "Let us linger here for a while."

"As you like it, sir." Abijah hopped down from his horse.

Finnegan stood petting the gelding for a moment. "The apothecary in Pottsville told me today that Captain Bourne brought him money every month to purchase laudanum for Johanna Wetherill. What do you make of that, Abijah?"

"What is laudanum, sir?"

"It is good that you have never had acquaintance with it. It is a vile substance that is meant to ease pain, but often becomes a terrible habit. Miss Wetherill had made a habit of it."

"I see." Abijah stood holding his horse's reins and gave

185

the question some thought. "I do not know why Captain Bourne would pay for Miss Wetherill's goods, sir, but I suppose there are only two reasons someone pays for something."

Finnegan grinned a bit at the young man's attempt at deduction. He was rather proud to see his associate trying to perform as a proper detective. "And what reasons might those be?"

"You offer payment for goods because you want them, which we know is not the case here. You offer payment because you wish to make a gift of the goods, which, given what I have seen of Captain Bourne, seems unlikely."

Finnegan waggled one finger at his young partner. "Captain Bourne may seem quite prickly, but you should never disregard the possibility that a man will purchase gifts to gain the favor of a young woman. Even the Bible tells that tale more than once."

"Do you believe that is the case here, sir?"

"No. A month's gift of laudanum seems excessive for the type of favor Bourne would have been interested in and it is not overly...romantic."

"Romantic, sir?"

"Yes, the type of gift a gentleman gives a lady when he wishes to be in her good graces. It is referred to as romantic."

"Oh. Interesting."

"Yes, well, it is often of use to attempt to determine what motivations people may have for their actions."

"Yes, sir, I can see how it might be."

"And what is another reason you might conjure that could explain the captain's actions?"

"Well, sir, perhaps it was part of his duties."

"His duties?"

"Yes, sir. You have told me that Johanna Wetherill was, in

fact, the niece of Colonel McLeod. Colonel McLeod is one of the men who owns the railroad, is he not?" Finnegan nodded. "The railroad and the mines own the Coal and Iron Police. Perhaps Colonel McLeod gave Captain Bourne a commission to supply his niece with this laudanum palliative."

Finnegan scratched his chin. "That is an interesting thought, Abijah. I would be inclined to call it correct if Colonel McLeod had not led me to believe that he had no contact with his niece after she left Philadelphia."

"Perhaps he misled you, sir."

"Misled me?"

"Yes, sir. Can colonels not lie?"

"Actually, it has been my experience that they spend a great deal of time doing that very thing."

"Perhaps, then, we have our answer."

Finnegan smiled and nodded. "Perhaps we do. We cannot be certain until I inquire of Captain Bourne. Tie off your horse. I purchased a few boxes of ammunition for that new Winchester rifle, and it would serve you well to practice with it some." They walked their horses over to a fallen oak that they used as a hitching post. "I have seen many a man fall dead simply because he had no experience with his arms. No man practiced in the army." Finnegan laughed. "It was considered a waste of lead and powder." He laughed again and withdrew the Winchester from the scabbard on his horse, where it sat opposite the one that held his Spencer. "Not that it might have done much good; I never hefted a musket in the war that would place two balls in the same general location. Your civil war was a poor endeavor for a soldier interested in marksmanship."

"Was it not your war, too, sir?"

Finnegan hefted the rifle. "No. This was not my country, at the time."

"Did they ever have a civil war in Ireland, sir?"

"No." Finnegan dug a box of cartridges out from his saddlebag. "Ireland is not a country. It is a colony of the English lords. Before a people can have a civil war, they must have a revolutionary war, as you Americans did."

"Will the Irish ever have a revolution?"

Finnegan laughed more than usual at the question. "They have revolutions all the time, young Abijah, they just have no talent for it." He tore a chunk of bark from the fallen oak and handed it to Abijah. "Run that out to the other side of the meadow and prop it up so you can see it in the grass."

"Yes, sir."

The boy ran the hunk of bark out to the edge of the trees and Finnegan deposited some cartridges in his pocket. He paused to look one over and marvel at how much things had changed just since he was a boy. Before coming to America, Finnegan had never held a gun. The idea of his father being able to purchase a gun would have been absurd. If he had wished to steal one from the redcoat soldiers, it would have been an act of hubris too great to contemplate. An Irishman could be hung for simply staring at a redcoat's gun too long.

In contrast, practically the first thing placed in Finnegan's hand in the New World had been a gun. He had many unfortunate recollections of that gun, but he had good memories of it, too. Naturally, he had been fascinated with that first firearm. It was a rifled musket, designed to fire the new Minie ball that was to save the Union through improved accuracy. At the time, Finnegan had no understanding of such things. He only knew that in his new home, he had been handed, seemingly for free, an object of great worth and power. His ownership of such an object in Ireland would have been a capital crime. In America, it was a commonality. In the New

World, no one cared if you were Irish or English or Welsh. In the New World, everyone was in the same army, and everyone got a gun. Until their first engagement, Finnegan had found his introduction to America quite wonderful.

Toward the end of the war, cartridge arms had begun to appear on the battlefield. Spencers, Henrys, and a collection of other rifles were in the hands of the Union. The South had nothing that could even compare. They had been lucky to get the occasional case of smuggled Enfield's from England or copies of American arms built in France and brought in through the blockade.

Finnegan looked down at the centerfire round he held in his hand. It was the newest development. All the first cartridge guns had been rimfires, but this new Winchester had the priming compound hidden in a small cup in the center of the cartridge base. They were more reliable and, Finnegan had been told, allowed for more powerful arms. His dragoon had been converted to fire a cartridge similar to the one that the Winchester fired. He knew to a certainty that the cartridges gave increased range and performance. It was definitely more reliable. Perhaps the greatest advantage was that rain or humidity was no longer a concern. Percussion guns were near to useless in bad weather. With the new breed of cartridge guns, one man could kill another, rain or shine.

Abijah returned from placing the bark and pulled Finnegan out of his revelry. "Ah, yes, good job." With the rifle in hand, he strolled out halfway through the meadow away from the horses. "Here should do."

Abijah held up a few ragged pieces torn from a handkerchief. "For your ears, sir."

"Thank you, Abijah." Finnegan began working the cloth

into his ear. "I have been told that there are men working on guns now that load themselves."

"Load themselves?" Abijah smiled. "How on earth could that be?"

"I do not know, but that is what I have been told. It might have its advantages. One would not have to upset the sights from one shot to another, assuming the recoil was not too great." Finnegan handed the rifle to the boy.

Abijah looked the weapon over. "Do the sights operate as they do with the pistol, sir?"

"They do. You place the front sight on the target and nestle it in the rear sight. Press the butt firmly into your shoulder and work the lever evenly to avoid jamming the gun. It seems to feed quite smoothly, the few times I have fired it." Abijah brought the gun up to his shoulder and pointed it downrange. Finnegan made a few minor adjustments by pushing his head down a little and moving his hand farther forward on the forearm. "There, that seems fine. Load a round and fire." Abijah lowered the lever and brought it up again. His finger moved to the trigger, and he put pressure on it until the gun fired. The boy rocked back on his feet, but the piece of bark twitched, as well. "That is very good for a first try, Abijah. I believe you hit your mark."

"Did I?" He lowered the rifle. "It is hard to see with the smoke." He thought on it for a moment. "If a fellow did invent a gun that loaded itself, he would have to do something about the smoke, I should think. You would not know if you had hit what you were shooting at otherwise."

"Perhaps you will have to work that out, Abijah. I imagine inventing powder that did not smoke would be an excellent way to make your fortune."

"Perhaps that is what I will do."

"Reload your gun and try again, while you are thinking on it."

"Yes, sir." Abijah fired three more shots, and all hit either on or reasonably close to the piece of bark. "I like this rifle quite well, sir. It is pleasant to shoot."

"Yes, it is." Finnegan turned and looked east. He could hear a train coming. "Ah, let us go over to the tracks so that we may assess things as the locomotive passes."

"As you like, sir." Abijah placed the Winchester back in the scabbard and then ran to join Finnegan on the edge of the railroad cutting. "Sir, do you by any chance know what gunpowder is made from?"

"As it happens, I do." Finnegan withdrew a cigar from his new frock coat. "I once knew a man who spent many years working in a powder mill. He was a very humorous man, quite given to jesting. He claimed that having been almost blown up many times had enhanced his sense of humor. At any rate, he once explained to me the components of powder." Finnegan rolled the cigar in his mouth for a moment and then lit it. "Powder is made from sulfur, salt-peter, and charcoal. Mixing it together in different amounts gives you different kinds of powder." Finnegan puffed his cigar. "The powder used in cannons is not the same as that used in rifles or pistols."

"Which ingredient makes it smoke, sir?"

"I suppose you will have to be the one to work that out, if you wish to be an inventor."

The boy laughed as the train drew near. "Yes, I suppose so." They both stood and watched on the edge as the train came into the cutting, which had a curve to it. The locomotive charged past them almost unseen from the smoke and embers. When it was past, the cloud hung in the air for a moment before they could see the cars moving by a few feet

191

below them. The uphill grade and the relatively tight corner had forced the train to slow a great deal. Finnegan and Abijah both stood in silence until the train was completely past. "I have never seen a train pass below me, sir. That was interesting."

"It is often interesting to look at things from different vantage points." Finnegan knocked ash down into the cutting. "Do you believe you could have leapt from here onto the train?"

"Yes, I think that would have been possible. Though, I cannot say I would have cared to. Do you think you could have made the leap, sir?"

"I agree that it would have been possible. I believe there would not have been great danger of being injured, though there is always some danger with such a thing."

"Would you make the leap, sir?"

"It would depend on whether or not there was something worth leaping to on the train."

"What did the James brothers remove from the train they leapt to?"

Finnegan puffed his cigar. "As I recall, the railroad claimed they stole one thousand dollars in gold from the mail car safe."

"A thousand dollars." There was wonder in Abijah's voice as he spoke the words. "I should say that would be well worth leaping for."

"It is an important moment in a man's life when he first learns what he will leap for. Remember this day, Abijah. You will want to reference it when you consider leaping in the future."

"I will do that, sir."

"See that you do." They left the cutting and strolled back to the horses. "Abijah, remove that left scabbard from my gelding and strap it onto the right of your horse. From now on you may consider that Winchester your possession."

"Sir?"

"If you are going to perform the duties of an assistant detective consistently, you will find yourself in need of a good rifle, and that is an excellent rifle." Finnegan chuckled. "You should be proud to be starting your career packing a rifle stolen from a dead Coal and Iron peeler. Not every man can say that."

Abijah picked up the rifle and ogled it rather feverishly. "But, sir, you were so pleased to have a Winchester. Are you certain you do not wish to keep it?"

Finnegan shook his head. "No, it is best that you take it. I have been giving it some thought, and I prefer my Spencer. I know it is not supposedly as advanced as the Winchester, but I am not ready to part with it yet. I have a rather silly sentimental attachment to the weapon. I can still recall when I saw my first Spencer rifle. It was during the Battle of Gettysburg. I was fascinated by the way those lucky men who had gotten their hands on a Spencer did not have to reload from the muzzle. At the time, it appeared to be some sort of miracle."

"You procured your rifle at Gettysburg, sir?"

"Oh, goodness, no." Finnegan laughed, thinking back on it. "There may have been one or two men with a Spencer who fell during that battle, but I would not have been nearly big or strong enough to fight for their rifle. I believe most of them were collected by officers who made use of their privilege, since their muscle would not have been nearly enough, either." Finnegan patted the gelding while Abijah unwound the straps for the scabbard. "I bought my Spencer. I purchased it in '69, I think it was. I cannot hardly conceive of how it happened, but the company had gone bankrupt.

There was a time when men, myself included, would have traded their soul for a Spencer rifle, but that was apparently not enough to keep the firm in business. It folded only a few years after the war. I paid four dollars for my rifle at the bankruptcy auction. It is strange how one day something can be a miracle and seemingly the next it is only worth four dollars."

Abijah had the scabbard loose and had begun attaching it to his saddle. "What do you think the cost of this Winchester was, sir?"

"As far as I know, they sell for somewhere approaching twenty-five dollars."

"That is quite a sum, sir. Thank you. I cannot thank you enough."

"Oh, do not thank me. Thank the Coal and Iron peelers."

Abijah very carefully placed the Winchester in the scabbard and tightened everything down. "I will have to thank Captain Bourne when next I see him."

Finnegan laughed heartily and swung up onto his horse. "I would advise against that, Abijah. Captain Bourne may be so bold as to raise questions regarding the rifle's rightful ownership."

"Why would that be, sir?"

"Men like the captain are prone to such silliness. They often have a hard time appreciating how short life is and do not understand that our precious time should not be wasted on such trivial matters. Keep the rifle, use it with discretion, and thank the good captain for it in your prayers." Finnegan leaned forward and patted the neck of his mount. "This is a fine animal. You have a new rifle and I have a new horse. Not everything in this damned coal country is turning out to be a vexation."

★★

I<small>T WAS</small> mid-afternoon when the two made it back to St. Clair. They were slowly riding up Lawton Street, headed toward the stables. Finnegan might have noticed the strange man who stepped down off the boardwalk in front of a tavern and walked out into the street, but he had been woolgathering, planning his impending train robbery. He did not look up from the neck of his horse until the man with a rifle in his hands called out.

"Which one of you is Finnegan Gilhooley, the Pinkerton?"

Both Finnegan and Abijah reined up their horses and came to a stop. Finnegan stared at the man in the street, not certain if his question had been serious. "What?"

"Which one of you is Finnegan Gilhooley?" The man, who appeared to be somewhere in the neighborhood of fifty, but might have only been a well-used forty, hefted a trapdoor Springfield in his hands. He was not dressed like a miner, but instead sported a suit with an untied tie. His staggered walk betrayed how long he had spent in the tavern.

"For the love of sweet Mary..." Finnegan turned to Abijah. "Boy, ride around this fool and go to the stable."

"Sir?"

"Go."

"Yes, sir." Abijah gave his mare a small kick and turned off into a nearby alley.

"I am Finnegan Gilhooley. Do yourself a favor, sot, and get out of my way."

"You are Finnegan Gilhooley, sent here to kill John Siney by those damned Philadelphia capitalists?"

Finnegan put his hand under his jacket and felt the grip of his dragoon. "Do you wish to die in the street today, fool? Go back in the tavern so your corpse does not clutter up this avenue."

"I mean to shoot you down. I am the official assistant treasurer of the union, and I will not stand for you damn Pinkertons killing our union president."

"Sir, I am not in the habit of killing assistant treasurers, but if you raise that rifle, I damn well will."

The union representative cocked back the hammer on the Springfield. "After you are dead you should tell the other Pinkertons to stay home."

"What?" Finnegan saw that the rifle was raising. "Do not do that!" But the rifle continued to rise. Finnegan drew the dragoon and fired a shot. The assistant treasurer staggered backwards, and the Springfield fired. The gelding collapsed beneath Finnegan, and he fell down into the mud along with the animal. Finnegan pulled his leg out from under the fallen horse and got to his knees next to the horse's head. There was blood spurting from a hole in the animal's chest. The poor beast was clearly breathing its last. Finnegan patted the horse's nose and got to his feet. In front of him, some ten yards distant, the assistant treasurer was limping through the mud with a hole in his leg. "You bloody bastard. You've killed my horse!"

"I did not mean to." The assistant treasurer continued to limp toward the assumed safety of the tavern.

"You did not mean to?"

"No. I meant to kill you." The assistant treasurer began to fumble with the action of the Springfield in an attempt to reload the weapon.

"You meant to kill me, not the horse?" Finnegan began stalking toward the man.

"Yes, only you."

"It is your poor luck, then, sir." Finnegan walked to within a few feet of the man, brought up the dragoon and pointed it at the man's head. "That was a damn fine horse, you worthless son of a bitch." He cocked back the hammer on the Colt.

"I..." He held up the Springfield. "It is jammed." He cast the rifle down.

"Pick it up."

"I do not want it."

"Damn you, pick it up."

"You wish for me to pick it up so that you can murder me as you murdered John Siney." The assistant treasurer spit out the words with great truculence.

"Oh, to hell with you, coward." Finnegan dropped the dragoon's muzzle and fired a bullet into the man's shoulder. The assistant treasurer was twisted around and fell face down into the street. Finnegan began walking back toward his horse, but stopped when he saw the telegraph clerk standing on the boardwalk staring out into the street in awe. Finnegan took a step toward the clerk, shoved the dragoon back into his belt and pulled a cigar from his jacket pocket. "Was that succinct enough for you, young man?"

"That man who tried to kill you...he is a shipping agent for the canal company."

Finnegan struck a match on his belt buckle and lit the cigar. "And the assistant treasurer for the union."

"You did not kill him." The clerk pointed to the man in the mud who had begun to crawl toward the tavern as though it were all he could imagine doing with the rest of his life. "You took mercy on him."

Finnegan puffed his cigar. "He will likely die from his wound or suffer much while it heals. If it does heal, I may find him and shoot him again. He deserves to suffer, lousy horse killing bastard. When you get back to your office, inform Mr. Pinkerton in Philadelphia of what you have seen here, but be succinct."

"Yes, sir, but the service is free to agents of the railroad, as you know."

"Nothing in this life is free, boy. Do not waste words."

ABIJAH SAT on his side of the belfry smoking one of his hand-rolled cigarettes. Finnegan had just finished relating what had occurred in the street after Abijah had departed. "Oh, sir, that incident may lead to more trouble."

Finnegan nodded. "In all likelihood, it will. Although it should not; if the people of this godforsaken patch had any sense, they would give me a parade for shooting down a jackass such as that."

"Mr. Strother is a well-thought-of agent for the canal company."

"And the assistant treasurer for the union."

"Oh, yes, I had forgotten that he held that office." Abijah nodded. "Sir, there is not a doubt in my mind that this will lead to more trouble. There are already rumors that you have been sent here to assassinate John Siney. Now you have shot a high-ranking union official."

Finnegan scowled. "What the hell does the coal mine's union have a damned canal agent as one of its officers for? Cannot one of these damned miners assist in keeping the books?"

"I do not know, sir."

Finnegan waved one hand dismissively. "Never mind, it does not matter. It is nothing more than another annoyance in this place that seems to offer up nothing but annoyance." He shook his head. "Perhaps I should have killed him."

"Oh, I believe that might have made things even worse, sir."

"Yes, but it would have made me feel better. That half-wit shot the gelding, which, as you know, was apparently the only horse capable of any loyalty in the state of Pennsylvania. Worse yet, he made me shoot him in the street, and I try to avoid such ridiculous behavior. It is uncivilized to shoot people in public. Remember that as your career progresses. If men require shooting, it is best to do it in private. If nothing else, it allows you to be the one that determines what tales are told afterwards."

"Yes, sir. I will remember that."

"See that you do." Finnegan sighed. "We will sleep in shifts again, Abijah. Keep an eye on the window of my rented room during the night again, as before. I sense that the assistant treasurer may not be the only fool in this town."

Chapter 6

ST. CLAIR, PENNSYLVANIA
June 19th, 1877

FINNEGAN SAT STARING OUT OVER THE HIP WALL THAT surrounded the belfry. Below, he could see the streets of St. Clair and Mrs. Wallace's boarding house. The town had been quiet for most of the night. Only the yells of a few odd drunks could be heard, and then little to nothing. For some reason, the night reminded him of the night he had faced the James brothers in the Blue Earth Woods. Once the shooting had ended, the night was strangely quiet. Finnegan had stopped up his wound as best he could and began trudging back toward town. In the dark, it had been hard to say how much his wound had been bleeding. He had estimated that it would not be a problem, but he had estimated incorrectly.

When he tumbled to the road, he had rolled over onto his back and then taken small notice when the stars above disappeared as he fell into unconsciousness. The next thing he knew, he was being rolled about in the dirt and mud. Whoever was pushing on him was huffing and puffing and putting great plumes of breath into the cold air. Just as he did during any time of tribulation, Finnegan had reached for his guns, but could locate none of them.

"My weapons? Where are my guns?"

"I had to remove them. They are far too heavy. Even without them, I do not know if I can get you on the horse." The voice was distinctly feminine, which came as a great surprise.

"A woman?" Finnegan tried to make his bleary eyes work better in the darkness.

"Yes, I am a woman."

"You should not be here. There are men of bad character on this road. You should not be here."

"I know there are men of poor character on this road. For all I know you may be one of them, but it is too late for such considerations now."

"You should go."

The Samaritan gave up trying to roll Finnegan into a better position for lifting and left him in the dirt as she continued to huff and puff. "Are you the Pinkerton who was posted at the picket on this road?"

"Yes."

"What became of the two men posted with you? They are my cousins."

"The two Barlow men?"

"Yes."

"They went into Mankato for victuals and I have not seen them since."

"Mankato? They are probably dead drunk somewhere, damn their eyes."

Finnegan dug deep and managed to raise himself into a sitting position. It was quite unusual to hear a woman utter a curse. "Who are you, woman?"

"My name is Molly Meagher, and I came out here to bring my idiot cousins some soup."

"What in the name of St. Peter did they send you out here for? This is no place for a girl to be delivering soup."

"Well, there was no one else to do it. All the men are sitting pickets hoping to get a shot at the famous James brothers so they can brag about it for the rest of their days. I have never seen anything as foolish as this manhunt in all my born days. You men should be ashamed of yourselves."

Finnegan lolled around in a sitting position before catching himself. "Well, if I live, I will have much to brag about. I not only shot at the James brothers this evening, but was shot in turn."

"Oh, lovely." The woman got to her feet. "I am sure you are very proud of yourself."

"I cannot say as I have had the opportunity to develop an opinion on the matter, as yet." Finnegan felt around his body. "Where are my guns? Where is my rifle?"

"I told you, I removed them from your possession to help in my attempt to lift you onto my horse. Perhaps you would have had more luck reaching town if you had not elected to carry so many weapons on your journey."

"Perhaps, but I have found hindsight to be of little use."

"Can you stand if I assist you?"

"I believe so."

"Then let us try before the second coming occurs." She took his hands and leaned back to counterbalance Finnegan up to his feet. With that done, she ducked under one of his arms and supported him as they approached her horse. "It would serve Mr. Pinkerton well to hire smaller men to get shot on dark roads for him."

Finnegan reached out and managed to take hold of the saddle horn. "You know Allan Pinkerton?"

"Sir, I will show you a kindness and assume that your feeblemindedness is mostly the product of lost blood and your injury."

"Oh, thank you, lass. I appreciate that."

Finnegan was pulled out of his revelry in the bell tower when he noticed a dark form passing in front of the white-washed wall of the boarding house. There were two men below him, slowly moving toward the window of his rented room. He picked the Spencer up and set it on the hip wall in front of him. The gun was already chambered, so he slowly cocked back the hammer, depressing the trigger just a bit so that it would not make a sound. Under his breath he whispered in the hopes that his will would somehow change the behavior of the men below. "Do not do it, you daft bastards. Just go home and sober up."

In spite of Finnegan's whispered admonition, the two men continued to walk along the side of the building until they came to the window. When they reached it, one man put his face close to the glass, where he could probably see the shadowy form of the pillows Finnegan had piled up under the blankets of his bed. After taking a fairly long look, the man motioned to his partner and they both drew revolvers from under their coats. They turned and faced the window with the guns pointed toward it.

Finnegan took careful aim, using the hip wall as a rest. "I gave you every opportunity to change your minds." He heard one of the men cock back the hammer on a revolver just as he fired. As the man dropped to the ground, the pistol in his hand fired into the side of the boarding house. Finnegan worked the action of the Spencer and cocked back the hammer. Knowing that there is a tendency to shoot high in the dark and higher yet again shooting at a steep angle, Finnegan held low on the second man. The remaining assassin did not quite seem to know what to do or where the shot that had killed his friend had come from. He was not able to figure it out before Finnegan fired again. The second man dropped to the ground and Finnegan ducked down behind the hip wall. He pulled down the lever of the Spencer and left it open. Abijah was lying on the floor of the belfry, staring with wide eyes. "Good evening, Abijah."

"Someone went near your room, sir?"

Finnegan nodded and fished the round out of the action of the Spencer. "Two of them."

"They are...you got them?"

"I hit them both. I do not know if they are dead, but they will die presently." Finnegan held the Spencer round up in the moonlight. "Even wounded in the limbs, men do not last long when hit with a fifty caliber bullet." Finnegan pocketed the bullet and closed the action on an empty chamber. "You may go back to sleep, Abijah. I do not believe anyone else will attempt anything tonight."

"I may have trouble sleeping, sir."

"Whatever for?"

FINNEGAN SIPPED his coffee in Mrs. Wallace's dining room. The lady of the house had rather tentatively taken Finnegan's breakfast order and brought him his food without speaking a word. Earlier, Finnegan had asked Abijah if he wanted breakfast, and the boy had said he was not hungry. Now, the landlady was giving Finnegan the cold shoulder. Everyone was acting quite strangely. Finnegan suspected it had to do with the two dead bodies that had been discovered in the grass outside the boarding house just after the sun had come up.

Mrs. Wallace took a couple of slow steps into the dining room, looking a bit flustered. "Mr. Gilhooley?"

"Yes, Mrs. Wallace, what can I do for you? I must say these eggs are exceptional this morning."

"Um, thank you, Mr. Gilhooley. Sir, the sheriff is here, and he would like to speak with you."

"A sheriff?" Finnegan wiped his mouth with a napkin. "I must confess, Mrs. Wallace, I had begun to think I would come and go from this place without ever meeting the sheriff."

"He is here, sir, and he is waiting in the foyer."

Finnegan cleared his throat and took another sip of coffee. "Well, show him in, Mrs. Wallace. I would not want the citizens of this town thinking you are the sort of lady who keeps a sheriff waiting."

She stepped closer. "It will be all right, sir?"

"Of course."

"I imagine he wishes to speak with you about the bodies found outside."

"As rightly he should. What befuddles me a bit is that these are hardly the first bodies I have produced during my stay here and he has never shown any interest previous to this." Finnegan shrugged. "Please, show him in, ma'am."

"Yes, Mr. Gilhooley."

The sheriff of Schuylkill County came shuffling into the dining room with his hat in his hands and what could be termed a guilty look on his face, which was odd, because Finnegan was the one who had spent the previous night shooting people. "Good morning, Sheriff."

The sheriff was a fellow of average height and build. He had an average-looking face and an average-looking gun slung around his hips. All things considered, he was perfectly average, and Finnegan could only assume he felt blessed to have managed to slip out of the coal mines like most of those in the county who wore a badge. Right off, Finnegan figured he would be loath to part with the badge, and that might be a useful tool in controlling the fellow. "Good morning, Mr. Gilhooley."

"Would you care for some coffee? Mrs. Wallace always leaves an extra cup here. You might as well make use of it." Finnegan flipped the cup over and poured coffee into it. "I would assume you are here regarding the dead men on the side of the house?"

The sheriff set his hat on the table and picked up the coffee cup. "I...I am here regarding those men." He sipped the coffee. "I assume they were attempting to shoot you, when you shot them?"

"Sir, I have not admitted to shooting anyone and I see no reason to." Finnegan sampled his coffee again. "It has been my experience that admissions tend to complicate what could otherwise be simple matters. Who are the dead men?"

"One of them was a cripple who would have done anything to impress the union men and perhaps get a situation better than picking slate. The other... the other man may be the root of great trouble. He was a relative of a man named John Siney. Have you heard of John Siney?"

"I have."

"When word of this gets out...it could appear as though..."

"Appear as what?"

"It could look as though you were sent here to...to perpetrate some sort of crime against John Siney."

"But I was not. As it has turned out, a relative of John Siney attempted to perpetrate a crime against me."

"It may not matter what the facts of the case may be."

"Then there is small purpose in my contesting any given

accusation. I have little control over the stories other people may contrive. Regardless, it has nothing to do with my commission in this town. I could not care less about John Siney." Finnegan eyed the sheriff over his coffee cup. "Sheriff, are you only here talking to me now solely because one of the dead men found in the yard is some sort of shirttail relation to an important man?"

The sheriff squeezed his eyes shut and rubbed them. "Mr. Gilhooley, I spend most of my days auctioning bankrupt farms and feeding the few men the Justice of the Peace deems it necessary to keep in the jail. Captain Bourne and his men deal with most other business."

"All right." Finnegan nodded. "If that is the case...What is your name, Sheriff?"

"Orme. Sheriff Levi Orme."

"Very well, Sheriff Orme, if Captain Bourne normally handles such matters as dead bodies lying in the street, why are we speaking this morning?"

The sheriff quite obviously paused to ponder the question. "Captain Bourne requested that I speak with you."

"Because he is frightened of me?"

The sheriff pulled out a chair and took a seat behind his cup of coffee. "Yes, I believe he is. Does he have reason to be?"

"Some words may have passed between us when I was... irritated. It should not be enough to make the man fear to be in the same room as me. Frankly, I find this unprofessional."

"Be that as it may, I have come here to ask you about the incident."

"In the hope of hearing what? I agree that it is unfortunate that one of the men was a relative of John Siney. It may cause trouble for both you and Captain Bourne in the future,

R.F. Ryan

but I cannot remove the bullets from the men, so I do not know what it is exactly you wish to discuss."

"You could tell me that you will do your level best to stop shooting men. Oh, by the by, one of them, the relative of Siney, he was still alive this morning when he was found. He had crawled the better part of the way out into the street. He was hit in the lower back and stomach. He only passed an hour ago at the doctor's. Most of the town has been informed of this, but you have not?"

"I slept late. I was up until the wee hours."

"I see. How is it the window of your room is not damaged. I checked when I arrived. Did you open the window before you shot them?"

"I have not told you I shot anyone. Nor will I."

The sheriff shook his head. "What difference can it make? I obviously have no intention of bringing charges against you for...anything. You are a Pinkerton agent; how would I possibly get the county attorney to bring you before the bar?"

"That is not my worry. I simply prefer not to discuss specifics with you because you are local to this area, and I have learned that one local man tends to speak to another. This eventually results in all locals knowing everything. I prefer to keep my business to myself. As for your request that I make every attempt to avoid shooting men, I assure you, that is my constant policy. I have not shot a single man of this community who did not absolutely require shooting. Some of whom, I will be frank with you, sir, should have been shot long before I arrived here."

The sheriff scowled. "During my time in office I have not shot anyone."

"Perhaps you should be less discriminating. Since I have

208

been here, I have been accosted by an armed man in the street..."

"The union treasurer?"

"Assistant treasurer, by his own admission. Nevertheless, he forced the issue. Directly before that I was witness to a gang of drunken louts attacking a house full of women..."

"A whorehouse."

"Yes, which is why it was full of women. If it was not, I fear it would be wholly unsuccessful. At any rate, directly before that, I was in a barroom shoot out, was forced to kill a collection of moonshiners, and began my visit here being fallen upon by road agents."

"As I said, most of the duties of my office concern auctions and tax collection. Such matters as you describe, like the shooting of road agents, is not generally my business."

"Then you should not complain when other men see to it for you." Finnegan smiled at the sheriff. "Perhaps there is some way you can assist me in my work here so that I might be on my way sooner?"

"I would like that very much."

"Did you know Johanna Wetherill?"

"In what sense?"

"I have offered you no admissions, Sheriff, I would not ask you to offer any in return. You saw her about the towns within your jurisdiction?"

"She was well known in these parts."

"Would you be able to venture a guess as to who her murderer might be?"

The sheriff sat blinking for a long moment. "You are, in fact, trying to determine who sent the Wetherill girl to her fate?"

"I am. I believe I have been very honest regarding what I wish to accomplish in this town, sir. I only wish someone around here might believe me so that I could move things along more quickly. Now, did you know the Wetherill girl, and do you have any idea who may have killed her?"

"I did not know her well and I do not know who might have had reason to kill her. In truth, every time I ever saw the girl, she appeared to be rapidly approaching the grave of her own volition. I have a hard time imagining who would have bothered to push her along early."

"Can you tell me why Captain Bourne would have been purchasing her monthly supply of laudanum?"

The sheriff shrugged. "I suppose he may have simply been handling that particular business for Enoch McLeod."

"McLeod?"

"You are an assassin with a different title. I am an auctioneer with a different title. Captain Bourne, regardless of title, largely acts as an errand boy. Part of his duties include seeing to monthly invoices for men like Gowan and McLeod. Why should supplying the man's niece with poison be any different than paying his tailor? As far as I know, the money is considered part and parcel with the monthly payroll of the Coal and Iron Police, and they dispense it as instructed."

"So, there is no reason to think Bourne even knew the girl?"

"She was a whore, Mr. Gilhooley. Many men knew her. I would not venture to guess whether the captain did or not. If he did, I do not see what difference it could make now."

"Now?"

The sheriff stared blankly down into his coffee cup. "I do not recall when that girl was found, but it has been some time. When I was told that you had come here to find her killer, I, like everyone else, assumed it was a poorly constructed lie to obscure your real purpose. Now, you tell me that you are actually here to engage in this absurdity, and...I do not know what else to say to you. You could stay here a hundred years and kill every man in the county without determining who murdered that girl. I cannot imagine who would be foolish enough to send you on such an errand."

"Enoch McLeod."

"Ah, well." The sheriff sipped his coffee. "The wealthy are said to be strange. I suppose this proves it. Mr. Gilhooley, I wish you would tell me what you intend to do here, because I cannot conceive of what your plans might be."

"I intend to discover the murderer of Johanna Wetherill."

"So you said, but that cannot be done. I have never heard of such a thing being done, not even in your employer's nickel books. In my estimation, you have only two choices: you can spend the rest of your life here searching for a killer. Although, it is hard to say how long that life may be in a place where so many, many people wish you dead. Even a man of your skill is bound to run out of luck at some point."

"That has been suggested."

"Your second option is to select someone to be your killer, shoot him, and move on."

"That has been suggested, as well. You and Captain Bourne have much in common."

"We should. We have known each other since child-hood." The sheriff drained what was left of his coffee. "Bourne believes the populace is on the verge of rioting. If they are sending midnight assassins to kill Pinkertons, I am inclined to agree with him."

"They were not very effective assassins." Finnegan finished his coffee. "Perhaps I should ponder one of your suggestions, Sheriff. It may be that one of the dead men recently found outside my room would make a fine woman killer?"

The sheriff groaned. "Oh, if that is to be the case, let it be the cripple instead of Siney's...I forget what he was, a cousin, perhaps."

Finnegan rubbed his chin and decided to have a bit of fun with the sheriff. It was a slow morning and he had nothing better to do. "Perhaps I should say it was Siney? I could shoot him down and be on my way."

"No, that is not...you jest?"

"I do."

"That is not amusing, sir."

Finnegan was about to continue to jab the sheriff a bit more, but there was a knock at the dining room door. He dropped one hand to his Remington before answering. "Come in, whoever is there."

The door slid open, and the telegraph clerk stuck his head through. "Mr. Gilhooley?"

"You know that well enough, young man. Did you wire Philadelphia as I instructed you to do?"

"I did, sir, and you have received an answer. I have it here."

"Very well. Bring it over, then." The clerk stalked over and handed the yellow sheet to Finnegan. Finnegan flipped the young man a nickel.

"Thank you, sir."

"The service is free to agents of the railroad, your shoe leather is not. Now be off with you."

"Thank you." He scurried out of the room, clutching his nickel.

The sheriff eyed the telegram. "Perhaps you are being called back to the home office."

"Or perhaps Enoch McLeod has convinced the Philadelphia office to take up his original plan."

"What plan was that?"

212

"He felt it would be best to kill every grown man in Schuylkill County. That way the killer could not be missed."

"I do not enjoy your jests, sir."

"Then you should not remain in this house."

The sheriff slowly rose from the table and replaced the chair. "I take it there is no possibility of my convincing you to leave this town?"

"I will be on my way when my work is done."

The sheriff sighed in resignation. "If you like, I could suggest a feasible suspect or two."

"Would there be any reason to believe they are the real killer, over and above the fact that you would like them removed from the town?"

"Not particularly."

"I think you should be on your way, Sheriff. Mrs. Wallace is very discriminating about who she has in her house, and I am not certain your kind is welcome here. Good day."

Finnegan watched the sheriff disappear out the dining room doors. Once alone, he opened his telegram.

FINE WORK IN STREET. STOP. IMPORTANT TO REMIND POPULACE WHO REPRESENTS THE LAW. STOP. COME PHILADELPHIA IMMEDIATELY. STOP. WOMAN KILLER IN CUSTODY HERE. STOP. FORMERLY IN ST. CLAIR AREA. STOP. ROBERT PINKERTON. STOP.

Finnegan read the missive twice and then looked up to see Mrs. Wallace standing in the door to the kitchen, staring at him. "Bad news, sir?"

"No." Finnegan folded the telegram and placed it in his vest pocket. "It may be the answer I have been looking for."

"You may have found the man who killed the Wetherill girl?"

"Perhaps." Finnegan reviewed the look on the landlady's

face. "Oh, if it proves to be correct, I will be just as shocked as you, ma'am." He got up from the table. "I have to leave town for a day, Mrs. Wallace. Would you be so kind as to see that young Abijah receives a meal?"

"Certainly, sir. I have grown rather fond of the boy. Where are you traveling to, sir?"

"Philadelphia."

"You suspect the girl's killer is there?"

"It is suspected."

"If it proves correct, will you be returning to St. Clair?"

Finnegan thought on it for a moment. Normally, he would have boarded a train for Missouri the instant his work in Pennsylvania had been completed. "If the man in Philadelphia is the man I am searching for, I will return here to settle my affairs before departing for my next assignment."

"I am glad to hear that, sir."

Finnegan straightened his coat. "It was a fine breakfast, ma'am."

"I am glad you enjoyed it. Sir, did you kill the men outside, sir?"

Finnegan nodded. "They came here to kill me. It seemed to be the proper action at the time." He pulled his napkin from the table and wiped his mouth one last time. "Do you think I acted incorrectly?"

She shook her head. "No. You had no choice. I am sorry it happened, and I will be glad when all this madness is ended. I hope the man in Philadelphia is your man."

"So do I, ma'am."

FINNEGAN STEPPED OFF THE TRAIN, ducking to avoid the swirl of steam and embers that had blown his way from the locomotive. It was always a wonder to Finnegan that the majority of America was not on fire at any given time from the belching of locomotives. Somehow or other, the world had managed to gain a new form of transportation without paying what should have been the inevitable price.

Looking down the platform, he could see Robert Pinkerton waiting for him. Finnegan strolled over and extended his hand. "Robert, it is good to see you again."

"You as well, Finnegan." The younger Pinkerton smiled. "I have to admit, I would find it surprisingly ironic to discover your killer here while you are raising so much Cain searching for him elsewhere. Someday, a more efficient system for this sort of thing needs to be developed. Doing things this way results in so much wasted labor. It is unfortunate."

"It is." Finnegan adjusted his gun belt. He was traveling light. He had left his dragoon and rifle with Abijah and carried only his Remington and the Cloverleaf Colt in the small of his back. It was more than ample armament, but still he felt slightly underdressed. "You must feel a strong inclination that this is our man, Robert. I do not think you would have wired if that was not the case."

"I feel strongly that this may be our man, yes." They began walking across the platform. "We know to a certainty that this man killed a woman, a prostitute, here in Philadelphia. He mauled her quite badly." They walked down the stairs from the platform and Robert pointed to the brougham that waited for them. "He is known to have formerly worked as a miner and breaker man around St. Clair."

"Was he in the area when Miss Wetherill was killed?"

"We have no way of knowing." Pinkerton opened the door of the coach and climbed inside. "That is the reason I wired you, Finnegan. My father has informed me that several times in the past you have had great success gaining information from men such as this fellow held here. Do you believe you can obtain information from him?"

"Where is he being held?"

With both men settled inside, Pinkerton smacked the front wall of the coach, and the driver got the rig moving. "He is at the Eastern State Penitentiary. There may be a difficulty involved."

"What is that?"

"He waits at Eastern State to hang. I would think it is difficult to get a man to talk when he has nothing to lose."

Finnegan shrugged. "If that is the case, it does offer one advantage: no one will mind if the man expires during our interrogation of him."

"I suppose that is true." The two men sat in silence for a few blocks, contemplating the unfortunate work before them. Pinkerton decided to break the silence first. "How are things progressing in St. Clair?"

It took Finnegan a moment to figure out how he wished to respond. "It is difficult. I will be honest with you, Robert: I have little reason to believe I will be able to determine who murdered Johanna Wetherill if this man in the penitentiary did not kill her. I am not sure if anyone can determine such a thing so long after the act took place. I would assume this man at Eastern State was caught 'red-handed' as they say?"

"He was, in fact. The woman's...pimp caught him at the end of his vile act."

Finnegan pondered it. "The constabulary here in Philadelphia cooperate with you regularly?"

"Of course, there is not a man on their police force who does not wish to become a Pinkerton agent."

Finnegan smiled. "Men should be careful what they wish

216

for. I take it we know who arrested the man and we will be able to find the woman's pimp?"

"That should be no trouble, if it is necessary. If the man confesses, there should be no need of it, though."

"I only ask so that we may have a second option if the man does not confess." Finnegan scowled. "It is vexing that this scoundrel is about to hang for a number of reasons, not the least of which is that if he does prove to be the guilty party, I will not have the opportunity to have the man punished for Wetherill's death, specifically. I gave my word to Colonel McLeod that I would. I prefer to keep my word in such matters once it has been given."

"Some matters are outside your control, Finnegan. If it is any comfort to you, I am sure the good colonel is quite pleased with the regular reports we issue him. You are shooting a great number of his much-detested coal miners."

"Not all of them -- the majority of them, in fact -- are not coal miners. From what I can see, those men are generally too tired to engage in overly much murderous mischief. St. Clair is a strange place."

"How so?"

Finnegan thought on it for a moment. "I have never been to a place where the people seem to live in such fear. Even in the James brothers' hometown, the people are not so...terrified, seemingly by nothing more than the coming of the next day. They fear men like Gowan and the colonel. They fear losing their jobs and what little they have. They fear explosions in the mines, and now..." He paused to chuckle. "Now they fear having their men taken away and hanged. They truly live in a state of terror. I have not seen anything like it since the end of the war when your father sent us to Georgia. Do you recall those days, Robert?"

"I do. The rebels were afraid of the army, and I suppose

everyone feared those fools in their white sheets who could not admit their war was lost. Do you know that those men, supposedly led by that damned General Forrest, still pull negroes from their beds and hang them for nothing more than offending some southern woman or some such pretense?"

"I have heard that." Finnegan sighed. "Although, it may not be our place, just as now, to judge who hangs who based on what pretense."

"Finnegan, the Mollies were not simply lying in bed minding their own business when they were arrested. Every one of those men was clamped in irons after being caught in the commission of some crime or other."

The gunman nodded. "Yes, but was it the commission of a crime that had been suggested to them by our own James McParlan? You know as well as I do that Mr. McParlan would not be above such a thing. I do not doubt the Mollies existed before McParlan arrived in St. Clair, but I cannot help but wonder if McParlan transformed them into something worth making a fuss over."

"I cannot say, either, Finnegan. What I do know is that if the Mollies did not wish to burn, they should never have begun to play with the fire. At any rate, it is not our current business."

"I know it is not my business, but someday it may be yours, Robert." Finnegan looked at the only slightly younger man with a serious gaze. "In the years to come, I can only assume you and your brother will be taking control of this agency that your father has built. In many ways, it is a fine creation. There is no other alternative to make use of chasing evil men such as the James Brothers, and I am proud of the work I have done for your father. What I am saying, Robert, is that you should ask yourself if you are proud of what your family's agency did placing McParlan in St. Clair. You should ask yourself if you would do the same when you are in charge. Such questions are not my business and never will be, but they may be yours someday. That is all I would suggest."

"I have given it thought, Finnegan." Robert Pinkerton offered a sad smile. "I believe we have all given it thought." He forced himself to brighten up. "I am told you have made contact with that damned Sam Rooney in St. Clair. It must be good for the two of you to be together again. You were friends in the war, were you not?"

"Yes, Sam is an old friend. He has done a fine job convincing everyone in St. Clair that he is an indolent, besotted bartender. I imagine it takes hardly any acting at all."

Pinkerton laughed. "He is greatly talented in that regard. A pity he can only be counted on to play the one role."

"If you can play the one well enough, there is no reason for another." Finnegan leaned out the window of the coach to get a better look at the massive stone structure that was looming up in front of them at the end of the street. "That, in the distance, is the penitentiary?"

"It is."

"You Americans do dearly love to build castles, but you never seem to use them for anything other than hanging men."

Pinkerton leaned out his window to get a better look at the prison. "I suppose it does closely resemble a castle. I do not know if that is a uniquely American practice, though, Finnegan. I would imagine the prisons in Ireland and England are similar in appearance."

"Most of those were formerly castles, they have simply converted them. I was once told that the castles in Ireland were first built to keep the Vikings at bay. Perhaps something has changed over time. Castles were once meant to keep men out, now we build them to keep men in."

"Finnegan, have you not been sleeping well?"

"My apologies if I speak strangely. I did not get much rest this last night. I was up late shooting a couple of men who came to kill me."

Pinkerton cleared his throat. "I see." He moved around uncomfortably in the coach seat. "I am pleased to see you were quicker."

"Oh." Finnegan waved one hand dismissively. "Quick had little to do with it. They attempted to ambush me, as I had guessed they would. I was lying in wait when they arrived, and I was fortunate enough to dispatch both men with a minimum of difficulty. I used the Spencer the company purchased for me some years ago."

Pinkerton nodded, trying to not let his shock show too much. "I have been told the Spencer is a reliable weapon."

"I believe it hits harder than the new Winchester. Although, I have been told the '76 can match it or even better it. Have you tried the '76 Winchester, Robert?"

"I have not, as yet. I am under the impression it is meant for hunting game, even as large as buffalo."

"I have found a larger ball to be useful. It is best to knock men down so that they remain down." The coach came to a stop and the two men clambered out. Before them was a large gate with a guard acting as gatekeeper. It reminded Finnegan of the Schuylkill County jail, except for the fact that the guard was wearing a uniform and appeared to take his job much more seriously. The two men showed their Pinkerton badges and then made their way into one of the many cell blocks that radiated out from a central point in the middle of the structure. They walked down a hallway with two tiers of cells and a high arched ceiling. "On the outside it is a castle, on the inside a church."

"It is said that the man who built this prison wanted it to remind the prisoners of a church so that they might become penitent for their sins." Robert held a handkerchief over his nose in an attempt to blot out the smell.

"That may be effective." Finnegan glanced at a few of the inmates as they passed. "Of course, that assumes some of these men have seen the inside of a church to be reminded." They came to a cell on the first tier toward the end of the block and the guard sullenly pointed to the occupant. Finnegan nodded to the guard. "Do you have the key?"

The guard raised his eyebrows. "You wish to release him from his cell?"

"I may wish to enter the cell." Finnegan looked up and down the block. "What is in the center of this place?"

"We call it the yard. The inmates are allowed time outside every day so that they may recreate." The guard motioned down the block. "It is through that door. Oh, on one side of the yard there is the gallows. This one will be going there shortly." There was no sound from the man in the cell when the guard made his proclamation.

"Thank you, sir." Finnegan held out his hand. "The key."

The guard withdrew it from his pocket and handed it to Finnegan. "As you like, sir." He took the hint and walked back down the block, presumably returning to his post at the gate.

Finnegan and Robert stared into the cell where the inmate sat staring back. Robert spoke with the rag still pressed over his nose. "Markus Beresford?" The man only stared out of the cell toward the light of the cell block. "Mr. Beresford, we wish to speak with you." There was still no response.

221

Finnegan tapped the key on the metal of the cell bars. "Sir, you should know that you will speak with us today, whether it suits you to do so or not. It will save us all effort if you can find it in your heart to be agreeable."

"Agreeable?" The man slowly lowered his head to stare at the floor. "I have been nothing but agreeable in this place, and what has it gotten me?"

"Certainty." Finnegan put one of his hands around one of the bars. "Say what you like, there is little doubt left in your life. Most men have no idea what the future holds; you do. That is no small matter, Mr. Beresford."

The inmate turned toward Finnegan and sneered, showing that he was missing the majority of his teeth. "You may go to hell, sir. I do not deserve to be here. I am here, but where is that bastard Trotter. I ask you, where is he?"

Robert removed the rag for an instant. "Trotter? Oh, yes." He replaced the rag and turned to Finnegan. "That is the man who detained him."

The inmate's eyes grew angry. "That is the man who sold me an obstinate whore. What was I to do? You tell me what I was to do. That bastard sold me a whore who needed beating and then treats me thusly when I do what must be done."

Finnegan nodded and tapped the key on the bars again. "I take it you had been drinking, Markus?"

"I had been drinking. Now that I am sober, I can see that many of the things I did while drunk were improper. That has always been the way of it. That is the way of it with all men. I know that and so do you, so why are the men who sold me the liquor not in here with me? Why do you not hang them? Why not hang the men who sell spirits and obstinate whores and let me get back about my business? I have regular employment shoveling coal down at the docks. I am a good citizen, not a liquor merchant or whore peddler."

222

"Markus." Finnegan moved closer to the bars. "I wish to know when about you lived in St. Clair?"

He shook his head. "What the hell do you want to know that for?"

"It is of interest to me."

"If I tell you, will you let me out of here?"

"No, but if you do not tell me I may let you out of here."

"You may if I don't...you are a fool. Open the door or be gone."

"Oh, Markus, I believe you have spent your whole life much in the same manner. You are a vexing man." Finnegan inserted the key into the lock and gave it a twist. The cell door creaked open. "We shall have to see if we cannot make an adjustment to your character in the small amount of time you have left. When is it you are to hang?"

"I...I have today and one more. Then they take me out in the morning." The inmate stared at the open cell door as if it were a snake. "What are you at here?"

Finnegan pulled a length of small diameter hemp rope from his coat pocket. "I intend to save your soul, Markus, through the glory of confession. Only then will you be able to enter the kingdom of heaven." Finnegan charged into the cell, tossed Beresford against the back wall, and tied his hands with the length of rope. That completed, he began pushing the man down the cell block and out into the yard. "Markus, you may think that there is nothing left for another man to take from you, but you are mistaken. I intend to take the only thing remaining to you: two days."

"What?" He turned back with tears streaking down his face as Finnegan continued pushing him toward the scaffold in the corner of the yard. "You cannot. You cannot, I still have..."

"You have nothing now, you bothersome bastard. You are

uncooperative, so I see no reason to let you linger here among us. Be gone, be off, be damned." Beresford crumpled like a rag doll on the first step to the scaffold and rolled onto his back. "No, no, you cannot."

"It offends me, you louse, that you continue to breath the same air and live under the same sun as I do." Finnegan pulled the Remington from its holster and stuck the muzzle between Beresford's eyes. "Markus, I am not so picky as a judge or some finicky hangman. The rope and the bullet both have equal value to me." He cocked back the hammer on the revolver.

"What in God's name do you want to know?"

"Oh, now you wish to invoke the name of God? I have the sense he has lost interest in you some time ago, Markus." Finnegan felt Robert's hand on his shoulder.

"Finnegan, I believe he is attempting to cooperate."

"Ah, yes." Finnegan uncocked the gun and put it back in its holster. "Quite right." He stood up and straightened his coat. "Ask your questions of him."

Pinkerton cleared his throat and shoved his handkerchief in a pocket. The air was far preferable out in the yard. "Mr. Beresford, when did you reside in St. Clair?"

The inmate slowly stopped shaking and gazed up from his back at Robert. "I never did. I lived for a time in Tremont."

"Did you know a woman in that area named Johanna Wetherill?"

"I have never lived with a woman."

"No, I mean, did you..."

Finnegan sighed and pinched the bridge of his nose. "Did you kill a whore in St. Clair, Markus?"

"What? No? I mean to say, I do not believe so. They

claim I killed that obstinate whore on Walnut Street, but I do not recall that well."

"Oh, for the love of..." Finnegan gave the problem some thought. "Markus, can you get that gin-soaked wreck you call a mind working well enough to tell us how long you have lived in Philadelphia?"

"I have been here at least a year, sir."

Pinkerton groaned. "Oh, damn you." He scratched his chin. "So, any whore you may have killed in that time would have been killed here?"

"Yes, I swear it."

"Finnegan?"

"Yes, Robert?"

"Give me your gun, I wish to shoot this fool."

"They intend to hang him promptly, Robert. I am not sure it is worth your effort."

"I wish only to shoot him in some extremity so that he may understand what kind of vexation he puts other men through before he is hung."

"A fine thought, Robert, but that is not our purpose here."

FINNEGAN SAT SMOKING a cigar on one of the train platform benches. Robert sat on the bench opposite. Both men looked less-than-pleased with the way events had transpired. Finnegan knocked ash down to the platform and sat back. "Another dead end. What a pity."

Robert shrugged. "I suppose there is a possibility he is lying about the amount of time he has lived in Philadelphia."

Finnegan nodded. "Yes, it is possible. To be secure in our theory, you may wish to find that man Trotter and ascertain how long it is that Mr. Beresford has been purchasing prostitutes from him. I would venture a guess that Mr. Trotter is well known in the environs of Walnut Street."

Robert nodded. "Yes, that would be the thing to do to confirm it." He shook his head. "Sorry to have wasted your time, Finnegan."

"Oh, quite the contrary, Robert. I had as high of hopes as you that this man would prove to be the killer we search for. A damn shame he is not. In all honesty, I do not know how I will proceed from this point on. Shooting random idiots in St. Clair allows me to send you expense reports and charge you my salary, but serves little other purpose."

Robert pulled a cigar of his own out. "I suppose you are stuck in St. Clair until the twenty-first, at any rate."

"I am?"

Robert looked at him quizzically. "Oh, perhaps I forgot to include that in the telegram. I suppose I may have, since I was going to be seeing you anyway. Franklin wants you in Pottsville to act as a guard on the twenty-first. He is attempting to sweep together as many agents as he can, but wants you there, in particular."

"To act as a guard?"

"For the hangings, yes. He fears an insurrection."

Finnegan laughed and shook his head. "It seems all men fear insurrection these days. If these men wish to avoid such things, perhaps they should cease doing their level best to bring them about." He laughed a second time. "Just out of curiosity, if the populace of coal country does choose to rise up and lynch Mr. Franklin, what exactly does he believe I, or any other hired gunman, can do about it?" Finnegan took a long puff on his cigar. "I have hardly met a man old enough to shave his chin whiskers in this country who did not serve his bit for the North. They all have experience and they all, so it seems, have guns. If those men rise up, they will not be a rabble or even a rioting mob, they will be an army. They could burn Philadelphia, if they have a mind to."

"I believe Mr. Franklin feels that a strong show of force may deter the men of the coal patch from that very action. He wants the fearsome Finnegan Gilhooley. You have already killed many men in the patch. He feels seeing you there will make them reconsider any plans they may be fomenting."

"Fearsome Finnegan." He chuckled. "Men truly are slaves to alliteration."

Now it was time for Robert to laugh. "Yes, Finnegan, they truly are. I take it you have researched the meaning of the word?"

"I have recently obtained a dictionary that is quite comprehensive. I carry it with me amongst my traps."

Pinkerton grinned. "A gift, perhaps?"

"It was."

"It is remarkable how women behave. The world is full of men, and yet I have never known a woman to select a single one of them that she did not intend to modify or change in some way. You would think it would be far more efficient for the fairer sex to simply find one who already fit their criteria, but they never do." He continued to grin. "Has owning that dictionary made you a better man, Finnegan?"

"I have no idea what you are talking about, Robert."

"Oh, do you not?" Pinkerton lit his cigar. "Finnegan, I cannot say what kind of young lady this is you are courting with certainty, but I can say that she seems interested in modifying you. As I said, most gentlemen require some modification in the eyes of women, but in your case..."

Finnegan shook his head. "Robert, despite what your father would have the newspapers believe, I am no different from any other man."

"I think that is something you would prefer to tell yourself, Finnegan." Robert rolled his cigar between his fingers, contemplating his employee's history. "You have been hunting and killing men, for pay, your entire life. I do not think too many men can say they have ventured out in the night to kill the tax collector with their father. My father, as you know, is said to be the world's greatest detective, and yet, I barely saw the war beyond the railroad cars we rode on. That man you interrogated today is very nearly the only true criminal I have met. A man such as I am can be modified with ease. A man such as you...do you truly believe that this woman will change you into some sort of well-read farmer? A church deacon? Perhaps you will someday run for Congress?"

"Robert, I do not understand."

"No, I am certain you do not, and that may prove to be your undoing, Finnegan. Mark my words, if you attempt to transform yourself into what some sweet young girl wishes you to be, it can only lead to sorrow for you both."

Finnegan dropped his cigar to the platform and stepped on it. "How can a man know such a thing, Robert?"

"Through observation, Finnegan. My entire life, men have wondered how my father can possibly know the things he knows. It is not magic. It is not communing with the spirits. He knows what he knows from observation. I have observed the world, and I know where you are headed."

"I am headed to St. Clair."

"I believe you always will be, my friend."

SOMEWHERE DOWN THE creek bed an owl was hooting. It reminded Finnegan of the *Legend of Sleepy Hollow*. He could not help but feel as though his search for Johanna

Wetherill's killer had a few things in common with Ichabod Crane's predicament. Some things in life are simply unavoidable. Ichabod was bound to meet a horseman. Finnegan, it seemed, was bound to meet an endless parade of idiots who would make fine suspects for blame, none of whom could be confirmed. He was so far in contemplation that he actually jumped a little when Rooney stepped on a twig somewhere just up the creek bed.

"Good evening, barkeep."

"And a good evening to you, assassin."

"That is not an amusing jest, Sam."

"It is not meant to be." Rooney took a seat on the log just down from Finnegan. "Was it really necessary for you to shoot John Siney's nephew?"

"I have been told the young man was a cousin."

"In a week he will have grown into a son. The road to hell is paved with half-truths and dead relatives in this place, Finn. These fools will never stop trying to kill you now."

Finnegan shrugged. "Aside from digging coal, getting drunk, and threatening to strike, they seem to have little else to do. Dead relatives or not, I doubt they would stop trying to kill Pinkertons. They had a fine foundation for a grudge against us long before I arrived." He let out a deep sigh.

Rooney hung his head. "Finn, as you know, I could not care less who you shoot or who you leave living, but it would be best if we could remain less conspicuous, at least until after the payroll comes through."

"I have found a fine site for boarding the train. There is another useful place about five miles down the line for dismounting. Did you bring the map?"

"Here." Rooney pulled a map of the local Reading lines. He unfolded the map on the log while Finnegan struck a match.

"Here we get on board." Finnegan tapped the sheet with one finger. "Down here we leap off into some lovely tall grass, pleasantly free of rocks."

"Lovely." Rooney grinned while the match burnt out. "Finnegan, this should work quite well, but we cannot execute this plan if there are a horde of assassins chasing you through the woods while we try to catch the train."

"I am aware of that, Sam, but there is little I can do about it. It appears as though the situation is about to worsen, as well. You have met Franklin, the man in command at the Philadelphia office?"

"He gave me some rather useless advice before I came here."

"Well, he wishes for me to be by his side at the hangings."

"The hangings...you mean the hanging of the Mollies?"

"Yes."

"What in hell for?"

Finnegan let out a chuckle. "He believes I can save him from the mob when they attempt to hang the various hangmen."

"Is he under the impression you can smote an army? I do not recall a Finnegan mentioned in the Old Testament."

"It would seem that neither Mr. Franklin or any of the Pinkertons truly appreciate the amount of anger they have brewed up here or understand how these men operate."

Rooney returned his map to an apron pocket. "Yes, if a resident of this godforsaken place wished to visit some form of vengeance upon Franklin or one of the Pinkertons, their method would obviously be to track them down in five years' time and shoot them in the street in Chicago. These Mollies seem to enjoy taking their time. Of course, what is life without some task to keep one busy?"

"If I were a coal miner, I believe I would spend a great

deal of time striking, rioting, and plotting murder. Essentially, anything other than digging coal." Finnegan flopped around the lapels and tails of his frock coat, hoping the action would remove the coal dust he continually built up. "I will be pleased to leave this place."

"Have you spoken to your young assistant regarding our plans yet?"

"Abijah has always been more than willing to assist in all matters pertaining to my work. This will be no different. It is even more likely due to the young man's very practical nature."

"If you say so, Finn."

"He will give good service, I assure you." Finnegan stared up at the stars for a long moment and then turned back to his friend. "Sam, we have known each other a long time."

"We have. I have known you longer than anyone else, now that I think of it."

"Would you mind terribly if I asked you a question of a personal nature? I only inquire because our long association must mean we have a great deal in common."

The fake bartender shrugged. "I would not take offense to a personal query."

"Do you believe that a man such as yourself or I, a man like us, could ever marry?"

Without an instant's hesitation, Rooney proffered the answer. "Of course. Why on earth not?"

"You do not feel as though you would have difficulty settling into the more mundane existence of a farmer or some such fellow?"

"Naturally, that would be intolerable, but what does that have to do with the prospect of marriage?"

"I...you do not think that sort of life is a requirement for a married man?"

He shrugged. "I do not know for certain. I have known many a soldier who is married and still manages to fit in a great deal of excitement. I suppose it is possible, but I could suggest a much simpler solution."

"Such as?"

"Well, as an example, I am currently Gus Moody, benevolent barkeep. I could easily marry one of these miner's daughters and live quite happily for a time. When the drudgery of this place became a displeasure, I would simply resume my life as Sam Rooney and move on."

"You would leave the woman?"

"Men leave their women frequently. If she proved to be a very good woman, if she was an exceptional cook or the like, I might inquire as to whether or not she would be interested in waiting for me while I was off adventuring. Women being women, I would not think she would take me up on the offer, but that would be her choice, not mine."

"You would not feel remorse for having left her?"

"Ah, now I understand. There is a reason you cannot appreciate the efficiency of the plan. You do not imbibe the devil liquor, Finnegan. In the course of any man's life, he is bound to experience a bit of remorse for his actions, but the liberal application of whiskey quickly dissipates that particular malady. My advice to you would be that, if you wish to marry, you should take up drinking beforehand. That way, any decisions you are forced to make regarding the dissolution of the bond will not weigh on you so heavily, at the point when dissolution is inevitably required."

"Is it truly inevitable?"

"Finnegan, I would dare say that if it were not, you would not have asked the question. You are not a young man; I imagine if you had any real interest in farming, you would have tried it by now, wife or not."

Finnegan grimaced. "It does seem a loathsome profession. I have never understood how a man can dedicate his life to the spreading of manure."

"Indeed. I have often pondered that myself." Rooney got up from the log and stretched out his back. "The relative ease of tending bar wears me out after a long day. I cannot imagine how awful it must be to dig holes and drop seeds in them from dawn 'til dusk. It seems a far better thing to rob a payroll now and then and not be bothered with such foolishness."

"Now and then?" Finnegan smiled. "You are mistaking a singular job for a career, my friend."

Rooney grinned broadly. "Let us wait and see how the first robbery goes, then we may make informed decisions regarding future ventures."

"You are a disgusting man of very low character, Sam Rooney. You should be ashamed of yourself."

"I am, deeply, I assure you. It is a pity that I am also the best friend you have ever had."

"Ah, yes, now there is the real tragedy, I think."

Chapter 7

ST. CLAIR, PENNSYLVANIA
June 20th, 1877

Mrs. Wallace had presented the letter to Finnegan along with his morning breakfast. Whether married or widowed, all older women relish presenting single men with correspondence from young women. Mrs. Wallace had been exceptionally pleased with herself when she included the letter next to the cups on the morning coffee service.

"You will see you have post there, Mr. Gilhooley." She smiled slyly as she set down his bacon and eggs.

"Yes, I see that there, ma'am. Thank you."

"I see that it comes from a Miss Malinda Meagher. I assume you know that name."

Finnegan nodded and stared at the landlady quizzically. "I do. How is it that a person could receive a letter, at a boarding house, from someone they do not know?"

"I had not paused to contemplate that, sir." She hovered by one of the highbacked chairs. "The postal system is truly a marvel, don't you think?"

"I suppose it is."

"Mr. Wallace sent me many letters during the war, and I was able to send him letters back. No matter how his army marched around, those letters always managed to find him. How do you think they managed that?"

Finnegan shrugged and tried his eggs. "The mail runs by train, ma'am. The armies generally encamped somewhere in the vicinity of the railroad so they could better receive supplies. That habit made it much easier to deliver the mail, or at least that is what I would imagine."

"Do you intend to write back, sir?" If Finnegan was not mistaken, he thought she had a glimmer of blush on her cheeks as she asked the question.

"Write back to whom, ma'am?"

"The young lady who has sent you that missive."

Finnegan wiped his mouth. "I do intend to write back. Assuming the letter does not contain too serious of a rebuke from the information contained in my previous letter. The young lady in question is terribly fond of rebukes, and I sometimes wonder if she is not *too* fond of them. Now..." He set down his napkin. "Since you have asked me a question of a personal nature, would it be all right for me to ask one of you in return?"

Mrs. Wallace swept some of her grey hair behind one ear, grinning. "It would not be out of place."

"Why is it that all women seem to take such a great interest when they believe one of their fellow women may be on the verge of ensnaring a man?"

Mrs. Wallace shook her head. "Ensnaring is not the proper term, Mr. Gilhooley. The truth of the matter is that the season for romance is short in this life. Those of us who have already seen it pass wish for you young people to enjoy it as we did. The days when Mr. Wallace and I were courting are some of my fondest memories. What color is the young lady's hair?"

Finnegan took the liberty of rolling his eyes before answering. "It is of the golden persuasion, ma'am."

"Oh, the two of you would have lovely children."

"Does nothing require your attention in the kitchen this morning, Mrs. Wallace?"

"Just be quick about your eating so you can manage to write that girl back presently."

Finnegan,

I might have guessed that you would be unaware of the activities of your own employer. It is beyond comprehension how you could be, but if any man could, it would be you. I suppose you have spent the majority of your time plotting on some method for getting yourself shot again by the James brothers and have not had time to read the papers.

To help you avoid embarrassment the next time you have cause to catch up with your fellow Pinkerton agents, I will take the time to inform you of what your beloved Allan Pinkerton has been up to in the coal fields of Pennsylvania. To put it bluntly, your employer has perpetrated one of the greatest miscarriages of justice in the history of our country. It is a wonder that the good Lord, in his infinite judgment, does not choose to strike such a man dead for such an act. I trust his retribution is imminent, and you should explain that to him if you ever have cause to speak with the man again. Mr. Pinkerton has conspired with the coal and railroad interests in Pennsylvania to do nothing less that send twenty innocent men to the gallows. What is more, he has been very well compensated for his trouble. The most prominent attorneys and judges in this country have all declared what has occurred in Schuylkill County to be a travesty, although I cannot help but notice that none of them have lifted a finger to prevent it. I have always felt that hypocrisy is a greater sin than cowardice. Perhaps that is why I enjoy your company, as you evince neither.

I suppose it is not proper to rant to a friendly acquaintance regarding politics or the disposition of men's souls. Still, it upsets me to think of a man such as yourself being made a part of such a dirty business as the persecution of the Molly Maguires. It is my ardent hope that this letter finds you safe and warm, not encamped somewhere in the woods. I am very pleased to hear your wound has healed properly, and I know you will be pleased to hear that my entire family now enjoys good health. Father is considering joining with another bank and expanding the farm holdings. Mother is quilting without rest in preparation for two upcoming marriages of neighbor girls. My brother is considering a commission in no less than the Navy, if you can fathom such an oddity. What can a Minnesota boy know of sailing ships?

I have made inquiries of late regarding several missionary opportunities in the west. As always, father feels that missionary positions are not proper for unwed women, or married women, for that matter. From what I am able to glean from his lectures, the only proper position for a woman is in the kitchen of a farmhouse while her husband tends to livestock. I suppose I should not complain; many women of my age have no choices afforded them other than menial labor or unhappy marriages. I must remember to count my blessings. Perhaps I should not spend so much time contemplating what is not considered proper, but it appears to be my nature.

I can recall once informing you that I refused to spend my time worrying over your well-being when any dangers you were apt to face were the result of your own choices. I must now confess that particular declaration has proven difficult to carry through with. I think of you often and worry for your safety just as often. Please look to your own wellbeing while you

are out there in the world doing whatever it is
your employer continues to convince you to do.

Your friend,
Molly

Finnegan slowly folded the letter along the original creases and returned it to the envelope it had arrived in. With that done, he placed it in the leather carrying case he kept all of Molly's letters in. The carrying case went in his luggage next to the Blakeslee quick loader for his Spencer rifle. For some reason, he took enjoyment from seeing the two items next to each other.

FINNEGAN AND ABIJAH sat on the fence in the rear of the livery stable. They were both smoking and taking a moment to review the selection of mounts offered. Abijah adjusted himself on the fence rail and turned to his employer. "Did you sleep in your room last night, sir?"

"Yes. I got in late and did not wish to disturb you." Finnegan frowned. "Remind me to give Mrs. Wallace a few dollars for the repair of the wall in my chamber. One of those fools shot a hole in it the other night. On the inside of the room, it appears big enough to fit an apple in."

"You did not feel you were in danger sleeping there?"

"I did not sleep in the bed. I placed the pillows as before and slept on the floor on the opposite side of the room from the bed." He sighed. "I rent many beds, but sleep in few of them. How did you sleep in the bell tower?"

"Well enough, though I woke several times to reconnoiter."

"See anything?"

"No, sir. It was quiet."

"I do not believe this town is large enough to supply assassins every night."

"It would seem so." Abijah pulled his cap off and scratched his head. "It is a pity that the man in Philadelphia was not the killer we are seeking."

"It is a great disappointment." Finnegan shook his head. "When I began this endeavor, I did not believe sorting one specific killer from such a large number of murderers would be the greatest stumbling block. Although, perhaps I should have. It is rather similar to my main difficulty in locating the James brothers. Some days it feels as if I will be forced to shoot every man in Missouri before I have the opportunity to shoot at the James brothers again. It can be quite maddening."

"I can understand how it might be." Abijah pointed to the horses as they circled in the corral. "Are we going on another trip today, sir?"

"No, unless you can suggest some scoundrel for us to investigate?"

"No, sir. I cannot. I was only inquiring because of your interest in the stableman's horses."

"Ah, yes. I have been ordered to travel to Pottsville tomorrow to attend the hangings. I will require a horse for the journey, and I am hoping to procure an animal other than that damnable grey this man continually supplies me with. It is only a matter of time before the creature kills me or does something that leads to my death. I dare say even that donkey with an evil look in his eye would be preferable."

Abijah stubbed out his cigarette on a fence post. "Will I be accompanying you, sir?"

"No, Abijah, you will not. I know that during your time in my employ you have been witness to several unfortunate incidents, but there is no reason for a man of your years to see such a thing if it can be avoided. Hanging is a despicable way for a man to die."

"Have you seen many men hang, sir?"

"A few, most of them during the war. Uniformed soldiers were taken as prisoners while guerrillas and bushwhackers generally received the rope. They were men of the meanest character, but even they may have deserved better. A man rarely has a choice in such matters, but, given the choice, I believe I would rather stand in front of a firing squad."

Abijah scratched his head again. "Why is that, sir?"

"I cannot say exactly. Perhaps it seems like a soldier's death instead of the punishment meted out to criminals. I suppose, either way, the important matter is how a man faces it."

"How do you think the Mollies will face it?"

"Time will tell. I would prefer to find out secondhand from a newspaper, but my orders are clear." Finnegan knocked ash from his cigar. "I will give you an order as well. Do not venture far from the church tomorrow. If possible, you should spend the day in your bell tower with your new Winchester. It is hard to say how the people of this town, or the nearby towns, will react to the hanging of those men. It is a well-known fact that you are in my employ. People often fail to think or act properly when they are angry or frightened. If they cannot find a Pinkerton to vent their frustrations on, they may settle for a Pinkerton's assistant."

"I will keep a wary eye, sir."

"See that you do. As I have said, I will not be present to

offer you aid." Finnegan turned toward the corral as the stable keeper approached. "Ah, here comes that sharp horse trader." He hopped down from the fence and met the man halfway. "Good morning."

The stable keeper was a rather hulking fellow who had obviously spent a great deal of time with a large hammer in his hand mashing horseshoes into their proper shape and then affixing them to truculent animals who did not wish to be shod. He had a scowl on his face and sweat on his brow. "I don't see how any morning could be good while the likes of you lingers here."

Finnegan straightened up and hooked one thumb into his gun belt on the off chance the man wished to elevate the situation to an outright quarrel. "Sir, there must be some misunderstanding between us. I do not believe I have done anything to give you offense. Certainly nothing equal to what you have done to me, inadvertently as it might have been."

The stable keeper spit out a long string of tobacco juice. "And what is it you claim I have done to you?"

Finnegan pulled his cigar from his lips and chose his words carefully. "Several times now, sir, you have placed that grey mare in my possession. The animal reacts quite poorly to the sound of gunfire, and I dare say it has nearly cost me life and limb on a number of occasions."

"I only wish the beast had been more thorough." He wiped spit from his lip with the large paw that held his hammer.

"Sir, if you take umbrage with something I have done, I do wish you would come out with it." Finnegan moved his hand a bit closer to the dragoon under his jacket. The man's hammer was no 44 caliber Colt, but it still looked quite threatening when wielded by the giant.

"You, Pinkerton man, are ruining my business. Taking

the very bread from the mouths of my children, and you ask what it is I take umbrage with? I am sorely tempted to see if I could not pound you into the ground like a stake."

Finnegan took a puff of his cigar. "And I am sorely tempted to contact Barnum to see if he would be interested in purchasing a corpse of extraordinary size. Speak plainly, sir, what is it you claim I have done to you?"

The ogre spit out more tobacco and frowned. "You, Pinkerton man, have upset the natural order of the coal patch, and I will not stand for it. When the Raiders or road agents steal horses, the victims must buy new horse flesh from me. That is, until some bastard came along and shot all the Raiders and road agents." He took a deep breath and sprayed out more juice. "Drunks and loafers are notoriously hard on horse flesh. They require frequent remounts due to their apathy and abuse of their animals. That is, until some bastard comes along and shoots all the drunks and loafers in town. You ask me what you have done? You, Pinkerton man, have slit my throat by proxy."

Finnegan pinched the bridge of his nose. "I cannot imagine what sin I have committed that God should curse me with this town." He sighed. "Friend, certainly you cannot place blame on me for the unforeseen consequences resulting from my acting in my own defense."

"Why is that?"

"Because...Sir, I do not have time to sort out your absurdities. I have come here to procure an animal for use tomorrow. An animal other than that damned grey mare."

The giant grunted. "I will give you no animal, sir. Every time you procure a mount from me you do nothing but cause trouble and hurt my business. I will have no more of it. No one in this patch seems willing to stop or at least slow your progress shooting the majority of this town's citizens, so the duty falls to me."

Finnegan dropped his cigar down into the mud and manure of the stable lot. He motioned with one thumb to the corral. "Sir, that black gelding there. Do you recall how you came by it?"

The stable keeper pointed to Abijah. "Your boy there brokered a deal between us for that horse, as you well know."

"Did my young associate inform you as to how I came to be in possession of that animal?"

"Young Mr. Smith told me you killed John Egan and took it from his corral."

"Sir, I intend to come into possession of that animal again. Would you prefer to rent the animal to me, or should I obtain it in the same manner I did the first time?"

The stable keeper stood to his full height and glared down at Finnegan. "Sir, after I set my mind to a thing, I stand by it. No matter what men may threaten."

Finnegan pinched the bridge of his nose once again. "This is the only livery stable in St. Clair. Do you really intend to be so stubborn in this foolishness that I must shoot you to obtain a mount?"

"As I said..." The stable keeper was obviously growing tentative. "Once I set my mind to a thing..."

"Would you rent that black gelding to young Mr. Smith?"

The stable keeper looked past Finnegan to the boy on the fence. "Um...certainly. I have no quarrel with Mr. Smith."

"Very well then." Finnegan flipped a dollar to the man. "Take that in good conscience. I often handle the young man's financial obligations."

THAT EVENING, Finnegan treated Abijah to dinner at Mrs. Wallace's table once again. The landlady had prepared a fine lamb, and all parties present were enjoying it greatly. Annabel Lee was seated with the guests at Finnegan's request. It had been some time since he had seen the girl, and he was interested to see how she was progressing at being folded into the Wallace family. There was a new lodger at the table, as well. He was a short man with a set of thick glasses and a tweed jacket that featured a number of folded up scraps of paper protruding from the pockets. It appeared as though the man carried an entire loose-leaf novel with him in various places.

Finnegan sampled a potato and smiled at Annabel, who was seated across the table from him. He noticed that she had a very sweet face now that it had been washed properly and given a few days of rest and relaxation. "How do you like your new situation here, Annabel?"

"Oh, it agrees with me quite well, sir." She fairly beamed on the other side of the table. "I have my own room. It formerly belonged to one of Mrs. Wallace's sons, but he moved away some time ago to work in Pittsburg for the railroad."

"I see."

"It is a lovely large room with a dresser bureau all my own."

"That is lovely, dear."

"I know it may seem odd, but I always hoped to have a few drawers all my own someday."

Finnegan grinned. "And now you have a bureau all your own." He wiped a bit of lamb sauce from his mouth. "I am very glad to hear you are getting along well."

"I could not be happier, sir." She carefully cut a slice of lamb. "How goes your work shooting people? I am told you shot the assistant treasurer of the union the other day. I cannot claim to know what an assistant treasurer is, but I would assume shooting anyone with a title must be quite the feather in your cap." She popped the lamb into her mouth and offered a warm smile.

Finnegan cleared his throat. "That was an unfortunate incident."

"I am told the man still lives, sir. When last I heard, the doctor claims he will survive, although he may not regain the use of his arm." Abijah shrugged and tried the potatoes.

"Perhaps that will make him think twice before engaging in devilry with his remaining limbs." Finnegan glanced over to the new lodger. "It would be best for us to change the subject, young people. This is hardly proper dinner conversation."

The small man removed his glasses and gave them a scrubbing with one of the napkins. "Oh, quite the contrary." He replaced his glasses on his face. "I often find interest in items that most people consider to be inappropriate in pleasant conversation. It goes along with my profession."

Abijah leaned forward to see past Finnegan. "And what line would that be, sir?"

"I am a reporter, son. A journalist working for the *Police Gazette*."

Abijah's eyes grew wide. "Truly, sir?"

"Yes."

"I am very fond of your periodical, sir. I am unable to read it regularly, but I never fail to give it a complete review when I find a discarded copy."

The man nodded slowly. "Well, the paper appreciates our readership, regardless of how they find their way to us." He leveled his stare on Finnegan. "Sir, perhaps I misunderstand, are you somehow or other in the business of shooting people?"

Finnegan licked his lips. "I am not. These young people are merely unfamiliar with the intricacies of my work."

"What work is that, sir?"

Abijah fielded the question with the stock answer. "He is a detective in private employ."

"Ahh." The journalist sat back in his chair with a small smile playing across his lips. "You are a Pinkerton?"

Finnegan slipped a hunk of meat in his mouth. "Yes."

"Sir, you may be the very man I have come to this town in search of."

"I doubt that very much." He took a drink of his coffee. "Did you mention your name, sir?"

"McLerran Sinclair. Are you at all familiar with my work at the *Gazette*?"

Finnegan sighed. "I am not a regular reader of papers."

"Can you tell me your name, sir? From the forthrightness of your young friend, I can only assume you are not one of Mr. Pinkerton's clandestine agents."

"I am not." Finnegan sipped more coffee to fortify him for the fresh vexation he was about to face. In most instances, he would have simply told the man to mind his own business, but he did not wish to be rude to one of Mrs. Wallace's lodgers. The woman had been far too good to him for him to appear uncouth at her table. "Finnegan Gilhooley, at your service."

"Gilhooley." The journalist spit it out with a bit of awe. "Sir, I must say, it is an honor to meet you in the flesh, as they say. I...well, I have written a number of articles regarding your exploits."

Finnegan nodded. "I have been told that you newspaper

men generally write articles regarding men you have never met."

"Such is the nature of the business." He leaned forward over the table. "Sir, I would be very interested to know of your work in this area. Has Mr. Pinkerton dispatched you here to clean out the remaining Mollies? Oh, if that were the case..." He let out a small laugh. "If I could be the first to report that Finnegan Gilhooley is hunting Mollies in the coal patch, it would be quite a boon to me. After all, sir, you are the man who shot Jesse James."

Abijah leaned forward again to see Sinclair. "Mr. Gilhooley shot his brother, as well."

Sinclair sipped coffee. "Oh, yes, I seem to remember something about that. What is the brother's name?"

Finnegan gave Abijah a look that said his commentary was not required. "Jesse's brother is named Alexander Franklin James. You undoubtedly better recall his brother's name due to the human ear's love of alliteration."

"Alliteration?"

"Yes."

"I must admit, sir, I never imagined I would someday have the opportunity to discuss alliteration over the dinner table with Finnegan Gilhooley."

"It should come as no surprise. Alliteration is one of my favorite topics." He sipped coffee and returned to the lamb.

"Mr. Gilhooley, please understand that I am hesitant to bother you during a meal, but I would be eternally grateful if you could tell me specifically what your commission from Mr. Pinkerton involves presently. The newspaper readers of the country are simply insatiable for information regarding the Molly Maguires. I will not bandy words with you, sir: I have come here in the hopes of covering the expected rioting firsthand."

"Rioting?"

"As a result of the impending executions, sir."

Finnegan shook his head and returned to slicing his lamb. "I have great doubt that your expected riots will materialize, Mr. Sinclair. In all likelihood, these hangings will come to pass with nothing more than the weeping of widows and general regret of the populace that always accompanies such occasions."

"Oh, that would be a shame." Sinclair quickly realized he had misspoken. "Um, I mean only that I have traveled a fair distance to be here. Mr. Gilhooley, do you intend to be present at the hangings?"

"I will be there as a representative of the agency."

"And in the meantime? Are you indeed hunting Mollies?"

Finnegan shook his head once again. "I am not. My purpose here is no secret, sir. I have come to St. Clair to discover the identity of a man who murdered a young woman in this vicinity recently."

"A murderer?"

"Yes, Mr. Sinclair. The Pinkerton agency dispatches men to investigate all manner of mysteries. In actuality, this sort of work is much more common for us than this Molly Maguire business."

"Yes, well, I am sure you would have a better understanding of the policies of the Pinkerton agency than I do. It is only that I have never heard of a Pinkerton agent investigating a murder."

"The James brothers have murdered a score of men along with women and children. As you know, I have been searching for them for some time."

"Well, yes, I suppose so."

"Then it should come as no surprise to you to learn I am

in search of another murderer." Finnegan gulped the last hunk of lamb and placed his napkin next to the plate. "Mr. Sinclair, I am sorry I cannot be of more assistance to you. I find myself in St. Clair on a relatively mundane matter. I am sure your readers would take no interest in it."

Sinclair nodded slowly. "Perhaps. Uh, sir, you mentioned that you intend to travel to Pottsville for the hangings tomorrow?"

"Yes."

"Would you mind terribly if we rode over to Pottsville in the morning together? I would not normally trouble you, but to make it there I will have to leave at a very early hour, and I have been told that road agents frequent these parts."

Abijah leaned in again. "No need to worry about that, sir. Mr. Gilhooley has done a very thorough job of shooting the local road agents. The livery stable owner was complaining about it just today. Would you mind if I asked you a question, sir?"

"Um, feel free to inquire, my young friend."

"Why is it so many people are always being mangled and killed with axes in the city of New York?"

"Perhaps because Mr. Gilhooley is not there to shoot the rascals perpetrating that particular crime."

Chapter 8

POTTSVILLE, PENNSYLVANIA
June 21st, 1877

FINNEGAN AND SINCLAIR HAD NOT SAID MUCH TO EACH other on the ride from St. Clair to Pottsville. Finnegan had much on his mind and the newspaper man quite obviously did not spend much time riding in open country in the dark. The journalist spent most of the trip hanging off his saddle, attempting to discern what his horse was treading on and whether or not they were on the correct road. By the time the cold grey walls of the Schuylkill County Jail were in view, it was just before five in the morning and the dawn was not much more than a whisper of grey in the black sky.

Finnegan stood up in the saddle and looked over the hazy shapes that were already milling about outside the jail's front gate. "The crowd has begun to gather, Mr. Sinclair."

"Are they a crowd or the vanguard of a mob?"

"If they happen to become a mob, I am sure your paper will credit you with predicting it." He flopped down in his saddle and took out a cigar. "I believe it will be a long while before you and your fellow members of the press are to be admitted, Mr. Sinclair. What will you do to keep yourself occupied until half-past eight?"

"A good newspaperman never sits idle, Mr. Gilhooley. I shall keep busy interviewing these people who have gathered here. I will discover the temper of the working man, the wives soon to be widows, the friends of the condemned. All human activity falls within the scope of a true journalist."

"I see."

"And what is it you will be doing until the hour of doom arrives, Mr. Gilhooley?"

"I will be ardently hoping that none of the people you intend to interview do anything silly enough to earn a bullet here today. There are more than forty Coal and Iron men gathered inside the jail and about town, Mr. Sinclair. They have been brought here from Philadelphia and Pittsburg. They have no affiliation with any of the local people and they are all armed with Winchesters. It may benefit these people greatly if you would mention these facts to the citizens, sir."

"To dissuade them from doing anything foolish?"

"Yes."

"Foolishness often makes for finer newspaper stories, Mr. Gilhooley."

"Foolishness you do not survive leads to no stories whatsoever. Bear that in mind today, newspaper man." Finnegan gave his horse a small kick and left the journalist to his own devices. In the rear of the jail, Finnegan rode up to the clapboard structure that was clearly used as a stable for those who had business there. The small building was mostly open at the front with a roof that sloped to the rear as stables tend to. Despite the fact that the structure could easily hold ten horses, there were only two standing in the stalls. Finnegan leaned down close to the neck of his horse to look inside all the way to the rear wall. In the back of the place, he could see a man in a black suit that was far too clean for a stable boy. The man was standing on an upturned bucket so as to better peek out one of the stable's small windows. A Winchester was leaned by the man's legs.

"You there."

The man jumped and very nearly fell from the bucket. He had to grab the window frame to steady himself. Once safe, he slowly stepped down and turned to Finnegan. "Uh, yes, sir."

"What do you see back there?"

"Um, nothing much. Trees and the like."

"And you enjoy observing them?"

"Not particularly." He motioned around the stable. "I have been stationed here in case of trouble."

"I see." Finnegan swung down from the saddle. "Are you a Pinkerton man or a well-dressed Coal and Iron man?"

"I am a Pinkerton man, sir. Who are you?"

Finnegan led his horse into one of the empty stalls and grabbed a handful of hay, which he threw in after the animal. "I am a Pinkerton man, as well. You are here with Mr. Franklin from Philadelphia, I take it?"

"Yes, sir."

"Do you have any idea where I can find that gentleman?"

"I was told he would be in the sheriff's office within the jail if I had anything to report."

Finnegan nodded and pulled his Spencer from the saddle scabbard before closing the stall gate. "Please do me the service of looking after this horse while I am absent. It is a fine animal."

"Yes, sir."

"Also, be tentative about displaying or firing that rifle. It has been my experience that the men charged with preventing disaster are oftentimes the cause of it. Do you understand me?"

"Yes, sir."

"Very well. Can I enter through there?" Finnegan pointed to the small door in the rear wall of the jail.

"I believe so, sir. I have seen other men coming and going through there." The Pinkerton took a step closer to Finnegan. "Sir, you will be witnessing the hangings?"

"Perhaps." Finnegan paused to look over his rifle to make certain nothing had happened to it during the journey. "I was told to come here and present myself to Mr. Franklin, so I am here. You are sullen that you will not have a view of the proceedings?"

He glanced about again to make certain no one would hear. "Quite the contrary, sir. I have never seen a man hang and hope I never do. I must say, though, I would prefer to be inside the walls if some mayhem occurs out here. It would be very lonely to be the only Pinkerton out here if the jail is besieged."

A rather ragged rain slicker hung on the gate of the horse stall. Finnegan tossed it to his fellow Pinkerton agent. "It may behoove you to put that on over your fine suit. Keep that Winchester out of sight, and do not do anything to help the mayhem occur. Remain composed."

The Pinkerton slipped into the slicker and set his Winchester farther to the side in the back of the stable. "Yes, sir. I will do my best."

"Very well." Finnegan left the stable and made his way to the small door in the jail wall. He beat on the sally port, and it was almost instantly opened with a hoary, bearded face pressed against it. "Butcher." Finnegan grinned. "Now you man the rear door? I hope you do not consider this a demotion."

The ape's eyes squinted down. "Ah, the man with many badges. I recall you. What is your business here today?"

"I have taken a job in a laundry, and I bring the silk shirt one of the Mollies wishes to wear to meet his maker."

The ape squinted his eyes down. "I do not know if I believe you."

Finnegan chuckled. "I am here along with the other forty Pinkertons and Coal and Iron men. What the hell else would I be doing here in the grey damn dawn?"

The ape groaned and his face disappeared from the sally port. A moment later the door swung open. He no longer wore his bloody apron. Apparently, he felt the need to dress up for the momentous occasion. "You jest to damn much, Pinkerton, and it wears on my nerves. As you know, this is not my chosen profession, and I would prefer not to be here."

Finnegan walked through the door and into the jail's courtyard. "You do not wish to witness this historic moment?"

"Any daft bastard who would wish to see another man hang ought to get the rope himself, if you ask me."

Finnegan nodded. "I cannot help but agree, butcher." He looked over the courtyard and spied a clutch of Coal and Iron police who were standing around with their hands in the pockets of their blue coats with the fancy brass buttons. None of them appeared any more particularly intelligent than the next, so he chose at random. "You there!" They stopped gabbing and turned to him. "You there, the tall one, bring your carcass over here." Finnegan pulled his Coal and Iron badge from his pocket and held it up in the face of the approaching man. "You appear unengaged. You will man this door and admit no one who is not in possession of the proper credentials. Is that clear?"

"Yes, sir."

"Very well. Now go back and get your rifle from where you have left it."

"Oh, uh, yes, sir. Sorry, sir."

"Don't be sorry. Be quick, damn you." The policeman scurried off and Finnegan turned back to the butcher. "You may go if you like, sir."

The butcher looked a bit suspicious. "That is a fine favor for a Pinkerton to offer."

Finnegan laughed. "Perhaps you will hide me in your butcher shop if the townspeople do indeed riot."

The ape grinned. "Perhaps not that fine." He tipped his hat. "Good day, sir."

The butcher left through the door he had been guarding and the Coal and Iron man returned panting and proudly holding his Winchester. Finnegan gave him a sneer. "Have all of you been issued one of those?"

"Yes, sir."

"Mr. Winchester never had a better friend than the Molly Maguires."

"Sorry, what, sir?"

"Do you know where Mr. Franklin of the Pinkerton agency might be found?"

"Would he be the man in charge, sir?"

"I would hope so."

"I think he is gathered with the other men in the Sheriff's office at the top of those stairs, sir." He pointed to a wooden flight of stairs that extended up one wall of the courtyard.

"Good man. Keep a steady eye on that door." Finnegan crossed to the other wall and made his way up the stairs. At the top he found what might have been the only door in the entire jail that did not have a sentry that day. Finnegan swung it open, and half a dozen men swiveled to see who was entering. They resembled some sort of herd due to their matching black suits and black bowler hats. "Gentlemen."

One man shouldered his way through the assembled black suits and stepped to Finnegan. He wore glasses and had a neatly trimmed beard that stuck out from his chin like a dagger. Placed on the cover of a book he might make for the perfect villain. "Mr. Gilhooley?"

"Yes, sir."

"Benjamin Franklin." He put out his hand. "Thank you for coming. I know you have other business and Robert Pinkerton has informed me that you dislike to be sidetracked."

Finnegan shrugged. "I suppose it is not much of an imposition, and I doubt you will have cause to ask me to do this twice."

Franklin raised his eyebrows. "One would certainly hope not." His brow furrowed. "I am sorry we have not had the opportunity to meet before now. Robert Pinkerton speaks very highly of you and has great confidence in your abilities."

"The younger Mr. Pinkerton is always a pleasure to work with. I believe he is glad that this affair involving the Mollies is at an end and will not require repeating."

Franklin pulled Finnegan off to one side of the room a bit farther from the other bowler hats. When he spoke, his voice was lower. "If you continue to shoot men in the coal patch there may not be enough left for another six hangings when you are done. Good Lord, man, I know it must be justified, but I dearly hope you are about finished. It is only a matter of time before some damned newspaper man hears of it and makes us out to be murderers instead of men attempting to catch one. There are already whispers claiming that your real purpose in St. Clair is to kill a union leader named Siney."

Finnegan slowly nodded. "Sir, I assure you, I have never laid eyes on John Siney."

"No, and you are not likely to." Franklin cleared his throat. "As you might expect, we keep a careful account of Mr. Siney's movements. Him and a number of his associates. Currently, Siney is off some damned place in Kentucky trying to unite various mining unions into some kind of conglomerate designed to bedevil anyone trying to get anything done in this country. He is not even living in the coal patch presently."

Finnegan sighed. "I find such rumors vexing, sir."

"Yes, I have been told as much by Captain Bourne. He has sent me several telegrams explaining your difficulties and asking that you be removed from the coal patch for everyone's safety."

Finnegan let a small laugh slip out. "I have noticed that Captain Bourne is deeply concerned with safety." Finnegan felt the need to indulge in a bit of cruelty. "Sir, just to assuage Captain Bourne's anxiety, you ought to send him a telegram informing him that I have an excellent suspect in mind and intend to wrap things up in the coal patch before the end of the month."

Franklin's eyebrows shot up once more. "You do?"

"No, but it will at least shut the man up until the first of July. The fool is insufferable, sir."

Franklin frowned and nodded. "I might tend to agree with you. I told Bourne to be here today with his men, but he flatly refused me. He claims he and his men must remain in St. Clair to guard the town from insurrection. I could have forced the jackass into submission through General Pleasants, but I did not think it worth the trouble."

Finnegan motioned to the courtyard outside. "It is better to have men without ties locally, I believe, sir."

"Quite right, Mr. Gilhooley, quite right." Franklin smiled. "I believe I will send that telegram off to Captain Bourne. If he wishes to be obtuse, I might as well have a bit of fun with him." He took a deep breath. "Now, to the day's business. I understand you have spoken with one of these Mollies while he has been in custody. Thomas Duffy."

"You are very well informed, sir."

"It suits a Pinkerton man to be that very thing. Did you develop any kind of rapport with the man?"

"Somewhat, I suppose. There is no ill will between us that I am aware of. Well, beyond what must exist between men in our respective positions."

"Excellent. You are to be posted with Duffy. Keep a close eye on the man. Do your best to keep him tranquil. These men are being allowed to speak before their executions. We do not need them rabblerousing. We also cannot be seen to be keeping them from rabblerousing. The coal patch is a powder keg, Mr. Gilhooley. We must avoid sparks at all costs."

Finnegan nodded. "I will do my best to keep him peaceful and dissuade him from encouraging the crowd to violence."

"That would be much appreciated, Mr. Gilhooley. Mr. Duffy is unlike his fellow Mollies in some respects. It has been suggested that our agent McParlan somehow entrapped the man or simply pulled his name out of a hat. At any rate, there are rumors that the governor may pardon the man to placate public opinion. During your time with the Pinkerton firm, have you been forced to lower yourself to dealing with politicians?"

"No, sir, only killers, highwaymen, thieves, and prostitutes."

"A far preferable crowd to socialize with, I assure you. With your set, a man may get his hands dirty, but dealing with politicians soils the soul. I would not put it past our esteemed governor to issue a reprieve for this man after he has swung, so as to appease both sides." Franklin ran his fingers over his pointy beard. "Might there be some way you could come to the conclusion that the governor is the murderer you seek? You would be hard pressed to find a man more deserving of an early end."

"Sorry, sir. I have not, as yet, found reason to suspect him." Finnegan smiled and shook his head. "Shall I be off to look in on Mr. Duffy, sir?"

"That would probably be best."

FINNEGAN WALKED to the far end of the jailhouse block and leaned his Spencer against the stone wall. Someone had the forethought to place a few chairs by each cell so that visitors might speak with the condemned. Most of the other six men had relatives sitting in the chairs and chatting, or were patiently waiting for the next group to arrive. Only Duffy found himself alone.

Finnegan lowered himself into the provided chair. "Good morning, Mr. Duffy."

Duffy stood in the rear of his cell with his hands in the pockets of what appeared to be a new suit. "Mr. Pinkerton detective, you happened to be in the fine city of Pottsville this day and decided to stop by for a visit?"

"I arrived here purely by coincidence, just as you suggest." Finnegan sat back in the chair and looked over Duffy's cell. There was a platter with a perfectly good-looking beefsteak on it along with some fried potatoes. "You do not favor your breakfast?"

Duffy shrugged. "They said I could have whatever I wished, and I must say they prepared it perfectly. I simply have not felt hungry this morning. Would you care to try it? This may be an offer that is never made to you again. It is not every day you will have a chance to sample another man's last meal."

"I am afraid I do not have much of an appetite this morning, either. I cannot say I would feel quite right about it, even if I did." Finnegan pulled two cigars from his pocket. "Would one of these be more to your liking?"

"That would sit with me very well." He walked to the bars. "It is sad; I have bummed a fair amount of tobacco from you already, sir. Unfortunately, I have been out of work for some time and am currently without funds to reimburse you. Are you sure you wish to continue to support my habit?"

Finnegan found a match in his vest pocket. "It is a shame you have been out of employment." He handed the spare cigar to Duffy. "But you seem like a virtuous young man. I am certain you will be gainfully employed again soon." He struck the match and lit his cigar before holding out the match to Duffy. "Do you think you could get payment to me by the end of the week?"

Duffy let the end of the cigar glow red, then began puffing. "I give you my word, sir. If you are not paid by the end of the week, may you forever sully my good name."

Finnegan let out a cloud of smoke and sat back once again. "I cannot say why, but I trust you implicitly."

Duffy grinned and leaned against the wall of his cell. "You must be a damned fine detective, sir."

"In truth, detecting is not my usual occupation. Though you may have suspected that."

"It had occurred to me, although I must say, it is hard to imagine what your useful purpose truly is. If you are a tobacco salesman, you are very poor at that, as well."

Finnegan shrugged. "Mr. Pinkerton normally tasks me with locating men who are to be shot."

"Do you often locate and shoot them?"

"Frequently. I had amassed a fine record before I began chasing the James Brothers and this damned coal patch murderer." He puffed his cigar. "I imagine all men suffer runs of bad luck. This one will surely come to an end soon."

"That is surely true." Duffy held his cigar in his mouth and straightened his suit jacket. "I have been suffering a run of bad luck for the better part of a year now, but I can say with certainty that it will not extend beyond today. My advice to you, detective, would be to keep your chin up."

"A very optimistic outlook, Mr. Duffy." Finnegan took a moment to contemplate whether he should broach another topic. "You are certain, sir?"

"Ah." Duffy nodded knowingly. "You have heard the rumors of my impending reprieve?"

"I have heard there are rumors."

Duffy combed back his hair with one hand, looking somber. "Mister...what was it you said your name was, again?"

"You might as well call me Finnegan."

"Very well, and you may call me Thomas, if you like. Finnegan, as I said, I have been sitting in this prison for almost a year. I cannot help but think if the governor had an interest in pardoning me, he would have gotten around to it before now. I am sure a potentate such as the governor is a busy man, but it cannot take too much time to affix his signature to a single piece of parchment." Duffy rubbed his chin. "Is a pardon only one sheet, do you think?"

"I could not say; I have never seen one. I would think it should be a succinct document."

"Succinct?"

"To the point."

"A fine word, Finnegan. I shall have to remember that one."

"I have always enjoyed vocabulary."

"Who are these James brothers you so ardently wish to kill?"

"You have never heard of Frank or Jesse James?" For the first time, Finnegan was truly sad Duffy was about to die. His hanging would be the death of the last man who would not drive him batty.

"No, although I don't imagine I follow the careers of criminals as closely as a man in your profession would. They are rascals of low character, I take it?"

"Quite so."

"Well, then, I hope you fulfill your commission. Do you always shoot men, or do you send them off to be hung on occasion?"

Finnegan thought back on his record. "I have, in some instances, sent men off to prison. My primary solution is to shoot them, when it can be accomplished. I confess, I have formed a minor scheme to get the James brothers hung in Arkansas, but I doubt it will come to fruition. I do not believe I would feel right about it if I could hash out a proper method."

"It is better to shoot men than to hang them." Duffy carefully took a seat on his cot, next to his untouched meal. "Do not misunderstand me, it is not so much the dying that agitates me. What I would have preferred would have been a prompt trip. My trial ended many months ago. Giving a man this much more time to live, but forcing him to live in this damned cell in the meantime is unspeakably cruel. They should have dragged us to the gallows directly after we were condemned. This..." He shook his head disdainfully. "This foolishness strikes me as the kind of scheme concocted by men who have spent little time truly living. It must have been thought up by those bastards I see getting off the train to inspect the mines they own but never get dirty in."

"Those men were indeed the creators of this particular difficulty you find yourself involved in. You truly do not mind dying?"

Duffy shrugged. "It vexed me greatly at first. Now that I have had time to honestly contemplate it, I have come to wonder if Mr. McKenna might not have saved my soul. I suppose if I had been left to my own inclinations, I would have merely spent what remained of my life, before the black lung took me, in drunkenness and whatever other debauchery I could find funds for. This way...well, I have little to speak to the Father of before they take me to the courtyard."

Finnegan had to take a long moment to offer a response. "I suppose there is that small comfort in all this." He looked up the cell block. "You have no visitors today?"

Duffy let out a small laugh. "I never married, never had the money. My parents have passed."

"What of your uncle, the apothecary?"

"Oh, he was kind enough to provide me with this fine suit of clothes you see me in. Very thoughtful of him. I do not expect to see him today. It is for the best; he has never dealt with things of this nature well. He was so drunk at my father's funeral that he nearly fell asleep on one of the tombstones in the graveyard." Duffy laughed. "Did you tell him I have stopped imbibing?"

"I mentioned it, yes."

"Very decent of you. I am sure he had a laugh at that. He has always been far to sullen to suit me. Did he try to sell you one of his palliatives?"

"Yes, but I suppose that is his occupation."

"It is, and he is quite good at it. If you are not suffering from an illness, my uncle will surely invent one for you. Assuming you have funds, of course."

"Naturally." There was the faint sound of some weeping down the cell block and then a chuckle that sounded less than sincere. "The other men seem to have quite the collection of callers."

"Ah, yes." Duffy pointed down toward the other Mollies. "The one fellow down there, Munley, his father is here to see him today. I have been told the man walked all the way here from Gilberton. If memory serves, that must be ten or twelve miles. The man must have begun in the night to make it here now."

"It shows a great deal of loyalty."

"It does." Duffy waggled his cigar at Finnegan. "I am to die with him. Did you know that?"

"No. I have not been made privy to the arrangements."

"It is true. At one o'clock, Munley and I climb the scaffold together. Of all the oddities I have encountered of late, I must say: it is a strange thing to know who you will die next to."

"Do you know him at all?"

"We have spoken in passing once or twice. He seems an alright sort. I suppose I have no objections to dying next to him." Duffy grinned. "Given the choice, I would rather hang next to a stranger than a friend. Hopefully that would mean my friend never hung."

"Ah, that's the spirit."

Duffy stared down at his cigar. "Yes, I find myself in a

truly unique position. Few men know the time of their demise and the company they will keep at the end. Although, it will still come as something of a surprise since I do not own a watch."

"You do not?"

"I never have. I always meant to save up and purchase one, but I never got around to it. The whistle at the breaker always told me when to rise and when to knock off and that was enough to convince me to spend my money elsewhere."

"Well..." Finnegan pulled his watch from his vest pocket. "If you would like, for today, you may use mine." He sat forward and held the gold watch through the bars. Duffy took the timepiece with both hands very carefully. "You push the small button at the top to open it."

Duffy hit the button and smiled at the watch. "Oh, very fine, Finnegan. You must have given a pretty penny for this."

"It was a gift from my employer."

Duffy threw his head back and laughed out loud. "I will be damned. Are you telling me this is formerly the watch of Mr. Pinkerton?"

"It is, indeed; at least, he purchased it originally. There is an inscription, if you care to read it."

Duffy turned the watch sideways. "So there is... To F.G, in recognition of loyal and admirable service, A. P. Is that what you are, Finnegan? Loyal and admirable?"

"As reliable as the mail, Thomas."

"The inscription does not mention reliability."

"The other attributes can be assumed." Finnegan tapped ash from his cigar down onto the cold stone floor.

"What do you think Mr. Pinkerton would think of me holding this timepiece for the day?"

"He would not begrudge you it." Finnegan moved around in his chair and looked down the cell block again. "We have a fair amount of time on our hands. Would you like anything? I could locate a deck of cards, perhaps?"

Duffy shook his head. "No. I only play cards for money and, as I mentioned, I am without funds, currently."

Finnegan waved one hand dismissively. "Think nothing of it, I will stake you. Of course, I will have to insist that you pay me back with a half share of your winnings."

"Ah, an excellent offer and a proper encouragement to bet large. Find the cards, Finnegan, and prepare for a trouncing."

THE MINUTES and hours ticked by on Finnegan's gold watch. The two men played hand after hand of cards and discussed whatever various topics came to mind. They were slow to comment when the sheriff and a couple of deputies, along with a fair-sized entourage of priests and ministers, came to collect two of the other prisoners at eleven o'clock.

Duffy motioned down the cell block with his head as he contemplated his cards. "Which cells are they emptying?"

"It would appear the first two on the corridor."

"Ah, that would be Boyle and McGehan. Fine sons of Erin, them."

"To be sure." Finnegan stared down the corridor and was more than a little shocked when the two men emerged from their cells holding flowers. The men of the cloth begat praying for the soon-to-be dearly departed and the whole parade slowly made their way out of the cell block through the door at the end of the corridor. It was rather ominous when the large wooden door swung shut and blocked out the sunlight that had been pouring in.

A litany of sound began drifting in through the window in

Duffy's cell. First, there was a low murmur that sounded like the approach of a storm. Then, a small spattering of shrieks and wails that must have come from various family members in the courtyard. Finally, all grew quiet, and a lone voice could be faintly heard addressing the crowd. From inside the cell block, Finnegan could tell a man was giving a speech of sorts, but could not make out the words. "Who do you think that is, Thomas?"

"Sounds like McGehan."

"Would you care to go to the window to hear him better?"

"I would not." Duffy rolled yet another bummed cigar from one side of his mouth to the other and stared hard at his cards. "You may, if you like. McGehan and I are headed for a similar destination. I should have ample time to ask him the particulars of his discourse."

"Very well, then." Finnegan tossed down a couple of cards. "Two, if you please."

"Certainly."

For a moment, all sound ceased outside the cell block. Then, another voice, louder and deeper than the first, could be heard addressing the assembled witnesses. "I have nothing to say, gentlemen, only pretty much in the same way; nothing as regards my guilt or innocence. I forgive those that have put me here. I forgive them from my heart out, and I hope they forgive me. I forgive all this world."

Duffy tossed down a card. "Dealer takes one. Boyle is a very forgiving man."

"It certainly would appear so."

"You know, Finnegan, I cannot say what it is about that man Boyle, but I always thought that if any of us really were a Molly, it might be him."

Finnegan shrugged. "I would not be the one to say." There was a sharp crack like two pieces of wood being slapped together, followed by a dull thump. Finnegan looked up slowly from his hand. "Did you draw the card you were hoping for, Thomas?"

"In fact, I did. Although, I must say this is a poor time for my luck to change."

Another hour slid by as the men continued to play poker. The same money was generally passed back and forth between the two, with neither of them really gaining over the other. At the point that Finnegan had almost forgotten the sound of the dull thump out in the courtyard, the deputies and the sheriff appeared again. This time, the clergy were slower in arriving, but they did eventually come ambling into the corridor.

Duffy tossed down his hand. "Fold. Your pot."

Finnegan pulled the money across the mattress toward him. "Who are those two down there?"

"It must be Roarity and Carroll." He chuckled and began dealing the cards. "Did you know that they informed all of us as to our date and time of execution, but asked that we not inform the others?"

"Truly?"

"Yes. As though we have something else to discuss or someone else to discuss it with. I have to say, it is a bit discouraging to think that I will meet my end at the hands of men as silly as this." The second set of men began their walk toward the gallows and the sheriff, deputies, and holy men followed just as they had the first time. "At least they will be well-practiced by the time they get to me and poor Munley." He popped open Finnegan's watch and checked the time. "Does it go by slowly or quickly?"

"Always one or the other and never the one you would choose." Finnegan motioned down the corridor. "It is decent of someone to provide those men with the crucifixes and flowers to carry with them."

"Yes. They offered me a choice of items, but I declined." Duffy put Finnegan's watch away and dealt the cards again. A voice came drifting in from the window in the rear of the cell once again. "Ah, that would be Roarity, I imagine." He stared down at his cards. "My accomplice."

"Is he now?"

"Well, that's what Mr. Gowan said in court. From what I am told, me and Mr. Roarity went on quite the spree, shooting superintendents and breaker bosses down in Tamaqua."

"That is not how you recall events?" Finnegan scowled at his cards.

"Couldn't have told you the man's name by sight before I met him in this jail. Still have trouble recalling it." Duffy looked up from his cards and held up one hand as the voice drifted into the cell.

"Thomas Duffy is a man, I won't say for fear I might be lying, that I never seen him the third time before I seen him in the Pottsville jail..."

Duffy grinned. "There you have it. If you cannot believe a man while he stands on the gallows, when can you believe him?"

Finnegan removed two cards from his hand and tossed them down. "Two, please. Sadly, it is not me that requires convincing." He picked up two fresh cards. "If it were in my hands, I would let you all wander off. I cannot say what a superintendent is, but it sounds like a vile creature, and I see no reason not to murder one now and then."

"A pity you did not serve on my jury."

Outside, the first voice faded and was replaced by

another. "I have nothing to say, only that I am innocent of the crime I am charged with."

Duffy folded up his cards and stared at his newfound friend. "You have seen many men die, Finnegan?"

"Many."

"Do you not think it is a pity to kill men such as these without real cause? They are dying damn well if you ask me. Would it not be preferable to let such men live, or let them die for something worthwhile?"

Finnegan shrugged. "You are too young to have fought in the war." He shook his head. "Thomas, I have seen thousands, yes, thousands of men die for...nothing. Since it ended, I have read the opinions of, I do not know how many men, who have tried to explain what all those men died for, but I would suggest to you that whatever the quarrel was, they would have happily abandoned it the morning of a battle. I will grant you, I did not understand Americans so well then, but I never heard a soldier make mention of anything I have read from the learned men who began writing after the war. I never heard a soldier mention the negroes or whatever the hell states' rights are. All they ever discussed was their ardent wish to keep living. Some of them did, many did not. In the end, all men die for nothing, Thomas."

The younger man nodded solemnly. There was another crack followed by a dull couple of thumps. Both men did their best to ignore the sounds "Yes, I suppose so." He brightened a bit. "Still, I think it is important to die well, don't you?"

"Oh, yes. Most assuredly." Finnegan smiled. "I knew a fellow who ran away from every engagement our regiment fought in during the war."

"A deserter?"

"The chap never fully deserted, you see. He would

simply turn yellow and flee. After the fact, no one ever had the gumption to hang the poor devil, so all was forgiven, and he would return to the ranks. I asked him once why he kept fleeing in that manner." Finnegan folded up his cards, losing interest in them. "Being quite young at the time, I inquired as to whether or not he felt as though he could go on living, knowing he was a coward."

"I suppose that would be difficult to live with."

"Not for that gentleman." Finnegan laughed. "He explained to me that he could not give a damn less what people thought of him, and he intended to flee from every battle for as long as the damned Union insisted on having them. He said he felt dying in a foolish war was not dying well, so there was no reason to let silliness such as heroism or cowardice enter into it."

"It is an interesting view to take." Duffy tossed down his cards. "What became of the man?"

"He was kicked in the head by a surly mule two days before Lee signed at Appomattox."

Duffy laughed. "There is a lesson to be learned there, I think, though I have no idea what it might be." Footsteps could be heard approaching from down the corridor, so Duffy sat as far forward as the bars would allow. He glimpsed a priest coming near. "Ah, I believe it is time for me to cease tending to the needs of this world and consider the next."

Finnegan swept the cards together and set the full deck on the cot. "It is, my friend." He stood up from his chair. "I will give you some privacy." Finnegan turned and nodded to the approaching priest.

"This will not take long, Finnegan. It has been difficult to engage in much sin recently, given my living arrangements. Would you care to walk to the scaffold with me? It is not a long walk, but you may never have the opportunity to take another quite like it."

Finnegan considered the offer. "I would be honored, Thomas."

"Very well. I will see you when my soul has been properly cleansed."

DUFFY HAD NOT BEEN wrong regarding the length of time it would take to get right with his maker. Finnegan needed only to wander down to the end of the corridor, where he waited perhaps ten minutes. When the priest was finished, some sort of minister approached and Duffy spoke with him for a few minutes, as well. When that conversation finished, a third man in the clothes of a layman came to Duffy's cell, and Finnegan could hear the condemned man laughing just as one of his arms poked out the bars and motioned for Finnegan to come back down the corridor.

Finnegan walked to the cell and nodded to the new arrival, who wore a snappy three-piece suit and a grey bowler. "Sir."

Duffy was chuckling. "Finnegan The Pinkerton, I would like you to meet Arnold the Advocate. This gentleman represented me at my trial."

"Ah." Finnegan shrugged. "You will have to excuse me if I do not ask for your card."

Duffy laughed again and the lawyer hung his head for a moment. "I cannot blame you. Suffice it to say, there were extenuating circumstances."

Finnegan shrugged. "I suppose I have heard of worse advocates. The fact that you have come here today speaks well of you."

Duffy took on a more serious air. "It does, Arnold, truly. You should know I hold no ill will against you. You did the best you could for me." Duffy motioned to Finnegan. "You have not made the list of men I have presented to this gentleman here."

The lawyer looked to Finnegan. "List?"

Duffy nodded, looking grave. "Oh, yes, most assuredly. My friend Finnegan here is a professional assassin in the employ of the Pinkertons. Their motto is that one man's money is as good as the next, and the next man's money is even better. In keeping with that, I have contracted Finnegan here to murder the men who placed me in this unfortunate position. Do not misunderstand me, it is not that I am vengeful; it is only that I feel a man should give as good as he gets."

The lawyer spoke with a very matter of fact tone. "Thomas, somehow I doubt you have the funds to be hiring assassins."

"Oh, you might be surprised how affordable assassins are. Finnegan here mostly works in the public interest. He does not wish to get rich. He feels it would corrupt his character." Duffy pulled Finnegan's watch from his pocket. "How many murders will this buy me, friend?"

Finnegan took the watch and held it up for inspection. "It is a nice enough piece. I believe that will get you two dead men, or three if two of them happen to line up properly. Who would you like killed, Mr. Duffy?"

"Oh, let us make it Mr. Gowan and that damned judge who put the noose around my neck. If you can fit in a third, let's go with Gus Moody, a bartender by trade and a scoundrel of the highest order."

Hearing the alias of his fellow Pinkerton, Finnegan could barely conceal his surprise. "What is it the bartender did to you?"

"He was always stingy extending me credit, as if he knew I would someday hang and skate out of my tab. I feel it was a cold-hearted act and deserves another in return."

Finnegan pocketed his watch. "Payment has been rendered and accepted, Mr. Duffy. They are dead men."

"Oh, drat. I should have asked you to kill that Sunday school teacher who was so fond to rapping my knuckles. Now what was his name? Is it too late to select another victim?"

The lawyer shook his head. "Gentlemen, I hardly think this is a proper time for jesting."

"It is the only time I have, Arnold." Duffy put his hands through the bars. "Shake my hand and be on your way. You owe me nothing and you are not the cause of this. Know that."

The lawyer shook the young man's hand and turned to go without uttering another word. Finnegan waited to speak until the man was out the door. "Seems like a decent fellow, for a litigator."

"Yes, they are a pitiable breed, are they not?" Duffy put his head up to the bars when he heard the door at the end of the corridor creaking open. "Who goes there, Finnegan?"

"The sheriff and his men, Thomas."

"Ah, then it would appear our visit is at an end, and it is time to get to the business of the day. From the sound of things, there are a lot of people out there expecting an appearance from myself and Mr. Munley. I would hate to keep them waiting."

"I must say, Thomas, you are keeping your nerve beautifully."

"Ah, but there is the real problem, Finnegan. I have finally found something I have talent for, but I can only do it once. What a pity."

"Such is life, my friend." Finnegan nodded down the

corridor. "They are coming, Thomas. Straighten your suit and do not let them see you sweat. Do not give them the satisfaction."

"You can be assured of that." He adjusted his bowtie.

Finnegan turned to meet the lawmen. "Sheriff Orme. How have you been?"

The sheriff had a sheen of sweat on his forehead and his lip twitched once or twice. It appeared as though he did not enjoy executing his execution duties. "I did not expect to see you here today, Mr. Gilhooley."

"All the Pinkertons in Pennsylvania are here."

"Yes, well, I did not expect to find you chatting with Mr. Duffy."

"Mr. Duffy and I are old friends, and he has recently become a client of the agency."

"Excuse me?" Orme leaned forward to look into the cell.

"Mr. Duffy has traded a fine watch in return for a small portion of vengeance. Would you care to place the sheriff on your list, Thomas?"

Duffy smiled through the bars. "I cannot say as I have ever met the man. Have never seen him around my accommodations, either. I was beginning to wonder if this county had a sheriff." Duffy shrugged. "I was arrested by a gentleman named Bourne of the Coal and Iron Police. I suppose if you would care to shoot that son of a bitch for me, I would not mind a bit."

"On that score I may yet deliver."

"I'm afraid I will have to take your word for it." Duffy cleared his throat. "Shall we get about our labors, Sheriff?"

Orme wiped the sweat from his brow. "Yes, we probably should." He pulled a large key from his pocket. "Would you care for a flower to carry, Mr. Duffy? Some of the other men have requested them."

"I have never had any interest in flowers and see no reason to change now."

"Richard will bind your hands." The sheriff motioned to one of the men next to him who held a length of rawhide in one hand.

"Richard, I know. He has brought me many meals."

The deputy lowered his eyes toward the floor. "I won't make it too tight, Thomas. I promise you that."

"Much appreciated."

The sheriff fumbled the key into the lock and the door creaked open. Duffy stepped forward and the deputy affixed the rawhide. "All right, Thomas?"

"It will serve. I will not be wearing it long."

The sheriff wiped more sweat. "Remain here. We must do the same with Mr. Munley." He gave Finnegan a hard look. "Keep an eye on him."

Finnegan chuckled. "If the young man wished to attempt escape, I believe he would have tried before now."

Duffy stared at his bound hands. "I have often been called lazy, perhaps it was true."

Finnegan took a step closer to the cell as the sheriff moved two cells down to fetch Munley. That man's relatives and visitors had to be shooed away before the cell could be opened. Finnegan sneered. "The sheriff seems more upset than you, Thomas."

"Perhaps the election is near. A man can become near apoplectic when he fears he may lose his profession."

"Not having to worry regarding such things must be a great comfort to you." Finnegan shrugged.

"That is why I am so serene. I would go so far as to say that the only good thing about hanging is the way it dampens your worries." Duffy coughed into his hands. "You will walk with me, Finnegan?"

"All the way."

Duffy faked a smile. "I would recommend you stop just short of the trapdoor. I would not ask that of you."

"I appreciate that." Finnegan saw the young man's lip twitch. "Remain serene, Thomas. There is no need for fear. You are merely doing what all men must do at some time. Many have done this before you, many will do this after you. You depart today, perhaps I depart tomorrow. We will see each other again soon enough, Thomas, I assure you."

Duffy nodded and swallowed. "Feel free to take your time about it, Finnegan."

"Thank you for allowing me that."

The sheriff turned from Munley's cell "We are ready here. You will bring him, Mr. Gilhooley?"

"I will."

The sheriff wiped more sweat. "Then we should go."

"Very well." Finnegan nodded to Duffy. "I will be right behind you. Do you wish to speak to the people outside?"

Duffy shook his head. "I have nothing to say."

"It is better that way." Finnegan slapped the young man on the shoulder. "Remember to stand straight and keep your nerve."

"I will."

"Then let us begin."

With the sheriff leading the way, the procession made its way down the corridor and out into the courtyard. Finnegan had to squint his eyes when the door opened, and then stepped out into the springtime sun. It took a moment for his eyes to adjust so that he could make out the pale, frightened faces of the crowd that had gathered to act as witness. The majority of the faces looked far worse than Duffy or Munley. The visages of the crowd were tainted with something neither of the condemned had to carry at the moment. The faces of the crowd were colored with regret. There was not a one of them who did not wish they had stayed home at that moment. Four men had already swung, two soon would. It was a spectacle they would all carry with them to their graves.

A plankboard fence about four feet tall separated the spectators from the path the procession traveled. As they marched toward the gallows, the only sound that could be heard was the crunching of the men's boots on the earth of the courtyard. It took less than a minute for them to cross from the jail door to the steps of the gallows. Duffy's brand-new shoes squeaked as he climbed the rough-cut planks that formed the steps. It was new lumber, and Finnegan could see the sap still oozing from it. When Duffy made it to the platform, he turned and smiled at Finnegan. "Quite a sturdy structure."

Finnegan nodded. The gallows had been built as a long, thin platform with a line of upright beams with crossmembers. In the morning, six ropes had hung from the crossmembers. By the time Finnegan climbed the steps with Duffy, there were four remnants of ropes still waving in the gentle wind. They had ragged ends where the hangman had cut them. At the very end of the platform two nooses, still unused, hung in the June sunlight. Somewhere in the distance, Finnegan could hear a bird chirping. The entire courtyard was truly as quiet as a tomb. Finnegan pointed down to the end of the gallows. "I believe our destination is there, Thomas."

"It seems a likely spot." Duffy strolled across the platform as though it was a boardwalk with nothing more threatening than a mercantile at the other side. Finnegan followed dutifully. When they arrived at the second-to-last trapdoor, Duffy was careful to step to the dead center of it. "Ah, this should do nicely, wouldn't you say, Finnegan?"

"Indeed." Finnegan looked at the young man and saw that his face had turned as pale as the corpse he was about to become. Finnegan glanced over to see Munley shaking his head in response to a final offer to address the crowd. One of the deputies slowly placed the noose around the man's neck.

Duffy gritted his teeth and faked another smile. "Would you mind fitting me, Finnegan?"

"I suppose better me than a stranger." Finnegan took hold of the rope and draped the noose around Duffy's neck. He could see that the length of hemp fibers of the loop had been greased so as to let it slip more easily. Finnegan held the knot and gave the rope a tug. He left the barest bit of slack in it around his new friend's neck. "How does that suit you, Thomas?"

"As well as such a thing can, I suppose." He cleared his throat and surveyed the crowd. "I read in one of the papers that when we hang today, we will be martyrs to the labor cause." He chuckled. "I never was in the union. Thought it a rather silly outfit." He grunted. "Well, it has been fine spending the morning with you, Finnegan. You'll get me that money you owe me from the card game?"

"You may count on it."

"I should hope so. A fellow never knows when he may fall on hard times and need the extra funds." He swallowed hard. "Do not take this the wrong way, Finnegan, but I do dearly wish there was someone other than you to send me off."

Finnegan shrugged. "It makes little difference. This is something every man does alone whether he likes it or not."

"On that score you are correct." He looked over and saw that the men were backing away from Munley. "Well then, I see Mr. Munley is in a hurry, and since we are traveling by the same conveyance, I would hate to hold him up."

"Very well then. Goodbye, Thomas. Best of luck to you in the next world." Finnegan took a step back so that he was off the trapdoor.

"Goodbye, Finnegan. Best of luck in this one."

In the rear of the platform, a man stood next to a large wooden lever that was the obvious trigger for the trapdoors. Finnegan raised a hand to the man and nodded. The sheriff did the same standing by Munley. With the signal, the man heaved the lever forward and Duffy dropped. The platform was tall enough so that the young man disappeared entirely. In his place, as Finnegan stared straight forward, was a rope. There was no movement in the strand that cut vertically through Finnegan's vision. It did not waver to the left or right, it merely hung.

FINNEGAN WALKED to the end of the now-empty cell block. After Duffy had dropped, he had waited the roughly fifteen or twenty minutes it took to determine that the executed men were well and truly dead, but most of the crowd had elected not to. The onlookers, drawn by curiosity, and hopefully sickened and angered by what they had seen, wished to depart. Finnegan had watched them go out the main courtyard gate and wondered if they had learned anything. Would any of them take any action to see that something like this was not done to their friends and neighbors again? Personally, Finnegan doubted it, but then, no one had ever accused him of being an optimistic man. He found his Spencer leaning in the corner, just where he had left it. As he picked up the gun, he heard footsteps behind him. Turning, he saw the Sheriff.

R

The official was walking down the cell block with what appeared to be strong determination. That was, until he stopped short and grabbed the bars in front of a cell. He used the iron to support him as he retched onto the stone floor. Finnegan placed a cigar between his lips and struck a match to light it. If nothing else, the tobacco would keep the smell down. He let the sheriff finish and pull a rag from his pocket to clean his lips with before speaking to the man.

"Your duties do not agree with you, Sheriff?"

Orme slowly looked over at Finnegan, still bent over and holding the bars. "Someday, God willing, that sharp tongue will cut you, Gilhooley."

"What is it exactly that has you in such a dither, Sheriff?"

He dry-heaved and then leaned against the bars with one shoulder. "Damn you Pinkertons. It is all very well for you to come here and play your dirty tricks, then pack up and move on to the next sinful endeavor. What of the rest of us? I must continue to live here after this day, Gilhooley. Did you see the way they were all looking at me?"

Finnegan puffed his cigar. "They have reason to observe you closely. It is not every day you see one of your own hang his neighbors for no apparent cause." Finnegan snapped his fingers. "Oh, sorry, I forgot -- they were all dangerous murderers."

"Damn you."

"I believe you have damned yourself, Sheriff. When your day comes, will you be able to face it as well as Duffy did? He had no cause for worry on the scaffold. His soul was in no jeopardy. Is yours?"

"Damn you Pinkertons."

"Ah, yes, now I see. Your stomach is affected by an ailment common to men such as yourself. You had to do this evil deed today to keep your situation. Sadly, the job only pays enough to live, but not enough to run when something like this occurs. Now you must live in this little hell you have built for yourself. Duffy wished me luck, just before you hung him. I will wish you the same, Sheriff."

Orme ran his hand over his sweat-soaked face. "You believe they will come for us, me and Bourne?"

"They do not seem to have much else to occupy their time. As I said, I wish you luck."

Orme set his forehead against the bars. "Why were you jesting about shooting Bourne? Even you would not kill a man for a watch."

"You have just finished killing six men. Did you kill them for more?" Finnegan shook his head. "Perhaps I will shoot Bourne. The company expects me to shoot at least one more man before I leave town. It might as well be Bourne. Either way, it is none of your affair." Finnegan blew out some smoke. "That is assuming he is still available for shooting. The people of St. Clair may hang him from a breaker, yet. Good day to you, Sheriff."

Finnegan left the jail through the same side door he had entered through that morning and returned to the stable, where his horse still lingered in a stall. Finnegan found the same Pinkerton there, as well. The fidgety fellow was still staring off into the woods behind the stable. The only thing that had changed was that there was now an old man sitting against one of the pilings that held up the front of the stable roof. Tears streaked his ancient face, and he was doing his best to hide them. Finnegan approached the old man slowly so he would have a chance to clean his cheeks before looking up

"Sir, I believe I recognize you."

The old man nodded. "And I you. You are the man who was with Duffy all day."

"And you are the elder Mr. Munley?"

"Oh, yes. I was." The old man stared down between his feet. "Now I am the one and only Mr. Munley. They killed my boy today, as you know." He looked up into Finnegan's eyes. "Did you know Duffy?"

"I had only met him once before today. He had no one else to stay with him."

"It was decent of you to keep him company."

"It was good of you to come to comfort your son." Finnegan looked around the general vicinity. "I am told you walked here from Gilberton."

"I did, sir. Some eleven miles."

"That is a long journey for a man of your years." Finnegan pointed down toward the railroad depot. "Does the train run through Gilberton?"

"Near enough. Within a mile, I should say."

"Then you will take the train home."

"Sir, I cannot..."

"I will be more than happy to provide the fare for a fellow mourner. Your son stood up straight and showed no fear. Him and Duffy died as men ought to. You should be proud of your son."

"I am." The old man slowly got to his feet from where he was sitting by the piling. The operation took some doing.

Finnegan turned to the back of the stable where the spare Pinkerton man was still inspecting the woods behind the jail. "Hey, you there."

The Pinkerton turned and hopped down from the bucket he was using as a perch. "Yes, sir?"

"Which one of these nags is the sheriff's horse?"

"Orme?"

"To my knowledge, this county has no other sheriff."

284

"Right. Sorry, sir. As I recall, his is the tall bay with the white markings."

"Very well. When he emerges from the jail, *if* he emerges from the jail, tell him that he can find his horse at the train depot. Tell him it has been borrowed by Finnegan Gilhooley for the purposes of transporting one of the bereaved."

"Uh, very well, sir."

Finnegan turned back to the old man. "Can you ride, sir?"

"Well enough. Do you believe it is intelligent to borrow the sheriff's horse without asking?"

"Did he inquire to you regarding your son before he arrested him?"

"You make a good point, sir. To hell with the sheriff."

Chapter 9

SCHUYLKILL RIVER, PENNSYLVANIA

June 23rd, 1877

"SIR, IT MAY NOT BE MY PLACE TO ASK, BUT THIS SEEMS A strange way to search out a murderer." Abijah sat with his legs hanging over the bank of the river. He had been randomly tossing rocks into the current and otherwise killing time for the better part of two hours while Finnegan smoked and read. Other than the river and the railroad, there was nothing to keep the boy amused.

Finnegan slowly turned the page on his copy of *Faust*. "I offered to let you read the spare book in my kit."

"I cannot read a dictionary, sir." He shrugged. "I am not certain anyone can. That is not what dictionaries are for."

Finnegan eyed the boy quizzically. "If they are not for reading, then what are they for?"

"Well, what I mean is that a man does not sit down and read a dictionary for an hour as he would a newspaper or a nickel book."

Finnegan thought on it. "I do."

"That is because you have nothing better to do, sir."

Finnegan laughed. "Well, neither do you."

The boy sighed. "Sir, I do not like to bother you by being overly inquisitive, but I would very much like to know why we have been sitting out in the woods for two days?"

Finnegan set his book to one side and sat up a bit on the saddle he had been reclining on most of the morning. "Our purpose here, young Abijah, is twofold. First, we linger here in the country because when I enter one of the surrounding towns, I seem to inevitably find myself shooting the residents of said towns. Oh, speaking of which, what do you hear regarding the assistant treasurer?"

"It is said he has regained most of his faculties and is walking. I am told that it is reasonably certain at this point that he will live."

"That is for the best. It is all well and good to go about killing riffraff and other assorted troublemakers, but it is better to simply educate union officials."

"Educate them, sir?"

"The assistant treasurer will now carry his wounds with him through life, as I carry mine. When my hip aches, I think of Alexander Franklin James. When the treasurer's shoulder aches, he will think of me. With any luck, we will both learn from the experience." Finnegan paused to contemplate his cigar for a moment. "But, returning to your question: if I reside out in the woods, then I am not shooting men in St. Clair. It will not do to stir up trouble directly after something like the Molly Maguire executions. We must allow passions to cool for a time to avoid the bloodshed that inevitably follows when a man takes hasty action."

Abijah nodded. "I understand, sir, but is it not imperative that we continue to seek the murderer of Johanna Wetherill?"

Finnegan nodded in return. "It is, Abijah, and we will. Keep in mind, though: Wetherill's killer has been at large for some time. If he remains in the area today, he will still be here in a few days when we resume our search." Finnegan sat up all the way and snuffed out his cigar in the dirt. "Sit here for a moment; there is something else I wish to discuss with you today." Abijah dutifully approached and took a seat on a nearby stone. "Abijah, by this time you have surely noticed that most men in this life tend towards their own self-interest. There were, in all likelihood, plenty of people in St. Clair who wished to offer you assistance after your father passed, but were unable to do so because they lacked the funds or ability. They did not fail to proffer help because they are hard-hearted or because they dislike you, they are simply unable, and their own interests must be in the vanguard if they are to take care of themselves and their families. Do you understand that?"

He nodded somewhat sullenly. "I do, sir."

"Very well. What you must also understand is that many times looking to one's own interests is a debt a man owes himself. You must take advantage of the opportunities presented to you. Your father did not raise you up to this point so that you should not amount to something. You are the product of hard work, now you must work to make good on that investment. You owe it to your father and to yourself. Understood?"

The boy straightened and looked almost prideful. "I do, sir."

"Very well, then. Now, I will tell you something else that is important to remember. All men, even good men such as Mr. Pinkerton, look to their own self-interest and the interests of their families first. That is why Mr. Pinkerton has sent me here instead of coming himself. To him, in many respects, I am simply a tool, like the shovel and lantern your father carried. I am an object that Mr. Pinkerton can make use of to keep himself from danger or damage. In some ways, the work

I do is given to me as a kindness. In others, it is a curse leveled on me because I have no other choice. Such is life, young Abijah."

"I suppose I understand, sir."

"Of course you do. Any man who has picked culm banks to earn his bread would. All this brings me to my final point. Abijah, we have not been lingering here these past two days simply because I enjoy the scenery. We linger here so that I may know the near exact time the train from Philadelphia passes through that cutting with the curve in it. I wish to know the exact time because I intend to make the leap to that train."

The boy's eyes narrowed. "To what end, sir?"

"In two days' time, that train will contain the payroll for all the miners, breaker boys, mule drivers, and company store clerks in St. Clair. I intend to relieve them of it along with one of my associates. I will require your help to do this."

"My help?" The boy sounded almost awestruck.

"I will require you to leave me and my associate off here, so that we may leap to the train. At that time, I will need you to take the horses down the track farther to a place I have already selected. Once there, my associate and I will leap from the train, and you will meet us. If all goes as planned, the men running the train will be none the wiser that the payroll has disappeared, and the alarm will not be raised until the train reaches St. Clair." Finnegan raised a very strict finger to the boy. "No man or woman will be killed or assaulted in the execution of this plan. We will make use of quickness and bluster instead of the brutality so often utilized in such an endeavor. Will you assist me, Abijah?"

The young man gave the offer some thought before speaking. "Sir, I do not wish to be a part of the town losing its payroll. The men of St. Clair depend on it to feed their families."

Finnegan shook his head. "The men of St. Clair will get their pay, Abijah, only a day late." Finnegan chuckled. "The payroll for all the miners in St. Clair is nothing to the corporation that owns the coal fields. It will amount to twelve or thirteen thousand dollars at the most. It is a pittance to the men who sit on the coal company board. They will not even notice its loss on their books. The twenty-sixth they will put more money on the train and deliver it to St. Clair. They must. They cannot risk a strike or a revolt of some sort." Finnegan chuckled again. "If they are bright, the assistant treasurer and his union cronies will even convince the company to give every man a bonus for late payment."

"Truly, sir?"

"I would not lie to you about such a thing, Abijah. The payroll being late will make no difference to the men of St. Clair, but it will make a tremendous difference to us. That money will allow you to rise up out of your current condition. It will allow me to be something more than another man's shovel. This is the sort of opportunity your father would have wanted you to embrace, Abijah."

"Twelve thousand dollars, sir. That is a grand number."

"It is, is it not?" Finnegan took a bag of rolling tobacco from his pocket, which he had been saving for the occasion. He tossed it to his young partner. "While the payroll is a large number, a far grander number is what the coal and iron company would pay to have the Mollies hung. My employer, Mr. Pinkerton, was paid one hundred thousand dollars for that minor chore." The boy's eyes grew wide at the figure. "Now, recall, this same company did not proffer one thin nickel to assist you when your father passed. If I am shot down tomorrow, they will not so much as send a letter to my sainted mother. Now, I ask you, is one small payroll so much to take, considering how much we have already given?"

Abijah produced rolling papers and began fingering tobacco from his newly-acquired bag. He wore the look of a serious businessman considering his options. "Sir, if I assist you in this endeavor, will you assist me in leaving this place? I would very much like to pursue some of the opportunities you spoke of in the west."

"I did not know the man, but I believe your father would be very proud to hear you speak so, Abijah."

"I believe he would, too, sir." Abijah deftly assembled a cigarette and placed it between his lips. "It is hard to imagine that just a short time ago I was nothing more than a culm picker. Now, I am a detective in training and an aspiring train robber. It is remarkable what a difference a few days can make in a man's disposition."

Finnegan smiled. "I am glad to see you are excited regarding your new prospects. That is very well, given the fact that you must first perform a few chores in preparation for becoming a train robber."

"Chores, sir?"

Finnegan waved one hand. "Do not worry, there will be little labor involved. Only guile is required. I would venture a guess that the lack of required labor is what makes train robbery so attractive to those who practice it."

Chapter 10

ST. CLAIR, PENNSYLVANIA
June 24th, 1877

Finnegan stared up at the rafters of the belfry and slowly let smoke roll out of his mouth. He had, once again, spent the better part of the day out in the country, wasting time and monitoring the trains. In the afternoon, he and Abijah had returned to St. Clair and had enjoyed dinner at Mrs. Wallace's table. The only oddity was that Annabel Lee had been somewhat quiet while she served the food. After dinner, Finnegan and Abijah had retired to the back porch of the boarding house. After night had fallen, Finnegan had retired to the belfry and sent Abijah out on his final chore in preparation for the payroll delivery the next day.

Sometime around ten, Finnegan heard the clatter that signaled Abijah's assent to the belfry. The boy hopped over the hip wall and slid down to sit. He placed the bulging grain sack he carried between his legs. He loosed the string that held it shut and reached inside the sack. "As you requested, sir, two Coal and Iron helmets."

Finnegan grinned and took one of the helmets in hand.

"Very well executed, Abijah." He held up the helmet. "If nothing else, we will never want for a milk jug."

"Quite right, sir."

"Was it much trouble to obtain them?"

"No, sir. Two men set them down on the porch of the Coal and Iron house before stumbling off to answer the call of nature. They did not even pause to notice they had disappeared when they returned."

"And no one saw you?"

"Not a soul, sir."

"Very well done."

"Thank you, sir."

Finnegan took the helmets and placed them under the tarpaulin that hid the two Coal and Iron uniforms Abijah had stolen the previous night. The boy was proving to be a rather adept sneak thief. "Ah, the men in the mail car should be quite surprised to discover that the payroll is being removed by a couple of Coal and Iron men."

Abijah grinned. "I would certainly think so, sir."

Finnegan looked over the second helmet. "Very nice of you to find a couple that still have their chin straps. That will be helpful jumping to the train."

"Nothing but the best for our gang, sir."

"Gang? There are only three of us, Abijah. I do not know if that constitutes a gang."

"Did not the James brothers rob their first bank with only one confederate to assist them?"

"You have an impressive knowledge of my nemesis, Abijah."

"It is said that it is good to know your enemy, sir."

"Yes. I have been told that..." Finnegan ceased speaking when he heard the front doors of the church open somewhere

293

below them. He pulled his pistol from the holster where it laid nearby and motioned for Abijah to be silent. The priest seldom lurked in the church after dark, and it was surely too late for a service.

From the sanctuary below, the priest's voice bellowed up to them. "Young Mr. Smith, I would speak with you, and Mr. Gilhooley, as well."

Abijah leaned forward and whispered. "That sounds to be Father Mulvaney, sir."

Finnegan placed his Remington back in the holster. "I was unaware the man knew my name."

Abijah stared at him for a moment. "Sir, I doubt there are many between here and Philadelphia who have not become acquainted with your name recently. Especially Father Mulvaney."

"Why should that be so?"

"He performs the funeral rights."

"Ah..." Finnegan nodded. "Quite right, quite right." He stood and swung his gun belt around him before buckling it and pulled on his frock coat. "I suppose we should see what it is the good father would have of us."

"Yes, sir." Abijah moved some of his newspaper collection to one side and opened the trapdoor that led down into the church. "After you, sir."

Being unused to ladders, it took Finnegan a bit longer than the youthful Abijah to descend. Once back safely on ground level, he smoothed his coat and walked to the Father, who waited just in front of the doors. For the first time, Finnegan felt a tinge of regret regarding his use of the church as a staging area for both a murderer hunt and a train robbery. He offered his hand to the priest. "Finnegan Gilhooley, Father. I apologize that we have not been formally introduced until now."

The priest shook the gunman's hand. Father Mulvaney had black hair almost the same color as the flesh under his eyes. The man did not look well; as a matter of fact, he looked like a priest who had recently had a fair percentage of his flock shot or hung. "Hello, Mr. Gilhooley."

Finnegan gave the priest a closer look. "You were not at Pottsville for the hangings."

Mulvaney shook his head. "No, I left that to Father Strohm. Pottsville is within his parish, and...I thought I might be needed here."

"Yes, I understand, Father. I have been meaning to thank you for all you have done for Abijah. If not for your help, I shudder to imagine what might have become of him."

The priest shrugged. "That is only my Christian duty, my son. I would have done the same for any boy, although, I must admit, it has been pleasant having Abijah around. He is a bright boy with a quick wit."

"He is." Finnegan smiled at his young friend. "Father, what is it we can do for you?"

"Oh, I do not seek you for myself, Mr. Gilhooley. The lady you board with, Mrs. Wallace, she came to me in search of you. She said you were not in your rented room. Naturally, I assumed you were with Abijah in the belfry."

"Mrs. Wallace? Did she say why she requires me?"

"She did not, only that she wishes to speak with you." He glanced to Abijah. "You alone, sir. She feels the topic under discussion is not for the young."

Finnegan nodded. "I see. Abijah, return to your quarters and get some rest. We have a full day ahead of us tomorrow and you will have need of it."

"Yes, sir. Good night, Father."

"Good night, Abijah."

The three of them parted ways. Abijah returned to the

belfry. Father Mulvaney returned to the small house he lived in behind the church. Finnegan crossed the wide alleyway and entered the back of the boarding house. He could see that lights burned in the dining room. Inside, he found Mrs. Wallace sitting at the table with Annabel Lee. The girl appeared a bit upset, but nowhere near as much as the lady of the house.

Finnegan stepped to the table and placed his hands on the back of one of the chairs. "You asked for me, Mrs. Wallace?"

She took a cloth napkin and dabbed her eyes before speaking. "Mr. Gilhooley, after much crisis of conscience, young Annabel has something to tell you."

Finnegan arched one eyebrow. "Tell me?" He chuckled. "You may tell me what you like, Annabel. There is no need to fret over it."

The girl stared at him with one quivering lip. "I believe I should have told you sooner, sir. Told you when I first realized what I knew. I feel that I have wronged you by not speaking up sooner."

Finnegan smiled at her. "You can do no wrong to me, young lady. Go on, now, tell me what weighs so heavily on your mind."

"Sir, you have come to St. Clair to discover the murderer of the Wetherill girl?"

"Well, yes."

"Sir, I know who that murderer is."

Finnegan could not help but let his jaw drop. "I am sorry, did I hear you correctly?"

Mrs. Wallace patted the girl's hand and she continued. "Sir, when I was in the company of Mr. Egan, he..."

The girl turned to Mrs. Wallace. The lady gave her hand a squeeze. "You go on and tell Mr. Gilhooley, dear."

"Sir, when I was in the company of Mr. Egan, he would often bring me to town with him so that he might drink and then have me lead the horse home. Before I came into his company, the horse would often become lost, and once or twice Mr. Egan had been injured."

"Yes, I can see how that might occur ,but how..." Finnegan slowly pulled out a chair and lowered himself into it.

"Sir, on the night when Mr. Egan was jailed last, I was in town with him. As I could not enter the saloon he frequented and could not linger in the vicinity for fear of what the other men might do, I concealed myself and the horse on the edge of a large culm bank. We were hidden there all night, since Mr. Egan did not return until he was released the following day."

"All night?"

"Yes, sir." She glanced nervously between Finnegan and Mrs. Wallace before continuing. "Sir, from where I was on the edge of the culm bank, I saw the woman, Miss Wetherill. I saw her arguing with a man up by the breaker. They yelled awful things at each other and fought."

"Fought each other?"

"Oh, yes, sir. The lady, Miss Wetherill, she gave as good as she got, at least to start. The man took out his gun and shot her down, then..."

"He shot her? Just the once?"

"Yes, sir. He shot her and beat her with the gun. Then he just stood over the lady for some time. I watched, sir, as he went to the breaker and found an axe or a shovel, some such tool. He beat her more with both of those, sir. Beat the poor woman even after she was dead. Why would anyone do such a thing, sir?"

Finnegan leaned across the table. "Annabel, did you recognize the man who did this awful act?"

"Not at the time, sir. I had never seen him before. I did not see him again until I met you, sir."

"Met me? What do you mean?"

"The man who killed poor Miss Wetherill, sir, he is the man who came with you to Mr. Egan's place. He is the man that killed Mr. Egan. The man with the blue coat and funny metal hat."

"Captain Bourne?"

"That is what I heard you call him, sir. Yes."

Finnegan took a moment to contemplate all he had heard. "Annabel, why did you not tell me this earlier?"

"I am sorry, sir. Truly, I am. At first, I did not know if it would be proper for me to say anything regarding one of the men who rescued me from the company of Mr. Egan. I did not know if you would be angry with me for telling you. I did not understand you would even care to know until the other night at dinner, when you were speaking with the man from the newspaper. Since then, I have been at odds with myself whether to speak to you. Mrs. Wallace has counseled me. I hope I have acted properly, sir."

Finnegan folded his hands and leaned a bit further forward. "Annabel, this is a very serious thing. You understand that, child?"

"I do, sir, truly."

"And you are certain it was Captain Bourne you saw. It was night, Annabel. You were left alone and had seen a man do a terrible act. No one would blame you for looking away."

"Sir, there was so much moon it was almost as daylight. The two, the captain and Miss Wetherill, they were only a stone's throw from me, and...I could not look away. God save me, I could not." She hung her head and Mrs. Wallace put an arm around her.

Finnegan slowly leaned back in his chair. Even he had come to believe he would never really know the identity of Wetherill's killer. He drummed his fingers on the tablecloth for a moment and let the information sink in. Finally, he fell back to procedure. Even in a profession as rarified as his, it was important to have documentation. "Excuse me for a moment, ladies; I must fetch pen and paper. Annabel, I will write out a statement of the facts as you have related them to me, which you will sign. If Mrs. Wallace would be so kind, I would have her act as witness." The landlady nodded. "Very well, then." Finnegan stood. "It would appear I have finally made some progress."

FINNEGAN DROPPED down into the belfry with a thud. Abijah sat up just as the Pinkerton was shoving a cigar toward him. The boy took it and rubbed his eyes. "Sir..." He stared blearily up at Finnegan. "You seem in fine fiddle. What is it Mrs. Wallace wanted you for that has you in such a fine mood so late?" He yawned and beheld the cigar. "Is this for me, sir?"

"It is, young Abijah. We have cause to celebrate."

"We do?"

"This night, Abijah, this very night, young Miss Annabel has confided to me the identity of the man we seek."

Abijah sat up all the way and stared with shocked amazement. "Miss Annabel?"

"The night Johanna Wetherill was killed she was at the culm bank awaiting the return of that worthless cur we retrieved her from. She witnessed the killing, young Abijah, but has remained silent until now thinking it was not her place to speak up."

"Oh, well, sir, that is a piece of luck. I had begun to think you would need to pick some reprobate to be assumed to be the killer."

Finnegan laughed and lit his cigar. "You are not the only one, my young friend." He took a long puff and sat down, quite satisfied with himself. "Now, I not only have proof of the killer's identity, I will, in all likelihood, have the honor of shooting the scoundrel. I try to never take pleasure in the necessities of my work, Abijah, but in this one instance, I must admit to feeling a bit of glee at the prospect."

"Sir, who is it? Who did Miss Annabel see on the culm bank?"

"None other than our own Charlemagne Bourne, captain of the Coal and Iron Police."

Abijah flopped back and bumped his head on one of the trusses. "Bourne!"

"Indeed. I have to admit I was somewhat shocked to hear it myself. I would not have thought the man had enough initiative to walk to the top of a culm bank, much less kill someone when he got there. Apparently, he shot the poor girl up there then beat her with an axe and shovel to conceal his crime."

"Good Lord, sir." The boy grimaced. "Miss Annabel is certain?"

"She was quite close when the incident occurred, and she has had difficulty deciding whether or not to confide the information to me. I do not believe there is any room for doubt. If there were, the poor girl surely would have mentioned it."

"Captain Bourne. I will be damned." Abijah stuck his

300

celebratory cigar between his lips. "Will you be wanting to see to him tonight, sir?"

"Ah, there is the real luck of this, Abijah. Bourne is not in St. Clair tonight." Finnegan grinned. "He has gone to Philadelphia on the return train. On the occasion of the payroll, he travels to the city, spends the night, then returns with the money."

Abijah found a match for his cigar. "He guards the payroll, sir? Is there not the danger he will recognize you tomorrow?"

Finnegan shook his head. "Bourne does not guard it in the strictest sense. He merely uses the payroll as an excuse to go to the city and revel for a night. We have it on good account that Bourne always rides in the passenger car, ignoring his responsibilities as best he can. No, there will be no one in the mail car with the payroll other than a few railroad clerks." He puffed his cigar. "Now, this is where the true perfection enters in. We will relieve the clerks of the payroll without Bourne even realizing it has been taken. The alarm will be raised only when the train reaches St. Clair. It will take some time for Bourne to wire the sheriff in Pottsville and collect enough of his men to form a search party for the robbers." Finnegan grinned. "By the time he is ready to begin his search, we will have returned to St. Clair. That is when I will either arrest him so that he may face the rope, or gun him down when his cowardice moves him to flee."

Abijah nodded approvingly. "Sir, that is an excellent plan. With the arrest or possible shooting of the police captain, the robbery of the payroll may be forgotten, at least for a time."

"Yes. By the time the citizens of St. Clair have time to contemplate events, a new payroll will be arriving and

Bourne will either be in Pottsville or the grave. I feel the whole endeavor has a certain elegance to it."

"Truly, it does, sir."

"Mr. Pinkerton once told me that a proper detective uses pure logic to make determinations, but luck never hurts. In this case, he surely was correct. Get some sleep, Abijah. Tomorrow we will be concluding our business in this town."

Chapter 11

ST. CLAIR, PENNSYLVANIA
June 25th, 1877

THE DAY DAWNED CLEAR AND BRIGHT WITH FINNEGAN and Abijah already in the woods. They had loaded their various traps in the dark to avoid the prying eyes of the townspeople. By the time ten rolled around, they were in the small meadow they had lingered in many days previously. Finnegan pulled a jar of canned apples from his saddlebags, along with a hunk of cheese and some sausage. He set the various foods on a large stump created when the railroad had presumably needed a grand old tree for some mundane emplacement.

"Have something to eat, Abijah. We missed our usual breakfast with Mrs. Wallace, and you must keep your strength up."

"Yes, sir." The boy squatted by the food and picked up the canned apples. "These are quite fine."

"Yes, Mrs. Wallace does a nice job with them. She..." a branch broke somewhere in the forest and Finnegan's hand went to the butt of his Remington. He dropped his hand from the gun when he recognized the rider who emerged from the trees. "Ah, my associate. Leave your apples for a moment, Abijah. It is high time the two of you were formally introduced."

The boy set the jar back on the stump and stood as the newcomer rode up. "Well, I say, I know you, sir. You are Mr. Moody, the barkeep at the Crossed Keys."

Rooney brought his horse up to the fallen tree the other members of his party were using as a hitching post. "Indeed I am, young man, and you are Abijah Smith. Finnegan tells me you are quite the prodigy in the detective profession. Perhaps soon you will replace both of us in Mr. Pinkerton's employ."

"You are a Pinkerton agent, sir?"

Rooney dismounted, grinning. "You could say that. Although, in recent months, I have come to consider bartending my real calling in life. After our little outing today, I may purchase myself a proper saloon somewhere they have never seen my pretty face before and settle into domesticity."

Finnegan stepped to Rooney and shook his hand. "I thought you said you would always find a way to leave the farmer's daughter?"

"Men mature with time."

"You told me that only days ago."

"Some mature quicker than others." He clapped Finnegan on the back. "I see you have taken the time to bring breakfast, and I presume those bags draped about the boy's horse contain our uniforms?"

"You wager correctly."

"I would also assume we have ample time to eat before the train arrives?"

"Help yourself, Sam." Finnegan motioned to the food, and all three men sat down around the stump.

Abijah watched Rooney with a great deal of interest

while they began to eat. "Sir, you are truly an agent of the Pinkertons?" Rooney nodded with a mouthful of apples. "But, if you are a detective, why do you tend bar at the Crossed Keys?"

Rooney swallowed his apples. "I was posted there, young Abijah. Mr. Franklin sent me here and told me to gain some sort of employment that would allow me to keep an eye on the populace. I was meant to ferret out Molly Maguires and the tending of bar seemed a likely method for gaining men's trust. Ah, these apples are fine. It has been my experience that men are given to trusting bartenders, or befriending them, at the least. Of course, it was an excellent fit for me, since I know so much regarding the distribution and ingestion of alcohol."

Abijah made no attempt to hide his excitement at having discovered one of the locals was indeed a secret agent. "Did you assist Mr. McParlan in his activities, sir?"

Rooney shook his head. "No, I cannot say as I did, at least not to any great extent. I was as shocked as anyone when the arrests were made and McParlan was presented as the key witness." Rooney wiped his mouth with one hand. "I have to confess, I have always been a bit befuddled as to how exactly McParlan selected his Mollies. I was a bit worried that he might name me there for a while."

Finnegan laughed. "Have you taken to murdering superintendents in your spare time?"

"No, but most of the Mollies they hung the other day did not either, as far as I know." Rooney shrugged. "It is a strange world."

Abijah offered a bit of cheese to Rooney, which he readily accepted. "So, you found no Mollies, sir?"

"Oh, I suppose I could have guessed at a couple of fellows and slapped that label on them. From what I heard of the trials, that is all McParlan did. It seemed like something of a shabby trick to pull after he did it first, though." Rooney gulped the cheese down and shook his head. "No, after the trials I merely remained here to keep an eye on things and to report the general demeanor of the town to my elders and betters in Philadelphia. When those gentlemen grow weary of paying Mr. Pinkerton to pay me, I suppose I shall move on to the next bit of foolishness." Rooney reached out and clapped the young man on one shoulder. "Hopefully a bit more well-to-do thanks to today's labors, eh, Abijah?"

The boy smiled. "Yes, hopefully."

Rooney motioned around the general area. "I do not lament having my work here come to an end. I have never much cared for the coal patch. It is too damned depressing to sit around here slinging booze to these poor bastards who have no prospect but to trudge off to a mine, get black lung, or perish in a dark hole." He shook his head in disgust. "It would be far preferable to spend my days somewhere with a bit sunnier outlook." Rooney turned from Abijah to Finnegan. "They've sent that unrepentant sinner McParlan off to run the Denver office, but I think we should try for something better. From what I am told, Denver is a terrible place, some sort of frozen hell perched on a mountain top. Now, San Francisco, to hear others tell it, that town has potential. I am told they burn the whole place down every six months just to clean up from the parties."

Abijah turned to Finnegan wide-eyed. "Sir, could you truly be sent to San Francisco in your employ with the Pinkertons?"

Finnegan shrugged. "I suppose it is possible."

"I have heard the most wonderful things about California." Abijah sat back with a far-off look in his eyes.

"And I have heard that San Francisco is colder than a

well digger's backside." Finnegan waggled one finger at the boy. "A place is what you make of it, Abijah. Remember that when you go searching for paradise."

"Oh, yes, sir. I will."

Rooney chuckled and shook his head. "You are as much fun as ever, Finnegan. Here you have a poor boy who has never even left Pennsylvania, and you have ruined his dream of California with one sullen admonishment. Why not let the young fellow enjoy his whimsies while he still can?"

Finnegan stole a sausage for himself. "We will have to come to a compromise. I will teach the boy what is useful in this life, and you may fill what is left of his head with the silly reverie upon which you have based your existence."

Rooney grinned. "Oh, he'll be a fine fellow by the time we're done with him."

"He will be something, that is for sure."

Rooney grew a bit more serious. "Have you been teaching this youngster the basic skills of the trade?"

"Oh, yes. Not only has he learned a thing or two, but the young man owns his own Winchester already."

"A Winchester!" Rooney clapped his hands together. "How did a man of your tender years come to own such a thing?"

"Mr. Gilhooley obtained it from a dead Coal and Iron man and was then kind enough to make a gift of it to me."

"Oh, well, quite fortuitous. Especially given the fact that the other fellow no longer needed it." Rooney turned to Finnegan. "Are you still lugging about that old Spencer?"

"Sam, which of us is the gunman and which is the spy? I hardly think you have grounds to assess my choice of weaponry."

Rooney stole the last apple chunk. "Ah, but that is the glory of being a buffoon. I may expound on any topic that

307

crosses my mind without the least hint of shame at my ignorance."

ROONEY AND ABIJAH spent the next few hours espousing the glories of California, as they had both read of them in the *Police Gazette*. At some point, Finnegan brought them back to the task at hand. Both men changed into their borrowed Coal and Iron uniforms, complete with helmets. With that seen to, they both handed over their sidearms to Abijah's care and replaced them with a couple of converted Navy Colts that Rooney had been good enough to provide.

As Rooney slipped the Colt into his holster, he chuckled. "This is the first time I have had to make use of my gun belt here in the coal patch, and it is not even on Pinkerton business. Who would have thought?"

"That you would rob a train?" Finnegan queried.

"Well, yes."

"Every man who ever met you."

"Well, I suppose so, but that is all the more reason to be gladdened. I am finally living up to my potential."

In the far-off distance, Finnegan could hear the train. It was still many miles distant, but there was no missing the roar of the locomotive. "Ah, it approaches." Finnegan checked the thong on the Navy Colt to make sure it was secure. He looked over the cutting one more time. "All right. Abijah, before the train makes that curve down the creek, you should take the horses back down into the trees over there. When you are certain both Sam and I have made it onto the train, you will take the horses down to the meadow I showed you. You know the way?"

"I have it down pat, sir."

"Very good." He straightened his helmet. "Well, then, I suppose there is little else to discuss. Sam, any comments?"

"Oddly enough, nothing springs to mind."

"Grand. This is a fine plan. I see no reason..." Finnegan paused and turned to the east. "That is strange."

"What?" Rooney glanced around.

"The sound."

Abijah slowly rotated his head about. "I hear nothing, sir."

"Well, no. That is the problem, young Abijah. I no longer hear the train."

Rooney unbuckled his chin strap and removed his helmet. "Now that you mention it..."

"Ah, bloody hell." Finnegan pulled his helmet off as well. "That damned thing picked a fine time to have a fit." He ran to his horse and began digging around in the saddlebag. In a moment, he had his spyglass and was headed up to the top of a nearby rise with Rooney and Abijah close on his heals. When he reached the top, he used a tree as a rest for the glass. In the distance, roughly a mile off, he could see the train with the locomotive at its head. "It has stopped and..." He moved the glass a bit lower to see around a limb. "There is a great deal of steam rolling out of the engine."

"What?"

"The damned thing looks like it is aflame, but I think it is a great plume of steam."

"Here, give me the glass." Rooney took a turn looking. "The damn thing has dumped *all* its steam, Finnegan." The faint sound of gunshots drifted to the men on the rise.

"Is that shooting, Sam?"

"It sounds as such." He stared on for a long moment. "I see two men, no three, three horses with two riders. They appear to be fleeing."

309

"Fleeing the train?"

"Well, yes."

Finnegan scratched his bare head. "What in hell is going on down there?"

Abijah let out a laugh. "You truly do not see?"

Both men turned to the boy, but only Finnegan was curious enough to ask. "You know what is happening?"

"Well, of course. The train has dumped its steam, we hear gunshots and men are fleeing. It is obvious." He looked at his older compatriots, but they were still befuddled. "Sirs, someone is robbing the train."

Once again the two older men were dumbfounded. After looking from the train and back to the boy several times, Finnegan finally spoke. "But, that is *our* train. It is meant to be robbed by us. That is why we have taken the time to carefully plan the robbery and found this spot and the other down the tracks. We have procured these uniforms and seen to a hundred other minor details."

Abijah slowly nodded. "That may be, sir, but, in spite of that, someone else has apparently robbed the train and is currently escaping."

Rooney pulled off his helmet and scratched the back of his head. "Well, what are we to do now? I do not much fancy the idea of waiting a month for another damned payroll to come through."

Abijah squeezed the bridge of his nose as he had often seen Finnegan do during moments of vexation. "Well, since the two of you are agents of the Pinkerton agency, known far and wide as the scourge of train robbers, perhaps we should enter into pursuit of the robbers"

"Ah, yes." Finnegan began pulling his Coal and Iron uniform off. "I would very much like to shoot those bastards for robbing our train."

Rooney began to disrobe in a like manner. "Wait, gentlemen, are you suggesting we retrieve the stolen payroll we intended to steal?"

Abijah slapped one hand onto the top of his head. "Mr. Moody, or Rooney, or whatever your real name is, I am suggesting that we follow the robbers and deal with them in the manner Mr. Gilhooley appears to deal with most every man he encounters. With that done, we can keep the damned payroll!" Abijah sat silent for a moment, a bit embarrassed at having yelled at the older men.

Finnegan grabbed his Remington from his saddlebag. "So, you propose we find the robbers, shoot them, and keep the payroll?"

"Yes."

"That sound like a grand plan, Abijah. I dare say it is better than the original. It has less leaping, and more shooting involved, which I am more comfortable with." He pulled on his frock coat and swung up into the saddle. "Let us be off, gentlemen. I doubt those presumptive scoundrels down there will wait around all day to be shot at."

FINNEGAN RODE up to the open mail car. Inside, he could see what appeared to be both the engineer and the conductor staring down at a dead mail clerk. The two railroad men looked up just as Finnegan was flashing his Coal and Iron badge. "What has happened here?"

The engineer hung his head. "Kinda odd that you should ask. It was one of you that done this cowardly deed. Poor Connor here never did nothing to nobody that I know of. Don't know why the hell your man had to shoot him down."

"My man?"

"That no good Charlemagne Bourne. You all call him Captain. I knew him back when he was too dumb to muck out his daddy's horse stall."

"Bourne did this?" Finnegan was hearing a great deal about the Coal and Iron captain that week. "Why did he shoot this man?"

Now it was time for the conductor to speak up. "For no damn reason, mister." The conductor motioned forward toward the locomotive. "First, that Coal and Iron bastard comes up to the engine and orders Wally here to stop and dump the boiler. It'll take hours to get the damn thing up to pressure again. Then, he comes back here and starts beating on poor Connor until he opens the safe. Son of a bitch takes out the payroll he's supposed to be guarding and then the damn sheriff rides up."

Finnegan could not help but gape. "The sheriff?"

"Rides up big as Billy-be-damned. Connor says something to him and that damned Bourne shoots him for it."

Finnegan scratched one side of his chin. "You are certain it was the sheriff, Levi Orme?"

"I ought to know the bastard; I voted for him."

"Ah." Finnegan motioned over his shoulder. "I saw them leaving in that direction."

The conductor nodded. "They dropped down into the creek bottom over there and were beating hell toward St. Clair."

"Where does that creek bottom lead, gentlemen?"

Both men puzzled on it for a moment, but the engineer answered. "It starts up somewhere around the old Eagle diggings, as I recall. Near Old Slope."

Finnegan tipped his hat. "Thank you."

The conductor gave Finnegan a strange look. "Sir, how is it you happened to be so close by when this happened?

It's not every day the sheriff and a police magistrate rob a train."

"Uh," Finnegan shrugged. "I am an agent of the railroad; it is my job to monitor such things."

The conductor pointed to Rooney and Abijah, who sat some fifty yards distance from the train. "Is that the boy who lives in the bell tower and that drunken barkeep, Moody?"

Finnegan turned to look at them. "They are, but you should give the boy more credit, he's well advanced of his age."

"And what of the barkeep?"

"To call him a drunk is insulting to that better class of drunks." Finnegan turned his horse. "Can anyone on the train tap into the line and make use of the telegraph?"

The engineer pointed down at the dead clerk. "The only man who could have lays here."

"I see." Finnegan looked down the line toward St. Clair. "How long before you can get this heap moving again?"

"At least an hour or two," the engineer said, looking grim.

"Well, see to it as promptly as possible. When you reach St. Clair, inform the telegraph clerk there that he is to send word to the same place as always. Inform them that Finnegan Gilhooley is in pursuit and inform them who I am pursuing."

The conductor nodded slowly. "I assume that clerk will know how the hell to spell your name?"

"He should by now."

The conductor motioned down the line. "You want us to raise up a search party when we get there? You may need help."

"I have those two with me." Finnegan pointed over his shoulder. "They will be sufficient."

The conductor raised his eyebrows. "You mean the boy and the drunk?"

313

Finnegan smiled. "I have warned you about calling him boy, sir. Now, be about your business and I will be about mine. Good day." He wheeled his horse and took off in the general direction Bourne and Orme had fled.

FINNEGAN GOT lucky with the tracks. He had never been much of a woodsman, never been much of a tracker, but even he could pick out the marks made in the mud of a stream bed. Of course, it helped greatly that the creek was devoid of tracks other than those recently left by the sheriff and the captain. It appeared as though any fool could follow them, which was fortunate. Finnegan, Rooney, and young Abijah had only to glance to one side or the other on occasion to stay on the track, and it was perfectly obvious when the men had finally turned up out of the creek bed and moved toward the old Eagle breaker that sat on top of a small hill, like a tombstone marking the abandoned mine site.

Far from attempting concealment, both Bourne and Orme could be seen moving around in the old structure. Finnegan, Rooney, and Abijah all lay in the brush of the creek bed watching them as the sun began to sink.

Rooney slowly passed the spyglass to Finnegan. "That intrigues me."

"What is that, Sam?" Finnegan put the glass in one of his coat pockets.

"Those two up there at that old mill. They robbed the train today, bit the very hand that feeds them, and now, instead of running off to San Francisco, they have returned to the same damn patch they've spent their whole lives in. That intrigues me."

"That is something to ponder, I suppose."

Abijah scratched his head. "Perhaps they have not settled on a destination yet."

"It may be that the robbing of a train occurred to them rather quickly, and they have not as yet had time to formulate a complete plan." He sighed. "Regardless, it makes little difference for our purposes. They both have the same destination now, whether they like it or not."

Rooney pointed up the hill. "That sweet girl I see hanging out the wash at the boarding house truly witnessed that damnable Bourne killing a woman?"

"She did."

"And you came here to determine the murderer of that very whore?"

"I did."

"Finnegan, you are truly blessed."

"We can make a determination as to how blessed I am after those two are in the ground. Now, then, if you move to one side there, Sam, and I move to the other by that stand of scrub, we should be able to come at them from both sides and take them before they even fire a shot."

Rooney squirmed a bit in the brush. "You would propose ambushing them, just like that?"

"I would propose killing them in a manner that is both safe and effective for us."

He squirmed again. "I do not know if I would be all that useful to you in that capacity, Finn."

"What damned capacity would that be?"

"Well..." Rooney shrugged. "Well, you see, Finn, as it happens, I have never killed a man."

"What in blue hell are you talking about?" Finnegan stared at his friend in utter disbelief. "I have seen you shoot men. You shot some of those counterfeiters in Chicago."

"No, Finn, you shot all three."

315

"That horse thief in Indiana. You shot him."

"No, I shot at his brother, mostly on a lark. I knew I would never hit him. You shot the horse thief."

"During the war...the supply trains, Gettysburg, Virginia? We were both outside Richmond, for God's sake?"

"That was all you, Finnegan. Why do you think I was always at your side? You never miss, my friend. Standing by you, or more to the point, behind you, a man is often more safe than sitting in a church pew."

"How?" Finnegan shook his head. "Well, there is a first time for everything."

Rooney waved one hand. "I do not know if that is a good idea. In truth, the last time I found myself in such a situation, I faltered near to apoplexy. If the other man had not been quite so drunk, I may have perished."

"Well, a lot of damned good you are. Perhaps it is time you pursued your true calling in the priesthood if thou cannot damn well kill."

Rooney nodded. "Oh, I have considered it."

"Sam, I will not make this boy into a killer this evening. You would truly have me go up there alone?"

"Oh, I will go with you. You know I am no coward. I am simply informing you that I will be of no more use killing them than I have been in the past. It has never slowed you before. Hell, Finn, there are only two of them. You kill more men than that before breakfast some days."

"I will help you, sir." Abijah slowly motioned to the horses. "I have my Winchester."

Finnegan sighed again. "No, you will not. You will remain here with the animals. I hired you to assist me, not to shoot the local law officers." He turned to Rooney. "I am simply disappointed to discover that my associate has apparently been letting me do all the heavy lifting over the years."

Rooney appeared a touch perturbed. "I thought it was clear from the beginning that I was in charge of planning and strategy."

"Oh, really, that was clear?"

"The train was my idea. If not for me, you would still be casting about St. Clair in search of profitless murderers."

"The train *was* your idea, now that I think of it. Of course, we did not rob the train, so I am not sure how much credit you should try to take for that bit of brilliance."

Rooney grinned. "I would say this is preferable. What can be better than having someone rob a train for you?"

Finnegan shrugged and began backing his way down the bank to the horses. "You make a fine argument." He stood when he was out of sight of the breaker and withdrew his Spencer from the saddle scabbard. "He looked over Rooney's horse. "You did not bring a rifle?"

"I am a bartender, Finnegan. What would I be needing with a rifle?"

"It is not always easy being your friend, Sam." He handed the Spencer to Rooney. "Do you recall which end is the dangerous one?"

"Very amusing."

"Abijah, might I borrow your Winchester?"

"Certainly, sir." The boy carefully removed his new rifle from the scabbard and handed it to his employer.

Finnegan slowly worked the lever and chambered a round in the gun without a sound. "Remain here until I call out for you, Abijah. Then bring the horses up to the colliery."

"Yes, sir."

"Sam, climb the hill on the left side. Can you at least be counted on to show yourself to them to keep them from fleeing in that direction?"

"Of course." Rooney looked over the rifle. "Would you

care for me to fire at them a little? I'm a very poor shot, but I might be able to scare them a bit."

Finnegan squeezed the bridge of his nose. "Refrain from that unless it is wholly necessary. I would prefer not to be shot by my oldest friend today."

"Ah, well, we don't always get what we prefer in this life, Finnegan." Rooney chuckled and began moving through the brush up the lefthand side of the hill.

Finnegan looked to Abijah. "Do you now understand why it is so important to never indulge in liquor?"

"I am beginning to, sir."

"Give it your full consideration while I am gone." Finnegan began climbing the right side of the hill. It was not easy, but in the span of a few minutes he was able to climb to the outer wall of the breaker without much sound. Inside, he could just make out the sound of Bourne and Orme conversing. It sounded like any other conversation between old friends. An uninformed observer would never guess the two had thrown their old lives away that very day.

Peeking around the corner, Finnegan could see Rooney just as he made it to his side of the breaker building. With Sam in place, Finnegan began to slowly move down his wall of the structure. He stopped when he came to what had once been a doorway and was by then partially covered by the collapsing culm bank that surrounded the building. Peeking through what remained of the doorway, Finnegan had a clear view of both Bourne and Orme as they sat on one of the old breaker rollers. They were joking, smoking, and passing a bottle back and forth between them.

Finnegan put gentle pressure on the Winchester's trigger while he thumbed back the hammer. Noiselessly, he moved into a position where he had the front sight of the gun set in the center of Orme's chest with a good rest on the doorjamb.

It would take only an additional pound of pressure to fire and send the sheriff of Schuylkill County to the afterlife. Finnegan was not above such things, but for some reason, in that moment, he thought better of the notion and decided to give the fools a chance to decide their own fate.

"Stand and keep your hands where I can see them." He was close enough that he did not need to raise his voice.

Both men froze. Bourne sat bolt upright with the bottle halfway to his lips. "Ah, hell, Gilhooley."

Orme's face twisted into a sneer. "Goddamned Pinkertons."

Finnegan could see the poor decision forming in Orme's eyes. "Do not try it, Sheriff." In spite of the warning, Orme reached down to the revolver that hung at his side. Finnegan added the last pound of pressure on the Winchester's trigger and drove a bullet into the Sheriff's chest. Orme fumbled with his gun while he slid off the roller and fell into the coal dust that covered the breaker floor. Finnegan barely had time to assess what had happened. The instant the rifle had fired, Bourne had pulled his pistol and began firing at Finnegan. With no better alternative, Finnegan began firing at Bourne. He fired off at least seven or eight rounds while the police captain retreated back into what had once been the room that contained the breaker's steam works. When Bourne made it through the doorway, he slammed the door shut behind him and Finnegan fired into it once for good measure.

From the other side of the breaker, Rooney's voice rang out. "Finnegan, are they dispatched?"

Finnegan remained hunched by the old doorway. "One is. Bourne has run off into a room that still has a door on it. Can you see it from your side?"

"I believe so. There is a door leading out and a window."

"Well, shoot the bloody bastard if he tries to escape."

Finnegan glanced away from the door Bourne had disappeared into for a moment and spied a bag sitting on the floor. Orme had cast his hand upon it almost as his last act. Finnegan chuckled. "I believe the payroll is lying in the company of the good Sheriff in here, Sam."

"Ah, lovely. Let's get to killing Captain Bourne so we can properly see to the safety of the money. Do you intend to charge him, Finn?"

The walls of the room Bourne had retreated into were made of exceptionally heavy planks, but the door appeared rather thin and half rotted. Finnegan did not much fancy the idea of charging the armed captain cowering within. Thankfully, experience had taught him that there were other options. "No, we have a substantial supply of ammunition. I think it would be best to simply fire at him a bit and hope to score a hit. When we grow weary of that, it would probably be best to burn the breaker down around him. It is important to look to one's best interests at a time like this, Sam."

"That sounds like a brilliant plan, Finnegan. You begin shooting at the fool and I will bravely rescue the money."

Finnegan began slipping cartridges into the loading gate of the Winchester. "Somehow I knew I could count on you to take heroic action in that manner, Sam."

"There is no need for that foolishness." Bourne's voice sounded haggard behind the door. "No need to waste ammunition or go burning down this sad old pile of lumber."

Finnegan moved behind the doorjamb a bit at the sound of the captain's voice. "You are surrendering?"

"I have little choice. You shot me in the arm and my revolver is damaged. The spring has broken on the hammer. It is not much good to me."

"That brand-new Colt the coal company bought you?"

The surprise in Finnegan's voice was genuine. "That is a pity."

"I am not sure I could reload the damned thing anyway with only one good hand. I suppose it matters little, since you intended to burn the damn place down around me. Have either of you ever seen one of these places burn? With all the coal dust it is like a look into hell. It would still be burning a week from now if you lit it."

"Very good to know. Open the door slowly, throw out your revolver, and slowly walk out where I can see you, Bourne."

The door slowly creaked open and an instant later a gun came flying out into the coal dust. With shuffling steps, Bourne slowly made his way out to the center of the floor with his hands held up at shoulder level. He turned his head to look over at Orme. "Ah, poor bastard. I knew him almost from the cradle. I hate to see him like this."

Finnegan moved through the doorway and carefully approached Bourne, covering him with the Winchester. "Such are the wages of sin, Captain."

Bourne laughed and dropped his hands. "You may wish to be careful speaking as such, Gilhooley. I don't imagine you mean to turn that payroll in any more than I did."

"That is not the sin I refer to, sir. You murdered Johanna Wetherill."

Bourne nodded slowly. "So I did. I was informed that you had knowledge of it and intended to shoot me down. I came to the conclusion that it would be best to make off with the payroll and start somewhere new. As a true friend, Levi elected to come with me. This was not what we had hoped for." He shrugged. "But such is life."

Finnegan was a bit confused. "Bourne, I did not know

you had killed Wetherill until last evening. How is it you had knowledge of it?"

"I took the telegram from Franklin to mean..." Bourne sighed. "Your jokes to Levi at the hanging, he took them as an indication, as well. Damn it. I have never been lucky, and this is a fine example. How is it you came to know last evening?"

"Annabel Lee, the girl we retrieved from Egan's whiskey still, she saw you kill the woman."

"Truly?" Now the surprise in Bourne's voice was genuine. "She was present?"

"Just to the side of the culm bank."

"Well, that is the trouble living in a small town, no one ever gives you your privacy." Bourne looked over to the side and saw Rooney entering the breaker. He had to stare at the man for a long moment. "Are you not the barkeep at the Crossed Keys?"

"At your service, sir." Rooney slowly reached down and cast Orme's arm to one side before picking up the coal dust-covered carpet bag. "Ah, there is a good weight to this."

"As there should be. Have it with my compliments, bartender." Bourne winced and took hold of his damaged arm with his good one. "So, you are a damned Pinkerton as well, then? How many of you are there still slithering about St. Clair?" He looked back and forth between Finnegan and Rooney. "Ah, to hell with it. It makes no difference to me, now." The police captain stood up tall and closed his eyes. "This is as good a place as any, Gilhooley. Do me the favor of making it quick, eh?"

Finnegan shook his head. "No, I believe it would be of interest to the citizens of St. Clair to see you hang. In the best interests of the agency and the coal company, as well." Finnegan smiled. "I believe that is what those damned lawyers refer to as equal treatment under the law."

322

Bourne opened his eyes. "You are a cruel bastard, Gilhooley."

Rooney cleared his throat and held up the carpet bag. "Uh, Finn. Certainly no man has ever accused me of being bloodthirsty, but won't letting the captain here live interfere with some of our interests?"

Finnegan shrugged. "We would not be the first men to bring in a robber without his loot. Bourne tossed the payroll down a coal shaft and refuses to tell us where it is, no matter how much we beat him. Will it be necessary for us to prove that, Bourne?"

"You intend to hang me." He spit down into the coal dust. "Past that I care about very little. As I said, you may have the money with my blessing." He sneered at them. "You Pinkertons, you are a two-faced bunch. At least I was willing to take that money without subterfuge, like a man."

Rooney set the moneybag down and slapped Bourne on the back. "Funny you should mention that. If you were meant to live longer, I would tell you a hell of an odd tale."

I⊤ was slow going making their way toward St. Clair in the dark. They were forced to wind their way through a few miles of scrub brush and second growth forest before they could hope to reach the main road that ran to town. The only small mercy was that they were almost certain to not be bothered by highwaymen. Finnegan rode behind Bourne to keep an eye on him. Abijah, the only one who truly knew the way, and Rooney were in the lead trying to pick their way through the undergrowth as best they could. Rooney led the horse that bore Orme's body. Occasionally, the bartender detective would utter a curse when the animal became tangled, but other than that they rode on in silence. After the first few miles, Finnegan finally had to ask a few questions that had been gnawing at him.

"Bourne, would you mind speaking with me?"

The captain turned in the saddle. "I have little else to occupy me."

"You know I was with Duffy for the last of his hours?"

"Levi told me, yes."

"What did you arrest him for? What did you have him hanged for? He seemed an alright fellow, amiable enough. Why not pick one of the more vexing drunks in town?"

"I did not point my finger at him. Your man McParlan picked him. I never asked why. Never cared, truth be told. I never took much interest in what the Mollies got up to, certainly never cared to find out who might be a Molly or who was not. I did not much care when your man McParlan came to town. I thought if he wanted to hunt Mollies, that was his prerogative. I never imagined it would have much to do with me. I have never understood why there has to be such a fuss all the time in the coal patch. If the company would leave the miners alone so that they might drink themselves to death in peace, I imagine the miners would leave the company alone, for the most part. Foolishness. It seems my whole life has been spent in foolishness." He pulled his head back to avoid getting hit with a brush branch.

"Duffy asked me to kill you."

Bourne laughed. "Me? Out of all the men he might have picked, he asked for me to be put down? That is rather amusing. Duffy seemed a quick boy. I would have thought he could have appreciated that I am a very small fish in the pond that drowned him."

"I suppose you made an impression on him." Finnegan dug around in his coat and came up with a cigar. "I can see how a man like Duffy might want you dead. What I do not understand is why you could possibly want Johanna Wetherill dead. Why did you kill her, Bourne? There can be no harm in you telling me, now."

Bourne turned once again to see if Finnegan's question was a serious query, or merely another jest. "You truly wish to know?"

"Is it so surprising? When one ventures to investigate a crime such as this, these are the questions that haunt a man's mind. I would welcome a knowledge of why you shot the mail clerk. In truth, I understand none of it. You possessed the combination to the safe by right of being the captain charged with protecting the money. Why shoot the poor fellow?"

Bourne raised his eyebrows. "You, you who have killed so many still wonder about such things?"

"When I cannot comprehend a reason for killing, I question it, still."

Bourne sighed and turned back in the saddle so he did not have to look at Finnegan. "Very well, then, I will do you the favor of explaining. Perhaps when I am finished, you will do me a favor in return." He coughed into his good hand and continued. "I shot the mail clerk because he was an impertinent young cur. He made a comment regarding my character, and I was in a foul mood from having been placed in a position to steal money and flee. That is all. The young fellow simply chose the wrong moment to make a churlish remark. That is all there is to it."

Finnegan let the statement sink in before asking for an answer to the second part of the question. "And Wetherill?"

"There was more to it with the girl. She..." Bourne coughed again and stared back at Finnegan for a moment. "I knew Johanna for some time. I met her directly after she

325

came to the coal patch. I was charged with paying the local apothecary for her...medications. I was also charged with seeing to whatever other needs might flit into her fairly empty head. Numbering those would take too much time to enumerate. Suffice it to say, she was a woman with a great avarice in some respects, and a harlot grown accustomed to living far better than the station she found herself occupying in Crow Hollow."

Finnegan cupped a hand around his cigar to light it. "Why did the woman not return to Philadelphia? McLeod told me her family had cast her out, but there is seldom much that cannot be forgiven. Why did she remain here, living the life of a common whore when she could have thrown herself on the mercy of her mother back home?"

Bourne chuckled. "I am not sure what amount of mercy exists in the heart of her mother. If there was any, it was not handed down to Johanna. She was a spiteful bitch. As for why she remained here, I was always under the impression she stayed specifically to torture old Enoch. She hated that cruel old bastard and had more than a right to."

"What reason did she have to hate the colonel?"

"The rotten old letch compromised her at such an early age, his own kith and kin mind you, that she was barely out of the nursery, sir. From the time she was old enough to fall into his clutches she was, for all practical purposes, little more than the evil old shit's concubine." Bourne shook his head. "Even now, after all I have done." He laughed. "Some of which I have done to poor doomed Johanna -- even now, it sickens my stomach to think of what that girl's own uncle did to her." He wiped his eyes with his good hand. "Yes, she was a lowly whore of poor character even for a woman of her station, but I ask you, what else can a woman become when she suffers a life such as Johanna had?"

Finnegan spit down into the weeds. "I was unaware of the woman's history. Obviously, Colonel McLeod failed to inform me of his child rearing practices."

"Well, they were foul practices. I could hardly credit the knowledge, but Johanna had no reason to lie to me regarding them. I am mournful to think on it, but we became quite close over the time she was here."

"If that was truly the case, Bourne, why did you kill her? What reason could you have had, sir?"

"Ah, it was the laudanum, Gilhooley. Have you ever tasted of that liquid?"

"I have not."

"It is the most vile of concoctions. Truly, the devil in a bottle. That poison ate away at the woman over time. She began ingesting it initially because she claimed it quieted the horrid dreams she suffered from. As time went by, it corrupted her soul. I believe that, I truly do. The night I...the night she died, we met at the breaker as we had many times. She was in a quarrelsome kind of frenzy. She wanted me to go to Philadelphia and kill old Enoch. When I told her I could not, she cursed me for a coward and said that she was going to call on her uncle and have me removed from my position. He was wont to do such things for her. It was a sickening sort of trade they practiced." Bourne hung his head and stared down at the ground as it slowly passed beneath his horse. "She had made threats of similar stripe before, but that night...it put me in a rage. After all I had done for her, for her to speak so... it was as though someone else was holding my pistol."

They left the brush behind and moved into a small clearing. The road was visible not more than a few hundred yards ahead. Bourne reined in his horse. Finnegan did the same. "Do not stop, Bourne. You cannot put off what is coming."

"I do not wish to stretch things out, Gilhooley. I wish to ask you my favor, now."

"Ask."

"You say Duffy charged you to kill me for what I had done to him?"

"Yes."

"And old Enoch sent you here to kill me, as well, even though he did not as yet know it was me he wished dead?"

"Yes."

"Then, by God, be done with it." Bourne gripped the saddle horn and swung down to stand next to his horse. He gave the animal a small shove and it trotted up the trail to where Abijah and Rooney had stopped. "Show more character than I have, Gilhooley. Show a little mercy to me here at the end. I cannot wait for the scaffold as Duffy did. I know now that he was a better man than me. To face it like that. To sit for a whole damn year with the rope swinging outside his window every day. I cannot. The terror will consume me."

Finnegan stared down at the captain. "Why should I show you any mercy, Bourne? There is none in you."

"That is true, sir. But I know now that there is nothing free in this life. From mother's milk to God's grace, everything must be paid for in some manner. I will buy my mercy this very night."

Finnegan tossed down his cigar. "What is it you propose to pay with, Bourne? You seem to be at an impasse in that regard."

Bourne flashed a sad smile. "I will give you what only I can offer. You have been a curse visited upon me, Gilhooley, an angel of death sent to bedevil my final days. The curse was leveled on me by the men who had the right to cast it. As I stand here, I am the only man who has the right to place the curse on another. Do you agree? A man has a right to a dying wish, does he not?"

"I believe he does."

"Then I charge you to kill Enoch McLeod. Kill him for being a damnable cur. Kill him for what he did to poor Johanna. Kill him for being coward enough to charge you with killing me. Kill him because it is what you do and because it is right. Will you do that for me, Finnegan?"

Finnegan dismounted and led his horse forward to Abijah. He handed the reins to the boy. He had already taken charge of Bourne's horse. "Hold these animals, boy, and do not look."

"Yes, sir."

Finnegan walked back to face Bourne. The two stood only six feet apart. "Do you wish to turn away?"

Bourne slowly turned his back to Finnegan. "You may tell any who are interested that you shot while I fled."

"Very well." Finnegan drew his Remington.

"You will visit old Enoch for me, Gilhooley?"

Finnegan cocked back the revolver's hammer and leveled it on the back of Bourne's head. "Eventually all men have their due visited upon them. Goodbye, Bourne."

"Goodbye, Pinkerton. Perhaps we will see each other again in hell."

"We will all meet again in the sweet by and by." Finnegan fired.

Chapter 12

ST. CLAIR, PENNSYLVANIA
June 26th, 1877

It was near first light when Finnegan climbed the steps of the Coal and Iron house. Inside, he could see that all the members of the police, perhaps for the first time, were wide awake and sober. They stood in corners, leaned against walls, sat on cots, but they were all present to cast dark glares upon Finnegan as he walked to the main room of the place.

He rested his hand on the butt of his Remington as he looked the assembled men over. "Who commands here?"

One large fellow with a cup of coffee in one hand took a step forward. "I would think, since you dropped our captain off at the undertaker, you do, sir."

"Who are you?"

"Bannon Rourke. I am a sergeant, sir. I have been told you are a captain."

Finnegan glanced over the rest of the police force. None of them seemed interested in questioning his authority. "Are you the senior man here now?"

Rourke nodded and stared down into his coffee. "I am now."

"Then come in here and speak with me." Finnegan turned and walked into what had been Bourne's office. When Rourke was inside, he closed the door behind them. Finnegan handed his captain's badge to Rourke, who took it with the hand not occupied by coffee. "You will command here now, sir. I am promoting you. I do not know what will come of it. It may be that General Pleasant will send you back to the ranks when your superiors come to some conclusions regarding this place. What I do know is that, in the meantime, someone must lead here. Too much has occurred in this place recently for it to appear as though there is no form of governance present." Finnegan took a seat on the edge of Bourne's desk and pulled his hat off. "You men represent the law. At some point, there will be another sheriff and the coal company will sort you out, but until then you must conduct yourselves in the proper manner and keep some sort of order. Is that clear?"

Rourke nodded again. "What would you have me do, sir?"

"Patrol the town as you have always done. Make sure the taverns do not become too rancorous. Break up union meetings that suggest violent means. In short, do what you have always done. Nothing more, nothing less."

"Yes, sir." Rourke took a sip of his coffee and looked at Finnegan over the cup. "Sir, may I inquire of you?"

"You wish to know about Bourne?"

"I do, sir. I knew the man a long time, nearly all my life."

"What do you wish to know?"

"Did he take the mine payroll in his charge?"

"He did, along with Sheriff Orme. My men and I tracked them from the train to the breaker at the Old Slope mine. I killed Orme at the breaker and shot Bourne as he attempted to flee. That is all there is to it."

Rourke spit a hunk of grounds out onto the office floor. "They are bringing a new payroll today."

"That is prompt of the company."

"They are doing it to avoid a strike, not to feed the town's children." Rourke fished another chunk out with a finger. "But that is to be expected. It is a pity you were unable to reclaim the first payroll." The sergeant smiled. "Some fancy man in Philadelphia will have to switch to cheaper cigars for the day to make up the difference."

Finnegan set his bowler back on his head. "All men must suffer from time to time." He got up off the desk. "I will leave you to your duties, sir." He pointed one stern finger at the man. "Keep order here, but do not be too heavy-handed. Men must vent their passions. See to it that they are vented slowly and completely over the coming days. Can you accomplish that?"

"I can try, sir. I take it you will be on your way?"

"If conditions deteriorate here, I will be returning. Being as I have already shot the sheriff and the captain of your police outfit, I assume you would prefer I remained far afield from this place."

"You are correct, sir."

"Do your work properly and I will have no reason to return. Good day, Mr. Rourke."

Finnegan placed his books inside the valise he carried. He spread the books out and then placed his dragoon and clover-leaf Colt on top of the reading material. His spare shirts and other various traps would go over the guns to keep them from being scratched in transit. He had unpacked and packed the bag so many times that it was nearly reflex. Even with his current windfall, he could not help but wonder if he would ever cease to live out of his luggage. There was a soft knock and he turned to see Abijah linger outside the open door.

"Come in, boy. We have much to discuss."

Finnegan's young assistant strode in and stood just past the doorway. "It is time to depart, sir?"

"It is, indeed." Finnegan closed the bag and turned to face the boy. "Have you reached any decisions regarding your future prospects, Abijah?"

"I have given contemplation to several options."

"I have, as well." Finnegan sat down on the bed next to his bag. "I have given the matter some thought and have come to the conclusion that you may profit from a few more years of tutelage before going off into the world on your own." Abijah frowned and Finnegan held up one hand. "Do not take the assessment as a degradation. You are the most intelligent young man I have ever encountered. Soon you will grow into a very fine man; I would simply prefer that you spend a bit more time...seasoning, under the guidance of those who have your best interests in mind. If you are amenable to the situation, I would suggest that you travel from here to Chicago and take a position in the Pinkerton office there. I will see to it that you will be serving in the capacity of assistant to Mr. Pinkerton himself, as I did, at your age."

The boy's eyes grew wide. "Mr. Pinkerton himself?"

"Until our mutual employer deems it proper for you to engage in field work, of course."

"Field work, such as you do?"

"There are various types of work required. Mine is a rarefied profession. You should be able to pick from several different roles when the time arrives. Would you be amenable to this offer, Abijah?"

"Oh, uh, yes, sir. I would like that very much."

Finnegan slapped his hands on his legs and stood up. "Grand, then it is settled." He smiled at the boy. "In truth, my young friend, I will feel much better knowing you will be available to me in the future. It is often difficult for me to find associates that can be counted on."

The boy slipped his hands into his pockets and blushed a bit at the compliment. "Mr. Rooney seems quite dependable."

Finnegan chuckled. "Depending on Mr. Rooney often has a striking similarity to depending on luck. At any rate, it will be good to have you available." He took a step forward and patted the boy on the shoulder. "I will place the sum owed you for your work here on deposit in the bank when I reach Philadelphia. You may draw on it when and how you please. I would lecture you about spending your money prudently, but you have been on your own long enough to know all about that."

"Oh, yes, sir. I will husband every penny."

"Very well." Finnegan reached in his pocket and withdrew a stack of silver dollars. He pressed the money into the boy's hand. "Take this about town and settle any accounts I may have overlooked. Take special care to see to that damned stableman. I want no cause to have to return and deal with him further. Oh, give that telegraph clerk a dollar, as well. He has performed admirably and traded messages a man of his years should not be privy to."

"I will, sir."

"Good, then see to your duties and then pack your traps. You will travel with me as far as Philadelphia. We will see to your further transportation from there."

"Thank you, sir."

"No need for thanks, boy. You have earned everything you have. Now, begin. I must speak with Mrs. Wallace."

"Yes, sir." The boy scampered off in a rush, eager to be on his way.

Finnegan left his room and walked to the house kitchen. He knocked on the doorjamb and Mrs. Wallace turned away from the large pot of potatoes she was boiling. "Mr. Gilhooley." She took up her apron and wiped her hands. "I am glad to see you are safe. I heard you come in very late last evening." She smoothed the apron out. "And this very morning I have been told you killed the sheriff and that Coal and Iron man Bourne after they robbed the payroll train. Is it true they killed the mail clerk, young Mr. Anthony?"

"They did, ma'am."

"Then they deserved the justice you gave them. Young Mr. Anthony was a good boy from a decent family. His poor mother will be somewhat comforted to hear you dispatched the cowards that killed him."

"I am sure she will, ma'am. Might I have a moment with you in the dining room, Mrs. Wallace?"

"Oh, yes, certainly." She tossed a piece of wood into the stove and placed a lid on her potatoes. She entered the dining room and stood behind one of the chairs.

"Please, sit, ma'am."

"Oh, well, I suppose I can take a load off my feet for a moment." She pulled out the chair and took a seat, looking as though she enjoyed the rare experience of sitting at her own table.

"Mrs. Wallace, now that I have determined the identity of Johanna Wetherill's killer it is time for me to return to my previous commission."

The lady of the house sighed. "Mr. Gilhooley, I will tell you plainly, I was not heartened when you first took up residency here, but now I will be sorry to see you go. I cannot

335

thank you enough for bringing Miss Annabel into this house. She is such a great help to me."

"Yes, Mrs. Wallace, it is Annabel I wish to discuss."

"In what respect, Mr. Gilhooley?"

"It has occurred to me, Mrs. Wallace, that it is not correct to hoist the full responsibility of caring for a young lady like Miss Annabel onto you, ma'am."

"Mr. Gilhooley, regardless of what trouble it may be, I am more than happy to help the girl..."

"I know that, ma'am. All I suggest is that, since it is by direct action of the Pinkerton agency that this young lady has come into your care, it is only right that the agency should provide some funds for her care and board."

"Sir, I do not know if it is right for me to accept..." She watched as Finnegan produced a stack of bills and placed them on the table. "Oh, sir."

"That is five hundred dollars, ma'am. I hope you will accept it on behalf of the Pinkerton Detective Agency. If it is all right, I would like to correspond with you on occasion in the future to check on Miss Annabel and make certain you are both in good health and spirits."

"I...sir, thank you."

"Think nothing of it, Mrs. Wallace. It is my dearest hope that you and Miss Annabel enjoy every happiness." He smiled at her. "If nothing else, it is good to know that there will be at least two people in the coal patch who speak well of Pinkertons. Goodness knows, we have given the rest of the people in this town ample reason to speak poorly of us. Thank you for the hospitality you have shown me, ma'am."

FINNEGAN RECLINED on his preferred log and smoked a cigar while he watched Rooney approach down the creek bed. When his friend arrived, he pulled another cigar from his jacket and offered it. Rooney took it and placed it between his teeth.

"I take it you have seen to your responsibilities about town?"

"Hopefully they are seen to by now." Finnegan handed Rooney a match.

"You are a strange fellow, Finn. Always running off somewhere." He took the match and lit the cigar. "Why not linger a bit? Have a few more meals with Mrs. Wallace. Perhaps we could go fishing."

Finnegan raised an eyebrow. "Have you ever gone fishing?"

"I attempted it once, but it interfered with my drinking."

"A pity, to be sure." Finnegan shook his head. "No, I never much care to stay in a place once my work is finished."

"I simply do not understand the need for haste. Once you leave here, there is nothing for you to do but to return to Missouri and begin chasing rebel trash again. Oh, and I might point out that trying to kill all those fools for robbing trains rather smacks of hypocrisy now."

Finnegan grinned. "Sam, why would you say such a thing? I have never robbed a train."

"Ah, yes, but not for lack of trying." Rooney patted his friend on the back. "You are one of a kind, Finnegan. Do you truly intend to return to chasing the James boys? What of the farmer's daughter?"

"I believe you suggested a banker's daughter."

"They are all equal in my eyes. But what of it? You have your grubstake now. Do you not intend to more closely investigate the cries of petulant children and nurse cattle, or whatever it is husbands do all day?"

"Once again you paint a fascinating picture of domestic life. No, Sam, I do not believe I will give up the chase just yet. I promise to give it my full consideration when I am finished with the James contingent. There are some things a man must see through to the end."

Rooney nodded. "Finn, I have no idea what you are talking about, but that is hardly a rare occurrence." He pointed to the carpet bag that sat on the end of the log. "Would that be my share of the loot, Finn?"

"It is my dirty laundry. I donated your share to the church; I knew you would want me to."

"Oh, Finnegan, I always welcome jesting, but not in such a serious matter as this." He strolled to the bag and opened it. He raised his head smiling. "Ah, brilliant." He stared down into the bag for a long moment. "Finnegan, do you ever ponder the disposition of your soul?"

"Somehow, I doubt purloining already purloined funds can be classed as a mortal sin, Sam. Those Philadelphia millionaires have plenty. I am told Gowan's salary alone comes to some twenty thousand a year. Hard to say how much more he scrapes off in the meantime."

"Yes, I suppose so." He snapped the bag shut. "It could be argued, no matter what, that we are still far better men than McParlan."

Finnegan laughed. "That would not take much, my friend."

"What I mean, is that McParlan nestled in here and fed those men to the gallows. All the while, simply robbing a payroll to accomplish the same end probably never crossed his mind, or he lacked the grit to attempt such a thing."

"That is true, Sam." Finnegan patted him on the back. "You may take that money in good conscience."

"Oh, I would never let that enter into it."

"Good to know." Finnegan stood up and brushed the bark from his pants. "And what of you, Mr. Rooney? Do you intend to remain in Mr. Pinkerton's employ, or will you move on to enlarge your fortune elsewhere?"

"Oh, I will stay on for a time. I believe the decision will be reached when I discover where old man Pinkerton wishes to send me next. After the glamor of this place, I am not sure I could handle a diminution in the quality of my living conditions."

"Well, I wish you the best. I imagine we will meet again." Finnegan shook one finger at him. "Do your best to conceal the provenance of that money."

"Come now, Finn, I have been in this business long enough to know better than that. Ah, it has been good to operate with you again. Take care with yourself and take good care of that boy, Abijah. He is a rare find and has great potential."

"Yes, well, I shall have to do my best to make certain he never has cause to contemplate the disposition of his soul."

"What more can one man do for another? Goodbye, Finn."

"Goodbye, Sam."

Chapter 13

PHILADELPHIA, PENNSYLVANIA

June 27th, 1877

"HAVE YOU SPENT MUCH TIME ON TRAINS, ABIJAH?" Robert Pinkerton had immediately taken a shine to the young man that Finnegan spoke so highly of.

"No, sir. I had never ridden the train until yesterday, when Mr. Gilhooley brought me here. It is a strange sensation to feel oneself moving without a horse beneath."

Robert nodded. "It is unsettling at first. In time, you will come to enjoy it. Personally, I have come to love being able to read or see to company business while I travel. Rail travel is the future of this nation, Abijah. Now that you are in the employ of the agency, you will be able to play a role in bringing that future to fruition."

Finnegan shook his head. "You may skip the recruitment speech, Robert. The young man has already agreed to work for you."

"Leave me to my indulgences, Finnegan. It is rare that I get to speak with a new employee who has not been rendered cynical beyond redemption by previous experience."

Finnegan shrugged. "Sadly, such experience is normally required to make a decent Pinkerton."

Robert took the tickets from the railroad clerk and passed them to Abijah. "Be careful to keep these in your possession. You must present them to the conductor when you change trains, and occasionally while you are traveling. Make sure the conductor returns the ticket after he punches it. They have a terrible habit of keeping the tickets and leaving a fellow in a lurch if he does not keep an eye on them."

"I will be watchful, sir."

"When you reach Chicago, go directly to the agency. Do you have the letter of introduction?"

Abijah patted his vest pocket. "It is here, sir."

"Present it directly to my father's secretary and take no guff from anyone. Father always has a troupe wishing to speak with him, but that letter will place you at the head of the line. He wishes to personally see to you being settled in Chicago." Robert looked to Finnegan. "Both Mr. Gilhooley and myself have praised you enough that he may wish to take you home with him."

Finnegan stepped forward and took the young man's hand. "I look forward to working with you again soon, Abijah. Keep your wits about you, learn all you can from the men around you. Oh, and do not smoke too much."

"I will practice moderation in all things, sir."

"You are a good boy. I wish you well."

"Thank you, sir. For everything."

Robert and Finnegan shepherded the young man onto the train and watched it leave the station in a cloud of coal smoke and steam. When the boy was gone, they turned and began strolling off the platform. It would be several hours before Finnegan's train, bound for a more southernly collection of connections, would leave town.

"Robert, there is one detail that remains to be seen to from my work in St. Clair. You, of all men, know how I prefer to be thorough in my work."

Pinkerton stopped on the edge of the platform and leveled a serious stare on the gunman. "I am aware of your dislike for loose ends. Although, I must admit to some difficulty in imagining what remains to be done." He chuckled. "Against all odds, you discovered the murderer you set out to find. By all accounts, either by skill or luck..."

"Admittedly, luck was the deciding factor."

"Yes, well, no reason to admit that too often. It seems to me you have exceeded every mandate of your commission, Finnegan. What can possibly remain?"

Finnegan shrugged. "In totality, what remains may be the crux of the matter, so to speak."

"Well, if you truly feel it is important...who would know better? What is required?"

"A small matter, but necessary. I would see to it this very day, but I feel it would be best to receive approval from your father before taking action."

"Approval? Father has always given you great leeway. He trusts your judgement implicitly."

"If it were any other matter I would take that as gospel. In this instance, I would prefer further instruction, as my action may affect the agency's relationship with a client."

"Oh. Well, then I would agree that we should discuss the matter with father."

Finnegan smiled. "I was hoping you might speak with him about it. Perhaps act as something of an advocate for the idea before I broach the subject."

Robert gave him a quizzical look. "I suppose I could act in that capacity. What is it, exactly, you seek permission for, Finnegan?"

Chapter 14

CHICAGO, ILLINOIS
September 6th, 1877

FINNEGAN SAT IN A RATHER SUMPTUOUS CHAIR IN THE lobby of the Palmer House. It was difficult not to describe every item in the hotel as sumptuous. It was Chicago's finest, and Finnegan had never had cause to enter its doors before. The desk clerk had been more than a little hesitant to even allow the gunman to wait in the lobby, but had finally acquiesced when he learned the Pinkerton's purpose. At first, Finnegan had been a bit annoyed to wait, but had grown to like the idea as he sunk into the fine chair. When Enoch McLeod came tromping down the stairs, he was almost disappointed to be forced to move.

The bear-like colonel strolled up to Finnegan, who stood and tipped his bowler. "Ah, Mr. Gilhooley. I asked old Allan for an escort while I am about town. I did not imagine you would be his choice."

Finnegan smiled. "I requested the assignment, sir. As it happens, I was in the area, and I thought you might prefer to spend your time with an agent you have a prior acquaintance with."

The colonel nodded, his beard bobbing. "You are correct. I would certainly rather spend the day with the man who shot Jesse James, as opposed to some of the dregs Allan chooses to employ."

"Very well then, sir. It is my understanding you wish to inspect some of the damage to the railroad that has occurred during the recent unpleasantness. Particularly the viaduct area and the roundhouse?"

"Yes. The roundhouse, because it is railroad property, and the viaduct area in the hopes that they have not yet washed the blood of that rebel scum from the streets."

"As you like it, sir. I have a coach waiting."

"Lovely."

The two men took the coach to the Halsted Street viaduct and spent a few hours poking around and gaping at the remaining signs left from the riot that had occurred there six weeks earlier. Mobs numbering in the thousands had squared off against a local militia of five thousand men, a great many of whom were Pinkertons. Elements of the Illinois National Guard and regular U.S. Army troops had been brought in, as well, to quell the violence and return order. Some twenty of the rioting, unemployed railroad workers had been killed when the shooting began. After that, the unrest had quickly dissipated. Unfortunately for Mcleod, it had rained several times since the insurrection, and he was unable to find any blood on the cobblestones.

When they were finished investigating the urban battlefield, they traveled to the roundhouse at the Chicago depot. The building was a massive structure. It housed a giant turntable that allowed for locomotives to be turned around inside it so that they could be used in different directions depending on what was required. Originally, it had been a marvel of engineering, but after the riots it was little more than a burnt-out husk. On the day Finnegan and Mcleod visited, the building was still vacant and unrepaired.

Mcleod stood in the center of the ruined turntable. Other than Finnegan, the colonel, and some pigeons, the building was empty. "This is a damned indecency, Gilhooley. A damned indecency." Mcleod held up his arms, motioning to the ruined structure. "We can find no workmen to repair it at present. These anarchists eating away at the railroad have all the local carpenters and machine men convinced it is a betrayal to take honest work." He lowered his arms and sneered. "Oh, if only I could hang some of the bastards to show them who commands here."

"It certainly proved effective in the coal patch." Finnegan took out a cigar and rolled it between the fingers of his left hand.

"It did, and I would do it again, every time these bastards threaten a strike." He formed an evil grin. "We had little trouble convincing the simpering governor of this state to bring in the Army. With any luck, that will be the standard from now on. If these animals wish to stampede like cattle, I see no reason not to slaughter them like cattle. Eventually, the coddling fools who run this country will come to agree with me. There will be order here." He turned to face Finnegan and straightened his jacket. "Tell me what transpired with Bourne."

"Bourne?"

"Pinkerton has told me that you accomplished everything you set out to accomplish in the coal patch. You found the man who murdered my niece and you shot him down, just as I had charged you to do. I have no complaints; I would merely like to know what look the bastard wore on his face as he fell.

345

I confess to feeling somewhat betrayed by the man. He had been charged with seeing to some of my niece's needs. Looking back, perhaps I did not pay the cur sufficiently. Curs are more trustworthy when they are well fed."

"He did appear to wish for more feed."

"Yes, I imagine that is why he took the payroll. I cannot help but notice *that* was not recovered. Perhaps he was not the only man longing for greater fodder."

"Avarice is in all men." Finnegan put the cigar between his teeth and found a match. "You are mistaken on one particular point, though, sir."

"What point is that?"

"I did not gun down Bourne to satisfy you."

"No?"

"My intention was to bring him in to hang. He made it known that he would prefer to be shot. He offered a trade to purchase a more merciful end."

"There is some great difference to your way of thinking between hanging and being shot? You are a strange one, Gilhooley."

"I was given an important commission to see Bourne dead; it was, originally, not specified as to how he should meet his end. I felt there would be some poetic justice in his hanging, since the charge was given to me by Thomas Duffy."

"And who the hell is Thomas Duffy?"

"He is no one, now. He was one of the Mollies hung in the coal patch."

"A strange man, with strange acquaintances. Why are you telling me these things, Gilhooley?"

"So that you may understand what comes next. Duffy asked for Bourne to be killed. Before he died, Bourne asked for another man to die. Surely, a man such as yourself, a man who can boast of a long and honorable career, can understand the necessity of honoring a last wish from a dying man."

"I suppose that depends on the request." A hint of fear flashed through the colonel's eyes.

"Bourne asked for your death."

McLeod stood up to his full, imposing height. "Mine? He asked that *I* be killed? Why? I barely knew the man."

"No, you did not. Bourne knew your niece well, though. We must all pay for our sins, Colonel. Bourne has paid for his. Now is your time." Finnegan pulled the Remington from his holster and cocked back the hammer.

"You...you insolent whore's son. You dare to threaten me? Who the hell are you to say what I owe to God or man?"

Finnegan raised the Remington. "I am the curse you brought on yourself, sir. If you wish to cheat the devil, you should not invite him into your home."

★★

FINNEGAN LOWERED himself into the chair in Allan Pinkerton's office. Across the desk, Mr. Pinkerton closed a copy of his latest book and slid it to one side of his desktop. "Ah, literature, Finnegan. The men who write this tripe can never seem to avoid the temptation of abject fiction. I can only hope I am not the only one who is not fooled by it." He folded his hands. "Tell me some truth, Finnegan; I am in dire need of it. Are you finished escorting Colonel McLeod?"

"I have escorted him as far as any man may."

"Ah, very good. Where did his journey end?"

"If you have need of him, he may be found at the depot roundhouse."

"Excellent. I will send a man there to see him so that

347

others may be made aware of his condition." Pinkerton pursed his lips and shook his head. "It is my theory that the poor man has fallen victim to assassination by copperheads."

Finnegan raised his eyebrows. "I believe the colonel would have preferred it that way."

"Of course, the Baltimore and Ohio, the Illinois Central, and the Reading will all wish to determine what is at the root of the colonel's demise. I will beget a full investigation."

"That should require many men, sir."

"And much investment from the railroads. I believe the colonel would have appreciated the poetry in that."

"He did not seem one for poetry." Finnegan stood and extended his hand across the desk. "I may not be one to assess such things, sir, but if you are not the world's greatest detective, you are surely one of the finest businessmen."

Pinkerton sat forward and shook his hand. "I have never claimed otherwise." He tapped the book with one hand. "As you know, I leave that to other men." The old detective smiled. "And what of you, Finnegan? As you know, I have never been one to issue orders. I have also abstained from asking too many questions. All I would like to know now, one old friend to another: are you traveling to Missouri or Minnesota from here?"

Finnegan grinned. "Why would I go to Minnesota, sir?"

"My son Robert has informed me that you may have pressing business there."

"Your son Robert would make a fine clothesline gossip if he wishes to change careers."

Pinkerton laughed. "The boy traffics in information, it is his birthright. I can hardly claim standing to chide him for it. Is it a banker's daughter?"

"Her father has varied interests, sir." Finnegan shrugged. "In truth, my plan is to go to Missouri and contemplate the matter further. You may rest assured that I will not shirk my duties in the meantime, and if I do decide on Minnesota, I will give you proper notice."

"I never expected less. Take care, Finnegan."

"Do the same, Mr. Pinkerton."

A Look at: Of a Different Stamp (Finnegan Gilhooley 2)

The West is changing. He's not sure he belongs in it.

Finnegan Gilhooley once struck fear in outlaws across the country. But with the James Gang gone and the frontier growing tame, the Pinkerton Agency has fewer enemies—and fewer uses for men like Finnegan. Assigned to babysit a wealthy naturalist chasing adventure in Montana, Finnegan expects boredom. What he gets is a war.

When a bloody conflict breaks out between rival cattlemen, Finnegan finds himself leading a band of vigilantes through the lawless wilderness, with his thrill-seeking charge at his side. As tensions rise and violence escalates, he must decide whether he's protecting justice—or just feeding chaos.

In a land without law, what makes a man right or wrong?

AVAILABLE JANUARY 2026

About the Author

R.F. Ryan lives in Montana with his beautiful wife and comparatively ugly gun collection. When he is not writing, he can usually be found out in the woods hunting. He's currently retired from a variety of odd jobs that have interfered with his free time, including (but not limited to): ranch hand, green chain operator, bounty hunter, private investigator, and process server. Robert has written over twenty books in multiple genres, both fiction and non-fiction, and has penned hundreds of outdoors-focused articles for websites and print magazines.

About the Author